# PRAISE FOR JERUSHA AGEN

"Jerusha Agen once again delivers top-level suspense and thrilling action. *Covert Danger* kept me looking over my shoulder and flipping pages. Fast-paced suspense at its best."

DIANN MILLS, BESTSELLING AUTHOR OF CONCRETE EVIDENCE

"Hang on! This action-packed story doesn't let up until the good guys win!"

NATALIE WALTERS, AWARD-WINNING AUTHOR OF LIGHTS OUT AND THE HARBORED SECRETS SERIES ON COVERT DANGER

*Hidden Danger* kept me reading and on the edge of my seat from page one through the end. Jerusha Agen writes a gripping suspense filled with danger, romance, and K-9s complete with a strong faith thread.

SHAREE STOVER, BESTSELLING AUTHOR OF FRAMING THE MARSHALL

"Fast-paced, explosive thriller. I couldn't turn the pages fast enough."

CARRIE STUART PARKS, AWARD-WINNING, BESTSELLING AUTHOR OF *RELATIVE SILENCE* ON *RISING DANGER*

"*Rising Danger* grabbed me from the first chapter and never let go. Don't miss this edge-of-your-seat story of suspense and romance."

PATRICIA BRADLEY, AWARD-WINNING AUTHOR OF THE *LOGAN POINT* AND *MEMPHIS COLD CASE SERIES*

# TERMINAL DANGER

# BOOKS BY JERUSHA AGEN

**GUARDIANS UNLEASHED SERIES**

*Midnight Clear* (prequel novella)

*Rising Danger* (prequel)

*Hidden Danger*

*Covert Danger*

*Unseen Danger*

*Lethal Danger*

*Terminal Danger*

**WINDY CITY WESTONS SERIES**

*Waylaid* (Spring 2025)

**SECURITY LEAGUE SERIES**

*Rescued* (Summer 2025)

**SISTERS REDEEMED SERIES**

*If You Dance with Me*

*If You Light My Way*

*If You Rescue Me*

# TERMINAL DANGER

GUARDIANS UNLEASHED  BOOK FIVE

# JERUSHA AGEN

© 2024 by Jerusha Agen
Published by SDG Words, LLC
www.JerushaAgen.com

All rights reserved. No part of this publication may be reproduced, stored in a retrieval system, or transmitted in any form or by any means—for example, electronic, photocopy, recording—without the prior written permission of the publisher. The only exception is brief quotations in printed reviews.

Library of Congress Control Number: 2024919971

ISBN 978-1-956683-38-7

Scripture quotations are from The ESV® Bible (The Holy Bible, English Standard Version®), copyright © 2001 by Crossway, a publishing ministry of Good News Publishers. Used by permission. All rights reserved.

This book is a work of fiction. Names, characters, places, and incidents are the product of the author's imagination or are used fictitiously. Any resemblance to actual events, locales, or persons, living or dead, is coincidental.

# ACKNOWLEDGMENTS

When God first gave me the idea of the character Phoenix Gray, I was enthralled and intrigued by her. I looked forward to the challenge of writing not only about her, but, eventually, writing *her*—getting inside her head to write her own story from her perspective. I clearly lack Phoenix Gray's predictive abilities, because I did not accurately anticipate the incredible challenge she and her story would be to write.

But, as usual, the Lord sent the help I needed at exactly the right time and gave me plenty of aid Himself to transform this story—the most difficult book I've ever written—from a mess to a powerful *message*.

Thank you to author Sarah Hamaker for your encouraging friendship and for the brainstorming help for the opening of this novel. I'm so thankful for the blessing of traversing the joys and pitfalls of this Christian writer's life with you!

Author Kate Angelo, I can see why writers go to you for brainstorming help. Thanks for throwing out ideas with little to go on when I needed to make sure this story idea could work.

Federal Special Agent Judy Adams, you came through again when I needed expertise and insider insights to make this story as realistic as possible. Thank you for always being available and quick to answer with wonderfully detailed information when I need help.

Thank you to my wonderful proofreaders, Natalya Lakhno, J. E. Grace, Vickie Watts, and Angelique Daley. Your response to my earliest version of the novel was such a gift of encouragement to me, helping me to see the amazing work God had done with Phoenix's story.

To Barbara Diggs, an incredible prayer warrior and Christlike inspiration—you have been a tremendous encouragement and challenge to me to walk more closely with Christ through the hard times and the good. May God bless you richly and continue to draw you closer to Himself.

Mom, you have to admit, this is definitely a book I couldn't have written without you. Thank you for lending me your intelligence when mine was lacking to make this story work and become all it needed to be.

Lastly, I need to thank the fans of the *Guardians Unleashed Series*. Your enthusiasm and love for each of the stories and characters in this series have been such a blessing to me. You've embraced these characters as family and friends and have waited a long time for Phoenix's book. I hope her story exceeds your expectations in all the best ways. Happy reading!

*Soli Deo Gloria*

*He is the Rock, his works are perfect,
and all his ways are just.
A faithful God who does no wrong,
upright and just is he.*

Deuteronomy 32:4

# ONE

The child would die. Every second wasted spelled her doom.

Phoenix Gray stepped into the FBI conference room armed with efficiency as her goal and her K-9 Dagian at her side. She scanned the seven occupants of the rectangular space.

Special Agent Wendy Arndt stood at one end of the long table, speaking with a man in his sixties who matched the online photo of Special Agent in Charge Jack Friet. Arndt wouldn't be a problem. She'd invited Phoenix to consult and knew to get out of her way, following directions without question.

Arndt had warned Phoenix when she'd contacted her four hours ago that Friet was bringing in his own FBI consultant and wasn't keen on Phoenix being there.

The new consultant was obviously the dark-haired man who sat at the table, poring over the files in front of him.

Other FBI agents filled chairs around the table. Their tense body posture and curious stares at Phoenix signaled they were paying attention, at least.

She scanned them quickly.

One woman, two men. Their expressions and subtle unintentional cues indicated they were competent and ready to launch into action on command. The exception was one tall, musclebound male who leaned against the wall behind the table and cast her a grin. A hotshot who likely wouldn't follow orders well and cared more about adventure than rescuing the child.

"Phoenix." Arndt approached with a smile on her round face as she glanced from Phoenix down to Dag. "Glad you made it so quickly." She didn't stretch out her hand for the ritualistic handshake.

Good. If she remembered that much about Phoenix's preferences, this investigation should move quickly.

"We're at fourteen hours."

And ten minutes. Many hours too late. Phoenix refrained from pointing out Arndt should have called her earlier when she'd realized they were stuck. But the agent had no doubt encountered resistance to the suggestion, if she'd brought it up prior to the one-a.m. phone call she'd finally made to Phoenix.

"Bring me up to speed." The information that there had been a kidnapping in this Chicago suburb at 1:14 p.m. hadn't been much to go on. But Phoenix typically wasn't given more intel until she arrived at the secure site.

"Right." Arndt glanced toward the man examining the files. "Willis Peterson kidnapped a seven-year-old girl from Bakerson Park at one fourteen p.m. A witness saw him as he put the child in the car and fled the scene. Didn't get the tags. The wit ID'd him afterward from his mugshot. No security cams caught the car or the kidnapping. He's a registered sex offender. Did time in Federal prison for kidnapping, assault, and murder of two other children twenty years ago, also in the Chicago area. Got out with an appeal. Evidence technicality."

Phoenix's blood boiled, the familiar fury rising in response to the injustice, the insanity of a system that allowed pedophiles and murderers free to prey on the innocent again and again. She cooled the reaction outwardly, allowing none of the emotion to reach her face while using it to increase her sense of urgency. "Who is the girl?"

Arndt's mouth flattened in a straight line as she met

Phoenix's gaze. "Rachel Simolen. She was at the park with her parents, enjoying the Saturday. She had slipped away, apparently to look for the ducks that are there in the summer. They thought she was with them. They say she was only gone for two minutes before they looked for her."

Rachel. Phoenix let the name sink in, locking it in her mind with the others. Too late to spare her trauma and suffering. Not too late to save her life.

"The files." Phoenix turned her head toward the FBI consultant who still hadn't looked up since she'd arrived. Not much situational awareness.

"Oh, yes." Arndt glanced toward the man examining the papers. "Agent Ross?"

He finally lifted his head, his gaze finding Phoenix. Mid to late thirties. Brown hair in low-maintenance combover style. Lean. Approximately six feet tall when standing.

"This is Phoenix Gray, our consultant from Minneapolis. Phoenix, Special Agent Callum Ross out of New York. He specializes in finding serial killers that target children."

Another obstacle. He would know only enough to get in her way.

"Ross arrived about ten minutes ago, and we just gave him the files." Arndt sent Phoenix a glance filled with the awkwardness that colored her cheeks.

"Let him finish, Arndt." Friet's growling tone filled the room and drew the attention of the agents.

"I don't mind sharing." Ross directed a small, closed-lip smile at Phoenix that appeared genuinely unthreatened. He could be temporarily masking the ego specialists usually had. "I'm finished with this file for now." He closed the black folder over the contents and slid it toward her at the opposite side of the table.

She stepped to the table and flipped open the folder. She drank in the information.

Peterson's former kidnappings, murders. His photo. Photos of the victims. Scenes of the crimes. His defense attorney's claims of childhood abuse to gain sympathy. Peterson's account of the abuse. Images and intel on his childhood home, his parents.

Phoenix rapidly assimilated the details, interconnecting them with the extensive information Cora had given Phoenix before she'd left Minneapolis. Phoenix had taken precious minutes to study the satellite photos of the Chicago suburb, the lists of local addresses, buildings—locations occupied and unoccupied.

Those minutes were going to pay off now.

"He has Rachel at the Green Valley Way Apartments building." Phoenix lifted her gaze to direct the statement at Arndt.

Dead silence filled the room. All the occupants stared. Even Arndt blinked for three seconds before she found her voice. But she would trust Phoenix's conclusion. "Do you know which apartment?"

"Call or access their database and find the vacancy on the ninth floor."

Arndt nodded and turned toward her team, but Friet would stop her before she could give directions.

"Wait a second." The SAC glared at Arndt as he delivered the predicted objection. "You might trust your consultant implicitly, but I'm going to need evidence this isn't some weird psychic vision before we bust into a random apartment."

"Ms. Gray uses logic and deduction, not psychic visions." Arndt's face turned a deeper shade of red as she faced her superior.

Irritation sparked behind Phoenix's ribs. She couldn't care less what Friet thought of her. The imbecile was delaying a rescue.

Keeping her features still, she pivoted toward the large SAC and leveled him with a dispassionate stare. "All his crimes against children are committed in apartments. He copies the site of his own childhood abuse."

Phoenix spoke clearly, but rapidly. Rachel couldn't afford this to take long. "He won't go far from the park. He'll remain within two-point-five miles. He'll choose a building with a private enclosed garage. The building's address must have a one and a nine. He will choose a floor between the sixth and ninth, with the ninth being most likely. He'll break into an apartment he verified was vacant and use it to hold Rachel."

Silence hung in the air when Phoenix stopped. Friet stared at her. His mouth shifted, revealing doubt.

He broke eye contact. "What do you think, Ross? Any merit to this?"

Phoenix aimed her attention at the consultant, keeping her expression locked to reveal none of the readiness sharpening her mind and senses—preparation to defeat the ignorance or arguments he would spout.

Ross switched his gaze from Friet to Phoenix. He watched her for a second. Two seconds. Three. Processing and assessment showed in his eyes. "I think Ms. Gray is spot on."

A rare feeling of surprise pulsed through Phoenix's system. She harnessed the emotion before it could get close to appearing outwardly. But she watched the consultant with greater interest. And suspicion. What was his motive for backing her up?

"Her conclusions are sound."

A guffaw came from the hotshot. The young agent pushed off the wall and strode closer to the table, looking at Ross. "How could she know any of that? And in only like two minutes of looking at that stuff?" He swung his hand in the direction of the folder on the table.

"I'd like to know the same thing." Friet crossed his arms over his thick chest and glared at Ross as if his consultant had become the enemy.

Behind Friet, Arndt gave Phoenix an exasperated look and walked away, rounding the table to stop by a seated male agent who had an open notebook computer in front of him. Good. Arndt knew to keep the investigation moving.

The consultant gazed at Phoenix again. Perhaps waiting for her to defend herself. He'd have a long wait.

"Ross?" Friet pressed, for once helping speed things along.

"The pattern of an abuser mimicking aspects of his own abuse is common." Ross kept his gaze on Phoenix instead of Friet as he explained. If he was trying to unnerve her with his attention, he'd learn the hard way that intimidation tactics never worked on her. "As is the tendency to take the victim only a short distance from the place of abduction. Especially in a case like this, when he knew he might be seen and time would be short. A five-minute drive or less is likely."

"But how could she know which apartment building he'd go to?" Frustration cinched Friet's voice. "There have to be at least twenty within five minutes of the park."

Ross stood and reached a long arm across the table for the folder he'd given Phoenix. He lifted it and checked the contents. "Number fixation." He looked up, again at Phoenix instead of Friet. "One and nine." The line of his mouth softened as he watched her, but his eyes sharpened, as if he was assessing her again.

A flicker of warning pulsed in her mind. The warning could be accurate. He could present a threat. He possessed a level of intelligence she didn't often see. People couldn't usually explain her knowledge and deductions. Especially with such quickness and ease.

"Her fixation or the kidnapper's?"

Phoenix transferred her gaze to Friet at that one. The man's immaturity was showing. Along with his pride, apparently damaged by Arndt's consultant beating his.

Friet's eyebrows drew together as he switched his glare to Ross. "What's the basis of this number theory?"

"Willis's childhood address seems to be the foundation." Ross looked down at the file. "Then the pattern develops with his apartment of residence during the previous crimes and the apartment where he lives now." The consultant glanced at Friet. "All were in buildings with addresses that include a one and a nine. He also favors apartments on the ninth floor, though that doesn't seem to be as necessary, especially if the apartment number itself has a nine."

Ross closed the folder and focused on Phoenix. "As for the building also having a private enclosed garage, that would be a precaution Willis could have taken so he could stow his car out of sight of the police in the event he was spotted during the kidnapping. Which he was." Ross set the folder on the table and continued to watch Phoenix. "Since he's a hacker, he could easily have infiltrated the building's database to learn which apartments are vacant without risk of being identified through a phone call or visit."

Impressive. Phoenix met his gaze with her impassive one. The man might have found Rachel without Phoenix's help, given a bit more time.

"We've got it." Arndt's excited tone pulled the agents' attention to her. "Brandon found the vacant apartment." She glanced at the agent sitting behind the computer screen. "Number ninety-three sixteen."

*9316. Peterson must love that one.* But he wouldn't for long.

Determination and fury crashed into each other within, sending sparks through Phoenix's torso as she spun away. Dag kept pace with her as she headed for the door.

"We'll meet you there, Phoenix." Arndt's call rolled off Phoenix's back.

She had an appointment to keep. An appointment with a monster.

## TWO

Adrenaline and tension radiated off the FBI agents, dressed in SWAT gear and night vision goggles, as they dropped out of the truck and dispersed to their assigned positions.

Callum hopped down behind them, not geared up beyond a bulletproof vest since he wasn't part of this office's SWAT-trained unit. But they'd given him NVGs and an earpiece so he could follow any chatter and communicate, if needed.

"Good luck." Arndt voiced the quiet sendoff from the back of the truck where she was going to stay, listening to coms and monitoring body-camera footage.

She'd invited Callum to do the same, but he had to see for himself that Rachel was found. That she was alive. Rescued.

He'd been surprised Phoenix Gray hadn't wanted to do the same. That was usually what drove people like him and her to do this work. Rescuing the victims. Seeing that they were safe and their killers brought to justice.

He hadn't expected her to leave the office as soon as she knew they would go along with her location for Willis and Rachel. Though Arndt seemed to think she'd meet them at the apartment building.

Callum scanned the area as he followed behind Victor

Hessin, the last agent in the SWAT team that would breach the apartment.

The sidewalk at the rear of the building, lit by lampposts, was clear. As was the blacktopped driveway by the garbage dumpsters as they neared the back door.

No sign of the mysterious woman with her tan K-9. Maybe she'd gone in the front entrance or would meet Agent Arndt at the van.

Neither option seemed likely for the take-charge woman who, given her performance today, could be the most intelligent person he'd ever met. He still didn't know how she'd assimilated so much information that rapidly and put it all together with seemingly perfect knowledge of the area.

The breacher at the front of the SWAT team opened their entry into the building, and Callum's focus homed in on the mission at hand. Rescuing Rachel.

He pulled out his Glock as he followed Hessin inside.

The team passed quickly and quietly through the hallways to the emergency stairwell. Other agents were posted at the front entrance and elevators in case Willis tried to make a getaway.

Which he might. The realization pumped more adrenaline through Callum's veins as he kept pace with the SWAT crew.

Posting agents at the exits was only a standard precaution. Kidnappers of children with assault in mind were usually so focused on their victims, they didn't think of fleeing until it was too late.

But that might not be the case with Willis. His fear response was flight, as seen in the documentation of his previous arrest when he'd attempted to throw himself from the third-story window of his apartment to escape the cops. He'd clearly learned from his mistakes, given that he wasn't using his own apartment for his crimes this time.

And he was a hacker. He could have accessed this building's security feed and monitored the cameras to see when the FBI arrived.

As Callum followed Hessin up the final flight of stairs, his mind raced through possibilities for what Willis could have planned. The ninth floor would give him room to work with. Time to flee his apartment at the first glimpse of the FBI's SWAT team at the building. He could have made a break for the emergency stairwell the agents occupied now.

A simple dash down a few flights would get him to another floor where the agents wouldn't look for him. At least not immediately.

Callum glanced over the railing, down through the opening between the many flights of stairs. Even now, Willis might be on another floor slightly below, waiting until the agents passed by.

The lead agents moved through the door to exit the stairwell. Callum felt a pull to linger, to wait in case Willis popped out from a floor below and tried to escape down the stairs.

But Callum's first priority was Rachel. He had to make sure they found her. Then he could worry about tracking down Willis.

To tell any team member of his suspicions right then would only distract them, potentially putting them and Rachel in danger. So Callum kept silent as he followed Agent Hessin into the empty hallway.

A camera aimed at them from its mounted position on the ceiling halfway up the hall.

Willis was probably watching the feed from his phone or some mobile device. He'd make a break for it in the stairwell.

Callum's muscles twitched. But there was no way he was going to go anywhere but to Rachel until he knew she was found.

*Lord, if it's Your will, please let Rachel be alive.* The prayer built on those Callum had prayed nearly nonstop on his flight from New York to Chicago. Prayers for her protection. survival, and healing. Prayers for justice. But only God knew what His answer would be.

The SWAT team paused in formation outside the apartment door marked *9316*.

Callum positioned himself with his back to the wall behind Hessin.

"FBI!" Friet's booming call cut the silence, instantly followed by a crack as the breacher broke through the door.

The agents charged inside.

Callum followed, weapon in his hand. He entered an unfurnished space that was likely supposed to be the living room.

"Clear!" The agents' shouts came one by one as they popped in and out of rooms.

Callum trailed their progress, staying out of their way.

They converged on a short hallway with doorways opening off of it.

"We found her!" Someone's shout preceded Friet's more formal confirmation on coms that they'd located the hostage.

"Victim is alive." Friet's firm tone had never sounded so sweet.

Relief and a surge of joy rushed through Callum. *Thank you, Lord. Thank you.*

He couldn't see past the five agents between him and the room where Rachel was found. But he didn't need to. She was alive. He trusted them to take it from there.

Callum peeled off, walking out of the apartment as he heard an agent ask via coms for delivery of a blanket.

That poor, precious girl.

The horror of what she'd been through twisted his insides, urged him to run after the perpetrator, but he held himself to a quick stride for the camera as he headed to the stairs.

He could've brought agents with him. Cued them in to Willis's likely avenue of departure. But if Willis was still monitoring the cameras, as Callum suspected, and saw a whole SWAT team headed his way, he might decide to get off on another floor and nab some hostages to keep the agents at bay.

Hopefully, seeing only one guy in a suit on the cameras wouldn't alarm the kidnapper as much.

Callum pushed through the door into the stairwell.

Footsteps echoed from below. Willis?

Callum took off, not worried about being seen in the camera-free stairwell.

Willis was likely headed for the underground garage where he'd stashed his car, as Phoenix Gray had predicted.

FBI agents were posted in a vehicle outside the garage to cover what they thought was an unlikely chance Willis would try to escape that way. They would probably catch him, or at least be able to give chase.

But if Callum could reach him first, stop him in the garage, and maybe even convince him to cooperate with the arrest, they'd all be better off. And go home without any more casualties.

The footsteps gave way to a creak. Then a slam echoed up the stairs.

Willis had reached the garage.

Callum pushed himself faster, just shy of tripping as he flew down the remaining flights. *Please let me be in time, Lord. Don't let him escape or put others in danger.*

Callum braked hard at the base of the final steps and peered through the window in the steel door that led to the garage.

Willis wasn't likely to be on the other side, waiting to ambush Callum, but he'd be stupid not to take precautions.

Empty, shadowed garage met his gaze.

Glock ready, he slowly opened the door and slipped through.

A noise—like an abbreviated yell—echoed through the cold garage.

Callum veered closer to the bumpers of parked cars and crouched as he continued toward the direction of the sound.

Movement. On the ground at the rear of a black car ahead.

What...

Callum raised his weapon as he approached, trying to make sense of the moving, shifting shape on the concrete floor.

The changing form became clearer as he neared. Two forms. Two people.

An obese man who matched the photographs of Willis Peterson, and...

A woman?

Was Willis attacking another victim?

Callum's muscles clenched, and his heart rate spiked as he quickly closed the distance between him and the figures, aiming his Glock.

But he froze six feet away.

Willis wasn't attacking the woman.

She lay on the ground beneath his heavy body, but she had her denim-clad legs wrapped around his neck.

She was choking him.

Willis reached for the woman's face with his free hand, flailing wildly.

She blocked his reach with one arm as the rest of her body appeared not to move.

The man's hand fell to the ground, then his body stiffened.

Callum lowered his weapon. "Ms. Gray."

The baseball cap lying on the concrete a few feet away, the blond braid that disappeared behind her back, and the lovely profile he'd seen in the FBI office revealed her identity. Even if Callum still couldn't believe the scene he was witnessing.

Apparently, Phoenix Gray had also predicted the kidnapper's escape plan and decided to wait for him in the garage. Had Willis attacked her, and she was defending herself?

She didn't move, not even a twitch to suggest she was surprised Callum was there.

"Ms. Gray, the FBI frowns on chokeholds unless they are absolutely necessary, justified use of force."

She didn't loosen the triangle choke or show any sign she'd heard Callum.

He stepped closer.

A growl snapped Callum's attention to his right.

A dog emerged from the shadow between two cars, its teeth bared. The tan dog stared at Callum with startling blue eyes as he rumbled again.

Callum didn't dare move with her K-9 threatening him. But he could still speak. "I'm going to have to insist you let Peterson go. The FBI can't handle a suspect in this way." Callum risked gradually angling his gaze away from the dog to check on Willis.

Phoenix unwrapped her legs from around his neck and planted her feet wide as she stood.

Willis lay on the ground, unmoving.

"Dagian." She delivered the single word in her firm, deep voice.

The K-9 stopped growling as Ms. Gray took a step toward Callum, stopping a few feet in front of him.

She watched him with eyes he hadn't been able to see clearly before, thanks to the cap she'd worn at the meeting and her distance from him then. They appeared to be dark blue.

And completely devoid of emotion.

A strange sensation, like a tremor, shuddered through him.

He'd looked into the eyes of many criminals—serial killers, rapists, pedophiles. But even the psychopaths and narcissists who lacked empathy for others showed emotion in their eyes. Hers were entirely apathetic, at least from what he could see. Maybe it was the dim lighting in the garage.

"Dag." She didn't look away from Callum as her K-9 passed him and stopped at her side.

Callum searched her unflinching stare for any hint of emotion—dark or light, good or evil.

"I am not the FBI." She continued eye contact for one more moment, no defiance or triumph touching her expressionless features or infusing her monotone delivery.

She turned abruptly and walked away, her dog sticking close to her leg. She stalked past Willis and snatched up her gray baseball cap without breaking stride. Placing the cap on her head, she continued toward the closed door at the end of the garage.

Movement pulled Callum's gaze toward Willis. The man moaned as he touched his head and started to push himself up.

Callum hurried to him, pulling handcuffs from his pocket to secure the suspect.

Phoenix Gray knew what she was doing. She'd only held her choke long enough to keep Willis out for a matter of seconds.

Callum glanced up from cuffing the man's wrists just as the sound of the overhead garage door opening reached his ears.

Phoenix Gray and her K-9 stepped out of the lit garage into the black world beyond.

But he could still see her in his mind's eye—the way she'd stared at him with the eerie impassiveness he'd only seen on one other face. The face in a photo that had haunted him forever.

A girl wrecked by evil beyond belief.

The girl he was too late to set free.

# THREE

The door of the building swung outward, blocking Phoenix's view of the person who opened it.

A young girl stepped beyond the door and turned to shut it. She twisted the knob, as if checking the lock.

Phoenix gave Dag two hand signals. He responded quickly, dropping to lie on the ground. And he would hold the stay.

Even when she attacked the child.

The girl started up the path to the quaint farmhouse.

Phoenix followed. Noiselessly. Gaining on the unsuspecting target.

Only two feet away. One foot.

She closed the gap, grabbed the girl around her small waist, and carried her backward.

The child didn't make a sound. She hooked her foot on Phoenix's leg and threw her weight downward, loosening her attacker's grip. The girl quickly walked her feet backward, pushing her hips into Phoenix and dropping her opponent to the ground.

Phoenix slapped the graveled path with her hands as she slammed onto her back.

Marnie looked over her shoulder, black shiny hair glinting in the orange sunrise that framed her small face. Her wide smile beamed brighter than the sunlight as she held Phoenix's leg in the break position.

Pride swelled in Phoenix's chest as she pulled her leg away and stood. Marnie had come far. She would be ready.

"Did I do all right?" The nine-year-old peered up at Phoenix.

"Yes." Phoenix gave her a second to process the affirmation before giving the critique. "Keep your hand planted on the ground until the attacker hits the ground or you could lose your balance."

Marnie's smile disappeared, but she nodded.

Phoenix drop-stepped around Marnie and grabbed her waist again.

Without missing a beat, the girl responded with tighter, quicker technique.

Phoenix hit the ground. "Well done." Practicing immediately with the correction would encourage muscle memory. Phoenix planted her feet wide and stood. "Dag."

The K-9 immediately jogged toward them, gracing Marnie with a rare tail swish.

The girl plunged her slim fingers into the fur at the sides of Dag's face.

His eyes slid nearly shut as she rubbed the sweet spot she knew he liked best. Marion was doing well teaching her daughter about dogs.

The five minutes allotted for this training exercise were expired.

Phoenix started toward the house.

"Phoenix?" Marnie trotted alongside Dag to catch up. "Can we maybe..."

Phoenix stopped. Turned to the child.

"Can I..." Marnie dropped her gaze.

The ten minutes of cushion Phoenix always allowed when stopping at the Moores' could be used for offering emotional and psychological direction. But Marnie would have to shed the timidity that had always threatened to define her.

Marnie took in a deep breath. Lifted her dark eyes to meet Phoenix's gaze.

Good. She was steadying. Gathering strength. Displaying courage she didn't yet feel. "I have the bad dreams more. Like every night. Almost."

The nightmares of the reality she'd suffered. A natural reoccurrence, given that Phoenix and the Moores had told Marnie one year ago of the danger she was in. After they'd told her, the nightmares she hadn't had for two years returned. Then they faded. And now they had apparently come again. Marnie's subconscious could be ready to make use of the memories.

"You remember what I told you."

Marnie nodded, her small mouth shaping into a frown. "If I face him and don't run, I'll see what he looks like, and I won't be scared anymore."

Phoenix watched her. Waiting.

Lines bunched between the girl's black eyebrows. "I try. I really try. But I wake up every time." She dropped her gaze again, and her shoulders pinched inward as one who wanted to hide the truth she was about to share. "I get really scared." She dug the toe of her hiking boot into the gravel. "Like so scared, I maybe scream."

Pain cinched Phoenix's ribs. Marion or Eli would have assuredly comforted her, given her the love she should have. That was key to her recovery, her survival of the trauma she had endured.

Phoenix's task was supplying the other necessities to help her not only survive but thrive. The child was too young to accomplish the challenge of facing the monster in her dreams. The representation of the monster who had murdered Marnie's mother in front of her four-year-old eyes.

Phoenix herself hadn't been able to face her nemesis in her nightmares until she was fourteen. Though she had always seen his face in every dream. And in every waking moment until she'd learned mental and emotional control. "You will face him someday."

Marnie looked at Phoenix, her brow still furrowed.

"Soon." At which point, they would learn the identity of the murderer and end the threat to Marnie. Phoenix reined in the desire to accomplish that mission now. Though born of her love for the child, the urge to pressure Marnie to do what she could not was counterproductive.

No matter. Phoenix would keep Marnie safe until that day.

Phoenix walked to the house at a quick pace, Dag falling into place beside her as Marnie hurried behind.

Phoenix's feet hit the top step of the porch, and the front door flew open.

"Phoenix!" Jackson's round face stretched to fit the size of his grin. "We played Safe Game!" He clapped his pudgy hands together as he jumped through the doorway just as his four-year-old twin sister appeared, bouncing on her toes.

"I won!" Missy exclaimed the news, her Afro twists bouncing with her body.

Marnie stepped in front of Dag and grabbed the children's squirrelly hands. "You know what Mom says." She guided the children expertly into the house. "We *all* win the Safe Game."

Their mother was spot on, as usual. Including her idea to have the children practice their emergency response drills as a game. The preparation would save all the children's lives if Marnie's location was discovered.

Phoenix walked inside behind the children and closed the door, turning the lock.

"Phoenix, good morning." Marion smiled as she walked around the kitchen counter, holding her four-month-old baby, Hannah. The sight of Marion with her own infant brought a rush of memories to Phoenix's mind.

Of the rescued baby Elijah had brought to Marion's house. The danger Marion had survived that had made her stronger. The love and protection she received from Eli that filled the weak spots in her spirit she had needed shored up.

Marion was a different person now. A woman of strength, confidence, and love that made her the perfect mother—foster, adoptive, and biological—to the growing brood of children she called her own. Her past didn't hold her down any longer. She stood on its shoulders to be the admirable, unshakable woman who stopped in front of Phoenix with a steady, unflinching gaze. Even though the facial scar that had tormented her long ago was in plain view.

"You find us in the chaos of getting ready for school this morning." Marion smiled. "Though I'm sure you expected that." She glanced at the four-year-olds running around her legs, then lifted her gaze to her eldest daughter. "Marnie, you, Joe, and LeBrae need to be on the bus in twenty minutes. I only just managed to get LeBrae out of bed, so he won't be helping. You and Joe better get the little ones fed now, and don't forget to eat, too."

"Got it." Marnie managed to snag the moving bundles of energy and direct them toward the stools along the counter as she called to her eight-year-old brother, Joe, and her two other five-and six-year-old siblings.

No argument this time. Marnie must have decided to heed Phoenix's counsel a week ago.

"Thank you for talking to her the last time you were here." Marion lowered her voice as she spoke. "Whatever you said, she's been a different girl since. At least when it comes to helping out with the children and following our rules. She doesn't even get upset when LeBrae doesn't help with the kids and chores." Marion shook her head with a smile. "You're a wonder."

Fondness for Marion wanted to soften Phoenix's expression, but she kept the emotion contained inside. Marion had an emotional resilience and courage that few could boast. She would handle Marnie fine on her own, eventually bringing the girl around with the love and ethical boundaries she and her husband gave the children.

But accelerating Marnie's growth was essential for her survival and future. The time it took Phoenix to teach Marnie that individual strength and power came from taking responsibility when others did not, from being a person others could depend on, from being capable enough to help those who couldn't help themselves—that was time well spent.

"But you're not here for my thanks." Marion's smile grew as she came close to reading Phoenix's silence. "We'll walk with you to the kennel." Marion snatched a blanket off the nearby sofa and wrapped it around Hannah as she followed Phoenix out the front door into the crisp morning air. "Your dogs did wonderfully while you were gone. Azami even approached Marnie yesterday after about twenty minutes of Marnie sitting in Azami's room."

Good news indeed. Phoenix wouldn't be able to travel at all if not for Marion's unmatched skill as a dog trainer and the way even traumatized dogs warmed to her.

After the abuse Azami had suffered at the hands of her original owners, she didn't trust men and shied away from most women. But Marion had rescued Azami and given the dog her first taste of kindness at the Forever Home dog shelter and training center. And Marion had introduced Phoenix to the cowering, trembling twenty-pound mix, correctly perceiving she was a dog Phoenix would want to adopt.

Marion's instincts for pairing dogs with humans and ability to see the potential in all dogs were unmatched. Which was why Phoenix trusted her to select K-9s for the Phoenix K-9 Security and Detection Agency.

But Marion hadn't accompanied Phoenix to talk about her dogs. The tension around the woman's mouth meant she had something more concerning on her mind.

Wasn't difficult to deduce the source of her worry. Phoenix wouldn't wait to speak until Marion asked the right question as she did with most people. Marion had enough burdens to carry with eight children currently under her roof, most of them with traumatic histories she bore as if they were her own. Phoenix could help alleviate this one burden. "There are no signs of unwanted visitors on your property or around the fringes."

Marion looked at her, clearly not surprised she and Dag had

made their usual check of the isolated property before coming to the house. "Oh, good." She let out a breath, but the stress in her features didn't lessen. "You probably saw the new cameras Eli installed in our woods. He keeps adding more. He's at work now, or he would've wanted to show you himself."

Marion stopped by the door of the kennel and pulled out a cluster of keys from her pocket, selecting one with her free hand to insert in the lock. "Have you heard anything from Agent Briar?"

"No."

"Oh." Disappointment weighted Marion's response as she entered the building.

Dogs barked excitedly at the sight of their beloved rescuer and friend.

Phoenix scanned the runs. Her gaze caught on Apollo, the black of his Doberman markings gleaming in the light as he stood still and dignified, watching her with his keen eyes.

The deep, repeated barks of Birger reached her ears above the others. The fluffy white Great Pyrenees hopped off the ground with his barks, his tail forming the shape of a wheel above his back. Any excuse to vocalize made his day, almost as much as getting to guard someone or his property.

Affection blended with relief, softening the tension around Phoenix's heart. The dogs were happy and well.

Azami wouldn't be in the runs, since Marion gave her a home-like private room in the quiet training section of the building.

"Do you think we'll ever find out who killed her mother?" Marion's question drew Phoenix's attention to her brown eyes, filled with the deep concern of a woman who loved Marnie as her new mother.

"I will."

Marion watched Phoenix a few seconds, her eyebrows bunched. Then she nodded, and her features finally smoothed. "I know you will. It's just hard to go so many years knowing our daughter could be..." Marion glanced away. "That someone wants to..."

Kill her. They both knew what Marion didn't want to voice. A target had been on Marnie's back since the moment she'd become the only witness to her biological mother's murder. The only one who knew the killer's identity. Information locked away in a terrified four-year-old's memory.

Phoenix understood Marion's frustration. FBI Special Agent Corrine Briar, the only other person who knew Marnie had been hidden with the Moores, did her best to keep her eyes and ears open, while Phoenix kept feelers out with her other FBI contacts. An attempt to find a killer hiding in plain sight. In an FBI uniform.

Phoenix would never stop looking for the man who was sure to want Marnie dead. If he could find her.

If Phoenix couldn't find him first, she would be there when the killer came calling. Unless, by that time, she'd managed to turn Marnie into her killer's worst nightmare.

# FOUR

"Morning, Vanessa." Callum smiled at the barista behind the counter of his favorite coffee shop in New York City.

"Same to you." She grinned. "Though you're not looking too perky today. Long night?"

He forced another smile, failing to shake the darkness of the case that still clung to him despite the rising of the sun on a new day. "You could say that. The usual, please. I think I need it more than normal this morning."

"Coming right up." She turned to call out his coffee order, then took the bills he handed her.

"How's Kimmie doing?"

"Great." Vanessa glanced up while the cash drawer opened. "Still likes her new school."

"Awesome. Tell her 'hi' for me."

Vanessa's white teeth flashed as she handed him the change. "I will. She keeps asking me about Jewel."

The memory of the unplanned meeting at the park when he'd taken Jewel for a walk lifted the weight that had been pressing on his chest since last night.

Five-year-old Kimmie was shorter than Callum's Great Dane, but the two had loved each other instantly. Kimmie could use more dog therapy in her life, considering the severe bullying she had suffered at her previous school.

"We should set up another walk at the park sometime."

"Yeah." Vanessa nodded. "That'd be cool."

"Okay. Have a good morning." He stepped out of the line of customers that stretched nearly to the door.

As much as Callum liked connecting with people and trying to be a bright spot in their day, relief lowered his shoulders and coursed through his fatigued limbs. He joined the cluster of about twenty people, crammed near the pickup section of the counter in a space meant to accommodate ten.

That was New York. He glanced at the seating areas of the coffee shop, trying to maintain more situational awareness than the average New Yorker. So many people, packed like sardines around small tables, most staring at the screens of their devices. Some talked on Bluetooth connections.

After fourteen years of living in New York City, he usually didn't notice the crowds. Especially at this coffee shop that he visited nearly every morning on his way to the FBI office up the street.

But today, so many faces, voices—so many people—made him feel...exhausted.

Why was he so tired?

He'd been called in the middle of the night hundreds of times during his career. It was part of being an FBI agent. The work didn't confine itself to standard nine-to-five hours.

And it shouldn't be due to the dark nature of the crime against Rachel. It had been his choice to focus on crimes against children for his entire FBI career, all fifteen years.

They'd rescued Rachel. Alive. She was safe now and reunited with her family.

Dwelling on the positives—the rescues or the justice when he apprehended the criminals—had gotten him through fifteen years of confronting the worst kind of evil the world had to offer. Years of understanding the minds of people who committed such crimes just enough to predict their behavior and stop them.

But the positives this time didn't seem to be enough.

An innocent girl had suffered. She would never be the same. It was a horrific wrong that could have been prevented.

He clenched his jaw as two people in front of him moved up to the counter and grabbed their drinks.

That was the problem, the reason for his strange weariness. Truthfully, it was a feeling that had been creeping into his psyche for months. Maybe longer.

Willis Peterson was yet another previous offender who'd already been caught for brutal crimes. He'd been put away. That should have been the end of the story. Justice served, and the criminal never allowed to hurt anyone again.

But he'd—

"Callum!" The barista's shout interrupted Callum's thoughts, and he stepped forward to take the coffee cup the guy slid onto the counter.

"Thank—"

Ear-piercing pops cracked the air.

Callum hit the floor, whipping out his Glock and rolling to face the front door.

Screams intermingled with gunfire as a masked male in a black leather jacket and jeans aimed an AR-15. At the counter? Or Callum.

He wouldn't wait to find out.

Callum scrambled closer to the toppled table in front of him and aimed around it to take the shooter down.

"You're gonna die!" The man shouted the declaration like a call of retreat as he spun and ran from the coffee shop.

Couldn't shoot the guy in the back.

Callum launched to his feet. "Everyone, stay down!" He sprinted to the entrance and pushed through the glass door.

He looked to the right where the shooter had run.

His gaze slammed into a wall of New Yorkers, the sea of moving people packing the sidewalk.

No sign of the shooter. He would've been swallowed up by that mob within two seconds.

Callum let out a puff of air. Security cameras would have a better chance of finding the shooter now. If they could catch him at all.

For the first time, Callum couldn't bring himself to care.

# FIVE

The clang of the barred gate sliding shut behind Phoenix was almost as satisfying as the patter of her companions' paws.

The four dogs chose to follow her through the house just as they'd wanted to join her for the perimeter check outside.

Azami stayed as close to Phoenix as Dag, though Dag kept to her side whereas Azami scurried back and forth in front of her feet. An impediment to walking at the speed Phoenix preferred, but not an unwelcome one. The sweet dog had clearly missed Phoenix and her home.

Apollo trotted ahead of Phoenix as far as access would allow after she opened each partition and door in the hallways that cut through the belly of the house.

Birger trailed behind, as usual, walking at his own pace and lingering in each location longer than he should to thoroughly inspect the rooms he didn't usually visit.

She stopped by the closed, steel pocket door and typed in the code using the numbered pad on the wall.

The door slid open, prompting Azami to dart behind Phoenix's legs.

Phoenix crouched in the doorway and let the nervous dog smell her face. She gently scratched Azami under the chin.

"Good girl." Phoenix used a steady, soothing tone as she rubbed Azami's small chest.

Phoenix rose and stepped into the room, allowing Azami to choose to follow or retreat as she felt comfortable.

Azami darted through the doorway, then relaxed her body as she followed Phoenix into the sparse room. A bed and lamp were the only furnishings.

Phoenix made quick work of checking the space and the adjoining restroom for any lurkers or evidence of intrusion. She didn't expect to find anything. The security system Cora had created and modified for Phoenix had never failed yet.

But relying on anything other than herself would be foolish. Since she'd been away from the house for seven hours and twenty-six minutes, a complete check of the entire property was required.

She guided the dogs from the room, and the door slid shut behind them. Continuing to the next hallways, they passed through more barred gates, checking the additional rooms, each equipped for specific purposes.

All were untouched since she'd left them.

All were ready.

She returned the way she'd come, leading the dogs through the gates and doors, past her locked bedroom they'd already cleared, back to the space where they spent most of their time.

The living room, one might call it. Though she didn't do much living there.

The space, furnished with a single armchair, three dog beds, and Azami's crate, sufficed for the limited time Phoenix spent there. She sat there in the evenings for the dogs, who needed a sense of home and time with her.

The living room was open to the large kitchen where Phoenix headed. She pulled out her large saucepan and prepared to make lemon shrimp risotto for brunch, since she hadn't eaten after leaving the house at 1:05 a.m. It would be a rare, leisurely meal at the house in the middle of the day.

But the dogs would need her to stay for at least two hours.

They needed more stability, more of her than she had time to give them.

As she chopped an onion for the meal, an itching sensation grew inwardly until it seemed physical, like an irritation along her spine she should scratch. It would be a pointless exercise, since the feeling only stemmed from the urge to accomplish all the tasks she would normally be completing during that time.

She harnessed the feeling, wrestling it into submission as she fought to be present for the dogs that settled around her.

Azami and Dag lay near her in the kitchen while Apollo and Birger settled on the beds in the living room where they could see her.

She could stay until the evening, but then she'd have to continue the search.

Memories pushed at the back of her mind.

She allowed one. It would fuel her, push her forward.

Rose appeared before her eyes, her blond hair stringy and wet as she ran through the sprinkler in her flowered swimsuit. Her giggles reached Phoenix's ears, cascaded into her soul.

Winnie yipped and barked playfully.

Their father's voice echoed nearby.

Mom touched Robin's shoulder.

Enough.

Phoenix shut the door on the vault of memories, bundling the emotions they wrought and aiming them at one target.

He would come soon.

She would find Rose.

It would finally end.

---

Callum released a decompressing breath as he sat on the park bench.

Jewel sat beside him on the grass, her large head even with his chest. She watched the people walking and jogging by on the paved path in front of them, probably trying to take advantage of the quickly waning hours of daylight now that the days were growing shorter.

He rested his hand on Jewel's neck and scratched the base of her docked ear. For probably the thousandth time since he'd met Jewel at a Great Dane adoption event, he admired the swirls of brown and black that created her brindle coat.

Felt good to think of something beautiful and good. Something other than the shooting he'd had to deal with all morning. Debriefing, investigating.

Poor Jewel hadn't gotten her usual noon lunch-break walk in the park. They'd both had to wait until some of the chaos had settled at two-thirty, and Callum could get away for the hour of so-called lunch without being missed.

All that effort, and they hadn't been able to ID the culprit yet.

Praise the Lord, only one person had been minorly injured in the shooting. It was further evidence that the man hadn't been a mass shooter. The attack had been targeted.

The coffee shop security cameras showed the shooter had entered the shop when Callum's back had been turned, twisted his head as if searching for someone, and then opened fire in the direction where Callum was standing.

A barista had stepped into the line of fire just then to set Callum's drink on the counter. Poor guy had gotten scratched by a bullet before he'd ducked.

"Looks like somebody's gunning for you." Agent Carney had made the pronouncement as soon as she'd seen the footage.

As much as Callum was flattered that the Special Agent in Charge of his unit at the NYC FBI office thought he was that important, he wasn't convinced. How could the guy have missed if Callum had been his target?

Callum had moved at that moment to pick up his coffee cup. But still, the man had an AR-15, plenty of ammo, and an easy target less than twenty feet away.

Callum sighed and dragged the hair off his forehead with his hand. A cold hand.

The weather was getting nippier now that November had arrived. Or maybe the coldness was settling inside him and moving outward.

If the shooter had been aiming at Callum, that likely meant one thing. He was yet another criminal who should've been locked away where he couldn't hurt people. Maybe one that had been imprisoned and then released.

Jewel's head dropped from under his hand as the big dog lay down.

Callum bent to give her a belly rub.

Shots pierced the air.

# SIX

Jewel yelped and crawled under the bench as Callum hit the ground, diving toward the end of the bench to see clearly behind it. He clutched his Glock as he peered into the foliage eight feet away.

A dark figure shifted in a bush.

Light flared with another shot, pinpointing the shooter's location.

Callum rolled away from Jewel, bullets whizzing past his left side as he leveled onto his stomach, braced his elbows on the grass. Fired at the muzzle flash.

A cry. A thud. The bushes swayed.

Callum launched to his feet and crept close, Glock ready. "Drop the weapon and come out, hands where I can see them."

No response.

He moved closer, his heart telling him to look back at Jewel. To make sure she didn't run off in terror. He might never find her again.

But one glance away, a second of dropping his guard, could mean both their deaths.

He kept his attention locked on the bushes, scanning for any sign of movement. He inched forward.

The bushes were directly in front of him. Still no sound.

Keeping his weapon aimed, he reached with his left hand to push aside the leaves of the nearest bush.

A moan.

Callum paused, then stepped farther into the plants.

A dark sleeve caught his eye. An arm was stretched out on the ground.

Callum squeezed around another bush.

A man lay flat on his back, crushing plants beneath him. Black leather jacket, black mask, jeans. The shooter from the coffee shop.

He groaned, trying to lift his arm. His other hand lay on his chest. Where blood seeped through his sweater.

Callum scanned for the AR-15. Wasn't on the ground.

He lifted his gaze higher.

The rifle hung from two branches of a small tree. Snatching the weapon, he switched on the safety and holstered his Glock so he had a free hand to hold the rifle.

He stepped nearer to the fallen man as he pulled out his phone and called for an ambulance. He phoned Carney next, crouching by the shooter.

"Ross?"

"You're not going to believe this, but I got our shooter from this morning." Callum reached for the man's ski mask.

"You're kidding."

He peeled back the cotton mask, starting at the base of his neck. "You were right. He was aiming for me."

"You mean he tried again?"

"Yeah." Callum tugged the mask over the man's ears. "We're at the park. I had to return fire."

"Got it. Who is he?"

The mask finally pulled loose, bunching on top of the shooter's head. His grimacing face hit Callum like a punch in the gut.

"Craig Schmidt." Another criminal Callum thought he had put away. For good.

Phoenix stared at Dagian as the K-9 slowed and pressed his nose to the ground.

Four more hours of searching last night, then five and counting that morning had yielded nothing. The same as the days and weeks before.

But this would work. Fanning out the search pattern from the starting point of the old house would work.

The house was almost exactly like the one he'd used for the original prison of his victims. Much more similar than the previous properties she'd found that had been vacant twenty-six years ago within the same county. She and Dag had searched every inch of the properties regardless, though some held cabins or larger, more opulent homes.

But the moment she had seen this one in person—the simple, aged two-story house, isolated in the heavily wooded area—she'd known she had found it at last. The place where he had taken Rose.

Two weeks of searching the property had yielded nothing. He had hidden her farther from the house than Phoenix had thought probable. But investigations of him and all his crime scenes since still led her to the same conclusion. He had to use burial. And this first one would have been close.

Dag lifted his head. Sniffed the air. Broke into a run.

Phoenix's pulse surged as she sprinted after him.

Dag only ran if there was a reason. He'd found something.

She dodged trees and jumped over fallen branches as she chased the tan blur.

A clearing opened ahead.

Where Dag stopped.

She slowed. Walked through the tall weeds and grasses in the clearing of thirty-two feet in diameter.

The overcast afternoon sky meant not much more sunlight touched the open land than under the trees.

She took two seconds to scan the clearing for surprises, then locked her attention on Dag.

His nose hovered over the ground. He rotated his body around the spot of interest. Swished his tail once.

He turned his bright blue eyes on Phoenix.

Her heart jumped into her throat.

He'd found human remains.

She walked to the spot, slipping her backpack off and dropping it on the ground.

"Well done." She gave Dag's head a quick scratch as she released the straps that attached the shovel to her pack.

He wouldn't need more praise than that. As Marion had observed during his training, with great astonishment, he wasn't like any other dog she'd met. He didn't perform tasks for an external reward of food, play, or attention. Doing what Phoenix desired was his reward.

He lay in the grass and watched as Phoenix plunged the shovel into the ground. Good thing temperatures hadn't dropped below freezing yet.

She dug quickly at first. The hole would be deep. A depth where no animal or human would discover the earth's secret unless they knew where to look. But not deep enough to have required heavy machinery.

After three and a half feet, she slowed. Not from fatigue. Energy pulsed through every fiber of her being, adrenaline burning through her veins, sparking with urgency that would drive her to dig with her bare hands if she had no shovel.

But she would not disturb what lay beneath the earth.

She controlled the emotions that powered her, leashing them as she patiently removed the dirt in layers. A careful inch by inch.

She switched to a spade she'd brought in her pack. Leaned over the hole she'd dug, four feet in length and width.

She glanced at Dagian behind her.

His gaze met hers. A glint shone in his blue eyes. Eagerness and awareness of the stronger scent he knew to find for her.

She was close.

She scooped up a half inch of dirt.

Ivory. A small bit of off-white color protruded through the dirt, exposed to the air.

Her heart rate accelerated. She halted her inward reaction to keep her hand steady and her concentration keen as she cleared away more dirt.

Until she could see...her sister.

# SEVEN

The undisturbed bones lay in recognizable formation. The correct height to be Rose.

No traces of clothing had survived the decay of twenty-six years, even though the pajamas Rose had been wearing were polyester fleece.

How Rose had loved that pajama set. The softness of the fleece material. A pale shade of blue. The perfect match for her eyes, the color of the sky on a cloudless summer day.

Phoenix halted the wave of sadness before it could wash over her. It would only distract her.

In the place of grief, the flame that burned constantly in the deepest recesses of her soul surged, growing hotter.

She bent over the grave, carefully clearing away more dirt. It had to be there.

Sunlight, emerging from the parting clouds, glinted off something. Metal?

Phoenix removed more earth to see the object better.

A disc-shaped pendant. Gold. On a chain.

She snatched it up.

There would be no fingerprints. There never were with him.

Tiny symbols were etched on both sides of the pendant in a

circular pattern that replicated the Phaistos Disc. It looked exactly the same as in her memories. In her nightmares.

Images, sounds, feelings hammered against the vault of her mind, threatening to escape and rush at her. She could face them. She had faced them all many times until she'd extracted every bit of information she could from them—everything she could use to find him.

They were no longer helpful to her beyond motivation when she needed it.

But the fire simmering inside her required no stoking.

She had found Rose.

And the grave had supplied exactly what Phoenix needed.

He would taste justice, at last.

---

"Mom?" Callum lightly rapped his knuckles on the open door as he entered his mother's room.

She sat by the window, looking through the glass as the sun lowered on the horizon and the daylight began to dim. Her position was a better sign than the days she wouldn't leave her bed in the corner of the room. But not great either, since looking out the window meant she was watching the park across the street from the mental health facility. Watching the children that played there.

"Hi, Mom." Callum grabbed the other chair, lying on its side on the floor in the middle of the room, and carried it to where she sat. "Terri said you were asking for me this afternoon." He set the chair down and sank into it.

She kept staring through the window. Or more likely, staring at the shadows of the memories that haunted her.

Terri, one of the nurses who had cared for Callum's mom the longest, had called to let Callum know his mom was having an episode. She'd thrown a fit, thrashing and screaming about Callum, calling for him.

But by the time he'd been able to leave the post-shooting

debrief and make his way there through heavy traffic, Terri had told him they'd been able to calm her. His mom continued to ask for him, though, with more tears and sadness than the panic of before. He just hoped he didn't make her worse now.

"Mom, it's Callum." He reached for her hand on her lap and gingerly took it in his.

Her skin was clammy, her hand limp.

He cupped it between both his hands. "I'm here, Mom."

Her head slowly turned toward him. Her greenish brown eyes, the mirror image of his, found his face. They widened. "Callum?" Fear edged her whisper.

His gut clenched. Would she become frantic again? "It's okay, Mom. We're safe."

"Callum, my baby boy. I'm so sorry." She suddenly gripped his hands between hers with a frenzied strength. "He's hurting you again."

"No," Callum kept his voice firm but calm, "he's not. He's gone. I'm safe. You are safe."

"You're screaming." She pulled her hands away, pressing one to her chest and the other to her cheek. "Oh, Callum. Why won't you stop screaming?"

The terror contorting her features reached behind Callum's ribs to wrench his heart. Nothing he said would convince her it was over. Not when her meds weren't working, and the horrors of memory became more real to her than the present.

"Mom, listen to me. Listen to my voice." He ducked his head to meet her gaze.

Her frantically shifting eyes paused on his for a moment.

"I'm safe. I'm not in pain." Except for the pain of seeing his mother in torment. "He's gone." And Callum would make sure he was gone forever for her, even though he would finish his sentence in eighteen years and be set free. He would never be granted access to Callum's mother.

"I'm sorry." Tears rapidly pooled in her eyes and spilled down her cheeks. "I'm so sorry." She leaned toward Callum, reaching for his hands. He gave them to her, and she squeezed them together in hers, pressing her forehead against their joined hands and washing them with her tears. "I'm so sorry." She repeated the same apology again and again.

His heart twisted painfully as he watched the woman who had never protected him, never stopped the abuse. But she couldn't. He'd known that then, too. Known he had to save her, not the other way around. And he had, once he'd finally grown big and mature enough to know how to escape.

But he couldn't save her from the prison of her mind. Only God could do that.

So Callum did what he always did. The only thing that could still make a difference.

He leaned forward to touch his head to hers over their hands and closed his eyes. "Father, please call Mom to You. Please take away her guilt and shame and set her free with Your forgiveness."

This was the kind of suffering Callum needed to prevent. But he was falling short.

How many mothers of abused and even murdered children were suffering like his own mother right now? How many would always suffer, never recovering from the trauma caused by criminals that were caught and imprisoned for far too short a time?

If Callum couldn't prevent this, the suffering of children and their families, then he was in the wrong line of work. It was time to recognize the futility of what he was doing. Time to admit he wasn't making the difference he'd set out to. Time to recognize that no one could.

# EIGHT

"Tell me that isn't what I think it is." Special Agent in Charge Rhonda Carney aimed her dark gaze at the stapled paper Callum held in his hands as he sank into the chair facing the SAC's desk. She sat on the other side, steepling her fingers as she lifted her attention to his face.

"If you think it's the report on the second shooting today, then I can't do that."

Her mouth curved into a smile that softened her dark eyes. "Glad to hear it."

Callum dropped the report on her desk and leaned back. He looked out the window behind her at the night scene. Lights twinkled and flashed on every skyscraper within view. But none of them were bright enough to banish the darkness.

"You're still going to give me bad news, aren't you?"

He returned his gaze to the woman who'd always been a fair, intelligent supervisor. Even a mentor for him when he'd first transferred to the NYC office, still at the beginning of his career as an agent. They knew each other well after fourteen years. "I think I'm done."

She sucked in a breath, as if caught off-guard by the declaration she'd expected. "Don't say that." She leaned forward, propping her elbows on the papers that littered her desk. "You're burned out, that's all."

He slowly moved his head back and forth. "I don't think so. It's...more than that."

"No, I've seen it before. If you have what it takes to stick it out in this job, you're going to hit this point sometime. Everyone does. Comes with the territory." She settled back in her chair and crossed her arms over her navy blue suit jacket. "You can't expect to see what we see every day and not have it get to you eventually. But you'll get through it."

"It's not that. I learned to live with the darkness of what we encounter a long time ago."

Her thick eyebrows dipped as she lowered her arms. "Then what is it?"

He scooted forward in the chair and rested his forearms on the edge of the desk, meeting her gaze. "We had put Craig Schmidt away. Permanently, I thought."

She stared at him. Then looked off to the side.

"He was out in the streets today, shooting people." And nearly killing Callum's dog. As it was, poor Jewel had been scared half to death. Thank the Lord, Callum had found her under a nearby bush. He'd be going crazy right now if she'd been lost.

He moistened his lips. "And Willis Peterson. The FBI had caught him, too. Convicted, sentenced, imprisoned. And he was set free to kidnap another girl. Would've killed her if not for a brilliant consultant the Lord provided just in time."

Carney picked up a pen and tapped it on the stack of papers in front of her. "We can't control the sentencing part of things. Or incarceration. You know that."

"I know. And that's the problem. Because what is the point in what we do if the criminals we apprehend are set loose to hurt and kill again?" He lifted his hand toward her as if she could answer the question.

"We stop them when we can, the best we can. The justice system has to take care of the rest, and we have to trust it will."

He sat back in the chair. "But it's not working. The bad guys are winning."

The pen stilled in Carney's hand as she studied him. "I didn't peg you as one of those guys who got into this business to win."

A wry smile tilted his lips. "Spot-on instincts, as usual. But I did get into this business to protect children. To prevent crimes exactly like the one that happened to Rachel Simolen. By someone who had already been caught and put away. And you know that's not the first time that's happened."

She frowned. They both knew it was the tenth case in two years they'd had of child abuse, kidnapping, or murder done by repeat offenders. The previous offenses weren't always the same type of crime or of the same severity, but the criminals still should have been kept behind bars, unable to harm anyone again.

"I know it's getting worse." Carney shifted in her chair. Then she met his gaze, her lips pursing together. "But, Callum, you do make a difference."

Her use of his first name caught his attention. They usually called each other by their surnames, as did all the agents at the office.

"I've never known anyone in this job who manages to keep caring as much as you do. You love every one of those kids. You feel for them in ways I don't know how you can stand." She looked down at the desk, her lips shifting as if she was trying to hold in her emotions. "You invest every time, in every victim, even though it hurts." She glanced up. Moisture shimmered in her eyes.

A lump pushed into his throat at the sight. Carney was always so stoic.

"That alone makes a difference." She sniffed and glanced to the side. "And you also have rescued more children and apprehended more violent child offenders than any agent in this office." Her voice deepened as she leveled him with a stern look. "You can't say that doesn't matter."

Unless it didn't. How many of those offenders were back on the streets now? How many had committed more crimes after he'd caught them? He'd be afraid to find out.

But clearly, he wasn't going to convince Carney. Nevertheless, he would still have to resign. The whole point was to protect children and stop the evil people who preyed on them. If he couldn't do that in this job, he needed to quit and find a way he could accomplish that mission. Or see if God had something else He was calling Callum to do instead. Maybe he'd misinterpreted his vocation from the beginning.

"Okay, before you continue down the path you're obviously still considering..." Carney's disappointed tone halted the doubt and questions growing in his mind. "Would you do me one favor?" The tilt of her head and her schoolmarm stare brought a slight smile to Callum's lips.

"Sure."

"Take some time before you make your decision."

He already had. A good six months of struggling with the growing sense of futility. But he nodded. "Okay. I can take a little more time."

"Good. Besides, you haven't finished your goal yet."

Did she mean protecting kids? That was the point he'd been trying to make himself.

"Didn't you want to find the Forster killer when you first became an FBI agent? I remember you told me that when you transferred here. You even worked on it for a while, didn't you?"

He nodded. Funny she'd mention it when he had just remembered that old photo of Robin Forster. The only survivor of one of the most atrocious crimes he'd ever heard of. The case was one of the first he had studied in criminal investigations training. And he'd never forgotten it.

"I wasn't going to mention this since you seem to be getting a little burned out." Carney's voice tugged him away from the image of Robin, still so vivid in his memory.

He landed his gaze on Carney, his chest pinching as it always did when he thought of Robin.

"But I got a call from the Minneapolis SAC, Karen Lining. She thinks they may have found the remains of Rose Forster, the Forster killer's first victim."

If Callum hadn't been sitting, he would have fallen flat on the ground. As it was, he seemed to have stopped breathing. "Are you serious?"

"Well, she sounds serious. She called to ask for you to come, since you specialize in these cases."

"And you didn't tell me?"

Carney's eyes lit with humor. "She only called this afternoon. Sometime between shootings, I think." Carney grinned. "You were busy."

"What makes them think it's Rose?"

"A K-9 cadaver team found the skeleton. The handler is a woman who's consulted on violent crimes against children before." Carney's eyebrows lowered as she seemed to search for the memory. "Phoenix someone, I think she said."

Phoenix Gray? It couldn't be. But it would make sense. The intriguing consultant clearly had an interest in the same crimes he dealt with.

As if he needed another reason to go to Minnesota.

He pushed up from the chair. "Tell Agent Lining I'm on my way."

A wide smile stretched across Carney's face. "I'll do that. Maybe this will change your mind about things."

He paused and met her gaze. "I'm sorry, Carney. But I wouldn't get your hopes up." He turned away and left the office, heading for the elevators as he pulled up the airline app on his smartphone.

Maybe, Lord willing, this would be his one opportunity to do something of lasting value before he left the Bureau. His chance to catch the perpetrator of the most heinous crimes Callum had encountered. To finally bring him to justice. And to make sure he could never hurt another child again.

# NINE

She was being watched.

Phoenix sensed the attention locked on her before she shifted slightly to see the person without turning her head.

A man started walking toward her, stepping out from the shade of the trees at the edge of the clearing. He'd been standing still, observing her.

The plainly styled, dark brown hair and simple black jacket, open over a brown sweater, made him quickly recognizable. Agent Ross.

He slowed to a stop four feet away, glancing at Dagian before returning his gaze to her. "Ms. Gray. Good to see you again."

Not something she heard every day. Only Marion and Eli seemed to have that reaction when she showed up.

She kept her gaze on him long enough to convey she wasn't intimidated, startled, or pleased by his appearance and greeting. Then she returned her focus to the FBI agents that documented the evidence in and around the grave.

Ross took another step closer, but she didn't look at him again.

Dag would ensure he didn't close the distance any farther.

"You found the remains? Or rather, your dog did?"

A rhetorical question if she'd ever heard one. Since he'd apparently been called in, he would also have all the pertinent information.

Her silence encouraged him to stay silent, as well. At least for a few seconds.

"What made you search here?"

The suspicious, investigative mind at work. She could respect that. Unless he was simply irked that she had found the evidence the FBI couldn't. She kept her eyes on the agents in the clearing as she answered. "My K-9."

He released a slight puff of air, as if a breath of amusement had escaped.

She angled her gaze his way.

His mouth slanted in a self-deprecating smile. "Good point. Would you be willing to share how you knew to bring your K-9 to this area?"

No irritation or condescension in his tone as he asked the question. Only a touch of amusement. Good-naturedness, even. But he couldn't be entirely without ego.

"I confess I'm amazed. No one has ever been able to find any of the Forster killer's victims." He lifted his shoulders. "And everyone had given up on finding his first."

Not everyone.

"Everyone but you, apparently." He pushed his hands into the pockets of his navy blue trousers. "What made you think you could find her? Here?"

Her. Phoenix had been talking to FBI agents all day after the first team had arrived to start documenting the bones and collecting evidence. No one had referred to Rose as a *her*, as a person instead of a body or an *it*.

Perhaps Phoenix could give him something. He'd learn the information from another agent regardless. "We searched all properties that were vacant during the likely timeframe in an expanding radius until we found her." She watched him, an unusual curiosity motivating her study of his face. It had been years since she'd met someone she couldn't predict at least two statements or movements ahead.

He returned the attention, that look of processing in his gaze. Somehow, the expression didn't compromise or sharpen the softness of his eyes that were a hue of greenish brown. "You started at the original property where he housed the victims, then broadened out to include all the nearby properties he could've chosen at the time? That must have taken months." He shook his head slowly, but his eyebrows pressed together instead of lifting in the amazed expression she would have expected to match his statement and tone.

Caution itched at the back of her neck. He was looking for motivation. Not doubting her find but wanting to know the *why* behind her actions. Wanting to know about her.

She'd have to keep a close watch on this one. Exceptional intelligence unhindered by ego or a desire to prove himself. No obvious tendency to assert dominance or take control.

Without the usual traits of law enforcement agents and men in general, he was an anomaly. A wildcard she might not be able to predict.

She would have to figure him out quickly, or he could become a liability to her and the plan she'd waited twenty-six years to execute.

That was not a possibility she would allow. No one was going to stand in her way.

---

Callum tried not to stare at the most fascinating woman he'd ever met.

Apparently, he hadn't needed to worry she'd leave if he stepped away to look at the burial site. He'd risked doing so when he had realized he would need to come up with a different approach to glean information from her.

That had been an hour ago, and she hadn't budged from the place she'd been standing when he'd arrived. She and her dog still waited there, silently watching the Evidence Response Team scour every inch of the hole and the grassy land around it.

The photographer had finished a half hour ago, and the site had been thoroughly documented yesterday and today before Callum had arrived. The ERT agents were now ready to begin the careful collection of the bones.

Callum crossed his arms over the ache in his chest as he watched an agent remove the first bone.

Poor Rose. Only eight years old. A precious, sweet, blond-haired and blue-eyed girl, living with her family in the Midwest. Innocent, happy. Until that night when a monster decided to destroy her world. Then her.

And her sister. Sometimes, he couldn't help but wonder—secretly to himself—which was the worst fate. Being killed after it all, like Rose, or going through the same torment and surviving. Alone. Like Robin.

She'd survived physically, at least. But had her heart—her soul—survived?

The image of Robin hovered in front of his eyes again, blocking his view of the grave. She'd disappeared after that photo appeared in the news. At least in the media. It was a rare case of even the public agreeing to give the ten-year-old child space and privacy to recover from the trauma that had rocked the nation.

Had she recovered? He wished he had tried to find out what had happened to her instead of focusing only on the case itself, studying it to learn the psychology of serial killers who preyed on children. Then studying every detail again and again in the hope he might someday be able to find and capture the wretched man who'd committed such evil against the Forster family.

Movement out of the corner of his eye made him look to his left.

Phoenix Gray and her dog walked farther into the clearing, stopping a couple of yards from the grave. Her gaze, shadowed under the bill of her charcoal cap, seemed to focus on the agents removing the skeleton.

Strange how someone who conveyed no emotion at all could have such an intensity about her. At least, it seemed that intensity was what he could sense when he had stood close to her at the edge of the clearing.

He hadn't been able to see her eyes clearly then either. Maybe he would be able to glimpse some emotion in them today. Perhaps satisfaction that she'd made this incredible find. Sadness over finding a child's body. Or, maybe, anger over the crime that had put Rose there.

But it wasn't only Callum's growing curiosity that made him move toward Phoenix now. He also needed to find out how she had known Rose would be there.

Her search process was logical and brilliant, enhanced by her apparently gifted cadaver dog. But how did she know Rose had been buried and that she was fifteen miles from the location where the killer had originally kept her?

Robin had led the police to that location, forcing the kidnapper to flee with Rose. Tragically, before the police arrived.

Most kidnappers with the intention of assault didn't travel far with their victims. Phoenix Gray had used that information to make deductions about Willis Peterson in Chicago. But nearly getting caught—like the Forster killer had been—could change that tendency in a heartbeat. She would know that, too.

Most in law enforcement had concluded he'd taken off on the freeways and transported Rose out of state. And the consensus of the investigators also supposed he'd burned the body or destroyed it with chemicals to avoid having the remains easily discovered.

What made Phoenix Gray think differently? Had her cleverness enabled her to form conclusions no one else could from the evidence? He'd seen her do that in much less time in Chicago.

People didn't search for months for a grave they couldn't be sure was there. From a murder twenty-six years prior. Not on their own time and dollar.

And no one did that without caring. A lot.

Why did she care about this case? About Rose?

He ventured closer to her, trying to seem natural as he stopped beside her and turned to face the same direction, toward the grave.

She didn't look at him. Didn't even turn her head or seem to blink, though he couldn't be sure from his angle.

But her dog walked around from her far side to stand between them. A silent message Callum wouldn't dare misinterpret.

Hopefully, the K-9 wouldn't take issue if Callum ventured a question. "There are other unsolved crimes, other killers that haven't been caught. Why Rose?" He resisted the temptation to look at her. Better not to seem confrontational.

She was silent. Was she going to ignore his question again?

She turned to face him, her dog following the movement in tandem, as if they'd practiced synchronizing in advance. "It's close to home."

Callum watched her, trying to see what he could of her face under the shadow of her cap. *Close to home.* Did she mean the case interested her because she lived in the area? Or it was convenient to search because the location was close to her home?

Phoenix Gray didn't strike him as someone driven by hobbies or convenient pastimes. There had to be more to her apparent obsession with finding Rose's grave than locale or even her involvement with the FBI, consulting on serial criminals who targeted children. Why would a civilian be doing that in the first place?

Had she meant something different by her answer? Did Robin or Rose—their story—affect her personally, as it did Callum?

The light shifted slightly, cutting into the shadow cast by the bill of her cap.

Blue eyes stared out at him. No anger, sadness, or even satisfaction in them. Not a hint of any emotion at all. No expression in the features of her face.

It was as if he were staring at the photo of Robin, taken after she had escaped the killer.

The eyes were the wrong color, and the features were different. Phoenix's golden blond hair was far from Robin's dark brown tresses. But she caused the same twist of his gut and pinch in his chest.

What had Phoenix Gray gone through to end up in the same dark place as the lone survivor of the Forster murders?

And why had it led her there, to Rose Forster's unmarked grave?

He wasn't going to get the answers from the mysterious Phoenix Gray. He'd have to find them himself.

He may not be able to help Robin, wherever she was now. But maybe, somehow, he could help Phoenix Gray. If it wasn't too late.

# TEN

A growing sense of urgency only seemed to intensify the ache that still filled Callum's chest. He peered at the screen of his notebook computer as he sat on the steno chair the hotel had paired with the desk along one wall.

The moon outside the uncovered window cast minimal light into the room, but Callum hadn't been able to pull himself away from the computer to turn on the lamps and close the curtains. He could see the illuminated screen just fine.

If only the information that appeared on it was helpful.

He scrolled back up in Phoenix Gray's standard FBI file, skimming past the details he'd read. Not much personal background was included, but her history with the FBI was all there. Or appeared to be. And it was as curious as he'd expected.

According to the file, she'd consulted on many serial killer cases, especially those involving kidnappings of minors. Several of the murder-kidnapping cases she was called in for fit the Forster killer's MO and were suspected to have been perpetrated by him. Exactly as in the Forster case, the FBI teams hadn't been able to apprehend the perpetrator or collect any evidence that could lead to a positive identification.

Phoenix Gray's involvement as a consultant in those cases

provided further evidence she had a special interest in the Forster killer or cases involving him. Though he still couldn't figure out why she had that interest.

He homed in on the dates of those cases, beginning with her first recorded consultation with an FBI investigation.

Eighteen years ago? That was before he'd graduated college.

He scrolled back up to verify he had read her birthdate correctly. Assuming the date was accurate, she was now thirty-six, two years younger than Callum. That meant she would have only been eighteen when she'd started consulting with the FBI. No average eighteen-year-old was invited for that job or allowed to do it.

But none of the details in her file explained why she would have been allowed to consult and what qualified her to do so. She apparently had three college degrees—two in psychology and one in criminology. And she'd achieved black belts in two different martial arts. The dates showed, however, that she'd achieved those impressive accomplishments after she had begun consulting for the FBI.

The standard file was not telling the whole story. Anytime that happened at the FBI, he knew what to do—use his clearance to dig deeper.

He backed out of her file, then clicked through to a separate search area that required him to log in again with additional credentials. Thank the Lord he had earned enough clearance to be able to see a few levels of classification beyond the standard files. Though if her information was top-level classified, he would hit a dead end.

He typed in her name and waited.

One result popped up on the screen. Sure enough, it was classified, but available to Callum's clearance level.

His pulse picked up speed for some odd reason as he hovered the mousepad arrow over the file with his finger. Phoenix Gray was so mysterious and intriguing. And he was about to find out why. Though he would've rather heard it from her than snooped in an FBI file.

But it couldn't be helped. If he was going to solve the Forster case before leaving the Bureau, he needed to investigate any suspicious people or peculiarities associated with it.

He opened the file.

The initial information duplicated the previous data he'd read.

He skimmed through it. Hopefully, there'd be something more in the file. Must be, since it was classified.

Whoa. His gaze froze on intel unlike anything he'd expected.

He swallowed. Blinked.

Looked again.

It couldn't be.

Phoenix Gray was a legally changed name, adopted when she was eighteen years old.

Her birth name was Robin Forster.

---

Phoenix and Dagian strode into the breakroom at Phoenix K-9 headquarters. The assembled agents hushed as they usually did when she first arrived, but their comfortable chatter would soon resume.

"Hey, boss."

"Hi, Phoenix."

The greetings from Nevaeh and Cora reached her ears as the smell of coffee infused her nostrils. Cora had apparently made Nevaeh's favorite caramel-flavored variety again. A regular habit now since the communications and technologies specialist had learned Nevaeh loved it.

Phoenix sat in her armchair at the far side of the seating area, scanning the room. Not that any of the protection K-9s in the breakroom would have allowed unwanted visitors inside.

Her gaze quickly took in the occupants as Dag lay on the floor beside her.

Sofia sat in the armchair at the front of the room, only her German shepherd Raksa with her for the late-night meeting.

Her Newfoundland water-rescue K-9, Gaston, was likely at home, enjoying the attentions of Sofia's adopted daughter, Grace.

Raksa lounged near Alvarez, Nevaeh's rottweiler mix, in the open area of carpet by the air-conditioning vent, which wasn't running due to the cool temperature outdoors.

Nevaeh and Jazz shared the long sofa, Nevaeh's PTSD service dog, Cannenta, sitting on the cushion between them. The corgi mix leaned into Nevaeh's shoulder, and the woman wrapped an arm around the dog's small body.

Jazz's protection and tracking K-9, Flash, stayed close to her as usual, the Belgian Malinois' front paws on her shoe as he stretched out on the floor between the sofa and coffee table.

Bristol sat opposite Jazz on the loveseat, the coffee table between them. Her explosives detection black Labrador, Toby, inched along the table at the front of the room, his nose lifted to check for the snacks that were only there in the mornings.

Cora sat on the other end of the loveseat, her narcotics K-9, Jana, resting her head on Cora's knee. A sign the golden retriever thought Cora was in need of comfort.

Phoenix homed in on Cora's face.

Her porcelain complexion was paler than normal, her eyes rimmed in pink.

Phoenix's stomach twisted. She hadn't wanted to tell Cora the topic of the meeting when she'd instructed her to assemble the team. But it would be better this way.

Cora always researched any topic Phoenix told her the meetings would focus on. She would have already performed the research necessary for the entire team to be brought up to speed on the case at hand. Without needing details from Phoenix.

She had known Cora would be deeply impacted by reading about the crimes associated with the case. But at least Cora would have spent most of her tears and strongest emotion in private and would be able to discuss it now.

The other team members darted concerned glances at Cora, then Sofia, and, finally, Phoenix.

Good. They were starting to look to Sofia as their leader. Exactly what needed to happen. They were almost there now.

Sofia, though Cora had told her the subject of the meeting per Phoenix's instructions, remained silent and focused on Phoenix.

Until Phoenix gave her a slight nod.

The petite woman's raven-black hair shifted on her shoulders as she received the message and scanned the other agents. "We're meeting tonight to bring everyone up-to-date on a big find for our agency."

*Our agency.* The possessive wording was an excellent sign. Sofia was settling into her role as the manager of the team and the agency.

"Dag and Phoenix found the remains of the first victim of the Forster killer, right here in Hennepin County."

The other team members looked as confused as Phoenix had expected.

"The Forster killer? I don't remember hearing about that." Jazz's new boldness and comfort with the team showed as she made the admission without hesitation or nervousness.

"Same, girl." Nevaeh nodded.

"I learned about it in a criminology class, or I wouldn't know either." Sofia glanced at Cora. "I still don't remember much, but you looked it up, right?"

Cora took in a slow breath as her gaze dropped to the notebook computer on her lap. "Yes. It's..." Her large blue eyes lifted to view the group, touching briefly on Phoenix as she moistened her lips. "It's one of the saddest, hardest things I've ever read."

"Do you want me to read the info?" Sofia's forehead furrowed with concern she used to not let herself feel for others. Her healed, stronger self could risk caring now.

Phoenix would advise Sofia to care deeply but to keep the emotions hidden so as not to allow others to use them against her. But each agent needed to heal in her own way and live as she saw fit.

"Thank you." Cora's next breath was still shaky. "But I've put it into my shorthand notes. I had better share it."

Phoenix's heart constricted behind her ribs. But Cora was always stronger than she thought. Cora needed to remember that, to practice using that strength. Her sadness would pass.

"The Forster killer is called that because he attacked a family with the last name Forster in Hennepin County, twenty-six years ago."

"Oh." Jazz's mouth circled around the word as her eyes widened. "We were just kids then."

Cora nodded. She would have been the youngest of them all —only three years old.

"He attacked a whole family?" Nevaeh stroked Cannenta's back, and the dog lowered to lie across her lap.

"Yes." Cora looked at the computer screen again. "He invaded their home at night when they were sleeping, though David Forster made it to the door as the intruder entered. The intruder shot and killed David Forster and his wife, Eve Forster, after he forced her to tie up her two daughters. He killed the couple in front of the children." Cora's voice shook with the last sentence.

Jana pushed in closer and placed her paw on Cora's knee, using the natural therapy instincts the dog shared with everyone as needed.

Cora stroked the golden's head as moisture filled her eyes. A tear escaped and tracked down her cheek.

A pang pierced Phoenix's chest. Sweet Cora. Too fragile and good for survival in this dark world. She wore her soft heart on her sleeve for all to see and take advantage of that vulnerability. Exactly like Rose.

Phoenix aimed a stare at Sofia.

She nodded. "I remember enough to take it from here."

The other agents pulled their attention from Cora to Sofia, but sadness lined their faces.

"He kidnapped the girls and took them to a house in the woods. Can't remember the exact location, but it was in this general area. No one knew where he'd taken them, though, or who he was for days. I think it was a really big deal in the news at the time."

"Yes." Cora sniffed. "The nation was shocked. Many law enforcement agencies were called in for the search and investigation."

"I'm afraid to ask." Bristol jumped her gaze between Cora and Sofia. "Did they catch the guy? Find the girls?"

"One of the girls escaped, right?" Sofia looked at Cora.

"Yes. Robin. The eldest." Cora pressed her lips together. "Though she was only ten."

How strange to hear Cora use that name. And the names of Phoenix's father and mother. Cora did so with great honor and compassion, of course. Which tempted Phoenix to indulge feelings she rarely entertained. Sadness, grief. But neither would serve any purpose there, now. Perhaps when it was all over.

Sofia nodded. "Robin managed to find someone at a nearby house who called the police. But when they got to the house where Robin told the cops he was hiding, the kidnapper had left with the younger sister."

"Rose." Cora inserted the name, her tone conveying the importance of the victim's identity, her personhood beyond being a victim in a long-dead cold case. Cora's soft, compassionate heart made her vulnerable, but it also made her an important asset to the PK-9 Agency. A necessary one.

"Please tell me they found Rose later?" Nevaeh dug her fingers into Cannenta's short fur.

Sofia shook her head.

"She was presumed dead." Cora's pained voice drew Nevaeh's gaze. "They never found her or the killer. Until Dag and Phoenix located her remains yesterday."

"You mean he got away with that? Destroying an entire family?" Bristol's ire flashed from her blue-gray eyes.

The same rage at the injustice, always simmering inside Phoenix, flared in response to Bristol's reaction.

No one answered. Not orally. But the silence and exchanged stares were the response.

"That can't be." Jazz shook her head, red ponytail swinging slightly with the motion. "How could he get away after a crime like that? What about DNA evidence?"

"They found some at the house where he held the girls, but they couldn't locate a match in any of the databases." Cora's tone welled with sadness.

"What about description?" Bristol stared intensely at Cora. "Was Robin able to describe him?"

"She did her best, yes. It must have been so hard for her. Such a brave girl." Cora's gaze dropped to her lap for a second, her empathy enabling her to grasp a fraction of the trauma, terror, and will to find Rose that Robin had experienced then.

Cora rallied and continued. "He had no eyebrows or hair. The police deduced from her description that he had shaved all of his hair to avoid leaving DNA at the murder scene. A forensic artist did a composite, and they checked it against the criminal databases and with all area security cameras. There were no matches."

"I've seen a lot of things..." Jazz's cheeks reddened with the anger that tightened her voice. "But that has to be the most awful crime I've ever heard of in this country. To destroy the safety of a child's home and murder their whole family? Then kidnap them and..."

"Did he..." Nevaeh slid her tongue over her lips as she glanced at Sofia and Cora, letting the sensitive question hang.

Cora nodded, smashing her lips together as more tears tumbled down her cheeks. It was too much for her sensitive heart to contemplate something as horrific as physical, sexual abuse, especially on top of the other crimes.

The sight of her tears wrenched Phoenix's heart. But no one would see that emotion on her face.

Regardless, Cora had suffered enough, likely imagining and reliving the crimes as if she were the victim through her vivid imagination and empathetic heart.

"He repeated the same crime multiple times after the first killings."

All eyes swung to Phoenix, almost as if shocked she was in the room.

Perfect. They were getting closer to where they needed to be.

But for now, she would wrap this up and give Cora time to gather her strength. "He's classified as a serial killer. He doesn't simply kidnap the child but always first kills the parents or authority figures in the child's life. Then he rips the child from the home, does his worst, and murders the child in the end."

"So he has more than kidnapping as his goal." Sofia narrowed her large eyes as she looked at Phoenix. "He's getting his kicks from destroying the illusion of safety the home and parents offer."

No surprise Sofia would make such accurate observations. The former CIA agent consistently displayed skill in quick psychological profiling.

"You said 'child.'" Bristol leaned forward to better see Phoenix. "Does that mean he doesn't take multiple children anymore?"

"Correct."

Sofia glanced from Phoenix to Bristol. "Probably learned from his mistake since Robin got away the first time."

It wasn't the only mistake he'd learned from and subsequently changed his tactics for the following kidnappings and murders. He wasn't adverse to modifying some elements of his attacks if needed.

But there was one element he would never change. Phoenix was sure of that. And she held that one certainty in her pocket—a gold disc pendant attached to a chain.

"So what are we going to do about this guy?" Sofia's black eyebrows pinched together as passionate anger sparked in her irises, apparent even across the room.

Cora looked at Phoenix, then responded with the other information Phoenix had instructed her to share. "Nothing more."

"You kiddin'?" Nevaeh shot a disbelieving look at Cora.

Pride in these agents swelled in Phoenix's torso. They were displaying one of the reasons Phoenix had chosen and assembled them. None of these women could ever be content with injustice or sitting on their hands. The lack of justice in finding the monster would disturb them to the point they would be ready to take action, if they were needed.

Their participation wouldn't be necessary if all went according to Phoenix's preferred plan. But if the killer responded differently than the most likely possibility, the team's passionate drive to catch evildoers and protect the innocent would be helpful.

"I understand how you feel." Cora met Nevaeh's incredulous gaze. "It bothers me, too. But Phoenix will be participating in the press conference tomorrow, where they're going to announce the discovery of Rose's remains."

"You're going to a press conference?" Jazz asked the question with a direct stare at Phoenix. Jazz had indeed come a long way after facing and conquering the darkness of her past. At least now, her boldness was fueled by trust in Phoenix rather than doubt and suspicion as before.

"The public should be made aware that the Phoenix K-9 Agency now offers cadaver services."

Sofia nodded, affirming Phoenix's statement. "It's an awesome new service. We can give closure to loved ones of people who have passed but haven't been recovered. And, hopefully, we can bring new evidence to light that can put away bad guys like the Forster killer."

"You think they'll find new evidence with the remains?" Hope lifted Nevaeh's tone.

"We can pray for that."

They all nodded in response to Cora's statement, Bristol tacking on an "Amen."

Strange how the team members had all become religious. That was the one aspect of their healing journeys Phoenix hadn't predicted.

But it didn't matter, so long as they all rose above their pasts, using their painful experiences to make them stronger.

Strong enough that they didn't need her anymore. A goal that was almost achieved.

But now it seemed she would complete her lifelong mission before moving on.

She had found Rose. The trap was set. Now, she would add the bait.

# ELEVEN

"The Phoenix K-9 Agency has found the remains of Rose Forster, an innocent victim of atrocities no one should have to suffer." The metal of the pendant warmed against Phoenix's skin, strange and foreign, as she stood behind the podium.

She was wearing a V-neck T-shirt and her tan leather jacket to the press conference at Minneapolis City Hall. Both clothing articles she never wore. But she didn't want to blend into the background today. She needed to catch attention. His attention.

Which was the only reason she was, for the first time, speaking to the press. "We are certain this discovery will lead to the apprehension of the criminal who ended her life and to justice being served."

She stared at the camera aimed at her. She couldn't care less what the reporters seated in chairs below the staircase thought of her or her words.

They would assume she referred to the FBI's hope they'd find evidence in the house on the property that would lead to the killer. The FBI wouldn't find a thing. He wouldn't make the mistake of leaving DNA at a location again.

But she wasn't talking to the press. She was talking to someone else.

She knew he had returned to the U.S. He would see the news. He would be watching, hating every moment, even without knowing who she was.

Applause surged through the audience, and several reporters shouted questions.

She ignored them, marching down the stairs with Dagian. She'd accomplished all she needed to.

Now she simply had to wait for him to take the bait.

He would do so quickly. He wouldn't be able to stand the disruption she'd created in his desire for completion. She had ruined the satisfaction he'd had in Rose's murder.

Pleasure rose up inside her as she headed for the hallway that led to the rear exit out of the building. She had waited a long time for this moment. Much longer than it should have taken.

At first, when living at her grandparents' house after her escape, she hadn't been able to sleep. Or to live one moment without fearing he would find her there. Her ten-year-old mind told her he would hunt her down and take her again.

Four years later, she had learned otherwise. Another home invasion, murder of a family, and kidnapping of an eight-year-old girl took place in Montana. At the time, no one seemed to consider it could have been done by the same killer.

But Phoenix did. She knew the moment she'd heard the details of the case on the news.

And at fourteen years old, she'd had to give up the hope that had replaced the fear he would find her someday. She had begun to look for him, to hope he would come, and prepare to handle him as she hadn't been able to before. To be ready to rescue Rose, to free her from the monster. But the news of his new crime, an exact repeat of the one before, meant Phoenix would never see Rose again. It meant Rose was dead.

When he struck again, killing another family and stealing another girl, Phoenix was sixteen. She was ready to do something about it. To stop the monster that had slaughtered her family and bring him to justice. But the FBI said she was too young to consult on the case.

At eighteen, the FBI finally allowed her to consult on another murder and kidnapping that matched his MO. She'd arrived too late and knew too little how to handle FBI agents to be effective, and he'd gotten away.

But three years later, when he killed another family and kidnapped their daughter, she was ready. The FBI agents who finally listened to her almost caught him.

And then she'd lost him.

As the years passed, longer than he would have been able to wait to kill and kidnap again, Phoenix searched for him. Monitored all kidnapping cases, assisted the FBI in any that remotely fit his MO.

Until she'd realized that almost being caught had frightened him. But he would never be able to quit. His desire, his need, to commit violence was too powerful for him to resist. He had to have gone elsewhere.

She'd expanded her search to outside the United States, connecting with CIA operatives in foreign countries. She learned of similar crimes being committed in Mexico. But when she followed him there, lack of communication and resources, corruption, and drug cartels interfered with every attempt to apprehend the monster.

She lost him again when he traveled farther south. But she kept trailing, never giving up, though kidnappings were so frequent in those countries that no one, even what law enforcement there was, seemed to care.

In between her work in the U.S. with the Phoenix K-9 Agency and other projects, she kept tabs on South American countries through the CIA, traveling to the sites when any operative thought a kidnapping could have been perpetrated by the monster.

And she continued to monitor and consult on cases in the U.S. with the FBI, constantly aware he could return one day.

Then, eighteen years later, news of a Canadian kidnapping that fit his MO hit the news media. Phoenix had attempted to interface with the Canadian authorities but hadn't been well-received. So she had searched for him and the child with Dag. And she'd returned to do the same three years later when he'd killed again.

But he was back now. On U.S. soil. She didn't know why, and she didn't care.

The family murder and kidnapping in Wisconsin three years ago was his work, without a doubt. Phoenix had been called in to consult, but too late. He'd had too much time to do what he always did. Disappear without a trace.

But he would not do that again. Not this time. Because she had the control.

She had the disc that hung from her neck.

He would be driven to calm the itch, to satisfy his need for the Phaistos Disc to be buried with a victim.

His obsessive love for the Phaistos Disc, or what it represented to him, had been obvious even to the child Phoenix had been when he'd taken them. He'd kept the pendant close at all times, fingering it with his gloved hands as he watched Rose. Until the day he'd hung it around her neck.

Phoenix hadn't known what the disc or symbols meant at the time. Only years later, when she was fifteen, did she think to look for information on what she had thought was some sort of medallion.

Discovering that the pendant was actually a replica of the Phaistos Disc hadn't been very helpful. Except that it indicated a fascination with unsolved mysteries or codes, since no one had yet to determine what the etchings on the real Greek artifact meant. Discovered in the early 1900s and thought to be from the 1600s B.C., the ancient Phaistos Disc, with its tiny symbols etched in a spiral design, could represent to him the mystery he wanted people to think he was.

Or perhaps he was obsessed with someone from his past, a family member or abuser, who had a fascination with ancient history. He could be frustrated by the unsolved mystery that made the symbols and their message feel unresolved. And he needed to complete the puzzle the only way he knew how. To kill a young girl and bury her with the disc.

Why he cared about the disc was one of the few psychological elements she hadn't been able to determine. Not conclusively. But she had deduced he'd buried the Phaistos Disc with Rose.

And Phoenix had been right.

She knew with equal certainty now that he would need to bury it again, with another girl. He had likely buried similar Phaistos Disc replicas with each of his undiscovered victims.

Now he would be driven by his need for completion to bury his original pendant with another target, likely a child he'd already identified and planned to make his next victim. Phoenix's actions wouldn't change that, beyond perhaps moving up his timeline.

But he would need to retrieve his Phaistos Disc first.

From her.

---

"Ms. Gray." Callum lengthened his stride to overtake the woman's fast clip in the wide hallway before she reached the doors only a couple of yards beyond her.

She stopped abruptly, swinging to face him with her K-9.

His chest squeezed at the sight of her impassive face, the void in her eyes. Knowing why didn't make it easier to see.

Though he could understand why he hadn't recognized her. Robin's girlish features had developed into the stunning high cheekbones, full lips, and perfect jawline of a beautiful woman. And she had drastically changed her hair color and eye color. Phoenix kept her distance from people and wore a baseball cap, probably in part to prevent anyone from noticing she was wearing colored contacts.

All clever tactics to ensure no one, not even reporters at a press conference, would ever recognize her as Robin Forster.

The outfit she'd donned for the press conference also seemed designed to prevent anyone thinking of young Robin. The fitted, tan leather jacket she wore with a pendant necklace, black V-neck shirt, and jeans emphasized her mature femininity more than her usual plainer, functional clothes. More misdirection for any observers.

Still, it was surprising she'd go on camera if she was in hiding. But was she hiding from the public or her family's killer?

He would think it had to be the public, given her fearlessness and the skills he'd witnessed. But maybe even this strong woman could be afraid of her childhood tormentor.

She certainly wasn't afraid of Callum, judging from the blink-free stare she leveled at him. While she waited for him to say something.

Her own love of silence prevented Callum from feeling embarrassed by his delay. But she would probably turn and stride away in another second if he didn't hurry up.

"I wanted to thank you for your words about Rose out there." He thumbed over his shoulder in the general direction of the lobby where the press conference continued. "Like you, I'm hoping you and your K-9 recovering her will lead to justice."

No change in her expression or the eyes that watched him.

"Now that the expedited DNA test confirmed the identity of the remains, I'm authorized to pursue this case personally." He met her gaze, hoping she would see in his expression the care and passion he would pour into the investigation. "I want you to know this is the only case I'm going to be investigating, and I won't stop until we get justice for Rose."

And for her, Robin. He fought back the urge to voice the addition, though everything in him wanted to say it.

Another instinct warred with his better judgment—to physically reach out to her and offer some gesture of comfort. He'd cared so long about the little girl who had survived horror beyond imagination. The girl who'd had the courage and intelligence to escape and try to save her sister. The girl who had lost everything.

But she wasn't a little girl anymore. She was a fierce woman. One who would probably break his arm or worse if he tried to touch her.

So he stuck with adding one more promise he hoped she would take to heart. "You can count on me. I'll find him. If he's still alive, he'll be brought to justice."

Still not even a flicker in her eyes. But she seemed to study him more closely. Unless he was imagining things.

"Yes. He will." Her deep voice stayed even, devoid of emotion.

But as she pivoted and left with her K-9, a shiver passed over Callum's arms. Phoenix Gray, the grown Robin Forster, was on a mission of her own.

And he didn't think anyone or anything would be able to stand in her way.

# TWELVE

"Good. Do it again. Bend your knees more." Phoenix watched the two fourteen-year-olds rep the choke defense for the third time.

A smile stretched across Keisha's face as she easily broke her training partner's grip around her neck.

Phoenix moved on to the next pair of girls, scanning the school gym that held the twenty-one at-risk teens who had shown up for the free self-defense class.

LaRen and Tori, the two volunteers who helped at the weekly class, had learned enough skills that they were able to offer tips to some of the teams.

"More head whip, Janelle." Phoenix walked past two more girls, her gaze traveling beyond them to check on Dag and Shequila.

The girl had balked at practicing chokes, clearly on the brink of a PTSD episode. Tori had guided Shequila to the bench along the wall, where the teen now stroked Dag's head as he sat beside her.

Dagian didn't have natural therapeutic tendencies, but he'd learned to offer his head for petting and his silent presence for strength and comfort when Phoenix asked him to do so.

Given Shequila's history with assault, Phoenix would have Cora bring Jana to next week's class, which would focus on more choke defenses. The golden retriever would be better able to offer the kind of support the girl needed, as would Cora.

Phoenix checked her watch. *3:25 p.m.*

Four more minutes, and she would dismiss the class. She would then take Dag to the house to decompress. He had tremendous physical and mental stamina, but not for dealing with people.

Phoenix had also had enough human contact for one day after instructing inmates training K-9s at the prison, coaching survivors of sex trafficking at the rehab home, and teaching a self-defense class at the domestic abuse shelter before arriving at the community center to instruct the teens.

But maintaining a predictable routine was essential. She had given him a week since the press conference. Approximately two days longer than she thought he could stand to wait before trying for his Phaistos Disc pendant.

He could have chosen to study her routine, the times and places she visited on each particular weekday.

But she hadn't seen him. And she would have if he'd followed her.

He could be waiting until next week, when the same days would repeat themselves and allow him to predict his best opportunity to attack and take the pendant. But since neither she nor Dag had detected an observer or tail, it was more likely he had chosen the other option she had anticipated.

He was planning to create a situation that would bring her to him.

Her smartphone vibrated in the pocket of her jeans.

She pulled it out and checked the caller ID.

*Marion Moore.*

Phoenix held the phone to her ear, glancing at her watch. She had two minutes to release the class, or they would run over. She never released them late. "Marion."

"Phoenix." The fear in Marion's voice surged adrenaline through Phoenix's veins. Something was wrong.

Marnie.

Phoenix stalked toward LaRen as Marion continued.

"I'm so sorry to bother you, but Marnie isn't home yet. She should've come home on the bus five minutes ago with Joe. But he said she never got on. She was on a field trip with her class today at Timber National Park. They were supposed to get back in time for her to take her usual bus home."

"Did you call the school?" Phoenix stopped by LaRen and circled her finger in the air, then pointed to the doors.

The woman nodded and turned to Tori, murmuring that they should end the class.

"Yes, I've called three times, but I keep getting a busy signal." Marion's tone pinched with worry. "It's not even going to their machine."

"I'm on it."

Dag jogged toward her as the girl he had comforted jumped up to join the others gathering their things.

"Thank you. I tried calling Eli, but he's at work, and he won't get his messages until tonight. I could pack up all the kids and go, but I know you can get there much faster."

Dag reached Phoenix in time to follow her through the door that led to the rear exit from the building.

"I'm probably overreacting, right? The class trip just ran a little late or something. They said it's an hour and a half to drive to Timber Park from the school."

Phoenix locked the steel exit door behind her and hurried to her white van, using the remote to start the engine and open the back for Dag to jump inside.

"Phoenix? Am I worried about nothing?" Marion's voice pleaded for comfort.

Far better to prepare her for the truth Phoenix would confirm shortly. "No."

Phoenix hit the gas and peeled out of the parking lot.

Eight minutes later, she pulled to a stop in front of the

Edison Elementary entrance and dropped out, remotely opening the rear double doors to let Dag free to catch up with her.

The small lobby was empty, but voices and ringing phones carried from the wide, shadowed hallway beyond.

Phoenix homed in on the sounds as she marched toward the light spilling through a window and open doorway.

A woman's raised voice hit Phoenix and Dag as they stepped into the room marked *Office*. "My daughter has dance rehearsal at four. If I don't get her there on time, she could lose her part in the recital."

"I'm sorry, ma'am." A woman with short black hair looked at the tall blonde who stood on the front side of the standing-height desk. "Principal Billings is getting their ETA right now." The middle-aged woman, whose nametag identified her as *Mrs. Chalmers, Office Manager*, spoke calmly. But the cluster of lines tightening the outer corners of her dark eyes betrayed her tension.

Four women and two men Phoenix deduced were teachers filled the space behind the desk, answering the incessantly ringing phones and offering similar statements. Stalling.

Two additional women stepped into the crowded space by the desk to speak to Mrs. Chalmers. Likely more parents.

A closed blue door labeled *Principal Billings* wasn't enough to hide the man exposed through the windows of his office, rubbing his forehead as he bent over a landline phone.

In a few quick steps, Phoenix rounded the open end of the desk and headed for the principal's office.

"Ma'am, wait!"

Phoenix recognized Chalmers' voice without looking back.

"You can't go in there." Chalmers' heels clicked as she hurried behind Phoenix, drawing the attention of the teachers. "The principal will speak with all of you as soon as he knows something…Stop!"

Phoenix gripped the knob, shot Chalmers a staying glance, and shoved in the office door.

Billings looked up, his eyes wide behind black-rimmed glasses. Panic lit his brown irises. But not because of Phoenix.

"I'm sorry, Principal Billings. This lady—"

"Is not leaving." Phoenix leveled Chalmers with a steady stare to match her even tone. There was no time to indulge the woman's nervous chatter.

Chalmers shut her open mouth, her big eyes shooting from Phoenix to her boss.

Phoenix turned her full attention on Billings, stepping close to the desk he sat behind. "Where is the bus?"

He lowered the cordless phone receiver, his stare riveted on her. "I…" He moistened his lips, his gaze flitting down to where Dag stood by her side. His head jerked up as if something startled him. "You're that woman from TV. The press conference. I remember your dog."

Good. That might help him trust her enough to be truthful. If he would stop being evasive. "The bus, Billings. You've lost one."

"Oh." He blinked. "I wouldn't say that." He reached up to adjust his glasses. His fingers trembled.

She held her stare. Silent.

"Well…" He dropped his focus to the papers scattered on his desk. Personnel files with contact information and an emergency protocol file folder.

"One of our classes is a bit tardy." He took in a breath and aimed his gaze a few inches from her eyes. "They went on a field trip to Timber National Park today, and they were expected back at three o'clock. But it's a long drive, and I'm sure they simply ran late or perhaps had a bit of car trouble."

His hand went to the phone on his desk. "Perhaps a flat tire. I'm going to call the teachers' numbers again." He threw Phoenix a shaky smile. "I'm told the cell phone reception can be next to none out there."

He was correct about the lack of cellular reception at Timber Park. And there was a possibility his theory of a harmless delay was also accurate.

But Marnie was on that field trip. Along with other children.

"How many students were on the trip?"

He held the receiver to his ear, his frown deepening as he probably heard only rings on the other end. "I'd have to check today's attendance record to be sure how many went. But there are fifty-one in the class." He slowly lowered the phone, shaking his head. "Still no answer on Mrs. Tegan's phone. She's the third-grade teacher. Her teacher's aide, Ms. Jennison, went along, as well, but my calls go directly to her voicemail."

"Have you called the police?"

His gaze shot to her face, dismay shifting his features. "I don't think that's necessary. Not yet. I'm going to give it ten more minutes. I'm sure they'll show up or call me back. I left messages with the teachers."

"Call the police. Now." Phoenix pivoted and left the office.

Dag matched her urgent pace as they exited the school and got in the van.

Billings could be right. But if he wasn't, the delay may have already been deadly.

# THIRTEEN

"There. The parking lot." Phoenix gave the direction to Roy Davis as he aimed the helicopter toward the rectangular, graveled lot at the entrance of Timber National Park. She checked her watch. *4:31 p.m.*

The sun, just starting to set, bathed the lot in a passing orange glow.

The lot appeared empty, but the east edge was bordered with trees thick enough to obscure anything beneath, especially through the dying orange, red, and yellow leaves that clung to their branches.

She'd beaten law enforcement to the scene with the helicopter, though Minneapolis police would have contacted the local Kewaunee County Sheriff's Office. Still a distance from Timber Park, they should arrive within ten more minutes if they took the situation seriously.

Phoenix gripped the strap of her trail backpack as the helicopter lowered. She would have preferred to fly herself, but Roy was a decent pilot. And she may not have been able to return his copter anytime soon. Depending on what she would find.

Phoenix peered at the hidden section of the lot as the copter dropped below the tree line.

A yellow school bus.

It waited alone by the border of the thick forest.

The class had never left the park.

Adrenaline spiked through Phoenix's system as the copter touched down. "Stay here. I may need you to transport wounded." Though she doubted there would be any to send with him. Not yet.

Her hiking boots hit the gravel as the blades whirred above her head. She held the door open for Dag to scramble to the front seat and jump out.

They headed across the empty lot, Phoenix scanning the surroundings.

Her nerve endings sparked, every instinct detecting and warning of danger.

Her gaze landed on the bus as she approached. No sign of occupants through the windows.

The folding door was flung to the side, hanging from one hinge. The door's safety glass windows were shattered into pieces that the laminate barely held together.

The theory that the class and teachers were lost in the park or waiting for help due to an injury was no longer viable. Phoenix's gut instinct was correct—their situation was far worse.

She slowed as she came within five feet of the bus.

Dag matched her controlled pace.

That smell. The odor she would never forget.

Blood.

Her stomach clenched.

Marnie.

She signaled to Dag to wait outside the bus. She wouldn't need him or her Glock. What had happened there was finished.

The perpetrator was gone.

She stiffened her jaw and climbed the steps to board the bus.

Three adults slumped in seats at the rear. Two women. One male.

Dead.

Phoenix scanned the remainder of the bus in seconds as she walked from the front to the rear.

Blood spattered the driver's seat and two front seats.

Children's backpacks and lunch containers littered the other seats and the floor.

She reached the bodies. Pressed her fingers to their necks to ensure her initial assessment was correct. No pulse.

The teachers and bus driver had met their deaths at the front of the bus and been moved, left slumped in the seats so they wouldn't be seen through windows.

The scene told a story Phoenix did not want to read.

Marnie had been kidnapped.

By the monster.

---

Callum dragged a hand through his hair as he stared at the notebook computer that sat on the hotel room desk. This couldn't be a dead end. Not yet.

The expedited results of the DNA samples they'd found at the house on the property where Rose's body had been buried were disheartening, to say the least. No match to the DNA found at the original house where the Forster killer had kept the girls before he'd fled with Rose.

There had probably been many residents at this second location in the twenty-six years since the kidnapping. Their use and cleaning could have erased traces of the killer's DNA and prints.

Or he had been more careful after his first location had been discovered, thanks to Robin.

But that meant no breakthrough in the case. No progress that would—

His phone rumbled on the desk beside his hand.

Agent Lining's number lit the screen.

He picked it up. "Ross here."

"I know you're focused on the Forster case right now."

And he didn't want to work any others. This was his last

case. He'd thought Carney had made that clear to the Minneapolis SAC when she'd sent him there.

"But we have a situation."

Whatever it was, Callum would have to say no. He needed to stay focused. There was always another case. One that would probably end up the same as the others—with him putting away a bad guy that would get out of prison all too soon to hurt children again.

But he wasn't going to be rude and cut her off.

"Forty-eight kids have gone missing in Timber National Park."

He straightened in his chair. Had he heard her right? "Forty-eight?"

"A third-grade class on a field trip."

He blinked. "And they're all missing? Or they just didn't return yet?" Could be a traffic accident or—

"All missing. Their bus was found still at the park. Their teachers and bus driver were murdered."

His stomach twisted. The poor victims. And their families. "I'm so sorry."

"I'm calling you because you know kidnappings and…well… the first officers on scene said a lady had discovered the bus and bodies before they'd arrived. She told them the children had been kidnapped by the Forster killer. Said to call the FBI."

Shock surged through Callum's bloodstream. "Wait. Was she—"

"Pretty sure from their description the lady was Phoenix Gray."

Callum shot out of his chair. "On my way."

He'd logged about one hundred prayers by the time he drove into the Timber Park lot two hours later.

Good thing the lot was built to contain many visitors' vehicles during peak season. Seemed every law enforcement and rescue vehicle within two counties was crammed into the space. Ambulance, fire engine, police cars, and unmarked SUVs and sedans like Callum's.

He pulled to a stop beside a large black SUV that had to be FBI issue and got out.

Headlights and flashing strobe lights illuminated the parking lot enough to see well without a flashlight or night vision goggles.

His gaze locked on the school bus.

A large area around the bus was cordoned off with yellow tape and illuminated with scene lights. Police CSIs worked behind the border in their hazmat suits. Some were crouched outside the bus, examining the ground and collecting samples from the vehicle's exterior.

White-hooded heads of others moved past the windows inside the bus. A bus where children had sat earlier that day. Where they'd expected to have fun—probably laughed, teased. And expected that their teachers would take them back to school, and they'd go home. Happy and safe.

His jaw tightened. That was where they should be. Home.

Was Phoenix right? Were they with the Forster killer?

Grabbing forty-eight children at once didn't fit his MO. What made her think—

A bark sounded. Close.

He turned around and looked for the source of the noise.

Light glowed through the windows of the building that stood to one side of the lot. Probably a visitor center now commandeered for the base of rescue operations. Two men and a woman in FBI jackets stood near the entrance, talking.

About eight yards away from the building, a group of women clustered near a white van. Something moved around them in the shadows. More than one something. Dogs.

Phoenix?

He hurried in that direction. He could first check in with the FBI agent running the recovery operation. But Phoenix would know more than anyone else about what was going on. Especially if she was the one who'd discovered the bus and murder victims.

"Lost?"

A woman's voice, accompanied by footsteps crunching in the gravel, made Callum stop. He turned to see the petite woman with dark black hair he'd glimpsed by the visitor center.

Her eyes narrowed as she planted small fists on her hips. "Special Agent Ross?"

"Yes."

"Your SAC called ahead. Understand you're an expert here to help us." The edge in her tone signaled she wasn't happy with that concept. And her use of *help us* carried more than a little sarcasm.

He kept his tone even and on the gentle side as he responded. "I'm sure you'll have everything well in hand. I'm only hoping you'll let me stick around and see if the kidnapper is the man I'm after."

She folded her arms across her zippered FBI jacket. Stared at him for a second. "The Forster killer?"

"Yes, ma'am."

"Nguyen will do. Special Agent Nguyen."

He gave her a single nod, hoping that appeased her enough that she would lower her defenses. "Do you know if Phoenix Gray is here? I was told she might have been the one to discover the bodies."

"You know Phoenix?"

He almost laughed at the question. Did anyone know Phoenix? He managed to keep a serious expression and answered the best he could. "We've worked together. And I'm handling the investigation of the Forster murders, now that she found Rose Forster's body."

Nguyen's arms lowered, and her tense posture relaxed. Interesting. She glanced away. "She was here. The description the local cops gave of the woman they talked to fits her."

"She's gone?"

"Seems so. No one has seen her since we arrived, and the cops said she disappeared after they started looking at the crime scene."

Why would she leave if she thought this was the work of the Forster killer? She had to have a good reason.

Callum tried to get in her perspective, her headspace. She'd just learned the killer of her family, her own abuser, was there. That he had kidnapped more children. At least she apparently suspected that he was behind it.

He connected her motivations to the facts he knew, her behaviors since he'd been able to observe her.

The answer clicked into place. She would go after the kidnapper.

Would she tell her team? She'd clearly called them to the scene, or they wouldn't be there. And she must have intended to use them in some way.

He glanced at Nguyen. "Have you asked her team where she is?"

Nguyen stepped to the side to see past him, probably locating the women and their K-9s. "I didn't know they'd arrived. I was inside."

"Agent Nguyen!" A shout came from a police officer who stood by the crime scene perimeter.

She raised her hand to acknowledge the summons and shot Callum a glance. "Ask them and report back to me." She spun toward the visitor center. "Blaine!"

One of the FBI agents standing outside the building looked her way.

"Go with him." She jerked a thumb toward Callum.

She still didn't quite trust him. Probably afraid he was trying to muscle in and take over her case. She was right he had the clearance and authority to do so if the perpetrator was the Forster killer. But he didn't need to manage a massive recovery effort with various law enforcement agencies, the park ranger service, and rescue personnel. He needed to be free to focus only on finding and capturing the Forster killer. If he was actually there.

The woman marched away as Callum waited a few seconds for Agent Blaine to reach him. After quick introductions and

Callum's brief explanation as to why he was going to talk to the Phoenix K-9 Agency team, they started toward the women and dogs.

They were moving away from the van when Callum and Blaine reached them.

"Excuse me."

Four stunning women halted and turned to face them, along with their four dogs.

"I'm Callum Ross, and this is Agent Danny Blaine. FBI. I'd like to talk to Phoenix Gray, but it seems she's disappeared."

A grin flashed on the face of the woman with a cloud of black curls around her head and a rottweiler beside her. "She does that a lot."

The tall redhead rolled her eyes and elbowed the other woman above the Belgian Malinois that fidgeted at the end of a leash.

"She hasn't disappeared. She's searching." The brunette with a black Labrador met Callum's gaze.

"Searching? For the killer?" Blaine's tone took on a slightly suspicious or defensive note.

Callum had a feeling he knew where that was heading.

"For the children." A woman with upswept blond hair and a calm golden retriever at her side looked at Callum and Blaine with big eyes. "She started out immediately after the police officers arrived."

Callum didn't know whether to be thrilled or disappointed. Phoenix Gray was prioritizing rescuing the children. That was best. But it also meant he couldn't talk to her and find out why she thought the Forster killer was the perpetrator. "Has she been in contact with you?"

"Yes." The blonde nodded. "She wants us to begin searching, as well."

"You?" Blaine's skepticism was written all over his face.

"Our K-9s are experts in SAR." The redhead answered his doubt with a bite in her tone. "That's search and rescue. We're the best chance those children have right now."

"But you're also not prepared to find a killer."

A snort drew Callum's gaze to the woman with the rottweiler.

"Wanna bet?" She grinned at Blaine, challenge flashing in her eyes.

"You're civilians. You can't go tromping through the woods after an armed killer. Agent Nguyen will never authorize that."

"What won't I authorize?" Nguyen approached the group, scanning the women and K-9s.

Blaine lifted his hand to indicate the Phoenix K-9 team. "They want to go searching for the hostages with their dogs. I told them we can't allow civilians to go after an armed and dangerous killer. That's why we aren't allowing any volunteer search and rescue teams in here."

Nguyen jerked a nod. "It's true we can't call in the usual civilian teams and SAR dogs because of the danger. But Phoenix K-9 is different."

"What?" Blaine's eyebrows lowered as his mouth worked.

"Still, I don't think anyone should go in alone. And you're not armed, correct?" She aimed her attention at the blonde.

"No, I'm not. The other ladies are."

Interesting. Seemed Agent Nguyen already knew that agent well enough to assume she wasn't packing under her jacket.

"Is Phoenix already searching?"

"Yes." The same soft-spoken woman answered Nguyen. "She's been on the trail with Dag for two hours."

"Okay. You can follow her instructions and join the search. We need your K-9s out there."

"Nguyen—"

She held up a hand in Blaine's face to stop his protest. "But I want an FBI agent or cop to go with each of your teams. More firepower if you meet the killer and a safety net for everyone. It's a big park." Her straight eyebrows dipped. "You're missing somebody. Amalia Pérez."

"It's Sofia Barrett now." The blonde softened the odd correction with a gentle smile. "She arrived before we did and started searching with her K-9."

A Phoenix K-9 agent had changed her name?

Nguyen mashed her lips together. "Fine. But I want you to loop me in and make sure you're all on channel three for communications with the rest of our rescue crews."

The other Phoenix K-9 agents glanced sideways at the blonde, as if they weren't sure they could comply with that directive.

"Phoenix said she would call you on her satellite phone."

Nguyen jerked a nod. "Good. I'll assign personnel to go with you in the next five."

A ring sounded. Someone's phone.

The blonde reached around to the backpack she wore and retrieved a phone. Looked like a satellite phone. An expensive model. She glanced at Nguyen. "This is likely Phoenix now." The woman pressed the phone to her ear. "Hello?"

Silence cloaked the group as she listened to someone on the other end.

If it was Phoenix, he would ask to talk to her.

The blonde's eyes widened. She looked at Agent Nguyen. "Phoenix found one of the children."

# FOURTEEN

The fool.

Phoenix's blood roiled, tumbling hot through her veins as she carried the boy up the graveled service road.

Dag had found the boy sitting in the tall grass along the trail they'd been on, too frightened to speak. Too frightened to do anything but throw his arms around Phoenix and never let go.

She held him securely, firmly. The best response to his tight squeeze around her neck that begged for security and protection.

No child should have to be this way. To feel such fear.

And he hadn't even tasted the full extent of the treatment the monster gave his intended victims.

The boy had only been kidnapped. Likely witnessed the shooting of his teachers and bus driver. Good thing for him he was male. That simple fact had saved his life.

Fury clenched Phoenix's jaw as she trudged on, the boy's legs dangling to thump against her thighs. Able to see easily through her night vision goggles, she watched for unevenness of the road to keep the boy's ride smooth.

That fool.

He should've tried for the Phaistos Disc first. He would have already been tasting justice now.

He was trying to ad-lib too much. Never his strength. He thought he was clever, capturing his target and luring Phoenix close with his pendant all in one strike.

It would be his undoing.

He'd taken Marnie and forty-seven other children.

He was out of his depth. Departing from his formula for the perfect crime that had enabled him to escape justice so many years.

Phoenix had altered his focus enough to make him misstep more severely than she could have planned.

He wouldn't win this time.

The boy whimpered against her neck.

Ten more yards, and the FBI car would reach them. Cora had given Phoenix the rescue operation radio frequency, and she'd heard on coms when the car departed from the base. For now, the PK-9 team would use that frequency to report their location and any findings, as well.

The rumble of an engine and tires kicking up gravel reached Phoenix's ears.

She moved to the side of the road.

Dag followed her as headlights appeared, the car cresting the top of the hill.

The black sedan slowed to a stop. The passenger door on the near side opened first, and a man got out.

Agent Ross.

She had expected him to be called in as soon as she'd told the police who had kidnapped the children. Hadn't anticipated she would see him. Not that soon. And not in the field.

His gaze hit her briefly before stopping on the boy. Ross's mouth pulled down into a deep, painful frown. "Hey, buddy."

A pang shot through Phoenix's chest. Sharp. Unexpected.

"You're safe now."

That tone. His voice. So achingly gentle and soft. But undergirded with strength that gave his words validity. She'd never heard a man talk to a child that way. To anyone that way.

The boy loosened his hold on Phoenix's neck and lifted his head to look at Callum. Seemed the boy was as affected by Ross's tone as she was. That, and the agent's comforting touch on the child's back.

"We're going to get you home, okay?"

The boy nodded, as if charmed by Ross's demeanor, and reached for the agent.

Ross smiled and took the boy in his arms as naturally as if he held children every day. And maybe he did. The man could be married or have his own children for all Phoenix knew or cared. Such information couldn't be more irrelevant.

Whatever the cause, he had the necessary skills to deal correctly with the child and return him safely to Base.

Phoenix turned to leave the road with Dag.

"Ms. Gray, please wait."

She paused and looked back.

Ross's voice returned to the even and neutral delivery that seemed to be his norm as he asked the other agent who had exited the car to take the boy. He murmured something to the child that made him stand on his own two feet and accept the other agent's hand to walk to the car's back door.

Ross turned to Phoenix and took a few quick steps to halve the distance between them. "I'd like to team up with you, if that's all right."

There it was. The pitch she'd just wasted ten additional seconds waiting for. "I work alone." She would swing away and leave, but he wouldn't give up that easily. So she paused, watching him through the yellow-green tinted NVGs. He could point out she had called in a whole team of agents and K-9s to assist.

"I know you can handle yourself, and I don't want to get in your way."

Passing up the confrontational approach in favor of the flattery technique. Now he would likely assert that Katherine Nguyen or another agent had ordered him to accompany her.

"I'm only here to make sure everything that happens is legal."

Not the excuse she'd thought most likely if he was trying to flatter her. She peered at him. He could be referring to the context of this rescue operation, that a law enforcement agent should be present for any interactions with the children and perpetrator. Or he could intend to reference the incident in Chicago, when he'd found her choking the kidnapper.

"Frankly, Ms. Gray," he gazed at her as intently as if he could see her eyes, which were covered by NVGs, "I think you know more about what's going on here than anyone else, and I want to find out what you know. I also want to help in whatever way I can. Even if that's only acting on the information you can give me."

He was good. Exceptionally diplomatic and convincing. But his lack of detectable artifice —even to her who excelled in spotting any trace of disguise or deception—led her to suspect his persuasion was effective because he was being honest. Speaking the truth.

If she was wrong, and he was more skillfully duplicitous than any person she'd met, this man could be a serious threat to her plans and even to the lives of the children. But she could deal with him then. For now, she would keep him close, where she could monitor him.

His aim was capturing the same killer she was after. If she let him pursue that goal on his own, she couldn't keep him from getting in her way. And he would miss his target like all those before him, sending the monster into hiding once again.

Not an option. "No flashlights."

The corners of his mouth lifted upward with a bit of a smile as if she'd announced he could come. He reached into the pocket of his navy blue parka and pulled out a pair of NVGs. "Agent Nguyen let me borrow these. And I've got my coms set." He tapped the earpiece he already wore.

At least he knew to be prepared. She turned away, facing the forest east of the road. She placed a hand on Dag's head, the K-9 waiting by her leg. "Go get them, Dagian."

He sprang forward, resuming his search with a lifted nose initially as he checked the air. He would lead them back to the trail they'd had to abandon when they found the boy.

She took off after him, maintaining a fast stride that kept Dag in view as he trotted through the underbrush.

Callum caught up quickly, branches and brush cracking under his boots as he moved parallel with her, two arm-lengths away. "How do you know the Forster killer did this?"

An obvious fishing question. She glanced at him.

The NVGs covered his eyes, making him a bit harder to read. But he had the intelligence and knowledge to have observed the same evidence she had.

"You saw the crime scene." She looked forward again, watching the brush in front of her to avoid tripping.

"Yes. Just briefly before I came out here."

"Then you know." Phoenix kept an eye on Dag's silhouette. The K-9 held a steady pace, leading them in the correct direction for the trail they'd left to meet the FBI transport.

"He shot the authority figures, the illusion of safety for the children."

Phoenix let Ross's statement go unanswered. He likely already knew the other details he seemed to want her to fill in.

"The shots were one through the heart, two in the head, as the Forster killer always does. No shell casings remaining. The children left all their personal belongings behind."

And he had chosen the Timber National Park and an entire third-grade class to draw his pendant to him. Or at least the person who knew where it was. But Ross had no knowledge of that additional evidence. And he never would.

"Those elements and others fit his MO, but why would he take forty-eight children? He's never even taken more than one child since...the first time."

His pause pulsed between them like a signal flare. Had he been going to say, *Since you were taken,* or something similar?

He knew.

She'd suspected as much at the press conference, when his demeanor and behavior toward her had shifted slightly.

He'd been professional with unusual kindness before then. But the look of sincerity and earnestness in his eyes when he had promised to find her family's killer, though without that wording, had indicated he'd discovered who she was.

He must have searched deep in the FBI records for that information. And he apparently possessed a high security clearance. At least he would know her history was classified.

He had better keep it that way.

"PT3 to Base." Cora's voice came through Phoenix's coms earpiece, joy and relief in her tone. "We've found a boy."

# FIFTEEN

*Thank you, Lord.* Callum offered up the silent prayer as he listened on coms to the Phoenix K-9 agent and Nguyen communicate back and forth about transport for the boy. The rescuer, who sounded like the blonde Callum had spoken with, had said the boy was unharmed except for a few scratches.

Realization, the blossoming of the suspicion that had spawned when Phoenix had recovered the first boy, solidified in Callum's mind. "He's letting them go."

Phoenix stalked on, keeping her head aimed toward the dog she'd called Dagian as the K-9 led them through the woods. They both seemed to know where they were going, though Callum hadn't been able to see any visual signs of footprints or a trail yet.

"You already knew that, didn't you?"

She kept walking without so much as a glance in his direction.

Callum had never met a woman who spoke so seldom. He was usually the quiet one in any group.

He had better follow her example, given how he'd nearly let slip that he knew she was Robin Forster.

She hadn't reacted at all. But she was smart. Brilliant. She'd have noticed.

He could go ahead and admit that he knew. Then he could ask her the questions he'd been holding back—especially what her prior experience and unmatched insight into the Forster killer told her he was doing and would do next.

But Callum doubted she would share that information with him anyway. He had better clam up and wait until she wanted to tell him something on her own. If she ever did.

He cast her a glance.

The yellow-green view through his NVGs did nothing to diminish her strong, determined profile and confident stride.

This situation must be so difficult for her, resurrecting memories of her unbelievable trauma. And right after finding her sister's body.

But she didn't seem rattled. She still showed no emotion at all.

When he'd seen her holding the boy in her arms on the service road, he'd been pleasantly surprised at the display of tenderness. Then disappointed when she'd spoken to Callum in her usual flat tone and didn't talk to the boy at all or smile at him. Maybe she'd only carried the child because he wouldn't walk. But Callum didn't want to believe that. Didn't want to believe she was as apathetic, passionless, and dead inside as she seemed.

Though it wouldn't be her fault if she was. It was the work of a demented man.

Could the Forster killer really have returned to this area? Right after Rose's body was recovered? The timing seemed too coincidental.

Unless that was what had brought the Forster killer there.

Of course. They'd dug up Rose's body. Maybe the Forster killer didn't want it dug up, either because of evidence he feared being found or for a psychological reason.

Many serial killers committed crimes in the way they did to

attain a sense of completion. To scratch a twisted, psychological itch.

When the FBI removed the remains, it could have created a sense of incompletion for the killer, reawakening that itch. That could be why he wanted to target another victim in the same area.

But no investigators had ever noticed a geographical component to the Forster killer's crimes before. Could it—

A bark startled Callum from his thoughts. Was that—

Phoenix took off at a sprint just as Callum realized it was Dagian, barking in the darkness ahead.

---

Phoenix raced through the trees, catching Dag in her sights. He had surged out of view just before he'd barked.

She slowed as she reached him.

A child sat on the ground in front of the K-9. A boy. His arms wrapped around his narrow chest, indicating either fear or cold. The temperatures hadn't dropped below freezing yet that fall, but meteorologists predicted a cold front moving in soon. Low forties were still too cold for the child in jeans and a parka with no gloves or hat.

Phoenix crouched in front of the boy, removing her NVGs to avoid frightening him further. "I'm Phoenix." She put her hand on the K-9 beside her. "This is Dagian. Can you tell me your name?" She scanned him for any obvious injuries.

A small scratch slashed one cheek. Likely an encounter with a branch in the dark.

"Hay..." The boy's voice caught, and his tongue slid over his lips. Thirsty. "Hayden."

Crunching footsteps neared from behind Phoenix.

Ross. She recognized the cadence of his walk. And Dag would've warned her of anyone else.

She reached behind her back to unclip the thermos from her pack. "Drink this." She handed it to the boy.

He gripped it with a solid hold and gulped the water. Good. He had strength left. And he was able to verbalize. His eyes held relief more than fear as he watched her and Ross over the thermos.

"Hi, Hayden." Ross's comforting tone came closer as he squatted next to Phoenix in front of the boy, his NVGs removed. "I'm Callum. We're going to get you home, okay?"

The boy nodded as he lowered the thermos, water trickling down his chin. He wiped it away with his sleeve. His natural reflexes were still intact. Excellent sign.

Ross would notice this boy was well enough to provide information.

She'd let him do the questioning, since he had the skill with children.

"Can you tell us how you ended up here?"

"He shot Miss Jennison and Mrs. Tegan. And Mr. Carlos. He was my favorite bus driver." Moisture glistened along the rim of the boy's eyes.

"I know. I'm sorry, buddy." Ross moved closer, shifting to face the same direction as Hayden. Then he sat on the ground next to him and put his arm around the boy's shoulders.

Phoenix stared. That, she had not predicted.

Hayden leaned into Ross, resting his small head against the man's chest as he quietly cried.

Phoenix stood and stepped away to report their find on coms. Nguyen responded that an FBI car was already headed in their direction on the service road. The wait time for transport would only be fifteen minutes.

When Phoenix returned to Hayden, Ross had the boy talking again, still in the shelter of the agent's embrace.

"The bad man made us walk forever and ever. Some of the kids got tired, but he said they'd be sorry if they stopped. And Marnie told us to keep going. But only when he couldn't hear."

Of course she had. Not a surprise, but helpful confirmation that she was unhurt and undaunted by what she'd witnessed.

Ross glanced at Phoenix. He wouldn't find the answer to his question there. He asked the boy instead. "Who is Marnie?"

Hayden looked up at Ross from under his arm. "A girl in my class."

Phoenix would have to ask the more precise questions herself. Now, before they would need to carry the boy to the service road. "Were you all on the Copper Hill Trail when he sent you away?"

He transferred his attention to Phoenix. "I don't know."

"Did you change trails more than once?"

The boy's forehead crinkled as he thought. "I think so. But he told other boys to go away before me. He pointed the way we were supposed to go and made us run. And he said he'd hurt us if we stopped or went the wrong way."

"How many boys did he send away, Hayden?" Ross interrupted with the question.

"I don't know." The boy lifted his small shoulders. "I don't remember."

"That's okay." Ross watched the boy, compassion shaping his features. "Can you tell me if any of the kids were hurt?"

"They got scratched by some branches on the trail."

Ross nodded solemnly, as if the news had been grave. "Okay."

Hayden would mention serious injuries if there had been any. Their kidnapper should know to keep them in good condition and not traumatize them more than necessary if he wanted them to keep walking.

The prints she and Dag had followed showed the children were made to walk on the Wiley Skunk Trail away from the parking lot, then eventually branched off onto the Copper Hill Trail. Dag had tracked the footsteps Phoenix had been able to see visually for one hour and fifty-three minutes until his nose had alerted to a fresher scent nearby, and he'd led Phoenix to the boy a quarter mile off the trail.

"Can you tell us what the bad man looked like?"

A shiver visibly coursed through the boy's body at Ross's question. "Scary." Hayden buried his head in Ross's chest.

The agent rubbed the boy's shoulder. "Okay, buddy. It's okay. You don't have to think about him anymore."

A crackle sounded in Phoenix's ear, then a voice. "Base, this is PT4. We've recovered another boy."

Phoenix caught Ross's gaze, aimed at her without the relief she'd have expected to see in his eyes. Instead, she read there exactly what she was thinking.

The kidnapper could keep them busy the rest of that night and beyond picking up stray boys. While he increased his significant lead with the other children.

The girls, he would keep. At least for now.

Well played.

But it was one move in a chess game he couldn't win.

She had come, with his precious Phaistos Disc, exactly as he'd wanted.

And that would be his checkmate.

## SIXTEEN

The FBI transport car was already five minutes past the ETA.

Five more minutes he could increase his lead.

"Wait here with Hayden." Phoenix directed the order at Ross as she turned with Dag to leave the service road.

"Wait a minute." Ross's tone was surprised, not commanding or offended.

So she paused and looked over her shoulder.

He held Hayden, the boy almost asleep against the man's chest. "Is this your way of losing me?"

She faced him more fully. Was that humor in the question? Hard to tell from his straight mouth below his NVGs. "There's no time to waste. Too many lives are at stake."

"I know. I can try to catch up with you after they pick up Hayden. But, to be blunt, I didn't think you trusted me that much."

To leave him alone with the boy, he must mean. He had a point. She didn't know anything beyond her own assessment of the agent. She hadn't had time to have Cora research him.

Dag growled slightly. An alert more than a warning.

The hum of an engine followed.

"Looks like we're both staying." Ross managed to deliver the observation without any trace of triumph as he removed his NVGs and looked up the road.

She took off her NVGs, as well, to prevent the sting of blinding headlights. She watched Ross as the sedan drove toward them. Yes, she would have to keep a close eye on this one. Couldn't remember the last time someone had kept her from doing something she'd intended.

Actually, she did remember. Her grandfather when she was sixteen, and she had planned to leave and hunt the monster on her own since the FBI had rejected her as too young. He'd done her a favor. She hadn't been ready.

But no one got in Phoenix's way now. Nor manipulated her into altering her behavior. If that was Ross's game, he would end up regretting he'd tried matching her in wits or skill.

The car pulled to a halt, and Phoenix switched her focus to handing over the boy as quickly as possible.

A man in an FBI jacket got out of the driver's side as the passenger door also opened near Ross and Hayden.

Another man exited the car. Elijah Moore?

Irritation burned a path behind Phoenix's ribs. How many tagalongs was Katherine going to send her? This wasn't a guided tour. Phoenix would have to call Katherine on the satellite phone before she sent another car with more tourists.

"This is Hayden." Ross spoke to Eli, incorrectly assuming he was there to pick up the boy.

"He's going to take him." Eli gestured to the agent who rounded the car and approached Ross.

Eli made a beeline for Phoenix. "I'm here to join the search."

"I already have one visitor too many."

Emotions swam in his dark eyes and tightened his usually smiling mouth. Worry, anger, protectiveness. Emotions that could get him and others killed. He was a skilled fighter when calm. Enough that she might allow him to stay if he were objective and detached. But he was clearly neither.

"I'm not a visitor, Phoenix." He met her stare head-on, as

usual. "You know I have skills if things get messy. I can help, and I won't get in the way."

"You're too emotional."

"Too emotional?" His voice rose, unintentionally proving her point. He stopped, angling toward Ross as the other agent loaded Hayden into the back seat.

Phoenix would have to make sure the driver stayed until Eli returned to the car. She didn't need a ticking time bomb out in the field. She already had to deal with the increasingly unpredictable Agent Ross. And while Eli was muscular and strong, he wasn't in condition to hike for eight to twelve hours straight, days on end.

"You are not in condition for this job, emotionally or physically."

Eli's jaw worked as he turned back to Phoenix. He took a step toward her, facing her down as he had once before, years ago in Marion's living room.

But now she knew him. Knew what he was to Marion and her children. Knew how he had put his life on the line for Marion and would do so again in a heartbeat.

"Phoenix," he took in a breath as he held his stare, "Marnie is my daughter. I either go with you, or I go on my own." His deep, slightly rough tone thickened, quiet but determined. "I know my best chance to find Marnie and the man who took her is you."

Phoenix didn't blink or react as she met his gaze. Measured his mental and emotional state.

Fierce, deep love sparked in his eyes—the driving force of the father's instinct to protect, which Eli had in spades. Unlike many fathers, he also had the training and ability as a cop in the St. Paul Vice Unit to enact that protection when needed.

He could be an asset. And he wasn't bluffing about going on his own if she didn't allow him to accompany her. He would be more of a liability then.

She lifted her gaze slightly to see over Eli's shoulder.

Ross had moved closer and stood six feet behind Eli, watching them.

"Keep up." She spun away and stalked to the edge of the road where she told Dag to resume the search. She slipped on her NVGs and quickly followed the K-9 into the forest.

No doubt the men behind her were sharing triumphant looks or some such camaraderie, thinking they'd bested her. She would let them have their belief they'd gotten her to yield to them. Such misconceptions could be useful.

The men crashed through the brush, hurrying to catch up. Good thing this wasn't a stealth mission. At the moment.

They flanked her as she continued after Dag, Ross keeping a polite distance while Eli presumed on their familiarity to walk within two feet of her. The FBI agent must have given him the pair of NVGs he wore. He would start asking his questions now.

"They briefed me at the base on what's been happening." Eli began right on cue. "Why is he letting the boys go?"

Phoenix didn't break her stride, still focusing on Dag in the distance. "Sending them out. They're decoys. Distractions." And it was working. Once again, they now had to backtrack over the same ground and then go beyond it to connect with the children's trail she and Dag had been tracking when they'd found the first boy. Sixty-three minutes that she hadn't been able to gain on the kidnapper's trail. Returning to the point at which she'd had to detour would take—

"Oh. But why only the boys?"

"You work Vice." The preference didn't hold for all abusers. But Eli would get the point, relevant in this case with that particular kidnapper.

Eli fell silent, except for the sound of his breathing. Already heavier than it should be. He may not last long. "Is he..." Another breath of air, but this one emotionally driven. "Is he hurting Marnie? The other girls?"

"Not yet."

"Phoenix?" A note of anguish mixed with simmering threat in his voice. "When?"

"Not until he feels safe. In the clear." She gave Eli one glance. "I will make sure he never does."

---

Callum lengthened his stride enough to catch up with Phoenix and Dagian.

They'd led the way for hours, never faltering or slackening the quick pace. About an hour ago, they'd reconnected with the three-foot-wide trail Phoenix said they had been following before they'd found the first boy.

Dagian's nose dropped to the ground then and hadn't lifted since, the K-9 scenting the trail of the killer and children.

Callum could see the footprints in the dirt most of the time with the aid of his NVGs. Three times, the prints had stopped. Disappeared.

But Dagian had continued on, holding his nose toward the ground as if the prints were still there. The scent apparently still was.

He had led them forward, reaching the point where shoeprints appeared visually again.

The Forster killer had evidently tried to wipe away the evidence of their trail. He likely knew it wouldn't lose any searchers completely but hoped it would delay them.

Thanks to Dagian and Phoenix, their little group hadn't been slowed at all by the attempt.

They should be gaining on the kidnapper and his hostages. Third graders couldn't walk as fast and as far as three adults and a K-9. And with a trail so easy to track, they hadn't had to pause or move slowly for Dagian to find the scent.

The kidnapper had a significant head start, given that time of death for the shooting victims was estimated between nine and eleven a.m. according to forensics. Agent Nguyen had conveyed over coms that Hayden and another boy claimed the killer had attacked as soon as they'd arrived at the park, before anyone got off the bus. Their testimony pinpointed the attack and kidnapping at approximately ten fifteen in the morning.

That meant he'd had at least six hours and fifteen minutes to travel before Phoenix had begun searching. But even if he walked the kids until they dropped, steady progress at adult speeds should mean the search party would gain on the kidnapper. Maybe reach him by sometime tomorrow morning.

Unless they continued to be diverted by the boys he'd sent off alone. The reports on coms of recoveries brought the total up to ten, assuming all had been relayed over the radio. None had been reported for some time now.

Had the kidnapper stopped sending them into the woods? Why stop at ten? Or perhaps there were more, and they were lost in the dark, waiting for rescue.

*Please help us find them, Lord. Help us find the boys and the girls with the man who took them. Thank you that you are in control of this situation.*

The reminder relaxed the tension that had been snaking through Callum, clenching his muscles and stomach.

Didn't help that he had nothing but his thoughts to listen to. After grilling Phoenix and introducing himself to Callum, Eli had grown silent as they'd pressed on.

And silent seemed to be Phoenix's natural state. Or adopted one for the persona she wanted to maintain.

He cut her a glance. All the good it would do, given she wore NVGs and never showed any emotion. But he couldn't help trying to see. Trying to understand what was going on in her mind.

What was she thinking? What was she feeling?

Contrary to her apathetic behavior, he believed she had emotions. She hadn't told Eli that the kidnapper likely had one girl as his target, and he would keep her no matter what. She hadn't said Eli's daughter could be the target.

The omission showed Phoenix was more sensitive to others than she let on.

Unless she knew Eli's daughter didn't fit the kidnapper's target type. Blond, blue eyes, sweet, and innocent. Judging from Eli's brown skin and black hair, that was likely the case.

Callum swallowed a sigh. Maybe he just wanted to think there was more behind Phoenix's protective shell.

Then again, she had shared her thermos with Hayden. Let him drink the entire contents, from the look of it.

Water would taste very good right about now. Callum had remembered to bring NVGs when he joined Phoenix but forgot basic trail gear. Hadn't given enough thought to how long they'd be searching without a break. He hadn't thought about much beyond getting to Phoenix, learning what she knew, and rescuing the children.

With ten boys recovered, that left thirty-eight kids still either with the Forster killer or scattered in the forest. Neither location offered much chance for survival. Unless they found the children soon.

Phoenix probably knew the gender split of the kids.

"How many boys are there in the class?" His voice cracked the stillness of the night, nearly startling him.

But Phoenix didn't flinch. Or look his way. "Twenty-seven on the field trip."

"Do you think he'll use them all as distractions?"

She marched on, apparently not intending to answer.

Dagian veered off the trail up ahead.

Phoenix suddenly quickened her speed to catch up with him.

Callum broke into a jog to stay with her, Eli's footfalls crunching behind him.

At the spot where the K-9 had veered off, a gap split the trees that bordered the trail. Where it connected with a service road.

Dagian skimmed his nose over the thinly graveled road, circling rather than moving in a straight direction as he had before. He lifted his head. Looked at Phoenix.

Had he lost the scent?

Callum's gut clenched.

Phoenix walked to the dog and looked down at the road.

She squatted for a few seconds. Then stood. "He put them in a vehicle. Likely a van."

Callum's heart sank. They wouldn't catch up tomorrow. Without a miracle, they might not catch up at all. Until it was too late.

## SEVENTEEN

"Thanks for letting me tag along." Ross glanced at the campsite Phoenix had selected, his gaze appearing to pause on the fledgling blaze she'd started in the firepit. "I'll see what I can learn at the base and get some gear so I'm ready for the long haul. Then I'll be back in..." He checked his watch. "Six hours."

She'd be gone in six hours. No need to point that out to him.

His mouth angled slightly, but his eyes smiled more. "A little earlier than that. I won't hold you up."

No, he would not. She wasn't about to wait for him to continue the search. She was already cutting the PK-9 shift shorter than normal by stopping at eight hours. But none of the PK-9 agents had planned on a search beginning that day. Jazz, Flash, Sofia, and Raksa had come directly from security details. They needed to grab six hours of rest and regroup as a team before going on long shifts in the morning.

"Well, see you in a bit." Ross dipped his head in a cordial nod and turned away, striding across the campsite toward the grassy area where visitors could park RVs near the service road. The FBI car sent to take him to Base should meet him on the road in the next five minutes.

She hadn't expected him to volunteer to leave on his own.

She would have to find out from Katherine later what exactly he did at the base.

Eli walked toward Phoenix and paused a few feet to her left. "Can I talk to you before the others get here?"

She held up a hand. He was right, the PK-9 team would arrive soon. Which meant she had to make a call first.

Phoenix swung toward the backpack she'd set on the browned grass and pulled out her satellite phone. Dialed the number she'd memorized.

He was slow to pick up. Though she doubted he'd be sleeping deeply at one a.m. Not with Cora gone on this search.

"Kent Thomson."

"Phoenix. You need to come out here." Cora would certainly have told her husband where she was going before she'd arrived at the park.

"Is Cora hurt?" The DEA agent's deep voice pitched even lower with intensity.

"No. You need to make sure it stays that way." Cora and Jana needed to be in the field, recovering children as quickly as possible. But Phoenix needed to stay on Marnie, the hostages, and the kidnapper. Phoenix couldn't be with Cora. Couldn't keep her safe.

Kent paused. Never one to take orders from others, not even Phoenix. But he would protect his wife. "I'm on my way. I'll be driving from Wisconsin." The location Cora had mentioned he was working a case.

"Get here in the morning. I'll keep her safe overnight." Phoenix ended the call and angled to meet Eli's impatient stare.

"I didn't want to ask this in front of the FBI agent. I don't know if he's trustworthy."

Ah. The question about Marnie's kidnapper.

"Everyone at the base is saying the kidnapper is the Forster killer, but could it be the FBI agent who wants Marnie dead? Maybe he's copycatting the Forster killer just like he imitated the other serial killer when he took out her mom."

A viable theory. One Phoenix had considered and discarded. The evidence didn't support it. "No."

Lines deepened in Eli's forehead. "Why not?"

"Too complicated and laden with unnecessary risks."

"But if it is him, he could've already…"

Killed Marnie. Eli was torturing himself with such thoughts. The reality was hard enough to handle.

"It's not him. If he knew where she was and where she went to school, he would have had hundreds of opportunities to kill her in ways that couldn't be tied to him. Ways that would look accidental." Phoenix bent to return the satphone to her backpack as she continued. "He won't kill her to keep her quiet in a way that exposes his identity and true intentions."

Phoenix straightened. "He wants her dead to keep his secret, to keep everyone believing he's a legitimate, clean FBI agent."

"You're right." Eli nodded. "I guess I'm not thinking clearly." He held up both large hands, palms out toward her. "But I won't let that interfere with our search." His characteristic grin, though a shadow of its usual vibrancy, split his black beard. "All I have to do is follow you anyway."

A growl made Phoenix jerk to the right.

Dag's posture relaxed, his tail lowering as he watched the dark trees that curved around the campsite.

A friendly.

A German shepherd emerged from the darkness, followed by a petite woman wearing NVGs.

Sofia grinned as she crossed the campsite with Raksa. "Quitting already?" She rounded the firepit and stopped close to the growing blaze. Pulling off her NVGs, her gaze landed on Eli. "I see we've got a visitor."

Eli extended his hand to Sofia. "Eli Moore."

Sofia paused only a second before returning the handshake. "Heard about you. Met your wife when we ran Raksa through his paces. Good work setting up the outdoor training equipment."

"It's all Marion's doing. I'm just the muscle."

Sofia chuckled, then looked at Phoenix. "The others aren't here yet? Slackers." She grinned at her own joke. "Oh, there's Cora." She jogged toward the road as headlights appeared.

"Does she always have that much energy?" Eli watched Sofia, likely feeling the weariness of his first SAR experience. And he'd only put in a few hours.

Phoenix might have to send him home tomorrow. But she would let his fatigue and soreness drive him to make that decision himself.

Cora pulled Phoenix's white van off the road and onto the dying grass.

Jazz, Flash, Nevaeh, and Alvarez piled out of the back as Cora emerged from the driver's side.

"You guys hitched?" Sofia's teasing tone carried into the campsite. "Cora, I can't believe you would help them cheat."

"Well, I couldn't drive past such beautiful dogs without stopping, could I?"

Jazz and Nevaeh guffawed at Cora's response.

"So the dogs are the beautiful ones, huh?" Nevaeh laughed.

"Here I thought it was Nev's curls." Jazz gave Nevaeh a playful shove as they walked into the clearing with their K-9s.

"Hey, Bris." Nevaeh cast her grin at Bristol, who approached with Toby from the opposite side of the campsite.

"Guess we're last in." And without the FBI agent Cora had said was accompanying Bristol. He must have returned to Base, as had Cora's shadow when she'd gone back to pick up the van.

Nevaeh laughed. "Only because some of us cheated, Sof says."

"Street smarts, girl." Jazz gave her childhood friend a high five.

"You must be Elijah Moore." Trailing behind the other women into the clearing, Cora greeted the newcomer as soon as she could.

"Eli."

"I'm Cora. Welcome." Cora's warmth was palpable even from the distance at which Phoenix watched the interaction.

"I'm so very sorry about your daughter, Marnie. I'm praying for her."

Eli nodded. "Thank you."

"I have a sleeping bag, other gear, and toiletries you can use. Would you like to come to the van with me and choose the items yourself?"

"Sure. Thanks."

Cora and Eli headed for the van as Sofia darted past them in the other direction, carrying a large cooler.

"Figured this is for us."

Cora chuckled. "Yes. Help yourself."

Jazz and Nevaeh joined the effort to unload the van, and the team soon placed folding lawn chairs around the fire.

Cora passed out sandwiches and bottled waters she must have retrieved from Base.

As the group sat in a circle around the warmth of the flames, Nevaeh chuckled. "You know," she smiled at Eli, "you're only the third man ever allowed at a PK-9 meeting. That's something you can brag about."

Sofia and Nevaeh laughed softly, exchanging looks full of fond memories.

Eli grinned, an attempt to push aside the anxiety that shone in his eyes. "I'm grateful for the honor."

Cora watched Eli across the fire, concern shaping her features.

Bristol wore a similar expression as she aimed her attention at Phoenix. "Finding ten boys isn't enough." Bristol's hand went to her slightly rounded belly automatically, covering the baby she'd been carrying for five months.

The burning wood crackled in the firepit, the only sound among the group for four seconds.

"Perhaps the police will recover more before morning." Cora's voice lifted with the hope she nearly always managed to keep alive.

"The cops are looking tonight?"

"Four tracking K-9s from local PDs." Sofia took the lead in answering Eli's question.

"Gary and Luger are probably with them. Good team." Eli was correct. The St. Paul PD's K-9 team was one of four units available to join the rescue operation.

"They'll search while we're off so there are always teams out there." Sofia turned her head toward Phoenix, looking across the fire between them. "Are FBI K-9s still coming tomorrow?"

"Yes." Phoenix had phoned Katherine before arriving at the campsite to coordinate the K-9 search efforts. "Three K-9 tracking units are supposed to come. I'll have them overlap with the end of our shift to keep all the dogs fresh and coverage constant."

"We can't ever let the pressure off this guy." Determination set Bristol's mouth in a firm line.

"Exactly." Sofia's eyes flashed in the orange light from the flames. "If he tries to relax, he'll feel us nipping at his heels."

"But we need to focus more on the kids than the kidnapper right now, don't you think?" Jazz landed her gaze on each of her teammates before stopping on Phoenix. "They're scattered all over the place. The forest is not a safe place for them to be, even if they aren't with a lunatic."

"I think Phoenix means for us to do both." Cora, sitting in the chair closest to Phoenix, stroked Jana's head as the golden retriever sat by her knee. "Phoenix will continue to track the kidnapper and the children still with him while the rest of us find the boys he sent away." She turned her big eyes on Phoenix. "Is that correct?"

Phoenix gave a slight nod. "Your first priority at seven a.m. will be to find the scattered children." She looked at each PK-9 agent, gauging their readiness as she gave the instructions. "Continue in a grid pattern to cover as much land as possible systematically. But be on the lookout for any sign of danger. There is no guarantee that the kidnapper will continue moving away from where he started. He may circle back, change directions. Be on guard at all times."

"Got it, boss." Nevaeh nodded.

"There have to be more searchers besides K-9 teams coming tomorrow, right?" Eli rubbed a hand down his beard as he aimed his gaze at Phoenix.

"No civilian volunteers, with or without K-9s, will be allowed due to the danger posed by the kidnapper. But during daylight hours, police and FBI personnel without K-9s will search on foot and in vehicles where accessible." Phoenix mentally sifted through the information Katherine had shared, isolating only what Eli and the PK-9 team needed to know. "Park rangers will search on horseback, in ATVs, and on foot. Helicopters, planes, and drones will be used for aerial search." Though with the thickness of the forest in most of the park, except for the rivers and lakes, it was an easy task to stay hidden from fliers.

The furrows on Eli's brow smoothed as she listed the help coming with the sun. Perhaps that would give him the peace he needed to sleep the few hours they had left.

One more instruction, then Phoenix would dismiss them. "If any of you encounter visitors, campers in the park, call it in and see that they are evacuated. The rangers evacuated all documented visitors already. But this time of year, when the visitor centers are closed, there may be campers in the park that the rangers aren't aware of."

Phoenix stood. "Plan to resume the search at seven a.m. Get sleep while you can."

The agents murmured among themselves as they left the chairs and went to prepare their sleeping areas. Most of them carried their untouched sandwiches with them, finally taking a moment to eat before they would rest.

"Ow!" Nevaeh's shout pierced the night, followed by a loud snap that made Alvarez bark.

Phoenix and Dag darted toward her, and the rest of the team closed in.

"Are you okay?" Jazz, closest to Nevaeh, gripped her friend's arm as Phoenix reached them.

"I stubbed my foot on something hard."

Phoenix scanned the dark ground for the threat, the danger that had caused injury.

A metal, U-shaped contraption lay on the thin grass. A bear trap.

Illegal to have in the park.

Sofia crouched down by the trap, studying it. She looked up at Phoenix. "This shouldn't be here."

No. It shouldn't.

There was only one reason such a trap would be there now. A present from the monster meant to disable any human or K-9 who tried to catch him.

If he wanted to take out Phoenix or her team, he'd have to do better than that.

# EIGHTEEN

Callum hit the backlight on his watch to check the time as the FBI car finally neared the park's main entrance lot. *1:45 a.m.*

He wasn't going to get much sleep riding the half hour to Base only to go back again to meet Phoenix no later than seven. If he hadn't needed more gear, he would've stayed at Phoenix's camp with the others. Especially to make sure she didn't leave without him in the morning. Maybe he should...

The thought of turning back right away died as the trees ended and his view from the front passenger seat expanded. Scene lights still illuminated the crime scene by the bus, and other lights had been added across the parking lot. But it wasn't the lights that made his mouth drop open.

The emergency vehicles that had been there when he'd left to join Phoenix in the search had multiplied, packing the lot at haphazard angles. Beyond the emergency vehicles stood unmarked cars, trucks, vans and the like, parked along the road for as far as Callum could see in the dark.

Yellow police tape had been stretched across the outer edge of the parking lot along the road. A border so the new arrivals wouldn't enter.

But people pressed against the tape from the outside, some

holding large video cameras and smaller devices they were likely using to take photos.

"Are those reporters?" Callum glanced at Mike Pinchert, the FBI agent driving the car.

"Some. Most are the families."

The families. Callum's heart pushed upward to lodge at the base of his throat as Mike squeezed the car between two county sheriff units.

Callum opened the front passenger door and got out, his gaze going to the line of people behind the yellow tape.

Parents, grandparents, guardians. The people who loved the kidnapped children.

He'd gotten so caught up in the search with Phoenix, he'd forgotten many would have come there if they could, desperate for news. Desperate to do something.

Hopefully, none of them would do something drastic in a foolhardy attempt to save one of the children. Agent Nguyen had better be managing them somehow to prevent that outcome.

"Nguyen is inside if you want to talk to her. They'll hook you up with gear, too." Watching Callum over the roof of the car, Mike tilted his head toward the visitor center they now called their base.

"Right. Thanks for the ride."

"You got it." Mike disappeared again to get behind the wheel. Probably going back out to continue driving one of the two service roads that wound through sections of the park. The headlights guaranteed the kidnapper would see the car and be able to stay out of sight, but perhaps one of the drivers would spot a boy who'd been sent away on his own.

As Mike drove away, shouts from the families drew Callum's attention. And twisted his insides. He'd go talk to them if he thought he could comfort them in some way. But he didn't have any good news to offer.

He'd do better to check in with Agent Nguyen and see if she

had updates she could share with the anxious and terrified parents.

Callum went to the rectangular building and opened the door. To a swirling ocean of activity.

Ringing phones and talking people combined to create a level of commotion that obliterated Callum's hopes of getting any sleep there.

Agents in FBI jackets darted around the open main room that took up most of the building, carrying papers and computers to other agents as if their lives depended on it. Intermingled with the FBI agents were officers in county uniforms, Twin Cities uniforms, and park ranger attire clustered in groups, answering phones, and diagramming on whiteboards.

If the parents could see inside the building, at least they would have the comfort of knowing law enforcement was hard at work, trying to save their kids.

Callum just hoped they were doing the most effective things they could, not unintentionally getting distracted by busy work and tangential concerns.

He reined in the urge to micromanage the operations. He only wanted to be sure the children were found as soon as possible, and his management skills and knowledge of similar cases could help with that goal. But he couldn't manage the rescue operation and follow Phoenix.

His gut and his reason told him she was their best chance, hands down, of catching the Forster killer and the children he'd kidnapped. Callum needed to stay with her.

Which meant he'd better get what he'd come for and try to find a corner somewhere quiet enough to grab a few hours of sleep before hurrying back to catch Phoenix before she disappeared.

He scanned the chaos for the petite Agent Nguyen. Couldn't see anyone with her straight black hair and take-charge demeanor.

His gaze caught on a closed door at the back of the room. An office? He headed that way, weaving through agents and cops who were much too busy to notice him.

Snippets of conversations reached his ears as he went.

"It's not like his other kidnappings…"

"Why's he letting them go?"

"He's already gone. On highway fifty-nine or beyond. I'd put money on it."

Callum reached the door and knocked, glancing back at the men and women who all seemed to have their own theories and questions. Could be a positive effort to investigate and uncover evidence to help predict where they would find the children and their kidnapper. But spitballing without follow-up and proof could lead to confusion and distracted focus, tempting people to act on theories instead of known facts and the rescue itself.

He knocked again. There was no way he'd be able to hear anything short of a gunshot from behind the door with the noise level in the main room.

The door swung open. An irritated Agent Nguyen glared at him. Then her eyes widened slightly, and some of the irritation dissipated. "You." She turned away and waved a hand past her shoulder that he took as an invitation to enter the small room with a desk, two chairs, a narrow bookcase, and…stuffed animals?

Not the plush kind children played with but the real kind. As in, actual animals that had died and were now preserved and mounted on pedestals and small tables, some smaller ones in glass cases. Must be displays used for educational purposes that were normally in the main lobby but had been moved to the office and crowded together on one end of the already small space.

A woman with curly blond hair sat with her back toward Callum as she faced the desk Agent Nguyen went behind.

The agent sat in a chair and aimed her dark eyes at the other woman. "You were saying your daughter never mentioned anyone strange at school or anyone following her home? Nothing like that?"

"No. Nothing." The woman's voice was likely higher pitched than normal thanks to the obvious strain tightening her tone. "And she always took the bus, or we picked her up. She never walked. Because it was...too dangerous." The woman dropped her head forward and sobbed.

Callum's chest squeezed at the wrenching pain this mother was experiencing. Since Nguyen apparently didn't mind him being present, he drifted toward the animals so he could see the woman's face.

After about a minute of crying, during which Agent Nguyen looked like she had to clench her jaw to keep from saying something, the mother lifted her head. Early forties, blond with blue eyes. She could be an older version of the Forster killer's usual victims. Was her daughter the one he...

Callum couldn't finish the horrible thought.

"I know this is difficult, Mrs. Kelly." Nguyen's tone was a far miss from sympathetic, but at least her words showed an effort. "Just a couple more questions. How long ago were you informed about this field trip?"

"Um..." Mrs. Kelly looked down at the damp tissue she twisted in her hands. "I think it was four weeks ago. Yes. That's when Mrs. Tegan, that's Anna's teacher, sent us a letter about the field trip. She was doing it as a special way for the children to study geology in nature." Her mouth crumpled. "All this for... for rocks." Another sob gripped her.

"Yes." Nguyen fired the sharp response like she hoped it would startle the woman out of her grief.

The mother looked up, biting her lip as if holding back the flood of tears that way. Apparently, Nguyen's technique actually worked.

"Was the field trip information only in the letter or was it posted or announced elsewhere?"

Mrs. Kelly blinked. "Um, I think it was only the letter. That's the only place I saw it. Oh, except for the reminder card Mrs. Tegan sent home with Anna the week before."

"Got it. You can go now. Thank you."

Mrs. Kelly didn't stand. "But what about Anna? Where is she? When will you get her back?" Tears pooled in the woman's blue eyes again as her voice thickened.

"We're doing everything we can to rescue your daughter as soon as possible, Mrs. Kelly. We will keep you informed." Nguyen stood. "Ross. Show her out?" The flash of exasperation in Nguyen's eyes and the fatigue that bordered them made Callum step toward the distressed mother without hesitation.

"Ma'am." He gave her a polite nod with a gentle smile. "You've been very helpful, and we'll use all the information you've been able to give us to find your daughter."

She looked up at him. "Are you, FBI, too?"

"Yes, ma'am. I just came from farther out in the park where expert teams with tracking K-9s are on the trail of your daughter and her classmates. I'll be rejoining them as soon as I can get what I need here."

"Oh. Thank God." Her eyes widened slightly, and she pushed to her feet. She stumbled as she rounded the chair.

He caught her elbow and guided her toward the door. He reached past her to open it, allowing the chaotic noise to spill in.

She paused and looked up at him. "You'll find her?" The fear, pain, and guilt in her gaze pierced through him. It was like looking into the eyes of his mother.

But this kidnapping wasn't Mrs. Kelly's fault any more than what he'd suffered was his mother's fault.

Anna's mother was a victim, too. A victim of the evil Callum had vowed to stop. And he would this time. "Lord willing, ma'am, we will."

She searched his eyes for a beat, then her lip trembled before she ducked her head and walked into the commotion of the rescue operation's hub.

"Nicely done. Close the door, Ross." Nguyen's sharp tone hit Callum's back.

He shut the door and walked to the front side of the desk, grabbing the chair as he reminded himself Nguyen had been going nonstop, wrangling the circus, managing media and parental demands for probably about nine hours. It was impressive she was still standing and no surprise she'd lost whatever civilities and manners she might have had at the start of the day.

Callum sat and crossed his leg over to rest his ankle on one knee. A relaxed posture he hoped might help put Nguyen at ease. "Are you interviewing all the parents, or did you select her for some reason?"

"Interviewing all of them. One by one." A task the agent wasn't thrilled with, according to her tone. Though he could hardly blame her. There must be at least twenty-five parents outside.

Her answer revealed she didn't suspect the woman's daughter could be the kidnapper's ultimate target. Maybe she didn't know about the Forster killer and the consistency of his target victims' characteristics.

"Great idea. It will keep them much calmer and more informed."

"That's the plan. And I'm hoping I'll get something from one of them that can shed some light on motive and opportunity."

Callum's ears perked at that. "You don't think this is the Forster killer?"

"Could be." Nguyen shifted in the chair, its oversized armrests, width, and high back emphasizing her small size. "Phoenix thinks it's him. Which probably means it is. But I've got people here pressing me for evidence of that theory and favoring other theories. They don't know her like I do."

Ah, so Nguyen had a history with Phoenix. Interesting. Sounded like the agent trusted Phoenix, too. "If it helps, I specialize in serial killers that target children and, as you know, I'm in charge of the Forster killer investigation right now. I second Phoenix's opinion that this kidnapper is the Forster killer."

"Based on what?" Nguyen lifted her dark eyebrows. "Phoenix took off before I could talk to her. I only heard through the grapevine she'd said it was him."

"The murder of authority figures, staging of the bodies, the number of shots to the bodies, close range, head and heart. The forest setting." Callum rested his hands on his crossed leg. "His previous illusiveness in wooded locations has made us conclude he's a skilled woodsman, which this kidnapper also appears to be. There are a lot of indicators. As well as some I suspect only Phoenix knows but isn't sharing."

"Okay." Nguyen took in a breath as she straightened and nodded. "That gives me more than I had. But why would he take a whole busload of forty-eight kids? That's the reason some say it isn't him."

"That's one of the anomalies I think only Phoenix and the kidnapper can explain."

Nguyen's mouth shifted in an angled line. "And I don't suppose she's telling you."

"Not yet."

"Well, don't hold your breath. She doesn't tell people anything unless she thinks it's absolutely necessary. More tight-lipped than the FBI." Nguyen leaned forward and laid her forearms on the desk, gripping her hands together. "At least I have some details now that I can use to pursue this as the Forster killer. If that's who this is, he could try to leave the park at some point with the hostages or he could stay hidden for as long as he can. We put up roadblocks and checkpoints on all the main roads that lead away from the park as a precaution. If he does try to escape that way, we'll catch him. But he could potentially leave a section of the park on foot where the land connects to privately owned property. Even some residential areas."

"I don't think he'll try to leave while he has so many hostages. It would be much harder to transport all those kids outside the park without being seen by someone in civilization." Though if he suddenly abandoned all the children except his actual target, he might flee with her. Callum kept that thought to himself for now. He'd rather learn what Phoenix thought of the possibility, with her keen insight into the Forster killer's mind. Even with only one hostage, this location offered advantages that could make the kidnapper stay.

Callum should mention the advantages to Nguyen, since she probably hadn't been able to go farther into the forest than the parking lot. "What I saw of the park today gave me an inkling as to why he picked it. The forest is so dense. Terrific place to hide if you want to."

"Tell me about it. It's even more effective for disappearing than you'd think. With the lakes and rivers, the ravines, valleys, and forested cliffs, missing person searches usually take three to four days. And that's when the people want to be found or, in some cases, have died and aren't traveling like this guy and his hostages."

Nguyen stared at Callum like she was about to say something more, but her gaze lifted above and past him to the door first. Then she lowered her volume as she spoke. "There are a few Timber Park missing persons who have been lost for years and presumed dead. Their bodies have never been recovered."

The information, though not too surprising, still struck Callum hard. He'd dealt with similar missing persons' cases at other large parks like this one, when abduction or violence to a child was suspected. They hadn't been able to recover the body of one of the children he'd tried to find either.

The wilderness, even when it wasn't the largest or most mountainous park in the world, could be both beautiful and terrible, especially when evil visited there. Then it became a hiding place for tragedy and sometimes, the darkness of humanity. A place that swallowed evidence and hid secrets that wouldn't be uncovered in a single lifetime.

It was a blow to Callum's hope for the hostages to learn Timber Park was capable of that, too. That it had the means to help a killer, a kidnapper, successfully hide himself and the children for a long time. While he had his way with them.

Although Phoenix had a convincing point that he wouldn't hurt them yet. Not beyond the trauma they were enduring through seeing the murders and being kidnapped.

She was right. He would be too concerned with keeping them moving and hidden, with evading the many searchers flooding the park, to do anything else.

And they'd better keep it that way. "I know we can't have volunteer searchers come in for this, given the danger. Are more FBI searchers on their way?"

Nguyen leaned back in the chair. "I have three FBI K-9 tracking teams and twenty agents assigned to come in tomorrow, and I'll get more if the search continues. We have three more K-9 tracking teams from Minnesota law enforcement agencies joining tomorrow, too, and you probably know there are four already tracking the kidnapper and searching for lost kids tonight while Phoenix's teams are off."

Callum nodded. "Sounds like you've got the ground search covered as much as you can."

"Aerial, too." She anticipated his next question. "As soon as daylight hits, we're getting drones in the air, search planes, helicopters. And, yes, the rangers are involved, too. They've got some aerial support, boats on the lakes, and I'm told some horseback mounted rangers will search in daylight hours."

Callum's concerns about the rescue operation faded as she outlined her plans. Nguyen knew what she was doing and was taking all the steps he would in her place. "Thanks for giving me the layout. I see you've got it well in hand, so I guess I'll get a couple hours of shut-eye before I go back out to meet Phoenix." He pushed up from the chair, weariness and overuse stiffening his muscles.

"Hang on, Agent Ross."

He paused as Nguyen also stood.

"There's a quid that goes with this pro quo."

He looked at her, waiting for her to explain.

"I want you to keep me informed about what Phoenix is thinking. What she's doing."

Incredulity and surprise pushed a laugh up his throat. He tried to choke it back, cutting the sound short rather than preventing it completely. "I'm sorry, Agent Nguyen, but how am

I supposed to know what Phoenix is thinking? You said yourself, she rarely shares information."

Nguyen's eyes narrowed slightly as she pressed her lips together. "I know. We go way back. Years. But she still won't tell me anything except what she thinks I need to know in her time and her way. I trust her. She gets unbelievable results. If she says she's going to rescue the kids and nail this guy, I believe her. But I'll need more information than that to keep other people happy if this search drags on as long as I think it's going to."

"I understand. And I wish I could help. But Phoenix doesn't trust me at all yet. She's not going to share her secret knowledge or thoughts with me." Though he hoped she would down the line.

"Phoenix doesn't trust anyone. I just need you to observe, and if she does reveal anything, report back to me when you can. Got it?"

"I'll do my best." Callum turned to go before she put him on the spot any more than she already had. He wasn't going to spy on Phoenix for her, if that was what she was getting at.

"Ross."

He paused at the door and looked back.

"Does she say she'll catch the guy? Rescue the kids?"

Callum thought carefully about Phoenix's very few words while he'd been with her. What she'd said to Eli. That she'd make sure the kidnapper never felt safe. "Not in so many words. But you know Phoenix."

Better than Callum at this point, perhaps. Hopefully, it wouldn't stay that way for long.

"Yeah." Nguyen rested her hands on her hips and jerked a nod. "She'll get him." Confidence slid into the agent's eyes, replacing the stress and doubt. "Tell her I'll do my best to give her time and room to work, would you?"

"I will if she'll let me." Callum gave Nguyen a smile as he reached for the door.

But it swung open, nearly smacking him as he took a quick step back.

"Nguyen?" A brown-haired guy stuck his head into the office. "Got a call Phoenix Gray is sending in a bear trap to be analyzed."

"A bear trap?" Nguyen's expression matched her disbelieving tone.

"Yeah. She said the kidnapper left it at a campsite as a booby trap."

The Forster killer had set booby traps for the searchers?

Lord willing, he hadn't had time to leave many. Or the hunters of the killer could end up becoming the hunted.

# NINETEEN

The slim figure moved back and forth, her shadowed silhouette breaking across the orange glow of the fire.

She stopped, wringing her hands.

Lying in a sleeping bag, Phoenix watched the pattern that had been continuing for twenty minutes.

Cora needed sleep. So did Jana. The faithful golden had followed Cora's pacing nonstop.

Phoenix silently got to her feet, and Dag instantly stood to accompany her as they made their way around the firepit.

"Cora." Phoenix spoke quietly before reaching Cora so as not to startle her.

Cora flinched slightly, then moved closer to Phoenix with widened eyes. "I'm so sorry." She kept her volume at a near-whisper. "Am I keeping you awake?" Her gaze traveled past Phoenix, likely checking the others to see if she'd awakened them.

Most of them still slept, though Sofia only lightly, ready to spring into action at the slightest sound. She would be awake now, but only until she saw Phoenix had the situation in hand.

"You and Jana need sleep."

"I know." Cora sighed. "A sound woke me, and then I

couldn't get back to sleep for worrying. So, I've been praying for the children." Her mouth curved in a soft smile. "Prayer is the best way I know to stop worrying about things I can't control."

Sweet Cora. So naïve to still believe in God. She had seen enough evil that she should have questioned the unrealistic theory in an almighty being who controlled all things, including human actions.

But Cora still remained sheltered from the worst kinds of evil. From the darkest, most perverted horrors Phoenix had tasted as a child and encountered repeatedly ever since as she pursued the criminals that did such deeds. Those were the realities that shattered any notions of a deity in control of anything.

People were animals that did whatever fed their desires, made them feel good. But people like Cora felt better if they believed in a loving God Who would protect them and help them through life.

Phoenix didn't need that kind of help.

But there was beauty in Cora's unmarred sweetness and naivete. It was as if Phoenix were seeing the woman Rose would have grown to be. The same silky blond hair, blue eyes, and hopeful, pure soul.

It made them vulnerable. Cora. Rose. That sensitive heart and innocence, shattered at the hands of a monster, had made Rose unable to cope. Paralyzed her with so much fear that she couldn't leave with Robin. Not before he came back.

Robin had to run and try to save them both the only way she'd known how. By getting the police. Who were too late.

Phoenix could do more for Cora. Had been able to many times in the years since she had taken Cora into her protection. "Kent is coming in the morning. He'll stay with you until this is over."

"You called Kent?" Cora's eyes showed surprise, then calmed with the trust she had in Phoenix and her ways. "Thank you, Phoenix."

"I want you to wait here at the campsite in the morning until he arrives. Sofia will stay with you."

Affection softened Cora's features as she watched Phoenix. She always welcomed and appreciated Phoenix's protection of her. Never resented it.

She was so much like Rose. Always trusting her.

"While you're waiting, research the kidnapped girls. Identify which one is blond, blue-eyed, small and delicate, and is thought of as sweet-tempered. Make calls if needed."

Cora nodded. "I brought the satellite router. I'll be able to use my smartphone for the Internet searches and calls."

Exactly as Phoenix had assumed. "Get sleep while you can." She turned away.

"Phoenix?"

Cora's soft tone drew Phoenix to angle toward her. "Do you think you'll be able to catch him this time?"

This time. Cora could be referring to the fact that he had never been captured in twenty-six years. But from the compassion lighting Cora's eyes in the glow of the fire, Phoenix thought not.

She knew.

With Cora's exceptional intelligence and intuitive understanding of people, she could easily match what she now knew about the type the killer targeted with the way Phoenix had always protected her and occasionally betrayed hints of fondness and pride in Cora through the years.

"Yes." Though if all went as planned, he would catch her.

---

Callum couldn't account for the eagerness that tickled his belly as the FBI car that had transported him to the campsite drove away, and he hurried from the road to the camp.

He rounded the Phoenix K-9 van and stepped into the clearing, scanning the circular area, his gaze skipping over several Phoenix K-9 agents, dogs, and Eli.

There.

Phoenix and Dagian stood by the doused fire in the pit. She

wore the large, gray backpack that never seemed to weigh her down, and the charcoal baseball cap. Her long braid dangled down her back, and her gaze went to her watch.

Callum couldn't help the small smile that shaped his lips at the sight of her.

Ready. Strong. No hint of weariness in her upright bearing. And eyes on the time.

Callum had made it with only five minutes to spare before her departure time of seven o'clock. And he had no doubt she'd leave without him. He had better tell her he was there. Although he doubted it would come as a surprise to the woman who seemed to notice everything.

"Ross, Moore." Her firm tone carried across the open space. "Load up. We're taking the van."

No surprise at all. Callum shook his head. She'd known he was there even though he hadn't seen her look his way.

She walked toward him and brushed past with Dagian.

At least the dog graced him with a brief stare from his bright blue eyes.

Callum should've known better than to expect a greeting from Phoenix. She was hardly a *Good morning* type of person.

Eli scrambled to follow her, carrying a backpack he hadn't had yesterday. "Morning." He gave Callum a weak grin, his eyes red-rimmed, and his gait stiff.

"Morning." Callum fell in step with him as they went to the van where Dagian was jumping in the back. Eli tossed his backpack into the rear while the double doors were open, so Callum slipped off the backpack he had gotten at Base and stepped up to put it inside.

Wow. Beyond the cooler, blankets, and camping gear stacked along the sides of the van, a desk stood, separated from the front seats by a barrier of steel bars. The desk held several computer monitors, what looked like a closed laptop, and some other electronic equipment he couldn't identity from where he stood. One large element appeared to be a sound board or control panel of some sort. Just what did Phoenix use the van for?

Dagian lay under the desk, a perfectly sized space for the dog.

"I'll ride back here. You take the front." Eli stepped up into the van before Callum could protest.

"You sure?"

"Yeah. I think she's sick of my questions. But you two speak the same language."

"We do?" Callum blinked at the man who ducked to move farther inside.

"Yeah. Nothing." He tossed a grin Callum's way as he reached the chair fixed to the floor by the desk.

Callum smiled in return before he remembered he was currently holding Phoenix up. She wouldn't thank him for that. In fact, she might drive away before he could reach the front of the van.

He hurried to the passenger door and opened it to slide inside.

She didn't look at him as she pressed a button on the dash labeled with an icon that looked like the rear door closure. She started the engine and backed the van around to face the road.

He waited until they were on the service road and headed in the correct direction to say anything. Though maybe he'd be better off saying nothing. Like Eli had accurately pointed out, silence seemed to be her language.

But she might be interested in his information. "Agent Nguyen gave me the lab results from the bear trap you sent to Base last night."

Phoenix stared out the windshield.

"No prints. And the model is too old to trace the sale."

She likely wasn't surprised by the news. If the Forster killer had left it, as was the prevailing theory, he wouldn't have been clumsy enough to leave any fingerprints or means by which he could be traced. He was an expert at leaving nothing behind.

The question was, had he planted more traps for unsuspecting searchers? Callum would ask what Phoenix thought, but he wouldn't get an answer.

So he settled in for a silent drive. He assumed her intention was to bring them to where they'd had to stop on foot last night, when the tracks showed the kidnapper had transferred the children to a van. Then they would attempt to follow the van.

Thank the Lord the other K-9 teams had found two more boys last night. Were those all the boys the Forster killer had released, or were there more? If others were lost, had they survived the night alone? He understood there were bears, wolves, and coyotes in Timber Park.

And then there was the cold. Last night wasn't as bad as it could have been with temperatures in the forties. Callum had heard FBI agents at the base discussing the unusually warm temperatures that were expected to dip lower soon. Below freezing.

*Father, please protect the children with the kidnapper and those on their own. And help us find them soon.*

Callum's gaze drifted to Phoenix.

She silently directed the van, scanning the tree-lined road.

*And please help Phoenix, Father. She's not an enigma to You. Please use me to help her, if You will. Let us catch the man who destroyed her and her family so she can find peace. In You.*

Callum continued with such silent prayers off and on as they drove for an hour.

Once they reached where the kidnapper had put the children in the van, Phoenix slowed down to keep the van's tire treads in view. She also stopped when any trail intersected with the road. Then she would get Dagian out and let him check for scents.

None so far had indicated the children had left the vehicle.

Callum kept watch through the passenger window, peering into the trees and underbrush for the next thirty minutes.

The drive would have been stunning and peaceful under different circumstances. The fall glory of the forest was something to behold, the leaves awash with vibrant shades of gold, burgundy, purple, and red.

But not that shade of red. A glimpse of a bold, deeply saturated red that had to be artificial made Callum grip the door handle.

"Phoenix, I see something."

She instantly halted the vehicle, and Callum dropped out the passenger side.

He rushed to the edge of the road where he'd seen the color break through tall weeds. "Hello?"

A muffled moan reached him before he spotted the movement.

A small, brown-haired head and hands parting the weeds. A boy. "Are you Phoenix?"

Callum's smile at seeing the boy faltered. "No." How did the boy know about Phoenix?

"Oh."

"I'm Callum. What's your name?"

"Phillip."

"Well, Phillip, we're here to help you. We'll get you home now."

Eli walked to them, a friendly smile on his face. "Hey, there. We've called for a car to come take you home. How would you like that?"

Phillip nodded. "I fell asleep here." Judging from the boy's slow blink, he was still sleepy. Much better than fear and panic. Though his lips were tinged with blue. He probably needed a blanket.

As if on cue, Phoenix appeared seemingly from nowhere with a blanket. How had he not heard her approach on gravel?

She extended the folded blanket to Callum, apparently wanting him to give it to Phillip.

Callum took it, and Eli helped the boy walk onto the road as Callum wrapped the blanket around his shoulders.

"How'd you get here, son?" Eli squatted in front of Phillip.

"A van. One of the girls had to sit on my lap 'cause there wasn't room." He wrinkled his nose.

Callum nearly smiled at the sign that the boy's normal, age-appropriate attitudes weren't damaged by trauma.

"But she was crying, so I guess she needed somebody."

Eli stood, exchanging a glance with Callum that held a glint of amusement. "I'm sure she did."

"Can you tell us what the bad man looked like?" None of the rescued boys had been able to give a clear description yet. They'd been too frightened. But Phillip, in his sleepy state, seemed relaxed enough that he might be able to face visualizing the kidnapper.

"He didn't have any eyebrows." Phillip touched his own eyebrows with a finger. "No hair on his head either. I saw when he took off his hat once."

Callum glanced at Phoenix instinctively, though she was sure to show no reaction. He recognized the description from the rendering he'd seen in the FBI case files that an artist had drawn from Robin's memory of her kidnapper. Phoenix would know from seeing him herself. It was the Forster killer.

A few more questions confirmed the man had dark eyes, likely the brown Robin had recalled of her kidnapper, and was wearing black pants, a dark brown puffer jacket, and a black beanie.

"He was really scary." Phillip dropped his gaze to the gravel. "Lots of the kids were scared, but Marnie said to be brave, and we'd get home soon 'cause somebody named Phoenix was going to rescue us."

Callum and Eli looked at Phoenix.

She watched the boy, no reaction or emotion showing in her immovable expression. Was she surprised Marnie had told the other children about her? That the girl expected Phoenix to rescue them all? And why did Marnie have such faith in Phoenix? The cool and detached woman did not convey the warmth or friendliness usually required for children to like an adult.

"Were you the first to be let out of the van?" Phoenix finally spoke.

"No." Phillip squinted at her, either because of the sunlight or trying to see her face under her cap. "He let lots go before me. Kept stopping to make them get out. They didn't want to go. 'Cause of the dark."

"Did he tell you to go in a specific direction?"

The boy nodded. "He watched us and pointed where we were supposed to run." Phillip glanced at Callum, then Eli. "I sneaked back after he drove away. He said he'd hurt us if we did that."

Callum stepped to Phillip's side and put an arm around his shoulders. "He can't hurt you now. We'll keep you safe."

The reassurance kept the boy calm as they waited for FBI transport. Didn't take long. There must have been a car out on the road between there and Base to arrive so soon.

Once Phillip was loaded, and the car turned to head back to Base, Phoenix silently returned to the van.

Callum and Eli hurried to jump in before she left without them, and she drove on, following the tire treads on the road.

If Phillip's story was accurate, the kidnapper had released boys along the way but not at any of the intersecting trails Phoenix had already checked with Dagian.

While she drove, Phoenix radioed in the information Phillip had shared about the other children being sent into the forest. More searchers, including some of Phoenix's team, would be sent to areas nearer that service road. Though if the kids had wandered overnight instead of staying put, they could be far away by now.

Callum initially wondered if the information about the other stray children would make Phoenix go from there on foot with Dagian, searching for the scent of the boys. But she apparently favored staying on the heels of the kidnapper and hostages.

A sound strategy. They couldn't let him get away. And especially not with his target victim or any of the other girls in the group he'd stolen.

A half hour later, Callum blinked his dry eyes, sore from all the staring and scanning their surroundings, looking for signs of children.

They'd only had brief breaks when Phoenix stopped to check intersecting trails. But it was—

Phoenix braked hard.

Callum braced his hands against the dash. "What—"

She was already out of the van.

He fumbled with his seatbelt, managing to get it unclipped to follow her.

She stopped at the side of the road, looking at something.

Callum hurried to her, scanning the weeds on the shoulder.

Crunching sounds behind him on the gravel made Callum glance back.

Eli and Dagian rushed toward them. "What is it?" Eli reached Phoenix's other side and glanced down at the ground in the direction she stared. "Is that—" He squatted by something...Rocks?

Callum hadn't even noticed the rocks, since there were plenty in the forest and along the road. But these were in a curious formation. Like they'd been stacked and arranged intentionally.

"This is one of the trail signs you taught Marnie." Eli looked up at Phoenix, hope lighting his face. "Isn't it?"

# TWENTY

"Yes." Phoenix lifted her gaze from Marnie's trail sign to the trees beyond it.

"I knew it." Eli nearly jumped to his feet. "She showed me after you taught her the trail signs so she wouldn't get lost in the woods."

It was the first marker Phoenix had seen thus far, though she'd been actively looking. Marnie must not have had opportunity to leave one before, when the children had been on foot. He'd likely watched her and the others too closely, or she'd feared another child giving her away.

The risk of leaving a marker was great. Any of the children other than his target were expendable to him. He wouldn't hesitate to kill one—to kill Marnie—if she became a problem.

But the reports from the rescued children showed Marnie was accomplishing two aims at once. She was helping the children survive with her encouragement and instructions, and, in so doing, she was making herself an asset to her kidnapper. She would be careful not to mention rescue by Phoenix when the kidnapper could hear. She would only let him hear her directing the children to do as he said.

Phoenix couldn't be prouder of the girl who had been paralyzed by trauma and terror when Phoenix first hid her with the Moores. She was rising above that now. Becoming stronger because of what she had experienced.

"They must have gotten out of the van here." Ross's calm tone was close as he stood beside Phoenix. "And then got back in?"

No. The sign was directional, the orientation of the rocks subtly pointing into the forest off the road.

There were no visible tracks, but some of the tall weeds showed bends and near-breaks. As if they'd been stepped on and then righted again to hide the trail.

Dag moved around Eli to smell the rock formation. The K-9 looked at Phoenix, checking if she was ready.

"Go."

His nose went to the ground, skimming through the weeds she suspected masked the children's tracks. He plowed through the tall grasses, picking up speed.

Phoenix followed closely, Eli and Ross crunching through brush and branches behind her.

"Did they go this way?" Eli's question carried ahead to Phoenix as she kept her gaze locked on Dag, breaking through the thick foliage.

The K-9 halted ten feet ahead.

She scanned the thick grass and trees in front of him.

No. Not trees. Trunks and branches. Reeds, grasses, and leaves intentionally placed to cover something. To hide something.

She moved closer and shoved aside two slim logs and leafy branches, revealing white paint and a door handle.

His cargo van.

"Is that the kidnapper's van?" Eli didn't wait for an answer. He clomped forward and threw aside more of the camouflage that hid the side and front passenger door.

He cupped his hands around his eyes and leaned against the passenger window. "I can't see in the back."

Phoenix went to the driver's side of the old model van and cleared the branches and leaves there. Tried the door. Locked.

"Looks like a grid divider in there behind the seats. I can't see past it." Eli's hope the children were still inside was going to be disappointed. Unless the kidnapper had left some because he'd dispatched them.

It was a possibility, but an unlikely one. He wanted them all alive to use as distractions for searchers. But if any had opposed him or gotten in his way...

Like Marnie.

Emotion clogged Phoenix's throat at the thought. She marched with Dag to the rear of the van.

Ross was removing the last of the camouflage that had hidden the two narrow doors. He looked through the windows. "Too dark to see anything."

Eli pulled on the handles. "Locked." He let out a frustrated grunt. "I could pick it if I had my tools with me."

Phoenix whipped her Glock from her holster and pushed past Eli. She slammed the butt of the gun into the left door's window, smashing through the untreated glass.

"Or we could do that." Ross looked at Phoenix, his mouth curved with that slight hint of a smile again that, though barely perceptible, still reached his eyes. "May I?"

She stepped back to let him get the angle to reach in through the window.

His taller height meant he could do so more easily since the rough ground beneath the van elevated the rear tires. He felt around for the lock. "Got it."

He pulled out his arm and grasped the handle before she could. He started to swing the door open.

He'd better not let Eli see the—

A crack sounded.

Dag barked.

Just as a log swung out from the trees, aimed directly at Ross.

Phoenix catapulted toward him, twisting her leg around his to take him down.

She landed on top of him as intended, instinctively securing him in a hold not necessary for a non-hostile. She let go of his arm and shoulder and pulled back enough to see his face. Check for consciousness. He could've hit his head hard on the way down.

He blinked. Greenish brown eyes fixed on her, their irises lit with surprise. Then the expression in them changed, softened, yet sharpened at the same time.

His gaze plunged into hers. Deeply. As if he could see...her.

A bolt spiked through her like an electric shock.

She rolled off him and onto her feet, landing in a ready stance two feet away. She watched him as he more slowly got to his feet. She refused to look away and let him think he'd shaken her.

The electric pulse was likely due to a physical reaction to the closeness. Some degree of attraction would be normal. He was a handsome man by most women's standards, and she had been on top of him, her palms pressed against his strong chest through the sweater. But a chemical reaction was neither useful nor safe. Not for her.

"Everybody okay?" Eli's question did not draw her gaze away from Ross.

The agent brushed off his dark cotton pants, then straightened. "Thank you." He aimed his gaze at her, sincerity filling his eyes.

A desire to break the contact made her turn away toward the van.

Unacceptable. She hadn't allowed herself to shirk from anyone or anything uncomfortable since she was a teenager.

No, it wasn't attraction she was feeling. It was something much more disconcerting. He'd targeted a vulnerability, a weakness she thought she had rid herself of years ago. A weakness no one had ever known about, and, thus, could never exploit.

Was he aware of what he had accessed within her?

"Looks like another booby trap, huh?" Eli pointed at a cluster of trees he was examining.

Phoenix walked to him and looked closely.

Rope was tied around several tree trunks, some of the rope slackened into a sling of sorts. The rope must have cradled the log and held it back just enough that it could be loosened by a trip wire attached to the doors.

"We'll have to use more caution from now on." In more ways than one. The thought simmered in Phoenix's tightening stomach as she returned to the van.

Ross had already entered the cargo area and was walking through it, stooped beneath the low ceiling.

No bodies or objects were visible from where she stood outside the van. The space appeared empty.

Marnie was still alive.

The rare tension knotting Phoenix's gut released. She would wait until Ross exited to enter herself and examine the area more closely. Far too crowded with him taking up most of the space.

At least he apparently hadn't felt any attraction in response to the physical contact between them. If he had, he would have responded like a typical male and tried to prolong the position or touch her inappropriately. Possibly would have made a crude or flirtatious comment.

But he'd only expressed gratitude for saving him from injury. That humility again.

She had never seen such a competent man not care if he wasn't in charge. Even when she, a woman, was taking the lead over him. Such an attitude could signal a lack of confidence. But he clearly had confidence in abundance. He would be intimidated by her if he were unsure of himself, as many people were. Like they did, he would recoil from her or challenge her to cut her down to his size. He clearly felt he had nothing to prove.

What had made him such a unique man? Full of confidence and skill with no ego to match it. Possessing a rare comfort in his own skin. A contentment and calm that defined him at all times, even though he appeared to genuinely care about the children and understand the danger.

But his knowledge of her background, coupled with the occurrence that had just taken place—the moment when he may have seen much more than she'd intended, much more than anyone ever had—that made him one of the most dangerous men of her acquaintance.

She would not let him get that close again. And she would make him forget what he had seen.

---

"How long ago were they here?" Eli's question drifted back to Callum as he followed behind the man who stayed close to Phoenix and Dagian.

Callum tried to spot the footprints they were tracking. The tall grasses that covered the open area were flattened and crunched, but he couldn't make out any distinct foot shapes.

"The tracks are at least fifteen hours old." Phoenix's answer was in a near-monotone as usual as she set a steady, determined pace.

The pinching sensation in his chest squeezed harder. He couldn't get over it—Phoenix Gray had saved his life.

If that massive log had slammed into the side of his head with the amount of force it had behind it, he could've been done for.

But Phoenix had knocked him to the ground. Then lingered above him, so close he could see her. Really see her, like never before.

His throat tightened as her face appeared in front of his eyes again, the way she had looked down at him. Looked into him.

She'd been even more beautiful up close. Breathtaking. That had been the first thing he'd noticed.

Then he had spotted the edge of her contacts, and the thought that he would love to see her real, brown eyes, had flitted through his mind.

But as he'd kept looking, focusing on her eyes, he'd found he couldn't look away. Didn't want to look away. Feelings he had no business indulging had surged through him, heating his limbs and running through his veins.

Then he'd seen it. The slightest tint of emotion in her gaze.

But she'd moved off him so quickly, he wasn't sure if he had imagined what he'd seen. Perhaps all he'd noticed was processing, thinking, assessing. That would be much more than he'd ever detected in her impassive expression before.

He had thought, for a moment, he'd glimpsed something more. Something strong and deep. Something soft...Vulnerable.

If only she hadn't pushed away so soon—much too soon for his taste. Though given her history with men, she was probably repulsed by the contact. Yet she had saved him anyway, without hesitation.

He watched her walk ahead of him now with Dagian. Strong, steady, purposeful. One thing he knew about Phoenix Gray was that she never acted on instinct. Saving him had been a conscious choice.

He'd have to try not to read too much into that. Maybe she wanted him around for some strategic plan locked away in that amazing mind of hers.

"Here." Her voice, so rarely heard, startled him from his thoughts. She held up a hand to halt them, looking at the ground in front of her.

Callum moved closer but saw only more flattened grass.

"He sent two more children away." She lifted her gaze to Callum.

His pulse quickened. Phoenix was asking him to do something?

Probably to call it in. He pressed the button on his coms earpiece and reported the news to Base. The Phoenix K-9 Agency teams, which Phoenix had directed to move into that area after they'd found the van, would follow the scents of the two boys who'd left the group.

Hopefully, the Evidence Response Team Callum had called in

would find something helpful on the van. But with the Forster killer's track record, he wasn't likely to leave any prints or DNA.

Callum had also warned the other agents on coms to watch for additional booby traps around the van and when following the trail of the hostages.

The kidnapper must have pre-planned that booby trap before he'd even kidnapped the children. Just as he must have scoped out the map, plotted his escape route, and decided where he would release children along the way.

He had known to pull the van off the road farther beyond where he wanted to hide it, then drive onto a trail barely large enough to hold it until he could back the vehicle into the thick foliage and unload the children where no sign of the van or footprints could be seen.

Marnie must have gotten away from him, maybe while he was camouflaging the van, to leave her trail sign on the road and double back before he missed her. What a remarkable girl.

A chopping sound drew his gaze to the sky. A helicopter passed overhead, one of several aerial search partners that had been flying all morning.

If the kidnapper had led the children through this clearing in daylight, he would have been seen. But he was too strategic for a mistake like that.

At least one of the pilots of a small plane had spotted two lost boys that morning, and the on-foot searchers had rescued three more. Callum had only learned of those recoveries when he'd called in the van discovery. Apparently, not all rescues were being reported on the main channel since there were so many agencies and searchers involved.

"Give them an additional note." Phoenix squatted by a small footprint, a clear impression in a patch of dirt. "One of the children released is a girl." Phoenix's eyes met Callum's. There was no emotion there, but he understood. As if she'd sent a silent message most people wouldn't receive.

But he did. And he knew what she meant.

If the Forster killer was starting to cull the girls, he'd begun something far more serious than subjecting more children to the dangers of the wild.

He would keep shrinking the number of girls until only one remained. His target.

Phoenix knew better than anyone what her fate would be.

God help her. God help them all.

# TWENTY-ONE

A snap behind Phoenix prompted her to check over her shoulder.

Eli stumbled, then righted himself, his form yellow-green through her NVGs. He should be able to see clearly in the dark with the NVGs he also wore. But vision wasn't the problem. His slumped shoulders and dragging legs made that clear.

She would not let him hold her back, as she'd said at the beginning. Nor would he want her to.

After hearing a girl had been sent away, he'd become grimmer and more pensive again. He hadn't peppered her with many questions beyond how she could tell the print was a girl's. The size difference between her print and the previous boy's prints Phoenix had found made the deduction obvious.

Eli should know Marnie would be fine if sent away. But perhaps he feared what would happen if the kidnapper kept her.

Ross's stride at the rear of their line had slowed to match Eli's pace in front of him. The agent's posture and relaxed, even stride indicated he'd done extensive hiking before. Fatigue didn't seem to be setting in for him yet, at least not visibly.

Dag continued to keep them on the correct scent trail, steady as always. As driven as Phoenix.

But even he would need a rest at some point, if only to ensure his scenting prowess stayed sharp. Two hours and five minutes more, and they would stop. Let the FBI trackers attempt to continue from there.

Since leaving the open clearing near the van, the rest of the children's scent trail had been slightly more challenging to follow. It wound unpredictably through the uneven, rough terrain of underbrush and thickly wooded areas, not confined to the park's designated paths or roads.

Dag had no problem sticking with the scent, but the FBI K-9s—

A ring sounded. The satphone.

Likely Cora or Katherine.

Phoenix reached behind her to the pocket of her pack and grabbed the phone. "Go."

"Phoenix? I'm so glad I got you." Marion's voice was as tight and strained as the last time they'd spoken. "I didn't realize until it was too late. I didn't know they would release the photo. I'm so sorry. I should've thought of this…"

Phoenix waited for Marion to calm herself. It wasn't holding up Dag or the search to let her panicked words spill out while Phoenix continued moving.

Marion soon reined in the constant string of words that didn't add much to what Phoenix had immediately deduced. The school had shared Marnie's photo with media outlets, along with all the kidnapped children's photos.

"I didn't know it until one of the other mothers told me about the kids' pictures being everywhere. Nationwide." Marion's tone took on a strangled quality, indicating the imminent arrival of tears. "It's supposed to help them be found. So people can identify them if they see any of them and report it to the police."

Marion sniffed. Took in a shaky breath. "He couldn't possibly recognize her, could he? She looks so different now. She was only four when…" Marion trailed off, the hitch in her breath evidence of more tears.

The tears weren't helpful, but the warning to Phoenix was. "You did the right thing, calling me."

Another sniff. "You don't think he would recognize her, do you?"

"Yes."

Silence followed Phoenix's answer. "But how?"

"The birthmark."

Marion sucked in a sharp breath. "Oh, no. You're right. It depends on which one they used, but if it's the one we had printed...you can see it in the photo."

And if the crooked FBI agent had seen the distinctive star-shaped birthmark on four-year-old Marnie's neck, he would instantly know he'd found his target. The girl he wanted dead.

"Phoenix, what do we do?"

Dag disappeared behind the trees ahead.

Phoenix increased her pace to bring him back into view. "I'll handle it."

Marion breathed in and out, more slowly this time. "Okay. Thank you. I guess he couldn't get to her anyway. Not right now." Fear cinched her voice, but she quieted for a few moments. When she spoke again, her tone signaled she'd regained control. "My poor girl is already in so much danger. This photo thing can't make that worse."

It could. If Phoenix didn't monitor the situation.

If anyone from the FBI team she had consulted with when Marnie's mother was murdered showed up for the search, Phoenix would recognize him. The media would have already broadcasted that her agency was helping with the rescue. Would he risk being identified by her?

He'd been smart and patient for five years. But the opportunity might be too much for him to resist. A positive identification of the girl and the scenario where he could again make the murder look like the work of a serial killer.

More agents were joining the search every day, brought in from other states. And Phoenix was not seeing most of them.

"Phoenix? You're making me nervous." Marion's voice trembled.

"I'll take care of it. I'll bring Marnie home." Phoenix ended the call as she stepped up onto a fallen log and dropped to the other side, then quickly dialed Katherine's number.

"What's the news, Phoenix?" Katherine's no-nonsense tone came across the line louder than Marion's weakened one.

"I need you to screen the FBI agents that have joined the search and any that arrive from now on."

"What?" Voices and shuffling sounded in the background. Then a noise like a door closing. The background grew quiet. Good. Katherine had gone to a more private location. "Screen for what?"

"For any agent that worked the Jacob Carlton serial killer case, when he was arrested five years ago."

A pause hung on the line as Phoenix navigated through branches and leaves on the ground, automatically choosing the quietest footfalls in between checking on Dag ahead.

"Do you know how busy we are here right now?"

Phoenix let another silence be her answer.

"Okay." Katherine puffed out a displeased sigh. But she trusted Phoenix. "I'll do what I can. When I can get to it. But no promises it'll be right away." The door opened again in the background, introducing more sounds of people and phones ringing. "And you'll agree to tell me what this is about later?" Katherine's way of reconciling doing as Phoenix said without giving up any authority.

"Agreed."

"Okay. Give me a call in the morning, and I'll see what I can do."

Phoenix disconnected and slipped the phone into her backpack behind her.

Crunching, approaching quickly. Eli would be trying to catch up now.

Phoenix slowed slightly without looking back.

Dag was holding a straighter line at present, so she shouldn't lose him at the pace that would allow Eli to ask his questions.

The man came up beside Phoenix, his breath puffing like a small cloud in the cold air before his face. "Was that about Marnie?"

"Yes." Quieter sounds behind her and an awareness of Ross's presence signaled the agent was also moving closer.

"I heard some of it." Eli's hushed tone still wasn't quiet enough for Ross not to hear.

The agent seemed genuine in his care for children, his commitment to rescue them and capture their tormentors.

But Phoenix's assessment of him and honed instincts could be mistaken. She couldn't be certain he was unconnected to the FBI agent who wanted Marnie dead.

He could even be unknowingly connected and used for the crooked agent's plans without consent.

"Aren't you going to tell me what it was about?" Impatience and worry made Eli's question louder.

"Later." Hard to send signals with one's eyes while wearing NVGs, but Phoenix added the slightest tilt of her head to indicate Ross behind them.

Eli, likely due to undercover experience, knew enough not to look at Ross. And to clam up.

"PT2 to Base." Sofia's strong tone came over coms. "Found a child. A girl."

Confirmation of Phoenix's identification of the print.

All the boys, the nine still unrecovered, were in the woods alone now. The clock was ticking down for them and for the girls that remained with the monster.

His lead was still significant. He had done well with his plan, his strategy to rapidly gain ground the first day, before anyone knew they were gone. And he was maintaining the lead with the diversions of the children he sent away and now the trail that was more difficult to track.

Marnie had to hang on until Phoenix could close the gap. If

she couldn't, or if he outsmarted the nine-year-old girl, Marnie wouldn't be the only one to pay the price.

---

Callum hadn't felt so weary physically since the Sawtooth Wilderness Loop, the four-day hike he'd gone on six months ago. He should've stayed in better shape. But his muscles seemed to remember the drill, even if they didn't like it.

Eli didn't seem to be faring so well. When Phoenix had taken a phone call about fifteen minutes ago, Eli had pushed himself faster to catch up with her. The energy output seemed to have been too much, as he'd lagged farther behind ever since.

Callum had been staying at the rear, but when Eli dropped so far behind, Callum didn't want to risk letting Phoenix get completely out of sight.

Now he walked between Eli and Phoenix, trying to keep his eye on both. Wouldn't be good to lose track of Eli, especially when he was looking more and more fatigued by the moment.

At least Eli surging ahead to talk to Phoenix had given Callum the chance to move closer himself. Just in time to catch Phoenix saying she would tell Eli something later. Callum had gotten the distinct impression she'd meant when he wasn't within earshot.

Disappointing that neither of them, especially Phoenix, trusted him enough to discuss whatever it was in front of him. But he understood. Phoenix had an abundance of reasons to be suspicious of everyone.

In this case, he was likely thought unsafe because of who and what he was. An FBI agent. Maybe they were discussing a crooked agent. It did happen, rarely. But once was too often.

Phoenix had saved Callum from that freefalling log, though. She must not think he was too awful, or she would've let him get clobbered. Obviously, she did approve of some people eventually, since she seemed to trust the members of her team and Eli. At least to a degree. She clearly didn't trust anyone with her emotions. She kept her real self completely hidden at all times.

But since it was possible for her to reach the point of accepting others and trusting them with some information, Callum would hold on to hope that he'd be in that circle eventually. She likely needed to do more research or see him in action longer before she would deem him one of the good guys.

His foot caught on something, nearly tripping him. Just a branch, lying flat on the ground among the flattened leaves. Apparently, his body had reached the point where he wasn't lifting his feet as high as normal.

Maybe seeing if he could last the incredibly long hike was part of Phoenix's test. He raised his gaze to find her and Dag ahead.

The K-9 jumped over a fallen tree like it was nothing and continued on.

Phoenix planted her hand on the horizontal trunk and effortlessly swung her legs over it to drop to the other side.

As Callum took advantage of his long legs to step over the log behind her, Phoenix suddenly stopped on the other side.

"Dag, wait." She squatted to look at the ground.

Callum moved closer as Eli clambered over the tree to join them. Callum scanned the ground, sprinkled with freshly fallen leaves.

A small bit of yellow, brighter than the leaves, nestled among them. Yellow and silver.

He crouched and picked up the small object with his gloved fingers. "I think this is a food wrapper."

"Beef jerky." Phoenix stood and moved in a half-circle outward, still looking down. "He had them stop here for two hours. Allowed them to sleep and eat."

"Thank God, he's doing that much." A note of relief eased Eli's tone.

Phoenix aimed her NVGs at Eli. "He wants them to have enough fuel to keep moving." As if her words were a reminder to all of them, she marched off again. "Dag, go."

The K-9 instantly trotted in front of her and skimmed the ground with his nose, apparently following the trail of the kidnapper and children when they'd left after their rest. Forty-five minutes later, Dag was still on the scent, leading the humans in the search.

Callum split his attention between watching his footing and keeping Phoenix in view up ahead.

She navigated the rough terrain expertly and so very quietly. Didn't know how she managed that. Or how she still held herself as straight and moved with the same precision and strength as when they'd started out that morning.

Seemed unbelievable she and Dagian could search for eight hours with only a few five-minute breaks.

But her apathetic exterior couldn't hide the intensity and drive that he could practically feel rolling off of her whenever he got close. Maybe that's why she could last so long without a trace of weariness. People could do incredible feats when the stakes were high and personally, emotionally significant.

Given who they were after—the man who had murdered her family—Phoenix's emotions had to be involved in the search, even if she didn't show any. There might be more than the driving desire for justice at stake, too.

She had taught Eli's daughter wilderness survival. Seemed to have mentored her in that way. The evidence that Phoenix did care about someone, that she had that ability and willingness to emotionally attach after all she'd been through, gave Callum hope.

But why Marnie? Did Phoenix have a special history with Eli?

They did seem to have some sort of understanding in their first meeting when Eli had shown up to join the search. Could there be a history—

A screeching yell pierced the air.

"What—"

"Dag!" Phoenix shouted the dog's name over Eli's broken

question as she veered left, breaking into a run as the K-9 dashed to reach her side.

Callum sprinted behind her, watching the ground to avoid falling over rocks and logs.

He glanced up as he ran.

Phoenix and Dag slowed.

He caught up as they stopped.

Next to a man lying on the ground.

Blood oozed onto the hand that rested on his chest. Just below a knife in his shoulder.

His brown uniform and badge showed he was a park ranger. He must have been out searching on foot, though he wasn't supposed to be doing that alone in the dark.

"I'm Special Agent Callum Ross, FBI." Callum knelt next to the ranger, trying to get a look at the knife and wound before he tried to do anything for it.

The ranger grimaced. "Kal Morris."

"Looks like you got into some trouble there, Kal."

"Yeah." The ranger sucked in a breath. "Came out of nowhere. Didn't see anyone. Like a branch hit me, but there was this…" He gestured to the knife with his hand.

"Another booby trap." Eli stood by a tree and held up a disconnected branch that was tied to a higher, attached branch. Loose enough to swing out once it was triggered.

Callum clenched his jaw as he took off his backpack and dug for the First Aid kit. How many more good men and women would get injured or worse before this was all over?

They had to find the Forster killer. Before he killed again.

## TWENTY-TWO

"None of them are a match to that team so far." Katherine's voice sounded as forceful as usual over the satphone, though she'd been working around the clock.

Phoenix watched Ross build a fire in the pit with the precut wood the park rangers had left at the site for visitor use. Clearly not the first fire the agent had built. "Keep checking any additional agents that join the search."

"Okay. Are you going to tell me why I'm checking to see if they were involved in that case?"

"Later." Still couldn't risk being overheard by Ross. Nor could she take the chance word would get out about Marnie's identity and thereby lead the murderous FBI agent to her.

Phoenix highly doubted Ross was connected to the crooked agent. But she wouldn't be caught unprepared.

"All right. I have enough on my plate right now anyway. Six more finds today, including the one girl Sofia recovered. The girl was too scared to tell us much. Didn't know anything helpful. Think the four other boys are out in the woods by themselves or with the Forster killer?"

The shadows along the edge of the campsite shifted.

A black Labrador, Toby, pushed through the trees, followed by Bristol.

"The girl's release indicates he's sent away all the males."

"Thought so." Phones rang in the background on Katherine's end. Likely frantic parents and reporters. "Cold front's moving in. Supposed to drop to thirty-four tonight." Katherine didn't need to spell out her meaning.

Nor was it news to Phoenix. The chilling wind was already blowing through the campsite.

Another danger for the children was increasing. Exposure to the cold. Whether they were alone or with the kidnapper, they may not have sufficient clothing and shelter to avoid hypothermia.

"Did Kanton pick up the trail where you stopped?"

"Yes." Phoenix had shown the FBI agent where to continue tracking before she went to the campsite. He and his K-9 would only need to stay on the scent trail, careful not to lose it. Then Phoenix would take the shortest route possible to where the FBI team left off in the morning, connecting with the scent trail at the farther point to avoid losing more time.

"Good. I've got the other K-9 teams searching for the lost kids, continuing from where your teams stopped. That's about all we can do until sunup. Keep me posted on everything out there."

Phoenix ended the call and slipped the phone into her backpack that sat on the ground next to Dag. She'd told the K-9 to lie down, encouraging him to rest.

Unfortunate they'd lost forty-five minutes of searching thanks to the detour of helping the park ranger. Given the extent of his injury and location in an area where the kidnapper had set at least one booby trap, Phoenix had to stay with the ranger until medical help and transport arrived.

After she'd led Dag, Ross, and Eli back to the search for twenty minutes, she still halted at seven p.m., the twelve-hour shift mark.

Dag could have continued longer, thanks to the break with the wounded ranger and the ride in the van that morning.

But Phoenix needed to assemble the PK-9 team and not overwork the women or their dogs. They all needed rest to be fresh tomorrow. And in the days to come.

"Hey, people." Nevaeh's greeting held the note of humor she usually had when with Jazz or the other women of PK-9. She and Jazz sauntered into the campsite with Alvarez and Flash on leashes. Alvarez looked like he'd reached the end of his energy, the rottweiler mix protection dog not used to such rough terrain. But Flash still sported an alert expression and eager body language, as if he could use a good run.

The women took off their NVGs as they approached the small, slowly growing fire.

"Hey, did you build the fire?" Nevaeh smiled at Ross who stood nearby, restacking the precut wood. Her newfound confidence with men, now that she'd conquered her worst enemy from her past, was obvious as she spoke to the agent.

"Tried my best." Ross returned her smile.

"Thanks. We didn't actually meet before, back at Base. I'm Nevaeh."

He nodded with a friendly expression. "Callum."

"I'm Jazz." The redhead held out her hands above the warm glow of the fire. "Ooh, that feels good."

"Told ya to wear your gloves." Nevaeh nudged Jazz with her elbow.

Jazz returned the gentle push. "Didn't need 'em. Some of us aren't cold all the time."

"Uh-huh. Tell that to your fingers." The two friends laughed.

Dag rose to his feet with an alert rumble.

Phoenix checked in the direction of his gaze.

Glimpses of white shifted in the shadows between trees as her van approached. Cora wouldn't be able to pull into that campsite as she had before. She'd have to park on the road and walk in.

"Hey, is that Cora?" Bristol looked at Phoenix as she approached with Toby.

"Yes."

"Cora's here, guys." Bristol glanced over her shoulder before heading toward the service road behind the trees.

Nevaeh and Jazz hurried to catch up, their dogs trotting along with them. "Hey, don't lift anything heavy this time." Nevaeh's warning to pregnant Bristol coasted on the wind to Phoenix.

She waited for the group to return, the tall, dark-haired Kent carrying the heaviest item—the cooler he and Cora had returned to Base to refill before driving to the campsite.

Phoenix stepped close to Cora as she neared.

"Phoenix, hello." The blonde stopped, but Jana continued on with Kent, a sign the golden retriever had bonded with the man a great deal in the year he'd been married to Cora.

"Did you identify his target?"

Cora nodded, fatigue showing in the slight shadows under her blue eyes. "I believe so." She pulled her smartphone from the fanny pack she wore around her waist. "I can show you her school photo." Cora tapped the screen a few times, then turned the phone toward Phoenix.

Blonde, blue eyes. Delicate. Sweet, innocent smile. Definitely his chosen victim.

"Her name is Anna Kelly. She's an only child."

Another trait he favored. Siblings could cause problems. As had Robin.

"Show me the photo of Marnie Moore that went to news outlets." When the photos were originally taken, Marnie had shown Phoenix several options. One of which was at an angle that hadn't revealed the birthmark.

Cora selected the photo and handed Phoenix her phone.

Marnie. Her smile aimed up at Phoenix.

Emotion compressed Phoenix's ribs. Affection, concern. And something she did not indulge often. A wish that the child had been dealt a better life.

But Marnie's smile was happy, an expression that had been rare at first. Then in the last two years, smiles had become more frequent as the girl grew in confidence under Phoenix's guidance and in the security provided by the love of her adoptive parents.

Marnie was not smiling now.

But when Phoenix found her, she would help the girl recover from this, too. Use it to become stronger than before.

That effort might be more complicated than Phoenix had expected initially, with only him as the obstacle.

There, clearly visible on Marnie's neck in the photo, was the dark birthmark shaped like a star.

The murderous FBI agent couldn't miss it if he'd seen the photo. And he would have, given the FBI's involvement in the rescue operation.

He wouldn't miss the opportunity to finally eliminate her, if the kidnapper didn't do it for him first.

"Phoenix?" Cora's blue eyes filled with concern. "Is there something else going on with Marnie?"

Phoenix passed the phone back to Cora. "Nothing for you to worry about." Because Phoenix would handle it, too. She wasn't about to allow a crooked FBI agent to interfere with her plans for Marnie or the kidnapper. No more than she would let Callum Ross, a likely legitimate agent, get in her way.

She scanned the campfire for the agent who was going to stay overnight this time.

He walked along the far side of the campsite, searching for something.

Traps. She'd mentioned when they arrived that they would have to clear the site for booby traps the kidnapper may have rigged.

The PK-9 team were doing the same with their K-9s, following the edge of the clearing and crisscrossing the campsite to clear the area.

Eli still lay on the ground where he'd sprawled as soon as

they had arrived at the campsite, his jacket bundled as a pillow beneath his head.

"Do you mind if I walk with Bristol? I want to see how she and the baby are doing."

Phoenix gave Cora a small nod. She'd prefer Cora wait until the site was completely cleared. But the woman was a valued member of the team, and sheltering her as much as Phoenix often wanted to would only make her timid and dependent on others.

Phoenix went to follow twenty feet behind Cora as the blonde fell in step with Bristol.

Dag reached Phoenix's side in seconds, abandoning his suggested rest the moment he sensed her concern. He never liked to be more than ten feet away from her, regardless.

Toby smelled the ground in front of Bristol and Cora as they walked, unable to keep from using his explosives-scenting nose at all times.

"How are you and the baby feeling?" Cora's question, full of caring sweetness, drifted back to Phoenix. At only five months pregnant, Bristol was in fine condition to work and handle long hours. But Cora's maternal instincts had kicked into high gear as soon as Bristol and her husband, Remington, had announced they were expecting.

"Pretty good today." Bristol's voice carried a smile. "I'm so thankful God saw fit to end my morning sickness before this rescue."

"Yes. That was certainly—"

"Hold it, Cora." Bristol's sharp command cut to Phoenix's ears.

Phoenix and Dag sprinted to close the gap between them.

Bristol held her arm across Cora's chest, keeping her from taking another step.

And Toby was sitting directly in front of her leg.

"Hey, guys." Bristol's voice was even and calm. "We've got explosives here."

## TWENTY-THREE

Callum instinctively held his breath as the woman who'd briefly introduced herself as Bristol Jones earlier shined a flashlight on thin wire she followed to the underbrush about three feet to her left.

It appeared to originate from a rock a foot to Cora's right. The poor woman still hadn't moved since Bristol had told her to stop.

The tall man who'd said he was Cora's husband approached her from behind and gently guided her back and away from the wire.

"Found it." The gathering Phoenix K-9 team seemed to lean in as Bristol spoke from the plants she squatted by. "IED with dynamite. No worries. It's an easy one."

An easy one? Who was this woman? He thought she did search and rescue, and maybe security given that the Phoenix K-9 Agency had *Security* in its name. The *Detection* part referred to the cadaver dog, trackers, and search and rescue, didn't it?

Unless it meant explosives detection, too. He became convinced that must be the case as he watched Bristol quickly and confidently disarm the bomb.

She stood and spun toward them, holding the wires she'd apparently cut from the explosives. "We're clear."

With her free hand, she whipped something out from the pack she wore around her waist. A rope toy with a ball on it.

The black Lab jumped at the toy, latching on to tug hard with his whole body.

Even though the Lab and Bristol must have experience as an explosives detection team, it was strange Bristol knew how to disarm bombs herself. Good thing she did.

*Thank You, Lord, for saving us from another close call. Thank You no one got hurt.*

He looked for Cora to verify she was okay. Her husband stood with his arm around her closer to the fire. Her eyes were slightly widened, suggesting she was still experiencing some shock, but she was getting the support she needed from her husband.

Everyone else acted as if nothing had happened at all. They laid out sleeping bags and broke open snacks and drinks from the cooler amid chatting and laughter.

The Phoenix K-9 Agency team was nearly as impressive as the woman who had started it. Made sense, if she had personally selected and assembled the agents, which he was sure she must have. Just how many impressive skills would a person need to qualify for employment by Phoenix Gray?

Learning her history as Robin Forster only began to explain a few of the mysteries that surrounded her. Every day he spent with Phoenix left Callum with more questions and unanswered curiosity about the enigmatic, incredible woman.

As he unrolled his sleeping bag and slid into it, the mysterious Phoenix Gray still filled his thoughts. And she didn't leave as he took off his watch, rubbed the rough line of skin around his wrist, and shut his eyes.

He slid them open. Seemed like the next minute since he had closed his eyes, but the scene he saw before him had changed.

Darkness still cloaked the camp, but all was quiet. No one moved or spoke.

The leaves clinging to the trees at the perimeter rustled in the cold wind.

A figure sat in the glow of the fire, embers floating in the air as if to touch their lone companion.

Phoenix.

Callum reached for the watch he'd set on the ground near his head. He pressed the button for the backlight. *10:14 p.m.*

It had been a little after seven thirty when he'd gone to sleep, he thought. What had awakened him?

His gaze landed on Phoenix again. Wasn't she going to sleep at all? She must need some rest.

Maybe she couldn't sleep. Too many memories or concerns. If she had concerns...

Hard to tell with the unshakable confidence she always displayed.

Or maybe she was keeping watch in case the Forster killer doubled back and tried to attack the searchers head-on. That would be highly unlikely. He'd have no reason to leave the children or risk getting closer to the people who were trying to catch him.

As if Callum were the moth and Phoenix the flame, he found himself getting to his feet, slipping on his shoes, and drawing close to her. He tried to walk softly to avoid waking the others.

Dagian growled, low and quiet, as Callum approached.

Phoenix put a hand on the dog's head as he lay next to her lawn chair. Her cap angled toward Callum slightly, but he couldn't see her eyes under the shadowed bill.

The crisp, cold breeze hit him now that he'd left his sleeping bag. Should've thought to pull on his jacket over his sweater. He went closer to the warmth of the fire and sat in a chair positioned on the same side of the blaze as Phoenix, about four feet from her and Dagian. "Having trouble sleeping?"

The crackling of the fire was his only response as she stared directly at it again. Of course she wouldn't answer a question like that. It implied weakness and emotional disturbance she wouldn't admit to, even if she were experiencing such a thing.

He tried a different approach. "If you think we should keep watch, I'm happy to take a shift." He gave her some time to reply.

Firelight glinted off something on her sweater. A necklace? A gold chain and pendant laid against the cable-knit, dark gray fabric. Looked like the same disc shape as the pendant she'd worn to the press conference. Did it hold significant meaning for her?

Another question for Phoenix Gray. But she apparently wasn't going to answer the simpler ones he'd already tried.

Okay. She was going to stay up for whatever reason she didn't want to share.

Maybe he could get her to share a little about one of the other burning questions he'd been holding back. "Agent Nguyen brought up the concern that the kidnapper will flee the park with the hostages. I don't think he'll try it with so many children, but maybe he plans to wait until he's gained enough distance on us, then leave the park with only his target victim. Do you think he'll try to do that?"

A pause. Then Phoenix's voice finally broke the silence. "No."

So confident and certain. He'd love to ask how she knew she was right, but there was no chance she would give him insight into her secret knowledge or reasoning process.

At least she had finally answered a question. He stifled a smile at what felt like a small victory. Maybe she'd answer another harmless one if he struck while the iron was hot. "Marnie seems like an amazing girl. The way the other kids describe her, she sounds like a real leader. Is she older than the others in her class?"

Silence again.

Maybe he hadn't found the right question. His one success drove him to try again. "Since you taught her how to leave trail signs, you must know her well. How did you get involved in her life?"

Phoenix turned her head toward him then. Firelight caught

her eyes under the cap. But no emotion showed there. Nothing he could use to gauge why she looked at him then. Except...it wasn't her expression or eyes, but he felt a change anyway. Like a shift, an increase in the intensity that flowed from her and aimed at him.

Had he hit some sort of nerve? Crossed a line? Ah, the danger there might be from the FBI, if his deductions had been correct from the brief snippets he'd heard of the exchange between her and Eli. He could change the subject. Try to dodge the sensitive topic. But he'd never liked subterfuge. She should know he'd heard.

"I overheard you and Eli earlier tonight. That phone call had something to do with Marnie, didn't it?" He realized she wouldn't answer that time, so he continued after a breath. "It sounded like she might be in some additional danger. Something to do with the FBI, I'm assuming, since you didn't want me to hear more than that."

Phoenix watched him steadily.

He watched her back. He had nothing to hide. "I'd like to help, if I can. She sounds like a remarkable girl. And she's already in more danger than any child should ever have to experience."

Phoenix kept her gaze on him for another two beats. Then she turned her head toward the fire. "She'll make it."

He could have imagined it, but a hint of determination seemed to undergird her firm tone. "I believe she will, with you protecting her." Words he probably shouldn't voice pushed up his throat. "I don't know how you do it, Phoenix." He probably should stick with the more formal and polite *Ms. Gray*. But it didn't suit what he was about to say. "I don't know how you keep going nonstop, physically and mentally, under these circumstances."

He sat forward on his chair so he could angle toward her. "I don't know how, from a distance, you can inspire a little girl to be strong and courageous in the face of a murderous kidnapper because she's sure you're going to rescue her." He let his admiration and amazement infuse his tone as he sought Phoenix's gaze.

But she still focused only on the fire.

"It's no wonder this team of impressive women and K-9s you've assembled will follow you anywhere and do anything for you."

"No."

Her sudden reply startled him into silence.

She landed her gaze on him, her eyes still unreadable. "For each other. The children. The victims." She faced the blaze again. "For justice."

He stared at her even though she didn't look at him any longer.

She'd given him a glimpse. The smallest of peeks into what lay beneath her impenetrable shell.

Did her words say more than she'd intended? In them, he heard her hopes, her loves, her passions, her dreams.

And they echoed his own heart's cries.

---

There it was again. The look in his eyes, even from four feet away—as if Callum Ross was seeing inside her.

The stirring within her rose. The pull toward him. As if he had accessed her soul, found the yearning there. And her subconscious believed he was the answer.

But he wasn't. Though she kept it deeply hidden in herself, the human need for connection was natural. Powerful. She did not need to heed her longing for it.

Connection, understanding, mutual love. These were for others. Not her. Even if she could find them in someone, those rarities she had not found in a human being since her family's massacre destroyed her, she would not risk the vulnerability and dependence with which they were inextricably linked.

He was going to speak. Verbalize what he'd seen in her, understood of her.

She couldn't allow that. "You should sleep while you can. We leave early."

Ross straightened, finally pulling his insightful gaze from her to glance at the fire. "You're right. But are you sure I can't take a shift of the watch so you can rest?"

The watch. He knew she was awake for a reason. Likely thought she was watching for bears or wolves. Or perhaps he thought she was watching for the kidnapper. But she knew as Ross did that the monster couldn't double back and return again to the children quickly when he had such a significant lead. Even if he took a vehicle, he would lose too much time and risk letting Phoenix catch up with him. No, he wouldn't come in person. Not yet.

Ross's intelligence allowed him to realize Phoenix's actions were intentional. But he didn't know she wasn't watching for danger. Couldn't know she wanted the kidnapper to see her through the trail camera he'd planted there. Wanted him to see the pendant.

She'd picked the most predictable campsite, closest to the scent trail they'd been tracking. Then looked closely for one of the trail cameras she anticipated he had planted at several campsites. He would want to watch as many search parties as possible to monitor their locations, distance from him, and their numbers.

But more than that, he wanted to find her. He needed to verify his plan had worked, that she had joined the SAR operation. And he wanted to monitor whether or not she was alone.

She'd located a trail cam hidden in the top of a bush among the trees bordering the campsite. And now she sat, framed within the lens of his camera in the firelight, openly wearing the pendant.

He would enjoy the feeling of power—the hunter watching his prey through a game camera.

And he would stay focused on her.

"Okay." Ross stood and bent over the stack of precut firewood next to Dag. "I'll take your advice, and sleep while I can." He picked up a piece of wood and reached to add it to the fire.

As his sweater sleeve pulled up, the orange light landed on a raised line of skin that slashed his wrist. The spot was normally covered by the watch he wasn't wearing now.

She hadn't expected to see that in the watch's place.

The thickened skin was unmistakable. A scar. Like those she'd seen on victims who had been bound with wire that had cut deeply into their flesh.

"Good night, Phoenix." He turned and walked to his sleeping bag, apparently realizing he shouldn't wait for a reply.

It was time to learn more about Special Agent Callum Ross.

Phoenix waited until he appeared to be asleep, then silently rose and went to her backpack, Dag following at her side. Retrieving her smartphone and the satellite router she'd told Cora to leave there, she sat on the cold ground. She wouldn't be so easily seen there by others who might wake.

Dag lay beside her, lowering his head to his feet.

Connecting her phone to the router, she accessed the Internet and logged in to the FBI database. A search of Ross revealed an impressive record of arrests, convictions, and rescues. All child offenders. Most repeat or serial criminals. He had been involved in such cases since the start of his FBI career, indicating a strong passion for dealing with that type of crime.

He apparently wasn't an agent who had been transferred to child sex crimes for administrative reasons. But he could be one who wanted to help because of a naïve, rose-colored perspective on the world that made him think he could sweep in and rescue all children so they could have perfect lives like his.

The latter possibility wasn't likely. He was far too insightful, uniquely intelligent in human nature, and genuinely compassionate toward victims. There had to be a reason for those traits. A reason why he was exceptional in his field. Why he could, perhaps, even understand her in some small way.

She navigated to another database and continued to search his background.

There. Her finger halted the scroll down her screen in the list of results. A court case.

*Pennsylvania vs. Terrell Smith.*

She opened the file and read quickly.

Callum Ross had taken his stepfather to court on charges of child abuse, torture, child endangerment…The list of dark, brutal crimes continued.

Anger burned in her stomach and surged up her chest as it always did when she heard of another monster destroying a child. She'd seen and heard of so many. But she never ceased to feel the fury, the horror, the drive to make the perpetrator pay. These were useful emotions. They drove her to act. Every day. For them.

She scanned the article, searching for the verdict.

Guilty on all counts. Forty-year sentence without parole.

She noted the year of the verdict. Twenty-two years ago.

According to Ross's file, he had only been sixteen years old when he'd taken his abuser to trial.

No, he wasn't an idealistic crusader who didn't know what he was dealing with. He bore the scars of experience.

Did he have unseen scars, as well?

When only a teenager, he had the courage to flee his prison and take charge of prosecuting his abuser.

He knew. He had lived through the horror. He had faced his tormentor and survived. Had obtained some degree of justice.

She cast her gaze to where he slept on the ground in the darkness just outside the firelight's reach.

That feeling she kept repressed pushed against her control, telling her to give him a chance. To let him in.

Perhaps he did understand part of her as no one else could. And yes, they were alike in some regards.

But a *chance* it would be. She never left anything to chance.

She didn't need the things her heart had secretly longed for since the destruction of her world.

She only needed to find the monster and finish this.

# TWENTY-FOUR

"Hey, Cal."

Callum started, jerking awake.

Someone shook his shoulder.

He sat up, blinking.

Eli's face was close, the man squatted next to Callum.

Darkness still cloaked the campsite except where the dwindling firelight broke through.

"Time to go." Why was Eli whispering?

Callum glanced at where the others had been sleeping. Still were sleeping, cozy in their sleeping bags.

"Is it three already?" He reached for his watch.

"One a.m., brother."

The watch face verified Eli's report.

"And we're pulling out." Eli thumbed over his shoulder as he stood.

Sure enough, Phoenix was lifting her pack onto her back at the edge of the campsite.

Dagian, standing at her side, seemed to be looking in Callum's direction.

Apparently, everyone but Callum knew they were leaving

right then. "I thought we were breaking for eight hours. This is only six."

"Eight's for the mere mortals, pal. Not Phoenix."

Callum glanced up to catch Eli's wry grin. Impressive the guy was handling it with a sense of humor, considering the physical toll yesterday's hike had taken on him.

"You can catch more sleep if you want, but the Phoenix group is leaving." He glanced over his shoulder. "Like right now." Eli wasn't kidding.

Phoenix and Dagian suddenly turned and walked away from the camp toward the service road.

Yikes. Callum yanked his legs out of the warm cocoon and started to roll up the sleeping bag. "Can you try to stall her 'til I can at least roll this up?"

"Stall Phoenix?" Eli's tone said it all. "Just leave it, man. Somebody else will take care of it."

Callum heeded the advice as Eli started to inch in the direction Phoenix had gone. Callum slipped on his watch and grabbed his jacket, then jogged with Eli to catch their leader.

"There she is." Eli's tone was slightly elated, as if he was afraid they'd actually lost her. Which, given Phoenix's remarkable abilities, was entirely possible if she'd intended to leave them behind.

But as they slowed and came up alongside her, Callum noticed she wasn't walking at her normal, fast clip.

A small smile touched his lips. So she did want them around. For some reason. Or at least she didn't have a strong enough reason to ditch them yet.

He pulled his NVGs from his pocket and put them on. Then immediately used the cover of them to check Phoenix's profile.

She didn't look their way or acknowledge their presence. But the fact she hadn't wanted to leave them behind sent a slow spread of warmth through his torso.

At least that and the jog to catch her took the bite out of the sharp, cold wind. Though he didn't know how long his fingers would last.

"Here." Eli smacked Callum's arm with something.

Callum glanced down at the dark objects in Eli's hand. "Gloves?"

"Cora brought 'em for you and me from Base."

"Thanks." He slipped on the medium-weight gloves, his fingers immediately grateful for the added coverage against the chill.

"Kind of makes you think, doesn't it?"

Callum gave Eli a glance. "About the children."

"Yeah. Is it too cold for them?"

"It does feel like it might be right at freezing." Or below, with the wind chill.

"Exactly." The worry in Eli's single word squeezed Callum's chest.

He had to offer the father some comfort. "I've been praying for them, Eli. I know God is holding them in His hands."

Eli turned his head toward Callum, his eyes covered with NVGs. "You a Christian?"

"Yes."

An unexpected grin split Eli's black beard. "Me, too." He braked and swung his hand out toward Callum.

Callum returned the handshake with a smile, as Eli gave his tricep a hearty squeeze.

Eli looked ahead. "I guess we'd better keep walking." His voice held a lighter tone as they hurried to keep up with Phoenix and Dagian, who had apparently resumed their normal pace. "I don't know how I'd get through this without Christ. I wouldn't make it."

Callum nodded. "I know what you mean."

"Good to know you're praying, too, man."

"Does your daughter belong to Christ?"

Eli sighed. "No. She hasn't come to faith. Yet."

"Maybe He'll use this to save her."

Eli turned his head toward Callum again. "I'm praying for that. And that He'll keep her and the other kids safe. Somehow."

"He is able."

Eli nodded. "And good. All the time."

"Amen."

They continued trailing Phoenix in companionable silence. But even the silence felt different, as if they'd both been strengthened with an extra gift of God's grace to carry them on. To intensify their faith that, somehow, God was working in these awful circumstances.

In the next hour and a half, Phoenix led them cross-country over ground they hadn't covered yesterday. Phoenix explained to Eli that she was taking the fastest, most direct route to intersect the location where the FBI K-9 team had ended their tracking of the hostages' scent trail.

Phoenix had apparently had radio contact with the K-9 handler before she'd started out, since she knew he'd left red markers on the tree and ground where he had quit. The FBI team's progress had been halted prematurely when the K-9 had scented a child, and they'd had to leave the trail to search. The rescued child had been another girl.

Once Phoenix located the red markers, she had Dagian pick up the scent trail. Then they followed the K-9's nose for nearly three hours straight. Long, silent hours of navigating dark, rough terrain through the thick forest as the cold wind ripped leaves from the trees, raining them down on the searchers.

With Eli being quieter than usual, the three hours had only been interrupted by finding one location where the kidnapper had let the kids stop and eat a snack for fifteen minutes.

Reports on the coms rescue channel had also broken up the monotony. Bristol had called in Toby's find of a boy. Then later, a drone spotted another boy huddled in a deep ravine, and rescuers were sent to extract him.

Only two more boys were out there alone, in need of saving. And nineteen girls, most of whom might still be with the Forster killer.

Callum silently reiterated the count as motivation to push his legs faster than they wanted to go. Fast enough to keep up with Phoenix and Dag, who had maintained the exact same speed since they'd started out with no signs of fatiguing.

Eli, on the other hand, seemed to grow more tired the longer they hiked, tripping over logs and branches on the ground as his posture sagged.

Callum's muscles weren't doing too well either. The soreness from the sudden overuse yesterday was starting to take hold.

Eli grunted.

Callum looked back to see him catch himself. Maybe he'd tripped again.

"How could the kids do this?" Eli turned his head toward Callum briefly, then down at the ground as he navigated the dark, uneven terrain. "I can't even do this. He can't expect them to walk forever. I can't believe they could've gone this far with just that one break."

People, including children, could do amazing things when they were afraid. When survival was on the line. And when they were driven by someone threatening cruelty if they disobeyed.

But Callum didn't want to voice any of those thoughts to Marnie's father. He was going through enough anguish as it was.

"What's he going to do when they can't go any farther?" Eli's question hung in the air as he stared at something.

Phoenix and Dag, sprinting out of sight.

---

Dag pulled right. Disappeared around a cluster of trees.

Phoenix picked up her pace to catch the K-9.

He came into view just as he shimmied through some brush.

She reached to part the plants and push through, but they gave way at her touch, falling to the ground. She paused and scanned the debris through her NVGs. Long tree limbs, dead leaves, branches.

The kidnapper's attempt to hide something he didn't want anyone to find.

The rapid footfalls of Callum and Eli approached behind her, then slowed. "Is that a manmade shelter?"

She let Eli's rhetorical question go unanswered as she ducked through the five-foot-tall opening in a square shelter made from branches, pine needles, and leaves that camouflaged perfectly with the surroundings.

A space of about six feet by four feet. Dirt floor. Large enough for small children, especially if they huddled together, as they would want to do for comfort and warmth.

Tiny once Eli and Callum stepped inside.

Callum stood close enough for his sleeve to brush Phoenix's jacket. If she didn't move away. Which she promptly did, moving to study the prints in the other corner of the shelter before the men destroyed them.

"Were they here?" Eli's desperation seemed to increase the longer the search went on. Understandable for a father who loved his daughter. But impractical for a rescue operation of this intensity and duration.

"They slept here." For about five hours, according to the older and most recent prints. "They left approximately twelve hours ago."

She was gaining on him. Three hours knocked off the fifteen-hour lead he'd achieved yesterday. But her gain would increase the longer she and Dag tracked him.

The footprints she'd seen on the scent trail they'd been following showed the children were growing weary. The staggered positioning indicated stumbling and dragging of the feet. They had been slowing dramatically, despite his efforts to scare them into speed.

Since children could match adult walking speeds, thanks to their bodies using energy more efficiently, Phoenix had anticipated she would not gain on the kidnapper the first day. The children had been fueled by adrenaline, fear, and fresh legs. Due to his diversionary tactics of releasing boys and driving the van, she had lost time instead.

But children didn't have the stamina of adults. Especially when they weren't conditioned for long hikes.

He had pushed them hard for too many hours without long rests. They couldn't continue traveling on adrenaline and the fumes of fear, and it appeared he knew that.

The shelter he'd constructed had allowed them to finally rest for hours at a time without chance of being seen in broad daylight from the air. But after walking them as long as he had without a full night of sleep, five hours wouldn't be enough to increase their walking speed as much as he would need. He would have to let them sleep again for more hours. Time that would allow Phoenix to gain on him. If she kept moving quickly.

She left the shelter, and Dag immediately appeared at her side, ready as always.

"Keep going, Dag."

He lowered his nose to the visible prints and followed their scent away from the shelter into brush and dead leaves that obscured them from view. But didn't eliminate the scent for the K-9 to track.

He led on through the thick trees for another twenty minutes, staying on the scent without deviation or pause, even through thickening deposits of fallen leaves.

According to the maps Phoenix had studied, they should reach the Voyageurs River at any moment.

The land sloped gradually downward under their feet. Then the trees abruptly stopped, giving way to rock-covered ground that tapered to…Voyageurs River. The wide river cut through the forest, one of many rivers and lakes in Timber Park.

Phoenix followed Dag as he kept his nose to the ground and walked across the baseball-sized rocks.

He paused in one area, circling and skimming the rocks with his nose as if he'd found a particularly intriguing scent. Or a concentration of them.

Then he moved away toward the river. He reached the water's edge. Stopped.

He lifted his head and turned to Phoenix as she went to him.

"Did he lose the scent?" Callum came within a few feet of her.

"It stops here."

"They didn't just turn and walk along the river?" Eli breathed heavily as he hurried toward them.

"No."

"Are you sure?" Desperation squeezed his voice. He spun and walked away, his NVGs pointed at the rocky ground as he searched for signs she was wrong.

Callum stepped closer to Phoenix, close enough to warm the cold air between them. "Phoenix," he kept his volume low, the turn of his head indicating he watched Eli through his NVGs to be sure the worried father was far enough away, "do you think he might have…"

Callum's mouth closed, then opened as he took a breath. Closed again before he continued. "I don't want to think it. But this is the Forster killer."

No more words were necessary to know Callum had thought of the same possibility she had. One she must consider, no matter how grim.

She gazed at the river.

The current was smooth and calm, causing barely a ripple on the glossy water as it reflected the moonlight. Even with the yellow-green tint of her NVGs, it was a scene stunning enough to be featured on a postcard.

But its beauty could hide a dreadful secret.

The tracks ending on the shoreline and Dag not scenting anyone in the water could mean only two things. The kidnapper had transported the children via boat, which would mean he'd gained more distance on them and would be difficult to find.

Or, he could have decided to lighten his load. Could have sent the children—all but his targeted victim—to their deaths beneath the river's glassy surface.

## TWENTY-FIVE

Dag veered back and forth over the rocks of the gently sloped shoreline. Rocks could be a challenging surface for locating a scent. But Dag was no ordinary K-9.

Phoenix kept her eyes on him, watching through the NVGs that allowed her to see well enough to search for visual prints in the mud that coated some areas along the shoreline.

The monster couldn't have suddenly ended the children's scent trail and then dropped them down again at another point along the river. But the patch of ground Dag had lingered on before he'd abandoned the scent was evidence of the kidnapper's actions. Dag would help confirm her deductions and find any outlying details she couldn't predict that would complete the picture of all that had happened at the river.

Dag swung into her path, walking toward the water. He'd scented something.

His nose pressed to the ground, lingering on one spot.

Phoenix moved closer.

He stopped smelling and sat, staring at her. He understood finding any scent was the goal at the moment.

She gently scratched his shoulders as she squatted to see what he'd found.

Footfalls clinking rocks together signaled Callum approaching. He'd been following her down the shoreline while Eli had remained at the location where the trail ended.

A faint, partial outline shaped the mud in the three-inch wide patch of mud. Shoeprints. Smaller. Likely female.

"Did you find something?"

"Two girls came out of the river." She stood, able to see the straight line of Callum's mouth but not much else with the NVGs he wore.

"*Out* of the river?"

She wasn't about to repeat the information. Or elaborate on what the tracks evidenced. The kidnapper had taken the children downriver. Not by walking through the water, or Dag would have easily scented them.

He would have had to—

"So he must have found a boat to use." Callum's observation came disconcertingly close to a completion of her own thoughts.

She looked his way, but he aimed his attention at the river.

"He could've stashed a canoe in advance or stolen one from the rangers' locked canoe racks. Then he could've tied up the waiting kids while he paddled downriver with maybe five or six at a time, since he couldn't fit them all in the canoe."

Phoenix stared at Callum. Impressive. The exact explanation she'd deduced. The patch of rocks that Dag had found so fascinating was the appropriate size and circular shape to indicate the girls had sat there in a bunched group, waiting for the kidnapper to return.

Would Callum know how to explain the rest of the kidnapper's actions and the two girls' tracks?

"He would have left the children he took over on the opposite shore, tied up so they couldn't run. And then he'd have had to walk up on the far shore and repeat the whole thing." Callum pointed at the tracks in the mud. "I suppose these show he let two girls go while he was at it. Probably hoping they'd keep searchers busy on this side of the river and give him more time."

The sound of rocks shifting against one another drew their attention to Eli, who trudged toward them.

"I don't think the kidnapper would have gone far from the children when he left them each time." Callum turned his head toward Phoenix. "He wouldn't have wanted to give them time to break free or be accidentally found by some ranger. And it makes sense why he rested them five hours at the shelter before coming to the river. If my figures are correct, they would otherwise have reached the river in daylight, between noon and one."

Callum directed his NVGs to the river. "He couldn't have risked crossing or traveling on the river at all in daylight. There's no coverage from trees. The aerial searchers could've spotted him." Callum brought his attention back to Phoenix. "Am I close?"

She wasn't about to tell him either way. Though she'd never seen anyone but her be able to make such accurate deductions so quickly based on the little evidence they had.

"Did you guys find anything?" Eli still sounded winded. Unfortunate that he was too stubborn to admit his physical limitations and voluntarily go home. But his growing desperation and determination meant he would assuredly attempt to continue on his own if Phoenix sent him away. In that remote and more treacherous area of the park, he would jeopardize his life and use the SAR crew's precious time when they'd have to rescue him.

"Tracks of two girls." Phoenix would give him a job to occupy his worried mind, at least. He didn't do well sitting and waiting. "Follow the shoreline downriver and look for more tracks along the water."

"Got it." Eli continued past them, veering closer to the water to do as she'd said.

"Don't you think the kidnapper would've ended up on the other side of the river after he moved all the hostages?"

Phoenix ignored Callum's question as she pulled out her satphone to contact Katherine for the nearest ranger canoe location and access code for the locks.

But the set of Callum's mouth caught her attention. His lips were slightly curved, amusement playing on them. Had his voice held a note of humor, as well? Recognizing she'd given Eli pointless busywork to keep him occupied?

As she obtained the information she needed from Katherine, half of her mind stayed on Callum Ross.

Amusement had never been anyone's reaction to her before. Her emotions didn't seem to know whether to be annoyed or to…enjoy it. Be warmed by it.

Neither response was useful. She stifled both.

How he could have gone through the childhood he'd had and find anything amusing was a mystery. One she didn't have time to solve.

She only had time to call Sofia and Jazz, the PK-9 SAR teams closest to that location, and have them move in to find the two lost girls.

Then she would retrieve canoes and pick up the scent on the opposite shore as fast as possible.

The monster's elaborate effort to hide his trail and lose her had failed.

The more he underestimated her, the more ground he would give up.

She would not waste the advantage.

# TWENTY-SIX

Callum plunged the oar into the water to keep the canoe gliding along the shoreline opposite from where they'd started.

Eli did the same, sitting in the bow of the canoe as he kept his NVGs aimed at the shoreline.

Phoenix followed silently behind them in a canoe with Dag. Probably keeping them in front of her so they couldn't disappear or attack her from behind.

Disappointment that she still didn't trust him sagged like a heavy weight on Callum's shoulders. Or maybe the feeling was entirely due to the fact they'd been traveling with the current for more than ten minutes and still hadn't found where the kidnapper had disembarked with the children on the other shore.

He hadn't thought the kidnapper would take the kids so far, one small batch at a time. He would have burned up a good part of his lead doing that.

Or had they missed seeing tracks somewhere along the beach? It wasn't as rocky on the far side of the river. A wider strip of mud formed the flat bank. If they missed the footprints, they would have to go back upshore and—

"Wait." Eli lurched toward the bank, nearly tipping the canoe. "I think I saw something."

Callum stuck his oar straight down into the water to brake and swing the canoe in a hard turn onto the beach.

Just in time for Eli to jump out without landing in the water.

Phoenix shored her canoe next to Callum. "Dag."

The K-9 leaped from the boat, outpacing Eli as the man jogged toward the trees.

Phoenix yanked her canoe the rest of the way on shore and stalked after the others.

Callum had to work to get his canoe far enough onto the beach to hold steady so he could get out from the stern. He scrambled to pull it all the way out of the water, then chased after Phoenix and Eli.

He caught up as they stopped. He went to Phoenix's side to see around her.

Eli crouched in front of a three-foot sapling.

No. Callum looked closer. Not a tree, but a branch, standing vertically in the ground. Had someone stuck it there?

"Please tell me you taught her to do this, Phoenix." Hope and the sound of unshed tears squeezed Eli's voice as he stared at the branch.

Callum looked at Phoenix. Hopefully, she'd answer that question.

"I did."

Praise the Lord. Another trail sign.

Callum scanned the area around the branch. Right where it was planted, small footprints showed in the wet ground.

They were a good twenty feet from the shoreline.

None of them could have seen the prints from the river. Between Marnie's marker and the shore, the ground was littered with leaves and strange lines where the dirt showed. As if the kidnapper had taken time to erase or hide the tracks.

"Marnie must be a very brave and smart girl." Callum voiced the thought as it passed through his mind.

Eli stood, removing his NVGs to swipe a hand over his eyes.

"She is." He swung his gaze to Phoenix. "Will the self-defense you taught her help her against this guy? Could it help her get away?"

Phoenix faced him, her NVGs hiding her eyes. Although they were sure to be expressionless, as always. "Yes."

"Then if she's okay, if she's not injured...why hasn't she tried?" Eli's voice constricted with the angst that strained his features. "Why hasn't she escaped?"

Phoenix didn't respond.

Callum's chest squeezed for the pain the loving father was experiencing. He didn't have an answer to alleviate it.

Did Phoenix? Was she moved at all by Eli's love for his daughter? Or was she more hardened and cold inside than Callum had hoped?

"There's more at stake than Marnie's safety." Phoenix's steady, impassive voice broke the silence. "She knows that."

At least Phoenix replied. Maybe she was moved by Eli's pain after all. It was a good sign. But her answer was as full of mystery as the woman herself.

More at stake than Marnie's safety? Callum opened his mouth to ask Phoenix what she meant, but she stalked into the forest with Dag.

Eli glanced at Callum, his eyes full of confusion Callum couldn't alleviate.

All they could do was follow Phoenix as they tried to figure out what she meant and struggled to trust God in the darkness.

---

"Find them, Dag."

The K-9 lifted his nose in the air, then dropped his head to the ground as he picked up the children's scent where there were no visible prints in the grass and weeds that led away from Marnie's marker.

The girl was doing well. The rest at the shelter, when the

kidnapper had either slept or left them alone could have been an opportunity for her to escape.

But he had likely secured her or the other children too well for her to free them, even in the time he was away. Or she'd realized they were too tired to run, to achieve the speed they would need to elude him upon his return.

Marnie had soaked up everything Phoenix had taught her, including one of the most important lessons—that her skills were not for her alone. They were for those who couldn't protect themselves.

If Marnie stayed true to Phoenix's training, she would wait to make her move until she was sure she could save the others and herself. She would only deviate if she couldn't control her natural fear response to the frightening monster who had kidnapped her.

But according to the rescued boys' accounts, she was in control. The trail signs were further evidence she was still thinking clearly, acting strategically, remaining courageous.

The monster had learned from Robin's unsophisticated escape during his first kidnapping. Since then, he had secured his victims thoroughly whenever he left them. None ever escaped.

But he had never kidnapped Marnie.

She would wait and plan, then act when she needed to.

Though now that Phoenix knew the monster had wasted his time trying to disguise his actions at the river, she might reach Marnie before the girl needed to take matters into her own hands.

Carting the children down the river and returning on the shore each trip would have taken him ninety minutes or more. Even with the half-hour it had taken for Phoenix, Callum, and Eli to reach the ranger's canoes, they had gained at least one hour.

With the children's continued fatigue, Phoenix would still have the advantage and would be able to close the time gap significantly, so long as Eli didn't slow her down.

But his energy had increased since he'd found Marnie's trail marker. He kept up with Callum as they followed close behind Phoenix.

She couldn't see prints in the thick underbrush and freshly fallen leaves, but Dag was having no trouble finding the odors he needed to track the children's path.

The K-9 led them up a steep hill, his nose lowered, still on the scent.

Breakage in the tall weeds and brush around the trees showed visible evidence that the children had climbed up the difficult incline. How tiring it would have been for them.

As Phoenix reached the top, her gaze landed on a four-foot-wide dirt trail that cut through the trees.

Dag waited on the middle of the trail, looking at Phoenix.

The scent had ended.

She scanned the dirt as she walked to Dag.

"Phoenix? What happened?"

She didn't look at Eli. Only at the evidence she hoped not to see.

There. Tire tracks. Multiple sets of different sizes.

"He put the children in a trailer attached to an ATV." Anger blazed heat through her torso as she lifted her head and stared at the tree-lined trail that faded into the forest.

That section of the park boasted the longest trails that allowed for the width of an ATV. If he had driven from trail to trail where they interconnected, he could have traveled late into the night, resting the children as he continued to gain ground.

He'd increased his lead all the more.

Longer for the children to endure before she reached them. Longer for their lives to be at risk.

And longer before she could bring the monster to justice.

# TWENTY-SEVEN

The loud rumble of the ATV engines, reduced to a hum by the helmet Callum wore, played in the background like the soundtrack for their pursuit of a killer.

Callum shoved his gloved hands deeper into his jacket pockets. Sitting still for two hours in the two-seater ATV while Eli drove had plummeted Callum's body temperature as the crisp wind bit through his jacket and chilled any exposed skin. But the full-face helmets were a blessing Callum was thankful they'd found for all three of them at the ranger station where they'd gotten the two ATVs.

Once Phoenix had discovered the kidnapper had transported the kids in an ATV, she'd called Nguyen, and the agent had directed them to the ranger station that was a twenty-minute hike north.

When they'd arrived at the unoccupied station and found the vehicles, Eli had said he loved driving ATVs, so Callum gladly let him get behind the wheel. Phoenix had chosen the ATV with a rear cargo carrier where she had Dag lie down.

Now she stayed in the lead as they followed another dirt trail the kidnapper had taken with the children in tow, according to the ATV tire treads. The distinctive tread pattern Phoenix had pointed out when they'd first connected with the kidnapper's ATV tracks allowed them—or at least Phoenix—to distinguish his route from other ATV tires.

Though spotting other treads on the network of trails in that section of the park was proving rare. Even the rangers didn't seem to have driven their ATVs around the area much, likely since it was the off-season.

The kidnapper had apparently taken advantage of the remoteness and cover of night to drive the ATV from one trail to the next at seemingly random moments, skipping past one intersection and turning at another.

But it wasn't random. Callum was sure of that. No more than the kidnapper's preconceived and prepared plan to use the ATV at that point in the kidnapping to gain time on the searchers pursuing him.

Having ATVs they could use to follow his trail was a Godsend. It might mean they wouldn't lose the amount of time he'd intended them to, though retrieving the ATVs at the ranger station and connecting with the kidnapper's trail had burned nearly an hour.

And they wouldn't be cutting into his lead, given that they couldn't drive any faster than he would have been able to.

Phoenix had to make sure Dag wouldn't bounce out of the cargo carrier on the rough terrain, and she had given instructions to all of them to look for any footprints that could indicate the kidnapper had released more children. She was sure to be watching for the kidnapper's tire tracks to halt, too.

If he'd managed to hide the ATV off the trail like he'd done with the van, they could miss where he may have made the children walk again or switched to a different mode of transport.

At least the full sunlight meant they could see clearly, even though the rays were broken by the thinning canopy of tree branches overhead.

A layer of leaves, likely fallen from the trees overnight in the strong wind, scattered across the trail and threatened to obscure their view of footprints and tire treads.

At least the good news Cora had reported over coms about an hour ago was buoying Callum's spirits. She'd found another boy, leaving only one more in the wild, waiting for rescue. They had no idea how many girls were also lost on their own, if the kidnapper had sent more away.

The winding trail straightened out in front of them, and movement a distance beyond Phoenix's ATV caught Callum's eye.

Something emerged from the trees and stopped on the trail.

Was that a horse?

Phoenix's brake lights lit red.

Eli slowed behind her, stopping when she did as they neared the large, brown horse with a tall rider on its back.

The man wore a brimmed hat and the park ranger uniform. "Hi, there. FBI?"

Phoenix and Eli killed the noisy engines.

But Phoenix didn't answer the ranger. Maybe Callum was supposed to do the honors. He pushed up the visor on his helmet. "I'm Agent Ross. This is Elijah Moore and Phoenix Gray."

"Of the Phoenix K-9 Agency?"

She slid up her visor. "Yes."

The ranger smiled. "Great work your team is doing here." He let the remark sit as if waiting for a reply. But after several seconds, he seemed to realize he wasn't going to get one. "I won't keep you. I thought I'd try hitting the trail from the north farther along and see if I could backtrack to the end of the ATV tracks. But there were tire tracks where I started, too, over on Gorge Trail about ten miles north of here. Seems he drove quite a long way."

Exactly as Phoenix had deduced he would. Frustration tangled in Callum's stomach. How long would the Forster killer manage to prolong the search and keep his lead?

"Given your report," the ranger looked at Phoenix, "I checked caves we know of and other shelters on my way here. No signs of use."

"Watch for signs of children elsewhere, as well."

Callum and Eli exchanged surprised glances at Phoenix's instruction. Apparently, Eli had also thought Phoenix wasn't going to say anything to the ranger.

"He'll be letting more go."

"Yes, ma'am." The ranger's hat dipped with his single nod. "We'll keep looking for them. We're checking ravines and cliffs, too."

Phoenix appeared to reach her hand toward the ignition to restart her ATV, though Callum couldn't tell for sure from his position behind her.

"Before you go…" the ranger's statement paused her movement. "Did you know there are three ATVs headed your way? At least, they seem to be trying to follow you. They're taking the same turns you did."

Maybe Phoenix responded with her gaze or a nod too small for Callum to see, because the guy continued.

"Saw them from O'Ryan's Bluff before I headed down here. They're moving fast. Maybe FBI reinforcements." He touched the brim of his hat. "I'll leave you to it now." He laid the reins against the horse's neck, and the large animal started to turn.

"Oh." The ranger straightened the reins again, pausing the horse as he looked over at Phoenix and then moved his gaze to Eli and Callum. "I assume you folks won't start a fire anywhere but in the pits at the designated campsites. We're having a dry fall this year. The risk of wildfire is high."

"We'll be careful." Callum gave him a nod.

"Great. See you folks later." The ranger left the trail on his horse, disappearing into the trees.

"So do we wait here for the other ATVs?" Eli looked ahead at Phoenix's back. "I mean, if we're supposed to join up?"

Phoenix didn't turn around. "If they can't find us, they don't belong out here."

A smile curved Callum's mouth. Classic Phoenix. Also full of truth, as usual.

"Base to PT1." Agent Nguyen's voice crackled over coms. A call for Phoenix.

"PT1, go ahead."

"I'm sending more searchers your side of the river. They should meet up with you soon if they can reach you by ATV."

So Nguyen was sending reinforcements. Did she think Phoenix was taking too long to find the hostages?

Phoenix wouldn't like the idea of backup. She already hadn't wanted Eli and Callum along.

"Roger, Base." Phoenix's voice didn't betray displeasure, or any other emotion, as usual.

Callum had never met anyone so masterful at masking her feelings and controlling her reactions. Her degree of self-discipline was unbelievable.

"And good news." The usual tension in Nguyen's tone lightened slightly. "The SPPD K-9 unit found the last boy. All twenty-seven boys have been rescued. Only minor injuries and mild exposure."

A surge of joy flowed through Callum's chest. "Praise the Lord." He spoke the words aloud without thinking.

"Amen, brother." Eli nodded in agreement, but his lips pressed in a firm, sad line.

Callum felt the burden, too, even as he silently prayed God would bring about the same outcome for the girls who'd been taken.

With the killer's horrible intentions and the fact that he kept staying ahead of them, a happy ending for all the girls seemed nearly impossible.

---

The ATV tracks stopped.

Phoenix hit the brakes. Hopped off the ATV. "Dag."

The K-9 jumped from the cargo carrier as Eli and Callum jogged toward her.

"What is it?" Callum looked at the ground as he approached. "Where'd the tire tracks go?"

Precisely. Her calculations had anticipated the kidnapper would have stopped driving somewhere in that area on Windy Forest Trail, well beyond the Gorge and Wolf trails. His tank would have been running low on gas after three and a half hours at the speed he likely drove.

She walked back up the trail, scanning the ground to find the tire treads before they had disappeared.

There. The tracks indicated he'd stopped.

A smattering of many small footprints showed the girls had disembarked from the trailer. Approximately eleven hours ago.

The shoeprints headed north, layering over his larger prints.

But where was the ATV?

She backtracked farther south, past the children's prints.

The tire treads doubled, overlapping. He'd driven there twice, the second time backing the ATV and trailer close along the edge of the trail.

Then...

The treads veered off.

She stepped to the trail's weed-lined border, Dag staying at her side.

A steep incline plummeted into a ravine. Carnage of smashed reeds, brush, and small trees along the slope told Phoenix what had happened.

Eli let out a low whistle. "Did he drive the ATV down there?"

"Not drove. Sent." Callum's deduction was correct, once again.

But had he thought of the other possibility? The monster may have sent one or more children with the ATV.

She couldn't see the ATV to verify. It must have swerved or rolled at the end, burying itself behind trees and brush.

She slid her gaze to Callum.

He watched her already, his brow furrowed.

Yes, he'd thought of it. But didn't want to say anything in front of Eli.

Now would be the perfect opportunity and timing for the monster to kill off a girl or two in such a way that would keep his pursuers occupied looking for them, finding them, and needing to recover their bodies. Needing to collect evidence of their murder.

If children had been sent down there with the ATV, their bodies would have been destroyed by the fall, likely requiring extensive time and effort for complete recovery and forensic analysis.

Dag barked.

Phoenix looked at the K-9.

He started to thread his way down the steep incline, his tail high.

She went down after him.

"Phoenix!" Eli's surprised shout drifted over her head as she scrambled down the slope, trying to keep up with Dag, though his four feet could handle the incline and rough terrain faster than she could.

Crunching and sliding drew her gaze up behind her.

Eli and Callum followed her path in single file. They'd better not slip and fall, or they would take her with them.

She hopped to the side, out of their path, as she continued to pick her way down as quickly as she could. She glanced ahead.

No Dag. He'd just been there, somewhere toward the bottom of the ravine.

She kept her eyes on the crushed path the ATV and trailer had created on their plummet down.

It veered off to the right, the ground ripped, plants and dirt torn up. The ATV must have tumbled. Rolled.

Her jaw clenched. If he'd left children in there...

Hot fury burned through her.

She pushed faster.

Dag.

He stood at the bottom. By the ATV and trailer.

The ATV was toppled on its side, and the trailer lay upside down in a jackknifed position, its back end facing Phoenix.

She hurried toward the wreckage.

Was that...

Hair. Dark hair.

And ivory skin. A hand, protruding through the leaves beneath the trailer.

A child was under there.

Phoenix slowed, her throat squeezing.

"Phoenix, is that—" Eli's voice choked behind her. "No!" His anguished wail pierced her heart.

She looked back.

Callum held Eli by the shoulders, preventing him from getting closer.

If it was her, he'd have to face it. See Marnie. Deal with the truth, regardless of how awful it was.

But at the moment, it was best for Callum to keep Eli out of Phoenix's way.

She walked to the trailer.

Dag barked again, his feet shifting with an unusual sign of anticipation.

A live find.

The pain squeezing her lungs loosened its grip.

She knelt by the trailer, pulled away the leaves and pine branches that covered most of the child's head.

No, children.

Two heads lifted and turned, blinking at Phoenix and the sunlight she'd let in.

Neither were Marnie. But they were both alive.

# TWENTY-EIGHT

"Thank you, Jesus." Callum dropped to his knees at the rear of the trailer where two girls twisted their heads to see him without releasing each other.

They were lying under the trailer, holding each other close in an embrace. No signs of blood or injury that he could see, but it was hard to tell with only their upper bodies visible.

Phoenix had stood and was calling over coms for transport with blankets, food, and water.

"Roger that." A male voice he didn't recognize sounded in his ear. "Agents close to you now and can provide transport. ETA five minutes."

Must be the agents on the ATVs who hadn't managed to catch up since Phoenix had kept driving, going at a faster speed after the ranger had told them the agents were coming. Seemed Callum was right—she didn't want reinforcements.

"Hey, girls. I'm Callum." He gave the two darling girls a smile. "We're here to help you and take you home, okay?"

They blinked at him, then looked at each other with wide eyes. The brunette whispered something he couldn't decipher to the girl with reddish hair.

"It's okay. You're safe now." He tried to soften his tone even more. "No one is going to hurt you."

Phoenix squatted next to Callum and stared at the children with her indecipherable expression. Not exactly the comforting inducement they needed to calm their fears. "Are you able to move?"

"Are you Phoenix?" The brunette stared at the inscrutable woman.

Phoenix paused a beat. Then finally answered. "Yes."

"Oh, good." Smiles lit both girls' faces as they released each other and started to crawl out.

Callum helped them to their feet, scanning them for injuries.

The redhead beamed up at Phoenix. "Marnie said a lady named Phoenix would come and rescue us."

Callum glanced at Phoenix.

No change in her apathetic expression. But she must feel something in response to that.

She took off her backpack and lowered it to the ground. What was she doing?

She unzipped her parka, slipped it off, and draped it around the redhead's small body.

Yeah. She did feel something.

Callum resisted the smile that wanted to show as he took off his own jacket to give to the other girl. Warmth filled him even as he lost the jacket.

Phoenix was still capable of feeling. Of caring. Of compassion, and love. Why that mattered to him so much, he didn't quite know. Other than it meant Robin Forster hadn't been completely destroyed by her family's killer.

"Did Marnie tell you anything else?" Eli came close, probably drawn by the sound of his daughter's name. When he had seen the girls weren't Marnie, he had stayed at a distance and sat on the ground, likely needing time to collect himself after the close call.

Callum could only imagine the torture it must have been to

the father's heart to think his daughter was dead under that trailer.

The brunette nodded. "She said to stop running once the bad man wasn't watching us anymore."

"Uh-huh," the girl with strawberry hair lightly gripped the brunette's arm, "and then to go back exactly where we came from. That's up there." She pointed with her free hand toward the top of the ravine.

The brunette wrapped her arm around the other girl's shoulders. "It was so cold, and Marnie said to find a shelter, so we went in there." She glanced at the upside-down trailer. "The bad man said he'd hurt us if we stopped running or if we went back."

Her brown-eyed gaze shifted to Phoenix. "But Marnie said he wouldn't because you would find us first. She told us to wait for you with each other and hide. We were supposed to never leave each other until you found us." She smiled, as if enjoying the story's happy ending.

Relief and joy swelled in Callum's chest. It was a happy ending. For these two girls.

Marnie's advice had probably saved their lives. They would have gotten too cold last night if they hadn't had each other for warmth.

Marnie's faith in Phoenix was unshakable. How much time and kindness must Phoenix have poured into the girl to build such trust?

He looked at Phoenix, who watched the girls without saying a word.

She had to be feeling great love and concern for Marnie, the girl who clearly trusted Phoenix with her life and so much more. That love for Marnie might be what was driving Phoenix so relentlessly, to search and keep going without breaks or sleep. Without discouragement or fatigue.

Perhaps love was an even stronger motive for Phoenix than the desire to catch the man who'd killed her family. Or maybe Callum was indulging in wishful thinking again, trying to romanticize the woman who could be as cold and calculating as she appeared.

But he couldn't believe that. He'd seen too much, sensed too much, of what hid behind the mask.

The rumble of engines halted his thoughts just in time, before he had to ponder why his heart seemed to be squeezing behind his ribs the longer he analyzed Phoenix Gray.

The sound of sticks snapping indicated the FBI agents were coming down into the ravine, out of sight until they rounded the trees toward the bottom and followed the ATV-cleared path.

"Hello." The guy leading the three agents in FBI jackets lifted his hand in a still wave as he approached. "Guess we showed up just in time." His gaze and smile aimed at Phoenix.

Callum inwardly winced for the man and his careless remark, implying he had come to the rescue. He'd have to spend the rest of his life trying to make up for that first impression with Phoenix Gray.

"Do you have blankets, water, food?" Phoenix leveled the bearded guy with her stare.

He blinked at her. Must've expected a warmer welcome. "Yes, we do."

"Take these two children south on this trail. Connect with Wolf Trail and take that to the clearing by Berry Ridge. A helicopter will meet you there."

The other two agents exchanged confused glances with their spokesman.

Phoenix must not like the look of them. Or their leader's attitude. Bringing in a chopper would mean the men wouldn't be alone with the kids nearly as long as if they drove back to Base. And it was a nicer idea for the girls, so they could get home much faster.

The bearded guy stared at Phoenix. "I thought we were supposed to drive them to Base."

Phoenix didn't break eye contact. "Change of plans. Transport them with the utmost care. I will call Base in seventy minutes, at which point I expect the children to be there."

Callum bit back a laugh.

The befuddled expressions on the men's faces were priceless. Clearly, no one had warned them about Phoenix Gray when they'd been sent as so-called reinforcements.

But the front man rallied and dug out another smile. "No problem." He glanced at the other agents. "Get them in some blankets and take them to the chopper."

They nodded and climbed back up the hill, presumably to retrieve blankets.

"We were actually sent to team up with you and your crew here." The bearded agent gave Callum and Eli a glance, still trying for a smile that looked a little forced. Couldn't really blame him. He wasn't getting the cooperation he'd probably expected when Agent Nguyen had sent him all that way. "I'll stick with you guys, and my partners can come back as soon as they drop off the kids."

"You'll be of more use elsewhere." Phoenix still stared at the agent without emotion, but the increase in intensity that emanated from her hit Callum where he stood a couple feet away. "My team is at capacity. Any more will only get in my way. That isn't going to happen."

The agent's smile faltered. He looked at Callum, then Eli, as if searching for some help.

Neither of them were foolish enough to challenge Phoenix on that subject. They'd both already had to fight for their own chance to tag along.

"Well, okay then." He cleared his throat, his smile shrinking to a weak curve of lips. "I guess I'll go with the others and call in. Maybe Nguyen will have a different assignment for us."

He backed away with another still wave. "You all take care now. And let us know if you want any assistance down the road."

The guy sounded a bit like a polite telemarketer. But at least he hadn't really gotten in Phoenix's face or blown up about it the way some agents Callum knew would have. Big egos were plentiful in the FBI.

A few minutes later, Callum, Phoenix, and Eli stood at the top of the ravine as the men drove off with the girls, gently wrapped in warm blankets and buckled into seats on the backs of two ATVs.

The memory of that first night of the rescue operation moved to the front of Callum's mind. When he'd ambushed Phoenix in a similar manner by arriving in the FBI transport car, and she'd initially told him she worked alone, clearly about to say he couldn't accompany her. But then, she'd allowed him to stay.

Why hadn't she dug in and sent him away like she just did with these agents?

The ATV disappeared from sight, and Callum turned to look at the enigmatic woman who, for some reason, had let him stay.

But she was already fifty feet up the dirt trail with Dag.

"We're gonna miss the bus, man." Eli smacked Callum's shoulder as he hurried past, handing Callum his backpack on the way.

Callum shook his head and slipped his arms through the shoulder straps as he scrambled to catch up with the woman who left him alternately confounded, puzzled, intrigued, and amazed every moment he was with her. The woman who was shifting his world a little more every day. And altering something deep inside him to such an extent that he knew he would never be the same.

---

Phoenix leaned into her stride as she followed Dag.

The K-9 tracked the girls' trail over terrain that grew increasingly rocky the higher they hiked up the steep hill that led to O'Ryan's Bluff. Would have been a challenge for the children to climb the incline, though they would have been fresher when they'd started out thanks to riding in the ATV trailer.

She checked her watch. *11:55 a.m.*

Sufficient time for the children they'd rescued to have

arrived at Base and been evaluated. Phoenix never would have handed the two girls over to three unknown men, even if they were FBI, except that they'd have to be stupid to do anything to the girls after the children had been recovered by witnesses to their condition. And shortening the duration the agents would be alone with the girls by calling for a helicopter was an added precaution.

She pulled her satphone from her backpack behind her and dialed Katherine's number.

"Phoenix, hi."

"Status on the two girls we found in the ravine."

"Right." The incessant ringing of phones sounded in the background, along with voices of people talking. "They made it in and seem mostly unharmed, other than mild exposure and some scratches. One of your teams found two more girls about a half hour ago."

"I heard." Nevaeh had reported Flash's find on coms. He'd located the two girls who had been released at Voyageurs River. The children had apparently been too frightened to disobey the kidnapper's order to keep running and had traveled a significant distance away from the river before hiding together.

"No matches to your case with the new agents that arrived today." Katherine paused as a man asked a question close enough to the phone for Phoenix to hear his voice but not the words he said.

"Yeah, tell them the search is progressing." Stress tightened Katherine's tone as she answered him. "And we've rescued four more children today."

Phoenix waited on the line another moment as she pushed up the rocky terrain that cut a wide path through the trees. Katherine would call her back if Phoenix didn't let her address the issue of her reinforcements.

"Phoenix, you turned away the new guys I sent you."

Phoenix let the pause hang. Katherine had more to say before she'd be able to let go of the frustration that edged her statement.

"I'm not surprised, but they volunteered, and I want more armed personnel out there if you're going to close in on him. Are you closing in?" A note of anxiety undergirded the question.

"I'll get him."

Katherine released an audible breath. "Okay, Phoenix. Keep me posted. And I'll take an ETA on that capture as soon as you have one."

Phoenix ended the call and shoved the phone into the backpack behind her.

"Hey, Phoenix?" Eli puffed a bit as he pushed up the incline to reach her side. "You said this is O'Ryan's Bluff we're headed for, right?"

She let her silence be the answer.

"Why would he lead them up to a bluff? There'd be nowhere to go from there. But he obviously planned his route in advance. Do you think he got turned around?"

"No." Though there was more than one possible answer to Eli's first question. The most likely being that the kidnapper had led the children down to the east or west near the top of the bluff using some path he'd found. He wasn't about to let them get boxed in when he'd clearly scouted and studied the park before the kidnapping.

Eli breathed more heavily as he kept up with Phoenix's pace. He had another question, or he wouldn't be trying so hard to stay with her.

His frustration about Marnie, his concern, had increased since they'd found the two girls. Since he'd feared, for a moment, that Marnie's body had lain beneath the trailer. The torment was written all over the lines of his face. "Why hasn't he let Marnie go yet? He's letting other girls go. Why isn't she one of them? He isn't planning to...keep her...is he?"

Phoenix paused, choosing her response carefully. "She's found a way to make herself useful to him."

Eli shot her a glance, eyebrows raised. "Useful? What do you mean?"

"Keeping the hostages calm, telling them to follow orders in his earshot. Promising him they'll be there when he leaves and returns."

"Why would she do that? Cooperate with him. Isn't it better if he lets her go?" Anguish pinched Eli's features as he turned his head toward Phoenix.

Callum's footsteps, crunching in the dirt that coated the rocky ground beneath their feet, moved closer behind her. It was fine if he heard her. He likely had the same questions as Eli, unless he'd already deduced the answers.

"Marnie won't leave the other children with him. Not unless she can perceive a way she could still save them by doing so." Phoenix crested the hill at last, the ground evening out under her feet in a clearing of flat stone that must lead to the edge of the bluff, judging from the treeless view of sunny blue sky straight ahead.

Dag kept his nose to the ground, following the scent forward toward the bluff. Odd the trail would keep going so far north to the edge. There must be a trail or way down on one of the sides closer to—

Eli stopped walking.

Phoenix paused a few steps ahead, angling back to him.

His eyes were closed, inner conflict shaping his mouth and lining his brow. "Marion said you were teaching Marnie to help others." He opened his eyes, landing his focus on Phoenix. "To not think about herself. That's a wonderful thing. It's what God wants her to do."

He pulled in a tight breath as his jaw clenched. "But part of me right now wishes you hadn't done that."

A yelp pierced the air.

Phoenix jerked toward the bluff.

As Dag plummeted off the edge.

# TWENTY-NINE

Callum sprinted after Phoenix as she dashed to the spot where Dag had disappeared.

Had he really fallen off the edge of the bluff?

Heart in his throat as he came to the edge, Callum nearly reached for Phoenix to be sure she didn't fall or intentionally dive after the dog.

He leaned to look over.

Dagian stood on a small rock ledge about twelve feet below, staring up at them.

Callum couldn't believe his eyes. The dog was all right? "Thank you, Lord." Callum breathed out the praise as he looked at Phoenix.

Tension vibrated off of her as she stared down at Dag. "Wait." She delivered the command in her firm, emotionless tone.

But Callum knew she was feeling plenty under her shell. The bond and partnership she shared with Dag was incredible. It was like they were an extension of each other.

He was surprised she hadn't already tried to climb down to the dog, though the rock face below them was a sheer drop with no hand—

Wait a second. Callum got to his knees to peer closely at the rocky face of the bluff below the drop-off. Were those spikes?

Glass. Shards of glass. How could that be?

But he couldn't deny what he saw. Sharp, jagged pieces of glass were interspersed with the rock all the way down to the ledge holding Dag. That didn't happen naturally.

Someone had to have forced the glass into the crevices of the rock face or even glued them in place intentionally. It was a setup.

"Did you see this?" Eli squatted at the edge and ran his fingers along what looked like the edge of a broken board. He tapped a nail head embedded in the wood, then stood. "There are broken wood scraps down there by Dag. The kidnapper must've built a platform. Probably covered it with leaves and branches to hide it."

Callum's jaw clenched. "And then had a child walk on it so any tracking K-9 on his trail would fall."

Eli got to his feet, his eyes smoldering. "The guy's a real piece of work." Eli looked over the edge. "Man, we can't pull him up with a rope, even if one of us goes down there. He'd get cut up pretty bad. Phoenix, you got any ideas?"

She still stared over the edge, either watching Dag or assessing and thinking, trying to figure out how to save her beloved partner and friend.

Callum's heart wrenched behind his ribs. He would not let her lose Dag. She'd lost far too much already.

And he wasn't about to let an amazing K-9 like Dag, or any dog for that matter, get hurt if he could help it.

He scanned the ledge where Dag stood again.

A medium-sized rock stood off to one side. Some of the wood scraps might be big enough to be helpful, too.

And, Lord willing, he was wrong in his rough guess as to how many feet down the ledge was.

"I think I'm tall enough." Callum slipped out of his backpack and let it drop to the ground.

"Tall enough for what?" Eli's tone signaled his incredulity. "To get cut to pieces climbing down there?"

"To lift Dag up to you two, clear of the glass." Callum shrugged off his jacket and quickly reversed it to cover his chest, stuffing his arms through the sleeves again.

"Oh, that'll help."

Callum's mouth twitched. Hadn't realized Eli was the sarcastic type.

Phoenix lowered her backpack without a word and dug through it. Hopefully getting some rope, since he didn't have any in his pack.

She pulled out a coil of rope and stepped close to Callum to hand it to him.

He took it from her, meeting her gaze. "Will he let me lift him above my head?"

The tiniest flicker, deep in her eyes, caught his attention. A hint of the powerful emotions she must be working so hard to mask.

His gut twisted.

"He will if I tell him to."

Callum swallowed back the urge to say something comforting. Barely kept from touching her arm or embracing her for the same reason. He nodded instead, a lump lodging in his throat as he turned, tied the rope around his waist, and went to the edge.

He scanned the rock face, as much as he could see it from directly above, and his target—the narrow ledge. Hopefully, it was big enough for him and Dag. And sturdy enough to hold them both.

"Maybe you can lower him down instead of needing to lift him up to us." Eli's suggestion drew Callum's gaze to the long drop beyond the ledge.

A network of brambles clustered on the only other outcropping he could see farther down, and the spikey tops of massive pine trees waited at the bottom. "Don't think so."

Eli grunted reluctant assent as he looked down, too. "Be careful." He took the rope from Callum, then walked five feet away from the edge and stopped, wrapping the rope behind his back and around his hip.

Good. With a strong guy like Eli anchoring the rope, Callum wouldn't have to worry about plummeting to his death down there. Lord willing.

Phoenix stood in front of Eli to add her own grip to the rope.

Callum nodded to her and crouched by the edge. The start might be the hardest part, trying to avoid the glass spikes as he went over.

Dag stared up at him. Seemed like he hadn't moved since the fall, but he couldn't be expected to stand still forever.

Oh, well. A few cuts were more than worth it.

Callum took a breath and carefully lowered off the edge, trying to extend his legs out in front of him as soon as he could.

Pain shot into his palms. Hadn't seen spikes at the very top, but the hidden shards he could see now that they were in front of his face sliced his skin.

He let go and gripped the rope instead, leaning far back as he walked his way down, the soles of his boots pressing into the rock and glass.

He checked beneath him as he neared the outcropping. Narrower than he'd thought from above.

But also not as far down. Maybe ten feet or a little less.

*Thank you, Lord.*

He waited until they lowered him farther than needed before he stepped his feet back and stood on the ledge. "Okay."

Phoenix immediately appeared at the edge above, her cap and slim figure silhouetted against the sunlight behind her.

Turning carefully so he didn't accidentally make Dag want to back up, Callum faced the K-9.

His sharp blue eyes stared up at Callum. And his tail wagged. Once. Twice.

Relief and another prayer of praise coursed through Callum. Dag had never acted aggressively toward Callum during the search, but he'd never been friendly either. First time Callum had ever seen him wag his tail at all.

Letting out a slow breath, Callum held out his hand.

Dag sniffed it for only a split second. Like he had no interest in an unnecessary ritual.

A chuckle bubbled up in Callum's throat. Dag really was like his human partner.

Callum scanned the dog's paws and legs. A bit of red dotted the dog's front leg. Looked like some blood. Probably a cut from the glass on the way down. But he was standing on it fine. It was a miracle he didn't have worse injuries and had landed on that ledge.

*Thank you, Lord, for watching out for him. And Phoenix. She's lost so much already.*

"Okay, Dagian. What do you say we get you back to Phoenix?"

Understanding seemed to emanate from the dog's blue eyes as he watched Callum.

"All right." Callum nodded. "Let's do it."

He carefully turned in place to see the rock he thought he'd spotted from above.

There it was past Dag, at the side of the outcropping. A little larger than he'd thought, which was perfect.

Though he'd have to get behind Dag to reach it. "Okay if I go past you here? I just need that rock."

The dog shifted slightly, but toward the rock face, as Callum scooted along the edge of the outcropping.

Callum tried not to think of the nasty fall that waited beneath him if he played it too close. He bent to grab the rock and pulled it to the right. It was heavy, but not too heavy to move.

He got on the other side of it as soon as there was room and pushed it a little toward Dag and closer to the rock face. But not too close. He'd have to keep his distance while lifting Dag to avoid cutting more than his hands this time.

He glanced at the wood scraps he had hoped he might be able to add to the rock to increase its height. But they were more broken up than they'd appeared from above.

The rock was nearly a foot tall. Hopefully that, combined with the depth of Dag's torso—also probably about twelve inches—would do the trick.

Before getting Dag involved, Callum practiced standing on top of the rock. It narrowed significantly at the top, creating a small, rounded surface that wasn't helpful under the circumstances. But if he kept his feet close together, he could maintain his balance. Hopefully.

He tilted, losing his footing. He stepped down onto the ledge, righting himself before he toppled off the outcropping entirely.

He blew out a breath as he looked at the unstable rock, then up to the bluff above.

Phoenix leaned over the edge, watching them. Amazing she could keep from telling him to hurry up or asking what was taking him so long. But, for once, he was grateful she preferred silence.

He knew she must feel the urgency of the situation. Feel hope that Callum would hand Dag up to her. Soon.

And he would. Using the rock as a stool was his only way to gain the height needed to lift Dag high enough for them to grab the K-9's harness and pull him up. Callum would make it work.

But he'd need to be closer, for balance and the few more inches of height. He pushed his makeshift stepstool toward the bluff, all the way until its wider base pressed against the jagged wall.

Dag shifted to the side to clear his path, thankfully not moving enough for Callum to worry about the dog stepping off the ledge. The K-9 seemed to have a better sense of balance and where the drop-off was than Callum.

"Okay, Dag. Ready for me to pick you up?"

The K-9 stared at him with steady blue eyes. Fearless.

Hopefully, he would stay that way when he was lifted off his feet.

"Lord, please help him stay calm and give me balance and strength." Callum peered up one more time. "I'm ready." He lifted a hand as he shouted up to Phoenix. "I'm going to lift him above my head, and you two grab his harness. Forget about my rope until he's up."

"Roger." Phoenix's voice was as strong as usual when she answered.

His rope slackened even more. Probably from Eli walking to the edge to help Phoenix lift Dag.

"Let's do this, boy." He crouched next to Dag and put his hands under the dog's middle.

No reaction that Callum could detect. The K-9 didn't even seem to tense up.

Lifting could be a completely different matter.

Callum tested lifting Dag off the ground, then set him back down.

Still no reaction. The dog didn't even look at him.

Okay. Should be a good sign.

A cracking sound jerked Callum's attention to the outcropping beneath his feet. Was that the ledge loosening? Maybe too much weight and movement.

His pulse sped up. Time to get off the ledge and onto solid ground.

Callum took in a deep breath and hefted Dag again, bringing him all the way up to chest level. Felt like he was about eighty pounds. Thank the Lord he wasn't any heavier than that.

Callum hurried to the rock and carefully stepped on top of it, pressing his feet together.

Keeping his knees slightly bent for balance, he adjusted his hands under Dag's torso to balance across his belly.

*Here goes.*

Callum lifted Dag straight up, the jacket across his chest brushing against the rock face and glass shards as he stretched. And waited.

"We can't reach!" Eli's shout dropped to Callum. "Too far from the ledge."

"This is as high as I can go!" Callum puffed out the answer

as he kept his arms stretched to the maximum. And reminded himself to breathe.

"Horizontally. Six more inches in." Phoenix barked the details.

Closer horizontally? He only had six inches between him and the glass shards in front of him. And the rock he stood on couldn't get any closer.

But maybe *he* could. Briefly.

"Okay!" He yelled loudly to be sure they heard. "In three...two...one!"

Callum leaned his upper body forward, stretching as high as he could with his arms holding Dag above his head.

Shards poked through his jacket, pressing into his chest. But Callum held his arms slightly farther back than his torso. Dag should be safe.

Glass pierced into Callum's skin as he leaned. Pricking, sharp pain.

"A little more!" Eli's shout hit Callum's ears.

He had to get closer yet. He shuffled his feet forward on the rock, wincing as the move pressed his chest farther into the glass.

The weight left his hands.

Callum looked up in time to see Dag disappear over the edge.

Just as Callum's feet slipped, and his whole body fell against the wall.

# THIRTY

Phoenix had never been in this position.

She stared at Callum, the FBI agent who sat on a blanket on the hard, stone ground at the top of O'Ryan's Bluff while Nevaeh tended to his wounds.

The tightening sensation that had begun to clench her ribs from the moment she and Eli had pulled Callum up from the ledge, and she'd seen his torn jacket and sweater, cinched harder with each passing minute.

She'd never allowed herself to get into this situation, where she'd be obligated to thank someone. To repay someone.

Other than perhaps with her grandparents, who took her in and raised her with the support she needed after the slaughter of her family. They'd made her the beneficiary of their life insurance policies and modest estate, though she had already been going to receive her parents' life insurance money as soon as she turned eighteen.

They'd ensured she would be provided for and gave her the means, once she'd built up the funds through investments, to live the life she did today and support the people and causes she considered most important.

But her grandparents had taken care of her out of familial

love and duty. Phoenix had no obligation to repay them beyond honoring their memories.

This was different.

Her gaze lowered to Dagian.

He lay on the ground, his furry side pressing against Phoenix's boot. His reclined position, a hint of fatigue, was the only sign that anything had happened to him.

Phoenix returned her focus to Callum. Yes. This was very different. Now she owed her most valued friend's life—her partner—to this man she barely knew.

And yet...she did know him. Better than she'd ever expected to.

He had shown her part of his soul when he'd risked his life to climb down on the unstable ledge. He'd risked pain. Intentionally subjected himself to physical injury to get Dag close enough for her and Eli to reach.

The red slices on his arms, bare below the short sleeves of his gray T-shirt, advertised the damage he'd taken. For Dagian. A dog that wasn't his own.

He didn't wince or make a sound as Nevaeh rubbed ointment on the cuts.

Nevaeh and Jazz had arrived within thirty minutes after Phoenix called them, knowing they were searching for lost children nearby. With Nevaeh's EMT experience, she knew the best treatment for the wounds and carried more medical equipment with her.

The former EMT paused, the antibiotic tube still in her hand, and looked at Callum's face. "What about under the shirt?"

He obviously had more cuts beneath the thin fabric, evidenced by the rips that allowed his skin to peek through. His cable-knit sweater had been in tatters and now lay in a heap on the ground as if returned to its original state as a skein of yarn.

Callum's gaze lifted to Phoenix as she stood to Nevaeh's right, watching him. Then he returned his focus to Nevaeh. "I'll take care of those later myself, if you'll leave the ointment with me."

He likely thought Phoenix would be disturbed or frightened by seeing him without a shirt on. She would have a right to be, given what she'd been through as a child. But she had subdued that fear along with all the others that served no useful purpose.

"Cora can bring you another jacket from Base when we make camp." Nevaeh placed the cap on the tube of ointment. "And maybe Kent will have an extra sweater you can borrow. And pants." She directed a pointed look at Callum's torn pants, though they weren't as damaged as the clothing that had covered his upper body.

At least the noon sun was warming the temperature enough that he shouldn't be too chilled in only his T-shirt at the moment.

"How long 'til our shift is done?" Nevaeh twisted her head to look at Phoenix.

"Two hours and ten minutes for you and the other teams." Phoenix had planned to track the hostages for two more hours with Dag, as well, since the K-9 had rested on the ATV for part of his twelve-hour shift.

But the plan would have to adapt now. "You'll stay here with Agent Ross until they arrive."

Nevaeh's curls bobbed as she nodded.

Phoenix lifted the satphone in her hand to call in a rescue unit.

"Phoenix, no." Callum's voice, firmer than usual, stopped her. "Don't." His eyes locked on hers. "I'm not going anywhere. Not until we find the children. All of them." Resolve intensified the green of his irises to a mossy shade as he held her stare.

He'd gone along with all her orders and directions so far. But she'd never mistaken that for weakness. He exuded too much confidence and psychological strength for anyone rational to make such an error in judgment.

No, his acquiescence was more like a lion's, resting among the pride until something required that he prove his mettle. His worth.

Callum had done that today.

Phoenix never said thank you. She owed no one. But she would find a way to repay Callum Ross. Starting with an early rest.

She switched her gaze to Nevaeh and Jazz as the redhead approached behind Callum with Flash. "Our group will rest here. You continue tracking where we left off."

"Got it, Boss." Jazz glanced down at Flash as the Belgian Malinois pulled toward the scent Dag had found as soon as he'd been lifted to safety.

Without being asked, the undaunted K-9 had immediately followed the children's unseen trail as it wound along the edge of the drop-off and then curved around to the western side. There, the ground sloped down steeply but gradually enough for the hostages to have scrambled down.

Phoenix had stopped Dag from tracking any farther, though she shared his desire to keep going. Jazz and Flash could carry on with the pursuit while Dag and Callum rested. "Continue for your remaining two hours, then make camp where you are. Report your findings and location to me via our private channel."

"Roger." Nevaeh popped up, closing one of her medical bags and taking it with her as she walked to her backpack.

Phoenix felt Callum's attention on her.

She met his scrutiny head-on.

"Thank you." The uncanny understanding in his eyes, that look as if he were seeing inside her again, constricted her ribs even more. As he thanked her.

She looked away.

---

Callum slowly, carefully rolled to his other side in the sleeping bag Jazz had loaned him since he'd left his at the campsite during the one a.m. rush. He grimaced as the cuts rubbed against fabric with the movement. They burned enough as it was when he was just lying there. Trying to sleep.

He reached for his watch on the ground beside him.

*2:16 p.m.*

He and Eli had moved to a darker location under the trees about forty feet from the bluff's edge to try to get some rest. The air was crisp and cool in the shade, probably in the mid-forties.

Looked like it was working for Eli. The man slept soundly, his breathing nearly at snoring depth as his ribcage moved up and down.

Phoenix hadn't even bothered to lay out her sleeping bag this time.

Callum sat up and scanned the area under the trees. Couldn't see her.

He checked farther away, out in the open where sunlight bathed the bluff.

There she was, sitting on the flat stone that formed most of the ground in the clearing.

Dag lay beside her as she rested her hand on his shoulders.

Praise the Lord, they still had each other. The fall from the bluff could have ended so differently.

Callum pushed to his feet and walked toward them. The bright sunlight fell on him like a warm and comforting blanket, since he still wore the tattered T-shirt that was too cold for the temperature.

Dag stood as Callum approached. But his body didn't look as tense and on-guard as usual.

When Callum was only a couple of feet away, Dag wagged his tail and closed the distance between them.

Surprise coursed through Callum and brought a smile to his face as the K-9 reached his nose to nudge Callum's hand. He petted Dag's soft head. "Hey, there, bud. Are we friends now?" He slid his hands to the dog's shoulders and continued rubbing down his back as Dag turned so his side pressed against Callum's legs. "We bonded, didn't we?" Callum's gaze found Phoenix, watching from her seated position on the ground.

She sat with one knee up in front of her and the other leg

relaxed on the ground. A position she could rise from quickly if needed. "You have a dog." It was a statement, not a question.

But the closest thing to a conversation starter he'd heard from Phoenix, so Callum wasn't about to let it slip by. He smiled at her. "Jewel. A female Great Dane rescue. My neighbor is spoiling her royally while I'm here." Callum bent over Dag as the dog stayed close, seeming to enjoy the petting. "Is Dagian a rescue?"

"Not in the standard sense." Phoenix went silent as usual after the statement.

It was surprising she'd answered at all. That the reply was cloaked in mystery was expected.

"He followed me while I was in Mexico."

Callum's gaze jumped back to her. She was offering more information? He tried to keep the shock from his face.

"A feral dog who didn't trust humans."

Callum watched her. Waited for more. But she turned her head straight ahead again, apparently looking at the blue sky beyond the bluff.

He couldn't let it stop there. He was actually having a conversation with her. He had to keep it going, see if he could get her to share more. Already, what she'd said told him a lot. A dog alone on the streets, trying to survive, had picked Phoenix to like. Phoenix to follow. "But he trusted you."

She looked at him. Said nothing.

"I noticed you don't give him commands. You don't tell him to 'find' or 'search' or German commands I've heard before."

She turned her head away, gazing straight ahead. She would never answer unless he asked a direct question. If she even did then.

"Why don't you use commands like other K-9 handlers?"

"What I say is irrelevant. He knows what he needs to do."

Callum looked down at Dag as he rubbed the dog's furry neck. He really was almost as amazing and intriguing as his human partner. "I've never heard of a dog like that before."

Callum stepped around Dag and lowered to sit on the

ground a couple feet from Phoenix. He hid a wince as the movement rubbed his pants across his cuts.

"Your wounds are keeping you awake." Another statement where someone else might have asked a question.

"Or the daylight, I suppose."

Dag lay down between them, warming Callum's chest with the additional sign the dog trusted him. If only Callum had been able to win Phoenix's trust that day, too.

"You should sleep while you can."

"Yet you don't."

She didn't respond and didn't look at him.

Never explained. Rarely rested. Never cried. Never showed fear.

What drove Phoenix Gray so relentlessly? Was it the desire to help others? To save them from what she'd gone through?

Or was it something more complex, like the woman herself? Could it be a desire to transform victims into survivors? A question he'd wanted to ask before pushed against his lips. Perhaps if he voiced it now, she might answer. "I've wondered how you picked your team members. For the Phoenix K-9 Agency."

He paused, not expecting a reply. Just taking time to put into words the thoughts coming together in his mind. "I thought it had to do with their impressive skills. Their experience. Their courage. But that's not the reason you chose them, is it?"

No response.

He hadn't thought she would give one yet. So he continued. "I'm guessing they were all wounded somehow. They all had something challenging they had to overcome. You helped them rise from the ashes of their lives."

There it was again. She didn't move or change expression. But he felt a reaction—a tensing, a current—as if he was connecting to the woman beneath her outer shell.

So he took a chance and said it all. "Like you did."

# THIRTY-ONE

She was used to questions. As soon as an FBI agent discovered who Phoenix was—that she had been Robin Forster, first victim and only survivor of the famous serial killer—the questions followed. People couldn't help their curiosity or need to express sympathy.

For some, a fascination with evil and so-called true crime caused them to pepper her with questions about the crimes she'd endured or about the serial killer himself.

A rarer few were more sympathetic and avoided probing questions, instead telling her how sorry they were as if they were somehow culpable for the murder of her family. Others pitied Phoenix and judged her as incapable of anything because of what she had endured.

But Callum had not followed the normal pattern. He had changed slightly once he'd discovered who she was, giving indications that revealed he had learned the truth. But he had said nothing directly to her, asked no questions. Hadn't even expressed condolences or pity.

Apparently, he had been thinking instead. Pondering, making silent deductions and observations. Much as she would have.

She turned her head to look at him over Dag, the dog who didn't trust anyone but her. Until today.

She met Callum's waiting gaze without flinching, as she always did when people revealed they knew she was the famous victim. But this time, she didn't feel the vulnerability, the sense of exposure that usually accompanied those moments.

She felt as she had when he'd looked at her like that before. Seen. Understood.

Which could be far more dangerous.

She had to even the playing field. "As you did."

A spark of surprise glittered in his eyes. Then a sad smile tipped up his mouth at the corners. "You researched me, too."

"And yet, you believe in God." It was the part of him that didn't fit. That could be disingenuous because it was so implausible, given his life history. The suffering and horror he had endured should have cured him of believing that a loving God controlled anything.

Callum stayed silent. But his posture and energy didn't shift as if she'd offended him. He still braced his hands on the ground behind him, the red cuts on his arms a stark contrast to his light skin. The wounds he'd gotten while saving Dag.

Her throat tightened.

"I didn't believe in Him for a long time." Callum's voice broke the silence, calm and quiet. He looked out beyond the bluff instead of at Phoenix. "I was so angry over the injustice of it all. What my stepfather had done to me. To my mom. How she'd been too scared and sick to help me. I had to do it all. To save myself and her from the bad guy."

He lifted one hand and brushed back the brown hair that had fallen forward onto his forehead. "Then when I was twenty-two, I heard about Corrie ten Boom, a woman who was sent to a prison camp with her father and sister in World War II because she and her family were helping Jews escape. The suffering she went through and witnessed done to her sister, father, and others was horrific. So similar to what my stepfather did to me. But some of it even worse."

Callum turned his head toward Phoenix. His eyes glittered with something she couldn't immediately place. "She was the only person in her family to survive the prison camp. And years later, she encountered one of the guards who had tortured prisoners in the camp. Do you know what she did?"

Callum's mouth curved in the beginning of a smile, but the emotion in his eyes wasn't happy. It was something more complex. Amazement and sadness blended into one. "She forgave him. She loved him. Her father had once told her that whenever we can't love in the old, human way, God can give us the perfect way. That's what God did for her. He enabled her to love the very people who had tried to destroy her and her family."

The fire that ebbed deep within Phoenix flamed hotter. She had heard such stories before about people forgiving those who'd hurt them. Cora talked about forgiveness a great deal. But barbarians like that—a guard who tortured innocent people and men who tortured children, who slaughtered families—they didn't deserve to be forgiven. They *shouldn't* be forgiven. They needed to be punished. They needed to pay for what they had done. And they needed to be stopped. Permanently.

Callum held Phoenix's gaze, as if he was trying to keep her there. "I saw myself in Corrie ten Boom's story, her suffering, and I wanted what she had found. Purpose and joy despite the horrors she'd been through. So I asked Christ to take over my life, to forgive my bitterness and hate toward my stepfather, and to give me what Corrie ten Boom had. And He did."

Callum's smile grew to full size. "That love, God's love, enabled me to let go of the hatred for my stepfather and other abusers like him. And it keeps me going, driving me to love others and to live my life for God's glory."

Even a man like Callum thought love and forgiveness was an appropriate response to criminals who preyed on children. He, of all people, should understand how wrong that was. He seemed driven to catch such criminals, as she was. Forgiving them wouldn't keep them from hurting others, and it wouldn't help their victims.

Callum's mouth straightened as his eyebrows lowered. He held Phoenix's gaze a moment longer. "What are you living for, Phoenix?"

The answer came quickly, always at the front of her mind, dictating the beat of her heart. "Justice."

---

Phoenix drove them faster and harder than ever through the darkness of night. Since they'd started two hours ago at eight p.m., Phoenix had seemed to push their hiking pace quicker with every hour.

She had let them have seven hours of rest this time. Maybe that was the problem, the reason she felt they had to make up ground.

Or it could be the update she'd received from the FBI K-9 team that had followed the hostages' trail while Phoenix and the rest of her team rested. The agent had reported that the kidnapper had sent away four more girls over the course of a four-hour hike. The tracks showed he'd released them one at a time, rather than in pairs.

But then the FBI K-9 had reached a rocky area and lost the trail of the hostages still with the kidnapper. The agent had said over coms it was as if the children and kidnapper had suddenly disappeared.

When Eli had asked how that was possible, Phoenix explained that the scent could have disappeared on rocks under the heat of the direct sun and wind. But she was likely having them cut through the woods with such speed to that location now because she thought she and Dag could pick up the trail again. There weren't any roads that would have saved them time in that area of the park, so this route was the quickest way they could reach the coordinates the FBI agent had specified.

Phoenix's urgency was probably only increased by the even

colder temperatures moving in. Already, Callum's fingers were chilled beneath his gloves as the air dropped into the mid-twenties. And he'd never been so grateful for a sweater and jacket, courtesy of Kent and Cora, whom they'd met briefly along the way.

All of Phoenix's SAR teams were now searching in the areas where the four girls had been released. The risks of hypothermia were heightened, especially for any girls alone. Hopefully, Marnie had instructed them all to find each other and share their body heat to keep warm.

At least Phoenix's fast pace provided exertion to help stave off the cold for Callum and Eli, especially while they'd been hiking up another steep hill for the past twenty minutes.

Phoenix slowed as Dag led the way to a flat rock outcropping.

Callum's muscles clenched. They did not need a repeat of the kidnapper's fake overhang booby trap.

But the FBI agent had described this one to Phoenix. The location where his K-9 had lost the scent, and the agent couldn't find any physical evidence of prints to follow.

Dag ran his nose along the flat stone, turning in a circle.

Phoenix crouched close to the ground, the angle of her head indicating she was examining the surface through her NVGs.

Eli watched Phoenix silently, as well. Probably with even more tension and bated breath than Callum.

If anyone could find the tracks again, Dag and Phoenix would. If they couldn't...

*Lord, please keep the children safe and continue to watch over them as You've been doing all along.*

Dag lifted his head.

Callum's stomach twisted. The K-9 had lost the scent.

Or had he?

As if silently communicating with each other, Phoenix lifted her head, too. And looked in the same direction as Dag. To the northwest.

Dag took off.

In nearly the same instant, Phoenix sprinted after him, chasing him away from the overhang at an angle across the flat, rocky ground.

Callum and Eli hurried to catch up, reaching Phoenix and Dag just as they stopped.

By a line of shrubs? Or maybe it was one very long and tall shrub.

As Dag smelled the base of the plant, Callum pressed his hand against the shrub. The intertwined branches and leaves resisted the pressure. Too thick to go through to reach the other side. If there was something behind it, they might have to find a route that would take them around. But how long would that delay them?

Dag moved about another foot along the shrub where he sniffed a spot higher up on the plant.

He suddenly shoved his head into the shrub itself, and then his whole body disappeared.

"How—" The question that sprang to Callum's lips cut short as Phoenix pushed through after the K-9.

Callum glanced at Eli, whose open mouth showed he was just as surprised. Callum stepped to the same section where Phoenix and Dag had disappeared. Did look a little thinner there.

Callum plunged his arms through first, trying to part the branches.

Ouch. Not thin enough.

The scratchy branches pressed on his cuts through the clothing as he forced his body through the shrub.

He emerged on the other side, scanning for Phoenix.

She stood near Dag beyond some trees about ten feet ahead.

Eli grunted as he escaped the shrub behind Callum. "Must be easier when you're as small as those two." He shook his head at Callum before his focus jumped to Phoenix. "Did you find something?"

He jogged toward her, and Callum kept up, parting the thick layer of fallen leaves to reach Phoenix.

Her NVGs aimed their way. "We've got it."

"How could Dag find the trail when the other K-9 couldn't?" Eli's tone held a blend of wonder and hope.

"I've never seen another dog do what he can." Her pride was evident in the words, though she kept it from her tone. She swung toward Dag.

The K-9 watched her intently, as if waiting for something.

"Go."

He spun around and surged into the trees, not slowing like he often did to smell the ground.

Phoenix shot after him.

Callum launched into a run, keeping Phoenix close in front of him as Eli followed behind.

As they ran, Callum watched the ground. The leaves were flattened, visual evidence they had been trod on. By many small feet, maybe.

But Phoenix wasn't pausing to check.

Didn't need to when Dag had apparently caught a scent so strong he was moving faster than Callum had ever seen him go.

Dag led them on a chase of an invisible target for what felt like five minutes of hard running.

Then he dashed out of sight.

Phoenix kept going, leading the way as if she still knew where Dag was. She darted through the trees.

Callum stayed on her heels.

A glimpse of sandy color. Dag's tail?

The tan flash disappeared into the trees.

Then Phoenix slowed slightly.

Callum swerved around her, avoiding a crash by inches.

But his new position at the front allowed him to see what Phoenix must have.

Dagian. The K-9 climbed up tiers of rock layers that stacked like giant, moss-covered steps God had formed into a tower-shaped hill that was wide at the bottom and narrowed as it rose.

Phoenix started up the stone tiers, and Callum did the same beside her, lengthening his stride to take large steps as one would to climb three stairs at a time on a normal staircase.

Callum glanced back to be sure Eli had seen them.

The worried father was close behind, traversing the rock formation with energy he hadn't shown for days.

Callum looked ahead, up to the top tier, just in time to see the tip of Dag's tail as the dog vanished again. Was that a dark opening, far to the right?

Phoenix and Callum crested the rock formation at the same time, and he let her go first to what looked like a dark hole surrounded by brambles. Was it a cave?

Phoenix crawled through the four-foot-tall opening.

Callum got to his knees and followed as quickly as he could, his heartbeat speeding up. What would they find? Hopefully more of the missing, released children. Or…could it be the main group of hostages themselves? Maybe the kidnapper had left them and—

A small cave opened before him. Or a tunnel? Without a light source, his NVGs couldn't help him see much.

Eli crawled through the opening, and Callum stood to get out of his way, stooping under the short, stone ceiling.

A red beam lit the space. Perfect. Phoenix had a low-level red flashlight with her. He should've brought one, too. Didn't usually need them since the NVGs were so advanced at utilizing any available light source, no matter how dim.

Phoenix shone the beam of her red flashlight around the cave systematically and quickly to hit the high points, the edges and scope of the room where the armed kidnapper could be lurking.

Callum saw enough as he followed the lit areas with his gaze for his pulse to slow and his hopes to sink.

No children. The cave was empty.

Though it could have been far worse. They could have found injured or, God forbid, deceased children.

*Thank you, Lord, that we haven't had to find that. Please don't let any one of them meet such a fate.*

Phoenix worked her way to the middle of the cave, about six feet in diameter, then squatted, shining her red flashlight on the ground there.

"Was Marnie here?" Eli asked the question in a whisper, as if the cave's memory might hear him.

Phoenix kept examining the dirt in the same area. Then she stood and moved a few inches forward, still looking down. She took another step, then another.

Callum's chest clenched.

She was seeing something. What was it?

He pressed his lips closed, battling the urge to ask and interrupt her vital observation.

Maybe he could see something himself. He looked down at the dirt, cast in red light.

The ground had obviously been disturbed. Many small shoeprints crisscrossed over each other on the cave floor.

Phoenix must be interpreting some information from them.

"Phoenix, what is it?" Eli voiced the question Callum fought to hold back.

She turned and looked their way. "They escaped."

# THIRTY-TWO

"They got away?" Eli's loud voice bounced off the walls of the cave. "How?"

Phoenix pointed to the impressions in the dirt. "Marnie choked him until he was unconscious." Phoenix took one step to the right. "Here's the impression of the rope she used to tie his hands. She unbound the other children and took them with her."

"All of them?" Callum watched Phoenix from four feet away.

"Yes. Though three more were missing from this group than our known count. He must have sent them away while on rocks or somewhere the tracks were missed." Likely when the FBI tracking team had been following the scent trail or during the ATV drive, when leaves could have obscured visual signs, and Dag wasn't tracking. Though if the kidnapper had sent the children away at other locations where no visible tracks could be seen, Dag might not have informed Phoenix.

The longer the search continued, the more the K-9 homed in on the hostages with the kidnapper. On Marnie, perhaps. Even Phoenix wasn't always certain what Dag was thinking or what drove his instincts. But they were always exactly what was needed.

"How long ago did they escape?" Callum moved closer, appearing to study the ground through his NVGs.

"Approximately twelve hours."

"But what happened to the kidnapper?"

She turned her head toward Eli to answer him. "Marnie didn't hold the choke long enough to be lethal. He released himself from the rope with his knife, gathered the ropes and all other physical evidence. Then left."

Anticipation pumped Phoenix's pulse faster. This was it. The move by Marnie she'd been waiting for.

They would be able to close the gap more rapidly now. Everything would fall into place.

"Do you think he's caught them again by now?" Callum's voice carried the concern she couldn't see past his NVGs. And the belief that a group of eight girls with only a brief head start could never evade a skilled woodsman and serial killer.

"You don't know Marnie."

Neither did the monster. Underestimating her would be his downfall.

---

Callum had to remind himself not to hold his breath as he followed Phoenix, Dag, and Eli through the leaves and trees that had closed in around them as they tracked the escapees.

They'd been following the scent trail for about a mile, and Callum's heart had pounded hard the entire time. At any moment, Phoenix could announce that the prints showed the Forster killer had caught the children.

It seemed certain he must have by now. They were following a trail that was twelve hours old. Even if he'd lain in the cave for a half hour, though he probably hadn't taken that long to get free, he'd had plenty of time and opportunity to catch up with eight small girls.

Callum could see the tracks himself, pressed into the fallen leaves and bare patches of dirt where the girls had clambered up steep slopes, then half-walked, half-slid when the ground slanted downward.

The girls had escaped during the daylight, Phoenix had said. The kidnapper wouldn't have needed NVGs like Callum required to see the evidence of where the girls had gone. He could have run after them and...

Callum's throat swelled as he tried to push away the thought of what could have taken place if the kidnapper had caught Marnie.

After she'd taken his hostages, including his target victim? After she'd choked him and foiled his plans? With everything Callum knew of the Forster killer, he believed without a doubt the man would kill Marnie. At the least.

If he'd already found her as Callum suspected, he already would have murdered the poor girl.

Eli seemed to understand the danger Marnie was in now, almost greater than when she'd been the Forster killer's hostage. The girl's father hiked at twice his usual speed to stay right with Phoenix, urgency in each step he took.

He and Phoenix were actually getting pretty far ahead. Callum's stride had apparently slowed under the weight of the foreboding clouding his mind. The dread of what they might find at any moment.

Phoenix had to know. She anticipated everything and knew the Forster killer better than anyone. She had to know he would kill Marnie when he caught her. And that he had to have caught the girl.

Although Phoenix had said Callum didn't know Marnie, as if there was something spectacular about the girl that would enable her to survive. To best the vicious killer who also happened to be as at home in forests as a marauding bear.

Marnie was astoundingly mature, clever, and courageous for a nine-year-old. That was obvious through the stories the children told of her coaching them and the trail signs she'd left for Phoenix.

But to keep herself and seven other girls hidden from the

Forster killer with only a thirty-minute or less lead? Callum didn't know how anyone, with the exception of Phoenix, perhaps, could do that. Certainly not a nine-year-old girl.

Yet, two things kept Callum's heart beating quickly as he trudged after the others, not letting him give up hope entirely.

Phoenix didn't act like she knew she was looking for a body. The body of the child she had, for some reason he still wanted to know, taken under her wing and mentored.

Then again, Phoenix never showed any emotion. And in the dark while she was wearing NVGs, his attempts to read her in the way he'd been able to a couple of times was impossible.

But there was one other reason that a rhythm of hope continued to beat beneath the dread that pressed on his ribs. God. He could do anything. He could save Marnie and the other girls during daylight hours, when these tracks had been made as the girls fled the killer.

And He could save them now, in the dark, when Callum desperately prayed that God had kept Marnie and the others safe and was still keeping them safe, right at that very moment.

"Phoenix?" Panic edged Eli's voice. He, Phoenix, and Dag stood still up ahead.

Callum's throat closed as he jogged to them. "What is it?"

Eli swung his head toward Callum. "The tracks stopped." He jerked to Phoenix again. "Where she'd go? What do we do?"

Callum put his hand on Eli's arm, squeezing his bicep through his jacket.

Phoenix didn't move, her attention on Dag.

The K-9 walked quickly away, a few feet from the last visible tracks. His nose brushed the ground.

Then he kept going in a straight line, like his nose was following an invisible trail.

"He's got it. The moss." Phoenix stalked away to tail the K-9.

"What?" Eli's tone still twisted with worry and confusion.

Callum gave a gentle tug on Eli's arm to jar him from his shock and keep him moving before Phoenix and Dag left them behind. "I think she means Marnie must have had the girls jump to this moss. So they wouldn't leave shoeprints."

An audible puff of air signaled Eli was breathing again. Then he let out what sounded like a choked laugh. "Of course she did. That kid."

Surprise filtered through Callum, loosening some of the tension and washing away much of the foreboding. Okay. Maybe now he was starting to understand what Phoenix had meant when she'd said he didn't know Marnie.

Seven hours later, still following Marnie's trail, Callum's disbelief was transitioning to a growing sense of awe.

Phoenix had been right, as usual. Marnie was an incredible girl. Very like her mentor.

Callum kept his eyes on Phoenix and Dag as the pair, cast in yellow-green through his NVGs, led the way through thick pine trees. They were still on high ground, traversing a cliff-like series of large hills that demanded stamina and hiking skill to navigate.

How had the children kept going?

The scent trail Dag followed showed Marnie had managed to keep her band of girls moving the day before. And she somehow hadn't left a physical trail the majority of the time.

The moss that ended their visible trail shortly after their escape had only been the first in a series of clever methods Marnie had used to obscure or eliminate the girls' tracks.

The next time Phoenix and Dag momentarily lost the trail, Dag had to search for a bit before he'd found that the girls must have walked or crawled along fallen logs and tree limbs to get off the ground.

Then later on, they'd climbed some trees. Phoenix speculated they'd done so to sleep and hide for several hours. The branches of the oaks that looked to be about 150 feet tall were plenty large and sturdy enough to hold the small girls.

The visible prints had appeared again after the hidden detours, but if Callum hadn't been with Dag and Phoenix, he never could have stayed on the trail.

Marnie was doing a better job hiding the trail of eight kids than her adult kidnapper. Lord willing, that would mean the Forster killer had lost track of where they were long ago.

The steep downward slope beneath Callum's feet drew his attention to the sharp descent that required him to angle his body toward the incline. Moving down the slope sideways, he looked ahead to the bottom.

A river cut through hills on both sides, though the near side flattened out to mostly level ground for about four yards before the waters' edge.

Just ahead of him, Phoenix and Dag reached the bottom, followed by Eli.

The K-9 turned left. His nose skimmed the ground as he appeared to stay on the scent.

Good. Hadn't lost them again.

Callum trailed the others, checking for tracks as he walked.

Shoeprints showed the girls had been there, walking parallel with the river but about ten feet from the water's edge.

Tension crept behind Callum's ribs again.

Having her progress stopped by the river could have interfered with Marnie's ability to evade the kidnapper. If she'd continued to follow the river, looking for a bridge or some way to cross, or had decided to double back, she could have met with trouble. Could have walked right into the path of the Forster killer.

"Where'd they go?" Eli stopped ahead of Callum, but beyond him, Dag and Phoenix had kept walking.

Callum lengthened his stride to reach Eli. "What is it?"

Eli pointed at the browning grass and dirt. "The tracks stop here again."

Sure enough. The footprints suddenly disappeared.

But there was no reason to panic. Dag had always been able to recover the scent so far. And anytime Marnie managed to hide their prints was a very good thing. If their trail was invisible to anyone without a K-9, the Forster killer wouldn't be able to catch them.

"Don't worry. Dag will find them." Callum watched as the K-9 headed back in their direction, Phoenix behind him.

His snout low to the ground, he swerved farther away from the river, then circled back. He passed a few feet in front of Eli and Callum as he headed straight for the river.

The K-9 lingered there, his nose skimming the shoreline. Then he reached the four or so inches down to the water itself. What was he looking for in the river?

He lifted his head abruptly and turned to Phoenix, staring at her.

Callum's pulse picked up speed. Had he found something?

Phoenix closed the distance between her and Dag, looking at the water. "They crossed here."

Callum and Eli hurried over.

Eli squatted at the river's edge. "The water's too dark to see anything. Can't make out any prints."

Squinting at the murky water, Callum had to agree with Eli's observation. He couldn't see anything beyond the rippling surface.

"Dag doesn't need prints. He can scent them through water."

Callum stared at her, then looked at Dag. Was there no end to their surprises?

"He says they crossed here." Phoenix's firm tone ended all arguments. "So we cross here."

# THIRTY-THREE

He was there.

The creeping sensation that tingled along Phoenix's spine hadn't left since the first time Dag had growled to warn her of what her instincts had detected at the same time.

The monster was near.

Dag had rumbled a few more times after the monster had started to follow them, sixty-three minutes after they had left the cave to follow Marnie's trail. Once Phoenix had acknowledged the warnings, Dag had understood this was one enemy they were going to keep close. That Phoenix knew and was ready for him.

Now Dag swam ahead of Phoenix across the wide Silver River.

She kept her head on a swivel as she waded through the water that reached her thighs.

The monster had stayed out of sight so far. Not difficult to do when he kept such a significant distance between them. But he was still too close for his own good. Much too close if she'd wanted to catch him.

"The kids will freeze after going through this." Eli's worried tone cut through her thoughts.

He wasn't wrong. The water was frigid. Phoenix hadn't taken much notice, since it couldn't compete with the fire burning through her. It would only flame hotter the closer he got. The closer she moved to the completion of—

"Won't they get hypothermia?" Eli wouldn't give up until she addressed his concerns.

She turned her head to look at him through her NVGs, his thick thighs pushing through the river a few feet to her left. "Marnie used the land bridge in the water."

"The what?"

"Land bridge. She used it as a raft for the children to sit on as she waded across, pushing them a few at a time. She was the only one who got significantly wet." Exactly as Phoenix would have instructed her to do, if she had been there. Marnie was doing well.

"A land bridge." The sound of water parting signaled Callum moved closer to Phoenix's right side.

She looked his way, noting the water was only knee-height on him.

"Is that how they didn't leave any prints close to the river even though they crossed here?"

"Marnie knows how to quickly construct a platform of sticks and branches to walk across. One then flips it on its side from the end so only one slim line remains behind. She made sure that was on the grass, not mud, where it could have been easily seen."

"Amazing." The awe in Callum's voice ballooned pride in Phoenix's chest. He was starting to get it. "You taught her that, didn't you? Did you teach her that Dag could track through water, too?"

Phoenix didn't need to answer that. Callum knew. But it had been up to Marnie to learn, to remember, and now, when the scenario was real and frightening, to apply everything Phoenix had taught her.

Five years of training could have been for nothing, could have been destroyed in an instant if Marnie had given in to fear or other overwhelming emotions. But she'd stayed true to her training. She was rising above her past, becoming unstoppable in her present.

She had even remembered to leave scent markers, invisible to the naked eye, for Dag to follow. Watching Dag closely as he'd followed the scent trail made Phoenix certain Marnie had rubbed her wrist on rocks and trees periodically to ensure the K-9 would find her.

And Marnie had intentionally waded across the river instead of floating with the other children, suffering the cold to leave her scent in the water for Dag to follow. Eli was correct, Marnie may be paying the price for that now, with the temperatures in the low twenties. But she knew the importance of getting dry in such conditions. She would do what she could. Time would tell if it had been enough.

Concern for Marnie's health, for the child's ability to keep going if hypothermia set in, knotted Phoenix's stomach. She allowed the concern to grow, to fuel her resolve to keep tracking until she found Marnie. Before anyone else.

It pushed her to hurry her pace, pick up her legs higher to move more forcefully through the water.

Dag reached the shoreline and tried to climb out. But the steep beach stood six inches above the river.

"Hang on, bud." Callum hurried toward Dag, surging ahead of Phoenix with his long stride.

He reached for the K-9 and hefted him onto the shore.

Dag shook his whole body, spraying water droplets cast in yellow-green through Phoenix's NVGs.

But her attention returned immediately to Callum. Pain seared in her heart as if someone were squeezing it behind her ribs.

Callum turned his back to the shore, staying in the water as his head swung toward her and then Eli. Checking on them as they finished crossing.

She angled away and plowed through the final five feet of

water. He would likely try to help her climb the bank if she was close to him.

He did wait, the feel of his gaze on her as she easily jumped from the water and planted her hands on the beach to lift herself out.

Once she got her feet under her and stood on dry land, she paused. Waited for Callum as he got out of the river. That irksome weight of obligation pulled on her, replacing the tension around her heart.

She took care of Dag. And he took care of her, in a way. They'd never needed another. They didn't now.

"Phoenix, you were right!" Eli's exclamation drew her attention away from Callum. Eli had already moved ten feet in, starting up the incline of another steep hill after Dag. Eli smiled back at her. "Dag found footprints."

The K-9 took off. But not away. He sprinted toward Phoenix, snarling.

She instantly dove to the ground, swung her body ninety-degrees to face the river as she pulled her Glock.

In the same second that a shot punctured the night.

# THIRTY-FOUR

"Take cover!" Phoenix's order hit Callum's ears as he scrambled for concealment in the trees that covered the hill.

Hadn't helped Eli. The man had fallen with the first bullet. Looked like it had hit him, though Eli had kept from yelling or making any sound.

Callum stayed low, darting from tree to tree as he made his way to Eli.

His yellow-green outline grew clearer as Callum climbed the incline, the muscular guy sitting with his back against a tree trunk wider than the other skinny trees on the hill. "I'm fine." He moved his hand from his thigh to his stomach, a Glock gripped in his fingers. "Go after the shooter."

"Stay with him." The voice directly behind Callum made him start and pivot.

Phoenix crouched there, Dag at her side.

How in the world had he not heard them approach? His senses were on high alert and usually didn't fail him so badly.

"I'm going with you." Eli grunted as he started to push off the ground.

"Stay put. You'll slow me down." Her NVGs angled to Callum. "Side wound."

She spun away and disappeared into the trees with Dag, headed up the hill instead of down to the river. Clearly intended for Callum to stay with Eli. And she was right, as usual. Eli could be badly injured.

Side wound, Phoenix had said. Somehow knew that, too. She must have seen him go down, though she'd been facing away at the time. Or at least Callum had thought she was.

It had all happened lightning fast, as all shootings did.

"Which side got hit?"

"Left." Eli grimaced as he unzipped his jacket. "Did he only shoot once?"

"Twice, I think." Callum pulled the jacket away from that side and lifted the hem of the fleece pullover Eli wore, layered on a white T-shirt. A contrasting, dark shade spread through the cotton. Couldn't tell through the NVGs if it was red, but he didn't have to. The splotch had to be blood.

"Probably took off right after the shots." Eli pushed out the words through his teeth as Callum activated his coms.

"F14 to Base."

"Base, go ahead." A woman's voice he didn't recognize answered.

"A searcher has been shot. We need transport and a medic ASAP."

As Callum went back and forth with the woman on coms to detail their location and set up a meeting place, he dug out the First Aid kit from his backpack.

Signing off on coms, Callum looked at Eli. "Think you can manage hiking to the trail for transport? I'll go with you and can help if you need it. I think it's a couple miles from here."

"I don't need transport at all." Eli leaned forward like he was going to get to his feet. "We should be helping Phoenix catch the shooter."

"Hey, hold on." Callum shifted in front of Eli, putting his hands on the guy's bulky shoulders but not pushing into him. "I think we both know Phoenix and Dag can handle whoever's out there."

Eli breathed a laugh as he sank back against the tree. "Yeah. She's something else, isn't she?"

An unexpected wave of warmth filled Callum's torso at the observation. Was it admiration? Or...affection. Callum couldn't help the smile that stretched his mouth. "That may be the biggest understatement I've ever heard."

Eli laughed again, then winced as his hand went to his side. "You sound like me when I first met her. Though I didn't trust her like you do. Hard to believe that now."

"You didn't trust her?"

Eli leaned his head back against the tree trunk and kept his grin. "Not a bit. But she didn't trust me either."

Callum chuckled as he pulled off his gloves to open the wrapper around the roll of bandaging tape. "Now that is not a surprise."

"Looking back, I'm glad. She was being smart. Like she always is. I was in her friend Marion's house. Just a scary stranger Marion had found out in the blizzard with a baby."

Callum lifted his surprised gaze to Eli.

"I had a legit reason. I was trying to rescue the baby from traffickers. But Phoenix didn't know me from Adam." He shook his head as his eyes took on a faraway expression. "Man, I thought for sure she was gonna blow me away for a minute there."

Callum stared at Eli, picturing Phoenix in a standoff with the man she thought was endangering her friend. The fact she had a friend was equally intriguing. And a hopeful sign.

"Still not sure why she didn't."

"She reads people well." Now Callum was guilty of a very large understatement.

"Yeah." Eli's grin returned. "Plus, Marion started kind of pleading for my innocence, even though we'd just met. She's my wife now." The glee in Eli's voice was impossible to miss. Then he laughed. "Can you believe I was stupid enough to threaten to take Phoenix's gun away from her? That was before I'd seen her fight."

Callum shook his head as he cut a strip of tape. "You were playing with fire."

"You aren't kidding. And that's only part—" Eli's head angled somewhere past Callum, like he was looking at something through his NVGs.

A threat? Callum spun around, his hand going to his weapon.

"Hey, Phoenix." Eli's greeting came at the same time Callum spotted Dag and Phoenix, approaching from below.

Callum's pulse slowed.

Eli could've said something right away. Especially since Phoenix seemed to have mastered moving with complete silence even in a forest.

She stopped by Callum. "Report."

He assumed she must be referring to Eli's injury. "I think it's just a flesh wound. No bullet hole that I can see, though it's bleeding quite a lot."

"Forget that." Eli straightened away from the tree. "Did you catch the shooter? Was it the kidnapper?"

"He's not a priority."

"What?" Challenge stiffened Eli's tone. Apparently, he still didn't back down from Phoenix.

"Marnie and the other children are the priority right now. Would you have me say otherwise?"

Eli's lips pressed together, his eyebrows lowered. "No."

Another faceoff won by Phoenix.

And she hadn't answered Eli's question. She always knew more than she shared.

Did that mean she had caught the shooter? If she had and it was the kidnapper, she surely would have said. Wouldn't she?

Callum hadn't heard any gunfire while she'd been gone. Maybe she had seen him, but he'd been too far out of range to catch without leaving Eli and the children's trail behind.

He bit back the questions that fought for release. Focused on what he could do now instead. Bandaging the wound. "I'll do what I can with the First Aid kit, but I'm no expert." He glanced up at Phoenix. "Did you hear the call about the medic transport in one hour?"

"We'll head there as soon as you get him bandaged."

"No way." Eli pulled away from the gauze pad Callum tried to place against his side. "I'm staying with you. We need to keep going. That had to be the kidnapper shooting at us, right?"

Phoenix seemed to watch him through her NVGs, but she didn't answer.

"Had to be." Eli pushed to his feet, prompting Callum to back out of his way and stand, too. "That means he's as close to Marnie as we are. We have to get to her first."

"You need to return to Base for medical attention." Phoenix's tone was as flat and matter-of-fact as always.

"Phoenix—"

"I won't allow you to slow me down."

"I won't slow you down."

A pause.

Callum knew what was coming. A Phoenix ending to the argument. Seemed like she often paused before delivering a final blow.

"Then you'll need to explain to Marion why we couldn't reach her daughter in time."

Whoa. The statement fell heavy in the air between Phoenix and Eli. Would Eli listen?

He was quiet for a few long seconds. Then he nodded. "I'll go back."

"Let Ross bandage you up. We'll start for the clearing in five minutes. It will take us at least seventy minutes on this terrain in your condition."

Eli sank back down to the ground. "I'll go alone so you two can keep following Marnie."

Callum glanced up at Phoenix before he moved closer to Eli to apply the gauze and wrap. Surprising she hadn't already said she was going to continue alone while Callum took Eli to the helicopter.

"You're in no shape to make it alone."

"Okay, then send Callum with me, and you stay on Marnie." Frustration tightened Eli's tone. "The kidnapper will keep going. He could catch up to her first."

"He won't."

There it was again. That certainty about things even Callum wasn't sure how she knew.

Unless...

Callum wrapped the bandaging tape around Eli's torso as deductions clicked into place in his mind. Of course. He should've seen it before.

The Forster killer was following them.

He needed Phoenix, needed Dag because Marnie was so effectively hiding her trail. He couldn't find his hostages without Phoenix now.

The irony of the situation hit Callum like a brick. Robin Forster, the girl the Forster killer had tried to destroy, was now his only means to getting what he wanted.

But Phoenix knew. She'd probably known a long time that the kidnapper was following them. Using her to find Marnie and the other girls.

That was how she could be sure he wouldn't continue on his own. Because she knew he needed her to find the hostages. But how would she—

"Base to all teams. Base to all teams." Agent Nguyen's voice came across coms, urgency edging her tone. "A wildfire has been reported two miles south of Frog Lake. The west wind is pushing the fire east. Expected to reach Silver River in five hours. If you are in the path of the fire, report in and evacuate immediately."

Callum glanced down the slope at the water below. "Isn't this the Silver River?" He looked at Phoenix.

She stared at him for a second.

All he needed to know the answer.

"We move out now."

Phoenix and Dag stepped to the edge of the clearing where the helicopter should land in...She looked at her watch. Three minutes.

Smoke rose above trees to the south, competing with the sunrise that colored the eastern sky orange and pink.

Switching to the rocky clearing instead of the original transport location farther west meant they'd been able to get out of the fire's path. But the walk there had been twenty minutes longer. She would still have time to return to Marnie's trail before the fire reached Silver River, obliterating the scent Dag would need to find her. So long as the helicopter arrived soon.

Leaves crunched behind her as Callum and Eli caught up.

"Stop here." She held her arm out from her side as a signal.

Callum had stayed close to Eli for the entire hike from Silver River, ready to help anytime the injured man stumbled or looked weak.

But Eli was proving strong again, able to hike over rough terrain for an hour and a half with only the few breaks Phoenix had forced him to take.

Still, Callum had reported at the last check that more blood was seeping through the gauze covering Eli's bullet wound. He needed medical support.

A chopping sound signaled the helicopter's arrival.

She glanced at the copter briefly as it came into view on the horizon, then lowered her gaze to scan the edges of the clearing.

Wooded on all sides, the round portion of land was naturally clear of tall plants except for a few ambitious weeds that found cracks in the flat gray stone that formed the ground. Not stacked and towering like some of the hills, bluffs, and cliffs, this extensive rock formation had spread in a wide diameter instead, managing to keep dirt and grass from burying it somehow.

Made it the perfect landing pad.

And a perfect place for a sniper.

She kept her gaze traveling across the fringes of the clearing, looking for any sign of movement. And keeping her ears tuned to any rumble from Dag.

The monster hadn't needed marksmanship before. Easy to hit close-range targets in home invasions.

But he'd invested in a rifle with a night vision scope to make that shot. The one that could have killed Eli. A difficult shot, through trees in the dark.

His poor marksmanship meant he could've hit her instead if Dag hadn't warned her, prompting her to dive to the ground.

But he wouldn't have wanted that. He needed her to find the girls. To find his target victim he wouldn't leave without.

And he wouldn't leave without the disc Phoenix wore around her neck under her jacket and sweater.

"Shouldn't we go out to meet them?" Eli raised his voice to be heard over the helicopter as it touched down.

"No." Phoenix wasn't about to let him be exposed in the open again. She wouldn't let Marion lose him. Not on her watch.

The fire inside her sparked as if someone sprinkled on gasoline, heating the flames several degrees hotter.

Phoenix hadn't anticipated the monster would try to pick off her companions long-distance. He'd never used a long-range weapon during his other killings and kidnappings. And his lack of experience had saved Eli's life.

He'd likely brought the rifle along to take out searchers if they got too close to him. Or to take out Phoenix.

But he couldn't do that now. Not when he needed her to help him first.

He'd aimed to eliminate her companions instead, thinking that once she led him to the children, he could easily kill her and take his Phaistos Disc.

She'd shown him just how bad an idea that was.

He had fled as soon as he'd shot Eli.

But she'd seen him.

A glimpse of his back as he ran from her.

The monster. Running. From her.

The memory of the moment gripped her—the thrill, the rage

that had fired within, nearly consuming her and forcing her into a chase that wouldn't end until she caught him.

But it was too soon. The wrong time. Wrong place.

So she'd stopped. Let him go.

But not before he saw her on a hill where he hadn't expected her to be. Above him. Ahead of him. Where he saw she was armed and could have shot him.

He shouldn't try picking off anyone with her again. He would know to catch her and only her when he wanted the pendant. He would wait for her to be alone and unsuspecting so he could attempt an ambush.

Phoenix raised her hand to the helicopter since no one had emerged from it yet.

A female medic dropped out and jogged toward them across the clearing, carrying her medical bag. "What have we got?" She glanced at the three people.

"He has a gunshot wound on his left side." Callum put his hand on Eli's shoulder.

"Okay, let's take a look." The medic set down her bag and opened it as Eli lowered to sit on the ground.

Dag growled.

Engines rumbled, overcoming the noise of the slowing chopper blades.

Phoenix put her hand on her holstered Glock as her focus cut to the west side of the clearing.

Three ATVs emerged from the trees and cruised across the stone, bouncing over the uneven ground. There was no groomed trail in that section of the park. The drivers must have found enough space among the trees to pick their way through the forest to reach the area.

They drove directly toward Phoenix and the others.

She didn't need to see their faces to know who they were.

The FBI agents so eager to join her search. Back again.

Plus another man on the back seat of one ATV whose silhouette she didn't recognize.

As they braked too close to Phoenix, the talkative bearded

one dismounted first and took a few steps to close the distance to her.

At least some of the distance. Before Dag's growl told him to stop where he was.

The man's fake smile flattened as he looked down at the K-9. He brought his gaze up to Phoenix. "Hey, we're the good guys. Nguyen sent us for backup since somebody's taking shots at you."

Katherine may have sent them, especially to cover all her bases, to guard against liability and blame down the road.

The man found his lost smile and tried to charm her again. "She told us to stay out of your way and let you give all the orders in the field. We'll just watch for bullets and shooters so you're free to search for the kids, okay?"

Let her give the orders. As if she needed his permission. And she didn't miss the unintentional implication he considered obeying her orders entirely optional.

She turned away, knowing Dag had her back, and pulled the satphone from her pack as she walked into the trees. Though if one of the newcomers wanted to follow her and eavesdrop, she wouldn't stop him. It would be the quickest way to get a definitive answer as to their true purpose there.

She felt Callum's gaze on her while she dialed Katherine's number. She glanced his way as she put the phone to her ear.

"Phoenix. Figured you'd be calling me about now. Yes, I did send you backup, though I know you don't need them."

"You cleared them."

"Yeah. None were part of the investigative team you wanted me to check for. Will you let them stay with you, at least for a little bit?"

"You're concerned you'll be blamed if you don't send backup after there was a shooting and something else goes wrong."

"Nailed it, as usual. I'm not a free agent like you, Phoenix." The obvious stress in Katherine's voice carried over the line. "Can you do me a favor and let them stay?"

"Tell me the fire report."

"Thank you." Katherine let out a breath. "Uh, latest on the fire just came in. It changed direction when the wind shifted. Warm front coming in from the south, so it's heading more north now."

Away from Marnie. That gave Phoenix additional time. And the new trajectory of the fire...if it held...could mean—

"They're hoping it'll end up hitting Juniper Lake. I guess they could try to trap it there and make it burn out. But there's also a rumor about a storm front moving in later today. Rain could help, but it's bringing strong winds that could change the fire's direction again."

"How many children are unaccounted for?"

Some calls reporting finds still weren't being broadcasted over the main coms channel. Phoenix had to make sure she knew the accurate count before she could execute the final stages of this operation.

"With the three you said must have been released earlier, we're at four left to find. Everybody's trying to cover ground at lightning speed now with the fire. As soon as the fire was reported, your teams got in front of it as close as they could and searched the area in its path before it spread."

Exactly as Phoenix had told them to do on PK-9's private coms channel. Sofia and Cora had both reported finding girls after that, two together and one alone for a total of three.

"Hey, Phoenix?" Katherine spit out the last words as if she was afraid Phoenix had ended the call. "Before you hang up, can you give me an ETA on finding the other kids and the kidnapper?"

"Soon."

"Real—"

Phoenix pressed the end button and slipped the phone into her backpack as she marched with Dag to the group at the edge of the clearing.

The bearded FBI agent gave her the fabricated smile. "What's the word? Can we stay?"

She walked past him to reach the medic.

The woman looked up from stuffing supplies in her bag. "He needs stitches."

Eli pushed to his feet. "No hospital."

Familiar phrase coming from his mouth. Same thing he'd said that Christmas Phoenix had first met the man.

The medic glanced at him. "The doctor at the base can do it there."

"Great. Then I'll come right back out here." Eli aimed his gaze at Phoenix.

"Not likely." The medic answered for her. "Not with that fire." She threw a glance at the smoke thickening in the sky.

"Phoenix?" Eli stepped close in front of her.

Dag let him. And so did Phoenix.

He met her gaze. "Bring my daughter home."

Phoenix let herself feel the full impact of his words. Of the raw pain and powerful love in his eyes. His great love for Marnie.

More reasons to get her back. She deserved a father like that, a home with a loving mother and safe, happy siblings.

Marnie would have all that Phoenix had lost.

She stared unblinking at the emotion in his eyes, letting nothing show in hers. But she gave him his answer. "I will."

# THIRTY-FIVE

Why wasn't she doing anything? Callum looked away from Phoenix to check his watch again.

A half hour had passed since they'd hiked to the campsite after the helicopter had left with Eli.

Callum had assumed Phoenix would immediately lead him and the other agents back to Marnie's trail so they could try to find her. He'd expected her to have a heightened sense of urgency, to drive them harder and faster.

But she'd led them to the campsite instead, two long hiking miles out of the way if they were going to connect with Marnie's trail again.

And all Phoenix had done since they'd arrived was sit on a rock in the center of the campsite. What was she thinking?

Sore and weary as Callum's muscles were, those sensations weren't as strong as the itch that tingled through him. The urge to run back to Marnie's trail and try to find her and the other girls before the wildfire or the Forster killer caught them first.

According to the communications coming over the general channel, the firefighters were trying to control the blaze, but the dry conditions, leaves on the ground, and the increasing wind were not helping.

At least the wind shift meant the fire wasn't currently aiming their direction or, more importantly, toward the area of Marnie's last known trail. But that could change at any moment. And who knew where Marnie had taken the girls after they'd crossed Silver River? She could have changed direction, gone somewhere that was now in the path of the forest fire.

But there Phoenix sat. Perfectly calm.

Not that she was ever anything but calm. He had just expected more movement at this point. More obvious intensity.

Dag was her mirror image, lying beside the two-foot-high rock where his partner sat. Neither of them slept, of course, though Phoenix had initially said Dag needed a rest when she'd announced they were going to the campsite.

Callum hadn't even sat down yet, which was probably foolish. But the itching sensation intensified to a twitch in his muscles as he watched Phoenix and Dag. Callum was a patient man, usually the calm one in any circumstances.

But Phoenix had the patience of a stone compared to him.

Unless she knew something he didn't. Again.

What was it? He pulled out the facts of the situation in his mind to review. If Callum's theory was correct that the Forster killer had been using Phoenix and Dag to find Marnie, then he might not be able to make any progress in following the girls on his own.

But with what Callum knew of the killer, the man would likely try anyway. He worked independently, never relying on others to enact his criminal schemes. Needing to follow Phoenix would already be making him feel off-balance and dependent on someone else. He wouldn't like that. He'd want to follow his original plan as much as possible.

That would mean he'd do everything he could to find Marnie and the girls, specifically his target victim, as quickly as he could. He wouldn't sit around and wait while Phoenix lingered at a campsite. He would try to pick up Marnie's trail where he knew Dag and Phoenix had left it.

And he'd be able to, since the children's footprints were

visible on the far shore of the Silver River where Eli had been shot.

Lord willing, Marnie had done a good job of hiding visible prints soon after that. Or she and the other girls could be in serious trouble. Even right now.

He stared at Phoenix. She would know that.

And she knew about the fire. The risk that it could change direction and target Marnie or that the girls could already have veered into its eventual path.

But he hadn't seen Phoenix make a mistake yet. No one was perfect, but she seemed to be awfully close. At least when it came to operations like that one.

If she was sitting there, peacefully, as if patiently waiting for something, she had to have a reason. Given the Phoenix he'd seen in action and even come to understand in some ways, he had no reason to doubt that she had this situation in hand, too.

Movement to the left of the campsite caught his eye.

The bearded FBI agent who had identified himself as Special Agent Tinney still paced back and forth, as he'd done since they'd arrived. The other two FBI agents who seemed to be under his oversight were restless, too, fidgeting with their phones and frequently casting glances in Phoenix's direction.

Mike Pinchert, the FBI agent who'd driven Callum to Base the first night, was the only one who seemed relaxed. He'd found a shaded spot to sit on the grass and recline against a tree.

At least the new guys weren't trying to pester Phoenix with questions or conversation. Maybe Tinney had figured out she wasn't going to respond in kind. Or he was heeding Agent Nguyen's advice to stay out of Phoenix's way.

Callum should probably listen to that advice, too. But his feet apparently didn't think so, since they led him in her direction.

As he expected, she didn't look at him when he approached.

Dag did the looking for her and gifted Callum with a swish of his tail.

The gesture of welcome, so rare from Dag, warmed Callum from the inside. "Hey, bud." He squatted next to the K-9 and rubbed his ears and neck.

Dag squinted his eyes in pleasure.

Callum chuckled and glanced up at Phoenix.

To see her watching him.

A different, more intense heat zinged behind his ribs. The reaction startled him almost as much as her attention on him. Was he developing…feelings for Phoenix Gray?

He couldn't be. But the odd trip of his pulse said differently.

Not good. He couldn't have feelings for her. Shouldn't. She would never return them or welcome them. Nor would he entertain anything romantic toward her when she wasn't a Christian.

For the first time, he broke the eye contact. He focused on Dag instead, giving himself time to process the alarming sensations spiraling through him.

So strange. He hadn't considered any woman in a romantic way for the whole of his adult life. He'd sought escape from his home situation through playing around with girls in high school. But after he'd grown and become a Christian, he'd stopped pursuing that sinful kind of pleasure and temporal comfort.

He wasn't against marriage, but God had never brought a woman into his path that he was interested in. Not in that way.

But there was no other woman like Phoenix. No other person like her. He respected her more than he could say. A respect that had grown with every day spent in her company.

And those moments they'd had a couple of times…the moments where he'd felt a connection so visceral he couldn't describe it. He'd never experienced that before.

Maybe that was what had thrown him. What was causing his reaction to her now—the feelings that seemed awfully like attraction and the beginnings of something else.

Respecting someone, connecting with her, and even feeling empathy as he did for the woman who had been Robin

Forster, were not the same as love. Christ-like love, perhaps. The love Callum needed to have and demonstrate to all people. But not romantic love—marriage, life-partner kind of love.

He let out a slow breath of relief at the safer conclusion he'd come to. She needed his Christ-like love. She needed to see what that kind of compassion and love looked like when he showed it to others, too.

She needed to see Christ in Him. Because as amazing as Phoenix was, as incredible as her ability was to survive what she'd been through, she was not well. She wasn't whole. She wasn't healed.

He lifted his gaze.

She still watched him.

And the void in her eyes where some hint of emotion should be proved his thoughts.

Phoenix Gray may think she had overcome her past. But the embers of the fire that had devoured Robin Forster weren't fully doused. The same destructive power still burned within her, devouring parts of her that should be free to truly live.

The only one Callum knew Who could end such inner torment was God Himself.

And only He could protect Marnie, the girls with her, and the others who might be in the path of the fire.

Callum stood and looked in the direction where the smoke had been visible when they were at the clearing. From the campsite, the trees were too close and tall for him to see anything beyond.

"I'm praying God will help the teams find the lost girls before the fire reaches them." Callum spoke the words out loud for Phoenix, knowing she wouldn't answer.

God had already enabled one of the drones to find two of the girls the kidnapper had sent away. They'd been located just when Phoenix had stopped at the campsite. Or at least, that's when the call had come in on coms. Those girls, hiding together, weren't in the immediate path of the fire, and a rescue team was sent to extract them. Should be only two more girls alone out there now.

And Marnie with her band of seven girls she was leading through the wilderness. With a killer at her heels.

Tension constricted Callum's muscles at the reminder. He looked at Phoenix, but she faced straight ahead, the bill of her cap hiding her face from his view since he was standing.

Sunlight glinted off something on her sweater. The pendant. She only seemed to wear it when they stopped to rest. Or maybe she was always wearing it beneath her layers of clothing.

Her fingers went to the disc, touching its rounded edges.

He hadn't been able to see it clearly at night in the dim light of the fire. But now, the sun revealed the design.

Small symbols—or maybe numbers—appeared to be etched into the gold, trailing around the disc in a spiral pattern.

Wait. Was that a replica of the Phaistos Disc?

He glanced away, moistening his lips. He shouldn't ask. Shouldn't pry. It could have sentimental value related to her family. She wouldn't want to share that, and he had no business asking her to.

His gaze drifted back to the disc. Something about Phoenix with a Phaistos Disc—one of the world's oldest unsolved mysteries—immediately spelled intrigue.

And why would she be fingering it? She was a woman who needed no crutches and refused to show even the slightest hint of vulnerability.

No, Phoenix Gray would not openly wear that pendant unless she wanted people to see it. And she would never finger it like she had a nervous habit except for the same reason. Did she want someone to think she had a dependance on the piece? Or wanted someone to see it for a different reason?

Could the Phaistos Disc be related to why she was spending so much time at the campsite instead of chasing after Marnie and the other girls?

The questions were too strong to hold back. "I see you're wearing a Phaistos Disc replica."

She kept fingering the pendant. But she was an expert at hiding reactions and inner emotions. She wouldn't want him to know he'd caught on to anything important. Or perhaps she was starting to trust him enough to not consider him a threat to whatever her plan was with the pendant.

He stuffed the latter, unrealistic and naively romantic notion in the back drawer of his mind. *Romantic* meaning imaginary or impractical, of course.

And just to remind himself he didn't need to be worried what she thought of him, he pressed again. "Does it hold some special significance for you?"

She looked up at him then.

And an electric pulse jolted his heart. *Lord, a little help here would be great.* Callum shouldn't be feeling such things for this woman. But he didn't even have time to think about the reaction until it had happened.

"Should it?"

He stared at her. Had he heard her right? Phoenix almost never asked people questions. At least not when he'd been around her. She made statements, knowing the answer already to any question she could have asked.

She was always so intentional in everything she said. What did she intend by asking him that question? Especially when she could have ignored him completely and stayed silent as she usually did.

Was she inviting him in? To engage in conversation with her or to try to guess at the inner workings of her mind and heart?

The way his heart pounded at the thought obviously meant that explanation was his preferred option.

But there were other, more likely reasons for her question. She could be trying to see what he knew about the Phaistos Disc, maybe that pendant replica in particular.

Which would mean there was significance to it. A lot of significance, if she wanted to confirm what Callum did or didn't know.

He'd better think of a reply that would get her to tell him more or to—

"PT4 to Base and PT1." A female voice spoke in Callum's ear through coms. Sounded like Jazz.

"Base, go ahead." Nguyen responded almost instantly.

"We've found two more girls by Ghost Canyon. Appear healthy. They report Marnie told them how to find each other and instructed them to stay together."

Callum closed his eyes as relief flowed through his limbs. *Thank you, Father.* Every lost child accounted for. Found and safe.

Those with Marnie didn't seem to be lost, since the young girl was taking care of them. And though Phoenix hadn't said, Callum suspected Marnie wasn't just wandering, evading the killer while helping Dag and Phoenix find her. She likely had a destination or some kind of plan.

She was, after all, like a young Phoenix.

And Phoenix never did anything random or haphazard.

After Nguyen worked out transport details with Jazz, coms went silent.

For only one second.

"PT1 to all Phoenix teams." Phoenix's tone didn't change as she spoke. "Come to me."

The hairs on Callum's arms stood on end. That was it.

He barely heard her specify their location as he finally realized what she'd been waiting for.

She was waiting for her agents to rescue the remaining lost children. So she could then assemble her team. Call them to her.

Was the move for their own safety, so she could be sure they avoided the wildfire? Or was it strategic for a different purpose?

Whatever the explanation hidden behind Phoenix's stoic façade, he knew one thing. Phoenix Gray was about to take action.

And Callum had a feeling it would be something to behold.

# THIRTY-SIX

He had returned.

Dag confirmed her instincts with a low growl.

Phoenix put her hand on his head, the dog standing by her side at the edge of the trees that surrounded the campsite. "I know." She spoke quietly, for Dag's ears alone.

The K-9 went silent, trusting her judgment and timing.

The monster had left after Phoenix had guided Callum and the FBI agents to the campsite. As Phoenix expected, he'd assuredly gone to try to pick up Marnie's trail himself, hoping he could find the hostages and retrieve his target victim on his own, then return to Phoenix.

He'd come back ten minutes ago—exactly in the time frame Phoenix had expected.

Marnie had foiled him again, hiding the visible signs of herself and her charges.

He still needed Phoenix. Which put him precisely where she wanted him. On her tail. At her bidding.

Phoenix angled toward the trees slightly and fingered the pendant she'd pulled out from under her layers to rest on her sweater, clearly visible since she'd taken off her jacket.

Had to make sure he saw it. Remembered his precious Phaistos Disc and how badly he wanted it.

Though that aim had allowed Callum to notice it, too. Recognize what it was. But he only saw it as the ancient Greek artifact that no one had been able to conclusively decode. Impressive he knew what it was, given so few people did unless they were in the archeological or history fields. Another sign of his intelligence.

His intellect could have led him to quickly decipher why she had the pendant, why it was visible now, and what its significance was. Since he favored silence, much like she did, Phoenix couldn't count on him voicing his thoughts if he had realized the pendant was associated with the kidnapper.

She'd had to ask—a startle tactic that she'd expected would reveal what he knew. And it had.

The surprise that had flickered in his eyes meant he hadn't been preparing to hide or reveal secret knowledge. And the subsequent time he took to answer further indicated he didn't have a ready conclusion.

But now that he'd noticed it, and she had highlighted the subject with her unusual reaction, he would ponder it more. With his level of intelligence and knowledge of the monster, Callum might be able to make correct deductions about the pendant and its significance.

But by the time he did, it would be too late for him to act on his conclusions. For him to prevent what Phoenix had planned.

She turned her back to the trees, allowing the monster to think she was sometimes vulnerable to attack. It would build his confidence. Assure him he would have the opportunity he wanted if he bided his time.

She scanned the PK-9 team members that populated the camp. She would give them five more minutes to rest.

Fifty-five minutes had passed since the final agents had come. Jazz and Nevaeh had arrived with Flash and Alvarez in the ATV with a trailer she'd instructed them to have the extraction team bring when they retrieved the last recovered girls.

Flash lay beside Jazz as she sat on the ground with Nevaeh. The Belgian Malinois held his head erect, watching Tinney and his associates who stood off to one side, talking quietly among themselves. Smart dog. And as Phoenix expected, Flash was as alert and ready to get to work as always.

Toby would have been the same had he been there with Bristol. But she had wisely heeded Phoenix's advice that she go home to avoid smoke exposure to her unborn child. She had sounded reluctant and disappointed on the satphone when Phoenix had called her immediately after the fire alert went out. But she was prioritizing her child, as she should.

Phoenix's gaze moved to Alvarez. The rottweiler mix rested his head on his paws in front of him as he lay a few feet from Nevaeh. Definitely more fatigued than Flash, but he had enjoyed a rest in the trailer during the drive there. And he hadn't been working as hard as Flash, since Alvarez was only along for security, not scent work.

Jana and Raksa appeared the most weary. The golden retriever slept with her head on Cora's lap as she and Kent sat on a blanket she had spread out for them.

Raksa had been panting a bit excessively when he'd first arrived with Sofia two hours earlier, despite the temperature only being in the low thirties. He also hadn't tried to play with the other dogs. A sure sign of fatigue for him.

But now, after his two-hour nap, the German shepherd was walking around, trying to forage in the underbrush along the trees and find something entertaining to do.

Any remaining fatigue for him and the other K-9s would fade when required. They would all rise to the occasion, exactly like their human partners.

That moment was now.

The monster was in place. Unwittingly ready to go where Phoenix wanted him and execute what he would think was his own plan.

The uninvited FBI lurkers would help with that.

Phoenix walked to the center of the campsite with Dag.

"Time to move out." She raised her volume, ostensibly to be heard by everyone in the camp. "Marnie will lead the girls to the ranger station near the east shore of Juniper Lake."

"What makes you think that?" Tinney was predictably the first, and likely only, person to question her. He approached with his two companions, arms swinging by his sides with a swagger that revealed more than his innocent expression.

"She clearly studied a map the kidnapper had and has been aiming for the ranger station since she escaped."

As Phoenix spoke, the fourth uninvited FBI agent, Pinchert, moved closer with Callum, the two of them having quietly chatted for the last half hour. Not surprising, since Callum had obviously known the FBI agent prior to when he'd shown up that day. The association and Callum's implicit approval in his demeanor around Pinchert was enough reason for Phoenix to leave the man out of her assignment for the others.

"That's great." Jazz voiced the observation, holding Flash's leash loosely as she watched Phoenix. Her study no longer held the suspicion it used to when she looked at Phoenix, but rather trust. "The kids won't be in the path of the fire if it keeps heading for the south side of the lake. Unless the wind changes again." She cast her gaze up toward the trees where the strong wind blew through the branches, stripping them of their remaining, dying leaves.

"I have a suggestion, if it would help." Tinney smiled, his tone friendly and laidback.

Phoenix turned her head toward him. He would offer to drive ahead with his companions on ATVs.

"How about I, Jenson, and Franks take our ATVs out there now. I think the trail we're by here runs part of the way to the ranger station, and we can go off-trail from there. We'll be able to reach the poor kids a lot faster that way."

Nice of him to volunteer so easily. So predictably. And his exclusion of Pinchert confirmed that Callum's apparent instincts about the fourth agent were correct. At least to a point.

She nodded. "Yes. I'll need to follow the trail in case the children went elsewhere or didn't make it to the ranger station. One of you take the ATV with the trailer for transporting the children."

Tinney's grin widened and reached his eyes for the first time. He swung a hand over his shoulder to beckon his men, and they strode to the ATVs parked at the edge of the campsite close to the trail.

Phoenix felt the stares of Callum and her PK-9 team members before she looked their way. Her acquiescence to Tinney's idea and sending him after the children would raise questions in the minds of those who knew her ways well. Which, oddly, included Callum now.

Her gaze pulled to him, as if of its own accord.

His eyebrows lowered slightly as they did whenever he was thinking hard, trying to solve a puzzle. Trying to solve her. To understand her.

But even if he had managed to do so in a few past fleeting moments, he wouldn't now. He couldn't.

Everything depended on Callum remaining in the dark until it was all over. Because he was the only one who had a chance—a slim but dangerous chance—of understanding her and the monster enough to figure it out. To know. To interfere.

No. She would not be stopped. She would finish what the monster had started.

Phoenix looked away from Callum as she gave the call to action to the PK-9 team, fueled by the fire within. "Follow me. We end this today."

# THIRTY-SEVEN

Something was off.

Callum watched his footing as he clambered up the steep incline through the trees.

Mike's heavy breathing told Callum the agent was close behind him.

Ahead of Callum, Jazz, Nevaeh, and their two dogs followed Phoenix and Dag. Next came Cora, Kent, and Jana.

Sofia and Raksa had been beside Phoenix and Dag at the front a few minutes ago, before the trees had thickened enough to make them travel single file. They must have dropped behind.

Callum glanced over his shoulder, looking past Mike to see if Sofia was there.

Sure enough, the petite woman now trailed Mike with her German shepherd. How she'd dropped back so far without Callum noticing, he couldn't figure out. But at least they hadn't lost her.

Given her apparent energy and conditioning, she must have moved to the rear to make sure Mike didn't fall too far behind. It was clear he wasn't in the best physical shape for that kind of hiking. Especially at the fast pace Phoenix had started them out at and continued to hold steady three hours later.

That part wasn't surprising. Speed and intensity were what Callum had expected from Phoenix during the hours she'd sat at the campsite instead.

Thanks to the quick pace, they'd crossed Silver River again after two hours of hiking and reconnected with Marnie's trail exactly where Phoenix, Callum, and Eli had left it.

For the next hour, Callum and the others had followed Dag as the K-9 tracked Marnie's meandering and hard-to-decipher trail. At least for human eyes. Dag hadn't seemed to falter or hesitate once.

Callum should probably be feeling confident and hopeful.

After all, Phoenix had declared when they'd left the campsite that they were going to end this today. And she never exaggerated.

Maybe he was overthinking her wording, but there were many different ways she could have meant that statement. And it seemed so odd for her to make such a declaration at all.

She usually didn't say anything when she left to start a new shift of searching for the kids. She simply expected anyone who wanted to go with her to follow along or be left behind.

So why had she said they were going to *end this*? And why did he have the feeling that her *this* might mean more than rescuing the children?

She would want to capture the murderer of her family, as well. That was obvious. Had to be a driving force for her during the days of searching, alongside her desire to rescue Marnie and the other children.

Maybe that had been the additional meaning behind her statement. That she was going to catch her family's killer and bring him to justice.

*Father, please let her do that. Let us catch this man today and end his evil deeds.*

The same mission had brought Callum there. Well, the children had become the priority once they were kidnapped. But finding and apprehending the Forster killer was Callum's last chance to accomplish what he'd set out to do when he had joined the FBI. To apprehend a criminal who preyed on children and to see justice done.

With the Forster killer's horrific deeds, even a lenient jury and judge would at least give him a life sentence without parole.

But they hadn't caught him yet.

Phoenix clearly had a plan, as usual. Whether it was to catch the killer or rescue the children, he wasn't sure. Hopefully both. But she wasn't going about it in her usual way.

Which was why an unsettled apprehension stirred in Callum's belly. Why would she have let other people go ahead of her to the location where she said Marnie would be with the hostages? Callum couldn't believe she would let someone other than herself rescue Marnie, with the possible exception of one of her trusted Phoenix K-9 agents.

Given Phoenix's history, the fact that she'd sent three men she didn't know to go after the girls meant she must think they wouldn't find the children. Or she had something else up her sleeve.

The Phoenix K-9 Agency ladies had given each other and their boss surprised looks when she'd sent the FBI agents ahead, too. Perhaps because she'd taken someone else's suggestion—something Callum had never seen her do before. And it was inconceivable that she would suddenly think Tinney—the FBI agent who gave off vibes of someone who wanted to be on the front lines only to steal the credit for success—knew better than she did.

Callum's attention was called to his feet as the upward incline, which had leveled off for a bit, abruptly dipped downward.

Kent and Jana stopped, and Callum had to pull up quickly to avoid running into Jana's back paws.

Farther down the slope, Phoenix's hand was raised as she signaled for the group to stop. "I'm leaving you now."

Leaving? Callum's breath left his lungs.

"I'm going to cut across difficult terrain the children wouldn't have attempted. Jazz, Nevaeh, and Cora, stay on the scent trail Marnie left. Depending on how far they've traveled, you may find them before I do."

Why hadn't she mentioned Sofia, too?

Callum glanced past Mike at the back of the line.

No sign of Sofia or Raksa. Where had they gone?

He angled forward again just in time to see Phoenix's cap tilt upward as she seemed to look in Callum's direction.

His chest constricted. Would she say he could go along?

"Agent Pinchert, you'll go with me."

"Sure." Mike brushed close to Callum thanks to the little space between trees as he scrambled to reach Phoenix below.

Was Phoenix ditching Callum now? So close to what she'd said was the end?

"Where do you want me?" The question came out worded exactly as he felt it, deep and irrationally painful behind his ribs. A question not of logistics and strategy for whatever she had planned, but of whether or not she wanted him with her.

"Your call."

The cryptic, emotionless answer was so Phoenix, but not the affirmation he'd hoped for. Still, it gave him permission.

"I'm going with you."

The bill of her cap dipped as she gave a terse nod. Then she turned away and started down a much steeper drop into what appeared to be a ravine. Although it was hard to tell with the tops of so many tall trees blocking the view of the bottom.

She wasn't kidding about difficult terrain.

But he didn't care if he had to climb a mountain. There was no way he would leave Phoenix at that stage. However things ended, Phoenix Gray was going to be in the middle of it and on the winning team.

The whisper of his heart told him there was a different reason he didn't want to leave her. And that he might not want to part with her when all of this was over. That if he had to see her no more, that thing she had altered deep inside him—his heart, his soul, or perhaps the part of himself that no one before her had ever seen or understood—might shatter, leaving him to pick up the pieces for the rest of his days.

---

It was good Callum had stayed with her. Phoenix needed another credible witness for the events that were going to unfold.

She lifted her oar out of the river and switched her grip to plunge it back in on the other side of the canoe.

Her gaze settled momentarily on Callum's broad back as the man sat in front of her, his greater weight sinking the bow lower than the stern where she steered. But Dagian, sitting in the middle, helped to even out the weight distribution.

Phoenix hadn't objected when Callum got in her canoe, one of two they'd found on the rangers' locked rack alongside Crystal River.

He hadn't asked. Simply stepped into the canoe as soon as they'd put it in the water and made his way to the front seat. At least he hadn't presumed to take the steering position.

But she knew he hadn't been presuming anything. Which explained why her heart rate had surged slightly as he'd gotten into her canoe, choosing again to go with her. To be with her.

Her heart had behaved similarly when he'd said he would go with her. No, he'd said *"I am going with you."* As if it were a constant state, something he had been doing all along and intended to keep doing. As if being with her was something he wanted to always do.

It shouldn't please her. She should be concerned. Alarmed. She should shut down any such intentions and interest immediately.

But she hadn't. And her feelings didn't want her to.

She had never allowed emotions to dictate anything in her life. Never gave them control. She wasn't about to let them take over and lead her away from what was truly important. From the lifelong mission she was on the brink of accomplishing.

But Callum could stay in her boat for practical reasons. His added weight at the bow would help ensure stability for Dag as they navigated the rapids ahead.

She pulled her gaze from Callum and checked on Pinchert in the canoe that lagged behind them.

No wonder. She and Callum had immediately fallen into a smooth rhythm, paddling perfectly in sync with one another. Along with the fast-moving current, they reached a high speed that Pinchert wasn't able to match.

No matter. She wouldn't lose the agent completely.

But she wouldn't slow either. She would gain two hours taking that direct and speedy route and arrive at the ranger station in thirty minutes.

Marnie and her charges would not be there by then. The age of Marnie's trail before Phoenix had left it had shown, from the few visible tracks and breakage of leaves and grasses, that the searchers were gaining rapidly.

Marnie and the other children were tired. Exhausted. Their speed had slowed with their growing fatigue, and Marnie had let the girls stop for frequent rests of increasing duration, in addition to their two sleeps of six and three hours. She wouldn't have the heart to push the children if they were tired and crying.

Marnie hadn't lost her tenderness and compassion for the vulnerable, something Phoenix encouraged. Marnie needed those attributes to motivate her to risk her own safety and comfort for others. To do the hard, cold, ruthless things to those who deserved it when needed for the sake of the vulnerable.

The sound of an engine drew Phoenix's gaze to the sky. A small fire plane flew overhead, one of several that had passed over the nearer Phoenix drew to the fire area. The plane aimed for the smoke clouds that rose above the distant bluff and trees.

The fire, too, was targeting Juniper Lake. But with the wind still blowing north, the blaze should reach the south side of the lake, rather than the eastern side where the ranger station was located. Where Marnie was headed.

According to the weather predictions and radar Cora had

studied while at the campsite, there should be time before the storm front arrived and changed the wind direction. Time for Phoenix to do what she needed to at the ranger station and then backtrack to Marnie. But if Phoenix got held up, the PK-9 team would be her insurance.

Marnie only needed to hang on a bit longer. The rescue she was waiting for would soon appear.

# THIRTY-EIGHT

Callum's breaths came short and quick as he pushed his burning leg muscles to keep going. He had thought Phoenix was setting a fast pace before. But since they'd left the canoes at Crystal River, she'd been hiking at a speed and intensity that stopped just short of breaking into a run.

Did she think the children were at the ranger station, and she wanted to make sure they were all right?

No, that couldn't be it. She wouldn't have sent Tinney and the other two agents ahead if she had thought the girls would be at the station before Phoenix made it there herself.

But she clearly expected something else. Something she wanted to be there for.

Or someone.

The pieces fell into place, clicking together in Callum's mind as he scrambled up the steep hill behind Phoenix and Dag.

The someone was—

*Pop-pop-pop.*

Gunshots.

At the top of the hill?

"Phoenix." The voice came from Callum's right.

He spun toward it. Thick shrubs and underbrush met his gaze.

Then movement. Sofia and Raksa appeared in sharp relief against the plants behind them. Where had they come from?

"Don't bother." Sofia shot Mike a grin as she sauntered past him up the incline.

Mike released his grip on his holstered weapon and cut a glance at Callum with raised eyebrows.

Callum shook his head, just as puzzled as Mike was by her sudden disappearance and reappearance. But he wouldn't get answers from down there.

Callum hurried to climb the slope behind Sofia, catching up as the woman and her K-9 reached Phoenix.

Sofia gave him a suspicious look, then silently checked in with Phoenix.

Phoenix jerked a nod.

Callum's chest warmed much more than it should at her sign of approval and trust.

"They were shooting when I got here." Sofia kept her voice low. "He's returning fire."

"Who's returning fire?" Mike's question drifted past Callum's shoulder.

But Callum already knew the answer. It shouldn't have taken so long for the details to connect in his mind.

The Forster killer must have been within earshot when Phoenix had given instructions at the campsite, telling them Marnie was headed for the ranger station with the other girls.

And Phoenix had known that.

After they'd all left the campsite, the kidnapper could have easily grabbed the extra ATV, which Phoenix had no doubt intentionally left available for him. He could have then driven to the ranger station, hoping to either beat the FBI agents there or forcefully take the girls from them.

It was brilliant. A masterful plan, executed so effortlessly by Phoenix.

"The Forster killer is here?" Mike's question broke through Callum's rushing thoughts.

Sofia must have indicated the killer was there while Callum had been distracted, trying to catch up with Phoenix's mind. "They've put the shooting on hold a few times, but nobody's moved." Sofia looked at Phoenix, mirth curling her lips. "Pretty sure they're afraid they'll break a nail if they actually try to get the guy."

"You didn't help?" Mike's tone was more quizzical than accusatory, matching the tilt of his head as he studied Sofia as if she were a specimen of human he'd never seen before.

Sofia gave him a look that was half pity and half amusement.

Phoenix had probably instructed Sofia not to intervene. Why, Callum didn't know.

Unless...Did Phoenix want to eliminate the Forster killer in a shootout?

"The fire must've jumped, or there's another one." Sofia's dark eyes were on Phoenix again. "There's some headed our way now. Saw it from up top when I was watching for you."

"We should call that in." Mike reached for the button by his ear to report on coms.

"No." Phoenix's sharp command made Mike halt and jerked Callum's attention to her. "You would endanger the firefighters. We'll stop the shooting first."

So she did plan to stop the shootout.

Phoenix moved her gaze over the three of them, her lack of expression telling Callum nothing. "Stay close, keep quiet, have your weapons ready." She spun and continued up the hill.

Callum hurried to follow Sofia, who was directly behind Phoenix, and pulled his Glock from its holster.

He had a strong feeling the gunfire would only end with the shooting of the Forster killer. By Phoenix or someone else.

It would be perfectly legal, since the killer was firing at FBI agents attempting to arrest him. Even if Phoenix had orchestrated the situation, she was only doing what any good officer of the law would if they had her strategic brilliance.

Creating a situation where the criminal could be captured was always the goal. If it could be accomplished simply by allowing the criminal space to use his own folly and evil tendencies against himself, all the better.

Phoenix's rush to reach the ranger station in time meant she wanted to watch. To see her tormentor and her family's murderer finally be stopped.

Callum understood completely. And he couldn't help but appreciate that, if things went according to Phoenix's plan, there would be no chance this serial abuser and killer could go free. No chance he could hurt anyone ever again.

Phoenix was allowing Callum to be part of the capture or final end of the Forster killer. She was trusting him that much.

His pulse beat quicker with the thought as they crested the top of the hill and thick forest spread out in both directions before his eyes.

His gaze caught on Phoenix as she crouched slightly and darted from tree to tree.

Shots cracked the air, much closer than before.

Exactly as Phoenix wanted it. The woman who didn't trust anyone. Who kept more secrets than he'd probably guessed and could maneuver and manage people more effectively than he would have thought possible.

Doubt seeped into his torso like cooling water as another possibility took hold of his mind.

Phoenix might not trust him at all. She might not care if he witnessed the Forster killer's last stand.

She could be maneuvering Callum like another piece in her chess game. A game he had only begun to understand.

# THIRTY-NINE

Phoenix darted through the trees, Dag matching every step.

The gunshots grew louder as she approached the FBI agents from behind. She could see two up ahead, lying behind a fallen log, using it for cover as they fired.

No return fire answered.

She reached a tree ten feet from them and stopped, concealed by the wide trunk. She peered around it.

The ranger station—essentially a small cabin—stood 100 yards away up a gentle slope. According to maps and GPS, approximately two acres of thick forest resided behind the log cabin. A bluff lay beyond the trees, overlooking Juniper Lake from a height of 500 feet.

Movement caught her peripheral vision, and Phoenix swung her head left.

Sofia stopped by a tree parallel with Phoenix. She flipped up the back of her hand, holding three fingers in the air.

All three FBI men had been there when Sofia had last observed them.

The sound of leaves crunching signaled Pinchert and Callum coming near. Pinchert dropped low as he passed Phoenix to join the other FBI agents, lying on his belly by the log.

Callum stopped and stood behind a tree to Phoenix's right. A revealing choice. One she shouldn't dwell on at the moment, especially since the action alone already activated the ache only he seemed able to conjure.

No. She had one aim. She would defeat the monster. She would have justice.

The flame within surged hotter, easily obliterating the ache, the longing that could never be eased.

Silence filled the air as the agents lowered their weapons and looked over their shoulders, alerted to Phoenix's presence by Pinchert appearing beside them.

If she had been the monster, choosing to ambush them from the rear, they wouldn't be looking at anything anymore.

"What happened? Was he already inside?" Pinchert's lowered voice still easily reached Phoenix.

Tinney pulled away from the log and shifted his upper body toward Phoenix, watching her as he responded. "No, we'd entered the ranger station and were inside when this guy ambushed us. The kidnapper, I guess. One of our guys got nicked. He's resting out of firing range."

An obvious fabrication. Tinney didn't look or tilt his head in any direction indicating where the other agent was, as most people would. The agent wasn't injured or hiding nearby.

"Were the kids inside the station?"

"No." Tinney glanced at Pinchert. "I think the kidnapper must have gotten there just before we did, and he hid the hostages out back. Then tried to take us out." Tinney's gaze went to Phoenix again. "That was his mistake. We opened fire, and we've had him trapped in there ever since."

Another lie. The monster had opened fire on them, pinning the agents down so they couldn't easily flee after they'd realized the children weren't there. The unexpected situation had prompted a new idea in their devious minds. They could use the opportunity to apply greater pressure that would accelerate the search for Marnie.

Phoenix's suspicions about the so-called agents were confirmed.

At least they deserved what would come to them. They had underestimated the monster.

She knew him, what he was capable of. What he would do.

Orange flickered at the rear of the cabin. Flames starting to climb the sides of the structure.

"There's fire back there." Alarm raised the volume of Pinchert's observation.

"That couldn't have jumped from the main fire. It's too far." Callum watched Phoenix.

She met his gaze. He was right. But a new fire could have been set by the missing third agent.

Would Callum figure it out? No legitimate agent would set a fire under those circumstances, even to force a suspect out in a standoff. The risk of a damaging wildfire was too high.

A pop burst the silence. Then another.

He was shooting from the cabin. Back in place. Ready for her.

The men by the log hunkered down and returned fire.

She felt Callum moving closer to her before she saw him.

He squatted next to Dag, low enough to avoid most bullets. Callum looked up at her. "Go around?"

Brave man. The flying bullets clearly didn't frighten him. And he didn't want to sit there any longer, doing nothing. A man of action, but not trying to usurp her authority over the operation.

A blend of respect and appreciation flowed through her. She hadn't thought a man like Callum Ross existed.

But it didn't change anything. It couldn't.

She gave him a nod. She swung toward Sofia and communicated through hand signals that she should approach from the west while Phoenix and Callum came from the east.

Sofia gave a thumbs up and took off without a sound. She might arrive at the ranger station before Phoenix.

But that wouldn't matter. As long as he had executed the predicted plan to make a clean getaway.

"Hold your position while we surround him." She gave the order to the other men, then sent Callum a glance as she brushed past him.

She picked up speed, Dag staying close as they darted through the trees to the east side of the hill where the incline sloped downward. Dropping below the cabin's elevation would help ensure they wouldn't be seen. Or shot.

Although there were no guarantees one of the crooked FBI agents wouldn't try to take them out. Callum was a more likely target for them, since they likely realized they may need Phoenix to complete their mission. But they might think eliminating Callum could make their job easier.

She hoped they wouldn't make the same calculated decision about Pinchert and take him out while he was alone with them. She wouldn't have left him if she thought it likely.

They wouldn't want to compromise their cover yet. Though they could claim the kidnapper's bullet from the ranger station had killed Pinchert. Hopefully, the agent knew how to handle himself if they decided to take that risk.

More shots cracked the air.

Good. The monster was still in the cabin.

Her inner fire blazed through her torso, coursing through her veins.

But heat also emanated from another source, blowing against her face. The fire from the cabin.

She crested the hill, angling toward the ranger station.

Bright flames consumed the tops of trees behind the cabin and clawed along the logs of the structure.

Perfect timing.

# FORTY

Callum stayed close to Phoenix, matching her quick pace and low crouch as they veered through trees toward the east side of the ranger station.

They reached the wall, both of them pressing their backs against the logs as Callum lifted his Glock in a ready position by his chest.

Phoenix turned her head toward him, her face close.

Their gazes locked.

He'd give anything to be able to read her expression. See some emotion in her eyes.

But she had let him come along. That had to mean something.

She faced forward again and quickly moved along the cabin, staying low with Dag at her side away from the wall.

Callum stuck with her, his eyes locking on the windowsill just ahead. Could be a way to get a peek inside. Or a way to get his head blown off.

Phoenix and Dag slipped under the window without looking in. Maybe she would check from the other side.

But Callum could get a look now from his angle if he

stretched his neck a little. He paused and peered through the bottom corner of the window.

Dark. The interior was too dim to see anything.

He glanced at Phoenix.

She kept going, headed for the side door a few feet beyond the—

A flicker of something caught the corner of Callum's eye. He jerked toward the window.

Someone stood by the glass, aiming a gun. At Phoenix.

Callum's heart stopped. He lifted his Glock, squeezed the trigger.

The loud blast reverberated in his ears.

Phoenix spun toward him, squatting.

The figure was gone.

Callum dropped low in case he was wrong.

Phoenix stared at him, no shock or question in her gaze.

"He was going to shoot you." The whisper came as raggedly as Callum's breathing. His heart still constricted at the thought of the scene he'd almost witnessed.

Phoenix. Shot.

She watched him a second longer, still no reaction.

Callum moistened his lips. "I think I got him."

She jerked a nod. "Let's go." She whipped around and darted to the door. Staying crouched, she reached for the knob above her head.

The door opened. She swung it in.

She would probably move to the side next, clearing the angles before entering.

She somersaulted through the doorway, and Dag dashed in after her.

Callum blinked. Of course. This was Phoenix.

He hurried after her more blindly than he should.

She stood in a wide stance with her Glock aimed at...

A man on the floor. A body?

A slam yanked Callum's gaze to the opposite side of the small cabin.

The door smacked into the wall as Raksa and Sofia burst through the doorway, her gun raised. Until she saw Phoenix and Callum.

She lowered her weapon, looking down at the man. "Heard the shot. One of you get him?"

Callum moved closer to the fallen man, the oppressive heat of the cabin making the air thick and heavy.

Black jeans, brown puffer jacket, black beanie that probably covered a shaved head. Everything Callum could see matched the description the recovered children had given.

He was the kidnapper.

Callum squatted beside him, wanting to see the man. The face no one had been able to identify, to link to the Forster killer, for twenty-six years.

He grabbed the killer's shoulder and tilted him back slightly.

The face was bloodied beyond recognition.

Callum grimaced at the sight. Had he done that? He'd aimed for the shooter's chest through the window.

He reached for the man's neck but halted when he saw the blood coating it. Callum grabbed the wrist instead, checking for a pulse to make the obvious conclusion official.

No pulse.

Callum glanced up at Sofia and Phoenix. "He's dead."

Callum released the wrist and sat back on his haunches as his gaze dropped down to the body. He never wanted to kill a human being, no matter how evil the person was. He'd only had to shoot three criminals during his career, to save other lives. Two had died from the injuries.

This was the first time remorse didn't fill Callum or make him question if he could have handled the situation differently.

The Forster killer, the most horrifically evil serial killer Callum had ever pursued, would never hurt anyone again.

Would Phoenix—

"Hey, we've gotta move." Sofia's remark drew his attention to where she stared.

Flames climbed up the inside of the rear wall of the cabin.

Not just the rear. The fire was suddenly consuming the front wall and trailing in from both open doors, eating its way up the sides. The wooden structure was burning fast.

"Go." Phoenix aimed the order at Sofia, who sprinted for the door Callum and Phoenix had used.

The flames weren't as high there as at the other doorway, so she and Raksa leaped over them.

"We should bring the body." Callum stood and glanced down at the Forster killer.

"We should go. Now." Phoenix didn't budge, though her gaze locked on the doorway where the flames grew higher.

She wouldn't leave until he did.

He clenched his jaw. He wouldn't let her or Dag be hurt for his desire to dot all the *i*'s. There were enough witnesses to confirm the Forster killer was dead.

He dashed for the door and jumped through. He spun around as soon as he landed near Sofia, his heart constricting as he waited to see Phoenix emerge.

Seconds passed.

Why was she taking so long?

He stepped toward the cabin.

Sofia gripped his arm. "Wait."

A tan blur flew over the flames in the doorway, landing outside. Dag. He would never leave Phoenix.

She burst through the growing flames and somersaulted into the landing, getting to her feet in one smooth motion.

"Call the firefighters." Her gaze met Callum's as she gave the order in a tone as even and apathetic as ever.

Never mind that the sight of her had jumpstarted Callum's heart at a rate that he was sure exceeded healthy limits. He reached to his earpiece to activate coms and call in the fire, but his eyes didn't stray from Phoenix.

At that moment, to his rapidly beating heart, she was the most beautiful thing he'd ever seen. And he never wanted to look away.

Never wanted to risk losing her again.

"Dag, now." The K-9 whirled away from the ranger station and darted through the trees, down the hill.

Phoenix sprinted after him, her feet flying, fueled by a different kind of urgency surging through her body.

The storm front was moving in, bringing a stronger wind out of the west.

She'd felt the directional change as soon as she'd left the cabin.

The wind would push the larger fire and the new blaze east. Rapidly.

Directly at Marnie.

The trajectory of Marnie's scent trail had begun to shift from northeast to hard east before Phoenix had cut across the challenging terrain to reach the ranger station as directly as possible. That route wasn't an option for Marnie with her young charges.

She would have been forced to turn sharply east and continue until the northern land became easier to hike. Only then could she have curved northwest and backtracked to the ranger station.

She would be approaching the ranger station from the southeast now. And she should be close. Within a ten- or fifteen-minute run for Phoenix and Dag over the rough terrain.

Phoenix could hear Sofia, Raksa, and Callum tearing through the woods after her.

The FBI agents would have seen her leave. They would come, as well.

Phoenix grabbed her satphone from behind her back as she kept up her running pace, eyes on Dag's fast-moving body, charging through the trees.

He knew the scent to find. The wind direction wasn't in their favor, but his unmatched instincts were. If Marnie was anywhere in the area, he would find her.

Phoenix punched the button for Cora's saved number and

put the phone to her ear. A trick as her whole body bounced with the impact of running on the uneven terrain.

"Phoenix?"

"Progress."

"Flash is still tracking the scent trail." A note of discouragement colored Cora's tone. "Jana doesn't seem to have located any air scent yet."

"Pick up the pace. As fast as Flash can follow the trail without losing it. A new wildfire is closer, coming at you and Marnie from the west."

Cora sucked in a sharp breath. "I'll pray."

Better to simply follow Phoenix's instructions. But she knew Cora would do both.

Phoenix lowered the phone and kept it in her hand as she ran. In case Cora and Jazz found Marnie first.

The crunching of branches and leaves drew her to check her peripheral vision.

Callum came up beside her, matching her speed. Silent, except for his measured breathing.

No questions. No challenge. Only…trust.

Her pulse sped to an unnatural pace for her running heart rate.

She'd never asked him to trust her. Never did anything to suggest he should or intentionally lead him to do so.

He should be more careful. Though given the relieved expression she'd caught on his face over the death at the cabin, perhaps he would agree she'd done the right thing in the end.

After all, he wanted the same thing she did. It was part of his life's ambition, his purpose, even if he didn't put it in the same terms.

He might be the only person alive who would understand.

That shouldn't matter to her. But the ache in her torso indicated that it did.

She clenched her jaw and pushed herself faster.

No. He wouldn't stop her. Nothing would.

She halted the mental battle and focused on Dag, the wind's

unchanging direction at their backs, the steep and rough terrain that, after six minutes of running, began to even out.

They were nearing the flatter land, the route Marnie would have taken with the exhausted girls.

In four more minutes of running, the ground grew smoother still, though still thick with trees and fallen leaves.

Dag sprinted out of sight. He'd found something.

Phoenix kicked up her speed, ignoring her tiring muscles and the challenge of getting enough air.

A bark. The sound of victory, carrying on the wind.

Squeals. Laughter.

Children.

Phoenix's heart soared, surging an abundance of air to her lungs. Triumph swelled inside her, almost painful as it pressed against her ribs. Tears would come if she'd let them, but she had programmed such outward signs of emotion out of herself years ago.

Even now, no one would see. No one would be able to exploit her affection for a child. She would not be vulnerable.

It was enough for Phoenix to know her love for Marnie had led her there. To Marnie and the others.

As Phoenix swerved around a thick cluster of trees, the children came into view.

Marnie hung on Dag's neck, her arms wrapped around him and squeezing like her mother had told her not to do.

The other girls surrounded the K-9, digging their fingers into his fur.

Dagian bore the treatment like the hero he was. He knew what the girls needed.

Marnie looked up at the searchers' arrival. Her gaze locked on Phoenix, and she let go of Dag.

The girl walked toward Phoenix slowly, calmly. She knew what Phoenix had taught her to do. Never betray vulnerability. And she knew Phoenix didn't like or welcome physical affection now that Marnie was older.

But as the girl neared, the moisture welling in her eyes and the way her lip caught in her teeth gave her away. She longed to be held.

Phoenix took a step forward and extended her arms.

Marnie flew into them, hitting Phoenix hard as she wrapped her small arms around Phoenix's waist.

Phoenix embraced the strong girl, pride and love surging through her.

Marnie was young. Too young to have to live without affection, support, and love.

Phoenix offered what she could.

"You came." Marnie's voice was muffled against Phoenix's jacket. Then she lifted her head, barely loosening her hold as she looked up with a small, watery smile. "You rescued us. I told them you would."

A lump ballooned in Phoenix's throat. A rare feeling. "Well done." She gently stroked Marnie's black hair with her hand, and the girl pressed her cheek against Phoenix again.

"I'm sorry, Phoenix." The words were quiet, but Phoenix could decipher them.

She wouldn't automatically tell Marnie she had nothing to be sorry for. Condescension never helped children learn or grow.

"I couldn't do it." Marnie released her hold and stepped back, her gaze aimed at the ground. "I knew if I held my choke longer, the bad man would die. And then he couldn't hurt us anymore."

Her dark brown eyes flitted up to Phoenix's face, then away. "But I just..." Marnie's small shoulders lifted, "couldn't do it."

Understanding and compassion squeezed Phoenix's ribs, though she didn't let either show in her eyes or expression.

Marnie was too young for the weight of such a decision—life or death for a brutal murderer. She would choose differently when she was older, if the opportunity arose then.

"You rescued the other children and yourself."

Marnie lifted her head, blinking up at Phoenix.

"Many of those he sent away are safe and well because of the advice you gave them. They were all found, alive. You did all you needed to do."

A beaming smile stretched Marnie's small mouth. "I did another thing, too."

Phoenix waited, her love for the girl making her content to rest her gaze on Marnie for a few more precious moments. That would bolster them both for the next threat.

"I faced him. The monster in my dream."

Phoenix's attention sharpened, her senses shifting into high alert. "You saw him?"

"Uh-huh. I looked right at him, and he went away. Just like you said."

"Could you recognize him if you saw him again?"

Marnie wrinkled her nose. "Sure. I won't forget. I'm not scared anymore."

"We need to go now." Phoenix scanned the surroundings.

Sofia and Raksa watched over the other girls twenty feet away as Dag made his way to Phoenix, likely relieved to be done with therapy duty.

Callum stood at a distance among the trees, his gaze on Phoenix and Marnie.

Where were the others? It was taking them longer to catch up than—

Dag growled, low and quiet as he reached Phoenix's side.

They'd arrived.

"Hey, you must be Marnie." Tinney's voice preceded his emergence around the thicker stand of trees, his remaining sidekick following close behind. "I'm FBI Special Agent Tinney, and your dad asked me to bring you to him right away." He donned a large smile. "He is so excited to see you, kiddo."

Phoenix put her hand on Dag to silence him, every instinct in her mirroring the K-9's. To protect Marnie. But this was the only way to expose and eliminate the threat.

Marnie glanced at Phoenix.

Phoenix kept her features immovable. Gave no indication Marnie shouldn't go. No cue at all.

Tinney took a step toward the girl, his hand outstretched as he smiled. "I've got an ATV, so I can drive you to your dad right away."

Marnie headed for the agent.

Phoenix waited until the girl was close enough. "Marnie."

She turned back, but Tinney grabbed her from behind.

And held a gun to her head.

# FORTY-ONE

Adrenaline pumped through Callum's veins as his pulse pounded in his ears.

Phoenix was more than capable of disarming Tinney herself. But when he was pressing the barrel of a gun into Marnie's temple? The risk was too great.

Phoenix must be thinking the same thing. She didn't move. Just stared at Tinney as he started to back away. She'd said something initially to Dag that Callum couldn't hear.

The K-9 held his position, too, his teeth barred as he rumbled a low growl.

"Don't you or your K-9 move, or she's dead." Tinney continued backing up, holding Marnie tight against him while he kept his Glock aimed at her head.

Movement in Callum's peripheral caught his attention.

Sofia and Raksa, about ten yards away from Callum by the other girls, slipped into the trees. Probably planning to go around to take Tinney as he left.

Looked like his intention was to return the way he had come, then use the ATV he'd left by the ranger station. Though the fire would have traveled this direction in the meantime. Maybe Tinney had driven his ATV part of the way there.

He likely wouldn't shoot Marnie. Not unless he felt forced to. He must want to kidnap her for some reason. Probably related to the danger Marnie was in that Eli and Phoenix had discussed so secretly. Questions swirled in Callum's mind, but he shoved them aside.

*Get Marnie safely away first. Grab Tinney and the other agent.* Then he could press Phoenix for answers.

Tinney hadn't looked in Callum's direction once since he'd walked on the scene. He'd seemed to only notice Phoenix and Marnie.

Callum was about eight feet away from Phoenix, tucked in the trees to the far right of Tinney's line of sight. He should be able to get around Tinney and Franks pretty quickly. Sooner than Sofia since she'd had to start from a greater distance.

As quietly as he could, Callum turned to his left and picked his way through the brush. He kept a thick layer of trees between him and the obviously crooked FBI agents.

Wait a second. Where was the third one? Jenson.

Was he lurking somewhere in the trees so the two visible agents would have surprise backup if needed? Or maybe his gunshot wound Tinney had mentioned had ended up being fatal. If Tinney had told the truth about that at all.

Getting closer.

Callum glimpsed Franks through the trees, the agent's back turned.

Callum slowed, taking each step carefully, trying not to make a sound.

Only a few more feet.

Tinney was still in front of Franks, both of them walking backwards as Tinney dragged Marnie.

Callum froze. He couldn't make a move for Franks without risking that Tinney would shoot Marnie. He'd have to wait. Let Franks pass by, then jump on Tinney from behind and disarm him. Hopefully before Franks could interfere.

Right. No problem at all. Callum took in a slow breath to ease the tension in his muscles.

Phoenix shifted into view. Ostensibly moving sideways to keep watching Tinney, but from the downward tilt of her cap, her gaze must be on Marnie.

Franks passed Callum, gradually moving backward.

Now.

Callum started out of hiding, but Tinney suddenly leaned forward.

Marnie's small leg appeared behind Tinney, and before Callum could blink, the big man landed on the ground.

Callum spun toward Franks on his left.

Just as the agent raised his gun.

Callum darted around the weapon and seized Franks' arm, twisting in a move that forced him to drop the gun and fall to his knees to lessen the pain.

Callum checked on Marnie. Although Phoenix would have helped her finish off Tinney.

He nearly did a doubletake at the sight in front of him. Apparently, Marnie didn't need anyone's help.

She lay on the ground by her would-be kidnapper, locking his arm in a dislocating position as she ordered him to drop his weapon.

Tinney resisted for a second. Then the Glock fell from his hand.

Marnie grabbed the weapon and aimed it at Tinney's neck as she scooted away.

Wow. Astonishment, akin to the wonder Callum had only felt when watching Phoenix in action, made him stare at the girl. But would Marnie be further traumatized by needing to defend herself? By nearly being kidnapped again? She hadn't had time to recover from the first—

"Zip ties anyone?" Sofia's voice jerked Callum's attention to the trees beyond Franks. Exactly where he and Tinney would have encountered the PK-9 agent, apparently, if they'd walked any farther.

She sauntered forward with Raksa panting at her side. "Nice

work there." She threw Callum a grin as she held up a black zip tie. "Want me to do the honors?"

Callum smiled and dropped the guy's arm. "Be my guest."

"Hands behind your back, pal. One wrong move, and my K-9 will eat you for lunch." Sofia's tone didn't lose much of the humor as she zip-tied the man's wrists. "Or I'll handle you myself, and you can decide which is worse."

Since she obviously had things under control, Callum turned away to check on Marnie.

The girl stood on the other side of Tinney as the man sat up.

Was he holding his arm against his torso? Hard to tell from behind.

In front of him, Phoenix stood with Marnie, gripping the Glock the girl had taken from Tinney.

Callum walked closer but stayed by Tinney in case he tried anything.

"Did you see what I did?" Marnie smiled up at Phoenix, her voice pulsing with excitement. "I got to use the armlock and everything." Marnie clasped her hands together in front of her, clearly over the moon. Apparently not traumatized at all.

"Well done." Phoenix didn't smile at the girl or reveal any emotion.

But Marnie bounced on her toes, beaming all the more at the two words of praise.

Callum shook his head. How did Phoenix do it? She'd taught the child to be much like her—a skilled, fearless warrior beyond most human's abilities. But freer and happier.

What would it take for Phoenix to be free and happy, too? Could she learn to show her feelings, to love and let someone love her, now that her family's murderer was dead?

It was over. The Forster killer was gone.

But would the torment he had inflicted on Phoenix's soul ever end?

"Send the helicopter to Ridge Point. We'll be there in ten minutes. PT1, out." Phoenix finished reporting the recovery of the children on coms just as Jazz, Cora, Kent, and their K-9s emerged from the trees by the rescued girls.

The children jumped up from sitting on the ground at the sight of the golden retriever and Belgian Malinois and rushed toward the dogs with smiles and laughter.

"It's Flash! Is that Jana?" Marnie's voice was still laced with the energy buzz from defeating Tinney on her own. "I've never seen her before. Can I go say 'hi'?" She glanced up at Phoenix, her smile chasing away the weariness that had shadowed her young face before.

Warmth ballooned behind Phoenix's ribs as she looked down at the special girl. "In a moment. Are either of these men the one from your nightmares?" Phoenix suspected the answer. Marnie would have already said if one had been him. But it was possible the girl could have missed a similarity because she hadn't been looking closely, or the years had altered the man's appearance.

Marnie shook her head, her nose wrinkling. "No."

"Are you certain? He could have changed since you saw him. His hair could be different. Or the beard could hide his features."

Marnie shook her head again. "No, this bad guy has blue eyes." She pointed at Tinney where they'd left him sitting on the ground, hands bound with a zip tie behind him. "The monster in my dreams has brown eyes. And he's really mean."

Apparently Tinney's meanness as an abductor and would-be killer couldn't compare. But it was logical. Marnie had seen the man in her nightmares murder her mother. He would be the meanest, most monstrous of all men in her mind.

"Go see the dogs now."

Marnie threw Phoenix a grin, then dashed off to greet Jana and Flash with the other girls. One would never think she'd spent days hiking the wilderness, trying to escape and evade a murderous kidnapper.

The most monstrous of men.

Rage surged through Phoenix's torso. Almost time.

"I'm sure you know. The fire is getting closer." Callum's voice shouldn't have startled her.

She'd known he was standing nearby, observing her and Marnie. Perhaps it was what he said. *The fire is getting closer.* As if he knew the intensity, the anticipation burning inside her.

She turned toward him, muscles tightening.

His greenish brown eyes were soft, thoughtful. Not sharp or wary.

The tension eased. He didn't know.

"How are we going to get the children to Ridge Point in ten minutes without running them into the ground? They're exhausted."

"Tinney's ATVs."

"His..." Understanding lit Callum's eyes. "So he did drive part of the way here."

"With the trailer."

A small smile lifted the corners of Callum's closed mouth. "You're incredible."

The words chinked her armor more than they should have. She didn't seek admiration. Never cared if she received accolades or hatred. The fact the praise came from Callum Ross should not trigger any reaction from her, emotionally or otherwise.

But he didn't act surprised he'd said what he did. He didn't blush or glance away. Didn't apologize or excuse the compliment.

He simply held her gaze, flickers of wonder and admiration sparking in his eyes.

His steadiness, his sincerity, seeped farther into the cracks of her armor, making her heart pound.

He had feelings for her. After she'd tried to push him away, ignored his questions, refused to tell him what he wanted to know. After she'd been intimidating, unapologetic, cold.

She hadn't treated the children with the tenderness he

showed them. She was an emotionless, expressionless void. A woman who clearly could offer him nothing.

Yet...His eyes said it didn't matter. Because he saw past the armor. Past the mask.

He saw inside her. Understood her.

Like no one ever had. And no one else ever would.

He understood too much.

She yanked her gaze away and marched toward her PK-9 team. It was time to leave.

# FORTY-TWO

Callum leaned toward the window of the rescue helicopter as it began its descent.

The parking lot at Timber Park's entrance was still lined with reporters and cameramen outside a temporary chain-link partition.

But other people crowded near the chopper as it lowered to the ground. Agents in FBI jackets and uniformed police officers pressed them back.

The civilians held out their hands in gestures that looked more like desperate reaches than waves of greeting.

"Mommy! I see Mommy!" The blond-haired, blue-eyed girl who sat on Callum's right leg pressed her face against the glass.

A lump clogged Callum's throat.

Phoenix, sitting in front by the pilot, had called ahead to inform Agent Nguyen that the children were in good enough shape to be greeted by their parents immediately upon their arrival. The kids would be checked out by medical personnel right after the greeting.

Callum wasn't sure if it was compassion or logistical wisdom that had led Phoenix to give the instruction. But looking out at the strained, desperately hopeful faces of the parents, he was grateful she had.

"I see my mommy, too!" The redheaded little girl who sat on Callum's left leg squished her friend to peer out the window.

The other girls made similar exclamations as they clamored to see out the windows.

Good thing the Phoenix K-9 Agency team members were bringing the rogue FBI agents back on foot and then by car, once they connected with the nearest service road where legitimate agents would pick them up. There never would have been room for all those adults and dogs, even in such a large helicopter.

Callum wouldn't have wanted the crooked agents anywhere near the girls in any event. He still didn't fully understand why Tinney had tried to take Marnie. But from what Phoenix had let him overhear when she'd spoken with Marnie, someone else had sent Tinney and the other men. He hoped Phoenix knew who the other person was, so she could end the threat against Marnie. He'd have to ask Phoenix about it as soon as he could.

But first, he had the privilege of reuniting some families.

The helicopter touched down between the parents and a smaller, blue helicopter Callum glimpsed through the far windows.

He stood, setting down the two girls just in time to face the mob of children who rushed toward him. He intentionally blocked the door behind him and held up his hands. "Okay, everyone ready to see your moms and dads?"

"Yes!" Their unified shout nearly burst his ear drums.

He smiled. "All right. We just need to wait until the pilot says it's safe. Then I'll open the door, and there will be a person there to lift you down. What are we *not* going to do?"

"We won't jump out."

He nodded, his smile growing as they echoed the instruction he had repeated several times on their short flight to Base.

"Exactly right. No jumping out, even if you see your mom or dad. Wait to be lifted down and then *only* leave the helicopter if you see your mom or dad. When do you leave me by the helicopter?"

"When we see mom and dad." Their response was more staggered than unified that time, but they seemed to get the message.

"Right." Callum looked toward the front of the copter, his gaze immediately going to Phoenix, though he could only see the outline of her headset beyond the seat's headrest. He had a better view of the pilot, who looked over his shoulder and gave a thumbs-up.

"All right." Callum grinned at the kids. "It's showtime." He pulled open the door, ready to stop the girls from jumping if they lost all self-control in their excitement.

Shouts of joy hit Callum like a wave of sound. Parents called their kids' names, straining against the officers who held them back to avoid a stampede.

"Mommy! My mommy's there!" A tiny brunette shouted next to Callum.

He handed her to one of the two FBI agents that came to help, and he watched as she ran to her mom and a man he assumed was her father. The joy on their faces echoed in Callum, swelling like a balloon in his chest.

The two FBI agents and Callum made quick work of lifting the other children down, letting them go to their parents in a fairly organized fashion.

"Daddy!"

Marnie's shout grabbed Callum's attention just as Eli appeared at the helicopter.

He reached for Marnie himself, lifting her and holding her close instead of setting her down.

She wrapped her arms around his neck and her legs around his waist. Had to hurt, given she was probably rubbing right over his gunshot wound, now hidden under his sweater.

But Eli's smile and closed eyes as he held his daughter close said he didn't care. Said he loved that girl more than life itself. And he never wanted to let her go.

"Marnie." A tear glistened on Eli's cheek, tracking into his beard as he said her name like a tender endearment. "I've got you, baby girl. I love you."

"I love you, too, Daddy."

Moisture filled Callum's eyes as he watched the reunion. *Thank you, Father.*

This job didn't get any better than moments like that. Few and far between. But so precious when they happened, when a child was returned home to loved ones, safe at last. And Marnie, despite everything she'd been through, was somehow more unscathed and unharmed than the majority of children Callum had rescued.

Phoenix must be feeling so proud of what she'd accomplished. Was she seeing the reunion?

He looked toward the front seats of the helicopter.

Both were empty. The pilot and Phoenix must have gotten out to watch the kids' return. Or maybe to check in at the base.

Callum hopped down, Eli and Marnie too busy hugging and talking to notice. He glanced around.

Parents and children laughed and cried together, some walking to the visitor center where the kids would get medical checks and probably be interviewed by Nguyen and other agents.

His gaze caught on the blond-haired, blue-eyed girl whose name was Anna, he'd learned on the flight to Base. Looked like her mother was Mrs. Kelly. The tall woman held her daughter's hand as they turned to go to the visitor center with an FBI agent.

*Thank you, Father, for sparing that child and her family.*

The Forster killer hadn't been able to enact his horrific plans on them. And he would never harm anyone again.

If only all the cases could have such happy endings.

But they didn't. Even when Callum apprehended the evildoers, they were released to harm innocent children again, far too often.

This was a rare victory. Assurance the abuser and killer couldn't strike again because he was dead.

But the next one would probably be like so many of the others—another reminder that Callum wasn't making a difference. That he wasn't able to protect children and permanently keep the criminals off the streets like he had set out to do.

Did Phoenix feel better now that her family's murderer was dead? Or did she feel it wasn't enough, the accidental way it happened? Callum wouldn't blame her if she'd wanted to see the Forster killer suffer, see him go to prison, get to speak at his trial and help to lock him away forever or sentence him to a final, deadly penalty for his crimes.

If Callum could locate her, he could try to find out what she was feeling. Though that would be a tall order to say the least.

A smile curved his lips at the thought as he walked around the nose of the helicopter to look for Phoenix at the front of the parking lot.

No sign of her.

Maybe she'd gone inside the base already. That would make sense, given how much she seemed to dislike emotional displays.

He headed for the visitor center, passing people going back and forth, all with lighter expressions on their faces, even smiles and laughter. The happy ending was marvelous for everyone involved.

As he stepped inside the base, he had to dodge a parent and child and at least two officers going outside. He had thought the place was busy and packed before.

It was even more congested and noisy now, though filled with joyous sounds that were like music to his ears.

He squeezed and excused his way to the office at the rear of the building. He knocked on the closed door and waited for an answer from within.

Impossible to hear anything with all the noise of the main open room. He knocked again and pushed the door inward, poking his head through the opening.

Agent Nguyen looked up from behind her desk, halting whatever she'd been saying to the couple that sat on the front side of the desk, the man holding one of the rescued girls.

"Agent Ross." Nguyen waved him in, her voice carrying a note of pleasure he'd never heard from her before, though she didn't actually smile. She got to her feet, her fingertips braced on the edge of the desk as she looked at the parents. "This is the FBI agent who helped rescue your daughter."

The parents both stood and hurried toward him with Molly, the redheaded girl he'd held in the rescue chopper, walking between them, her hand in her mother's.

"We're so very grateful." The girl's dad extended his hand. "Thank you."

Callum returned the handshake. "I'm thanking the Lord for the return of your daughter. I was only a very small part of this rescue. Phoenix Gray and her team are the reason your daughter and the other children are safe now."

The man released Callum's hand and turned toward Nguyen. "I keep hearing about this Phoenix Gray. Where is she? We would love to thank her."

Callum stepped toward Nguyen's desk. "I was going to ask the same thing. Have you seen her?"

"I thought she rode on the chopper with you and the girls."

Callum lowered his voice as he tried to be heard only by Nguyen. "She did. But I haven't seen her since we landed."

Nguyen shrugged. "That's Phoenix. She probably took off to avoid the press."

Callum's heart sank. Would she really have done that? Without a goodbye or…

He halted his ridiculous thoughts right there. This was Phoenix. Of course she wouldn't have stayed for a touching goodbye. What did he expect? It wasn't like they had a friendship or a…romance…or anything at all between them.

"Nice to meet you both." Callum dug up a smile for the family. "And your daughter." He left the room as quickly as he could and threaded his way through the people to exit the building. He pushed through the door hard. Where could she—

"Whoa, there." Eli's voice alerted Callum that he was about to crash into the man who'd apparently been trying to enter the base with Marnie. Eli released his hold on Marnie's hand to extend his big paw to Callum. "'Thanks' doesn't begin to cover it."

Callum took the offered hand. Then suddenly found himself yanked into a back-slapping hug.

As Eli pulled away, he gripped Callum's upper arm. "I owe you, brother."

Callum shook his head. "No. It was all God."

Eli nodded. "Amen to that."

"And, as I keep having to tell everyone, I was just along for the ride. You know that better than most. This was all God sending Phoenix to the rescue."

"Yeah, where is she? Marnie wanted to see her before we head home." Eli glanced down at the girl who slipped her hand into her dad's again and leaned into his side. "And I'd like to talk to her. She already saved my wife. Now I've gotta thank her for saving my daughter, too."

"I wish I knew." Callum glanced past Eli toward the red rescue helicopter they'd arrived in. "She must have gotten out of the chopper when I was helping with the kids, and I—"

Something was missing.

"Cal? You all right?"

Callum barely heard Eli's question. "There was a small, blue helicopter by us when we landed. I can't see it now."

"Maybe it's just hidden on the other side of the rescue copter."

"Maybe." The alarm bells sounding in Callum's mind pushed him to start in that direction. But a thought made him pause and turn back. "Eli, can Phoenix fly helicopters?"

Eli shrugged. "She flies her own private plane. Wouldn't surprise me if she flew copters, too."

"Thanks." Callum spun away and hurried toward the large red helicopter. He jogged around the nose.

A patch of empty gravel met his searching gaze.

The blue helicopter was gone.

## FORTY-THREE

The fire raged.

Phoenix stood at the edge of the bluff, looking down on the forest below.

Orange and red flames ravaged the trees, on a devouring path to Juniper Lake.

The fire to the east of the lake had diminished to residual smoke and blackened ash. Firefighters had been able to reach the blaze by the ranger station quickly enough to stop it.

But nothing would stop the fire that burned within Phoenix.

A few more minutes.

Then he would come.

She'd called Cora on the way there in the helicopter Roy Davis had dropped off for her that morning when she had let him know she needed it. Once Phoenix had Cora and the other team members' location, near the service road where they would meet the FBI transport vehicles, Phoenix knew where to land.

All she had to do was fall in behind the team, far enough away they wouldn't notice, but close enough to be nearer than the monster.

He was following them, his final hope to lead him to

Phoenix. He'd lost his target child. He would not want to lose his Phaistos Disc, too.

Dag and Phoenix had soon heard him trailing behind the team, as expected. Once she was sure he had seen her, she'd drifted away from the PK-9 team's path.

She led him back toward her helicopter. Time was of the essence.

But she wouldn't rush either. She'd waited far too long for this.

*Snap.*

The twig he stepped on gave him away as he moved toward her through the trees.

She breathed. Even, slow. Relaxed.

She'd practiced this moment in her nightmares. So many times.

The smell of his breath drifted to her on the wind.

A shudder started to ripple down her spine. She halted the response. Countered it with unwavering resolve.

It was his turn to fear.

She felt the heat from his body, inches away.

She leaned toward the drop-off, as if trying to see something.

His arm snaked around her neck.

She sprang into action, stepped behind his legs, lifted. Threw him to the ground hard as she spun.

She faced the monster.

Smaller than she remembered. Older. Just as repulsive.

He groaned and grabbed the back of his head, trying to sit up.

"Now."

At her command, Dag flew out from his hidden position in the trees where she'd told him to wait. He sprinted for the monster, who tried to get to his feet.

Dag knocked him to the ground and sank his teeth into the creature's arm. Dagian didn't take kindly to sitting by while someone attacked Phoenix.

The monster screamed. Tried to pull free from Dag's hold.

Phoenix watched. She could finish him. Right there.

Her fingers twitched with the urge.

But his scream traveled through her, finding the fire within and pouring like fuel on the flames.

Rose's screams answered his, echoing in Phoenix's ears.

No. He had to suffer first. For Rose.

Phoenix reached into the inner pocket of her jacket. Pulled out the syringe.

She marched to the monster and plunged the needle into his neck.

He would taste justice tonight.

---

"Phoenix never likes to stick around for glory or debriefs." Eli stopped by his black sedan in the shadows of the parking lot and smiled at Marnie. The girl slept with her head on his shoulder as he cradled her in his arms.

Callum should probably let them go home. But the unease in his belly urged him to ask more questions. "So she just takes off? Where does she go?"

Eli swung his attention back to Callum. "Home, I guess?" His dark eyebrows dipped. "Well, yeah. Because her dogs are home now. She'd want to feed them and take them out before it gets too late."

"Wait, what do you mean her dogs are home? Weren't they before?"

Eli shook his head. "No, they were with Marion. Phoenix always has them stay at our place when she goes away. All but Dag."

"Then how do you know they're at Phoenix's home now?"

"Marion called me. Said Phoenix phoned her this morning to tell her to drop off the dogs at the house. She gave Marion the security code to get in when Marion picked them up the first day of …" Eli glanced at Marnie and lowered his voice. "When this all started. I didn't get Marion's message until Phoenix sent me back to Base. My phone gets reception here. She was wondering if Phoenix meant she'd found Marnie. Phoenix had hung up before Marion could ask, of course."

Eli grinned. "I told her it was an awfully good sign she was about to find our girl."

"I guess it was." Callum mustered a smile for Eli as disappointment sank to join the unease in his stomach.

He lingered to help Eli get Marnie into the car without waking her, then waved as Eli drove off under the scene lights still being used to illuminate the lot.

His gaze drifted to where the blue helicopter had stood before. Probably Phoenix's means for a quick getaway.

Which she had every right to take. He shouldn't have expected anything else. She had left abruptly after the Chicago rescue they'd accomplished together, too. It was her style. Her way.

He knew that.

But the facts didn't assuage the surprise and dashed expectations he hadn't consciously recognized he'd had. What was he thinking? That she would say a tearful farewell? Or tell him she cared about him and wanted to see him again?

Callum clenched his jaw and turned toward the visitor center. Enough of that nonsense. Might as well check to see if Agent Nguyen was free for the debrief interview she'd want to have with him.

A quick glance inside at the people waiting on chairs outside Nguyen's office told him she wouldn't be available for some time yet. Which meant Callum was left without a distraction from the emotional soup that swirled through his system.

He returned to the cold air outdoors, alone with his thoughts. Something he enjoyed and found helpful.

Yes, it would be helpful to think through things. That always worked for him, bringing him back to logical reasoning that led to rational actions.

It was only natural Phoenix would want to get away as soon

as the rescue mission was completed. And after the death of the Forster killer.

She would have so much to process. The man who'd murdered her family and traumatized her was gone forever. And she'd gotten to witness his end.

Was she happy about that or sad? Disillusioned and lost? Or triumphant and relieved?

Callum's chest ached for her. It wouldn't be easy, processing the moment she'd probably waited for nearly her whole life.

If only she hadn't left so quickly. Maybe he could have tried to help her. Said something that could have—

Who was he kidding? She was Phoenix Gray. She wouldn't have wanted to hear anything from him and certainly wouldn't have discussed what she was feeling.

She would have masked it all behind her shell. Just as she had done so masterfully when they'd found the body. No reaction had so much as twitched a feature of her face or tinted her eyes. Even as she'd looked at her family's killer.

Not surprising, given how she was able to appear destitute of emotion under all other circumstances.

But she did feel. Callum knew it. She must have felt so many, hard things—and maybe some good things—as she'd looked at the murderer.

Whose face she couldn't see. None of them could. It had been too bloodied and destroyed for recognition.

So strange. Every time Callum thought back over what had happened as he'd prepared to tell the story to Nguyen, he remembered the same thing. He had aimed for the shooter's chest.

His aim, usually spot on, could've been off due to reflections in the glass, the dark interior, or the speed at which Callum had to react. But if he'd missed at that angle, he would've expected the shot to go wild to the left or right, hitting a shoulder. He didn't recall ever missing a target that far above where he aimed.

The queasy sense of apprehension returned, curdling in his

belly. He walked to the crime scene where the school bus had been. Where the teachers and driver had been murdered. And the children kidnapped.

Only crime scene tape remained. The bus and all other evidence must have been removed and taken to a lab for deeper analysis.

Why a school bus? Why a whole class of children?

Callum's gaze drifted past the scene to the woods behind. Why abduct them at Timber National Park?

The Forster killer was a skilled woodsman and always chose to take his victims to wooded areas, as far as they knew. But he'd never kidnapped the child in the woods before. It was always at a house. A home invasion.

Why the drastic shift?

Callum slowly turned, trying to take in the entire setting in the hope he would see or understand something he'd missed before.

The vehicles that lingered in the parking lot stood like shadows of the hundreds of people who'd been involved in the search for the missing children.

The Forster killer's first two home invasions with murders and kidnappings had made national news, too. And several law enforcement agencies had teamed together to search for the Forster children. They'd done the same for Janette Harrison, who was thought to have been his next victim.

But the scale of those operations hadn't been as large as this one. The abduction of an entire class of third graders at a national park—that was a crime no one would forget. A crime no one would allow to go unsolved. A crime that would require a perpetrator's arrest and conviction. Or his death.

Callum's gut tensed. His gaze went to the service road that emerged from the woods.

The vehicles transporting the Phoenix K-9 team and Tinney should arrive soon. Tinney and Franks, his only remaining FBI sidekick.

What had happened to the other one?

Had he become the Forster killer's way out of the tight situation he'd created for himself? The Forster killer could have slipped out of the park without the children. It would probably be easy for him. But evading arrest after that, from a rabid public and four other agencies hungry to capture him? With forty-eight children on the loose who could identify him?

That might be impossible, even for him.

Unless everyone was sure he was dead.

Then no one would search. The children wouldn't be asked to describe him for police artist renderings. Law enforcement agencies would count it as another win. A closed case.

The Forster killer could walk out of Timber Park and into an anonymous future. Free to kill again.

No.

Dismay clenched Callum's muscles. It couldn't be. The Forster killer couldn't be alive. Free to destroy more lives.

Did Phoenix know if he was alive or dead?

Desperation cinched Callum's throat. He needed to get his coms back so he could contact the Phoenix K-9 team.

They would know how to find her. She would be the only one who'd have a chance to locate the Forster killer if he was still alive. To catch him before he could hurt someone again.

The crunch of wheels on gravel yanked his attention to the service road.

Headlight beams passed across his eyes.

"Thank you, Father." He breathed the prayer as he hurried to the sedan that drove into the parking lot, followed by a black SUV, and...the white Phoenix K-9 van.

He needed to talk to the agency team, but he also needed to verify if the horrible theory taking shape in his mind was true. That took priority.

He held up a hand to the sedan's driver before the guy went to park.

The car halted under one of the scene lights.

Callum lifted his badge for the driver to see, and the agent nodded. Callum stepped to the back passenger door and yanked it open.

Tinney peered up at him, squinting at the light that poured in.

Callum crouched to see the other dirty FBI agent, too. "Where's your buddy? Jenson."

"He was—"

"Injured?" Callum interrupted Tinney's undoubtedly false reply. "Nicked by the kidnapper? I suppose that's why he didn't leave the ranger station with you."

Callum leveled a stare at Tinney. "He was doing something alone by that cabin, wasn't he?"

Something Tinney hadn't wanted anyone to know about.

The fire.

Callum had thought the kidnapper had started the fire. But maybe… "He was starting the fire."

Alarm flickered in Tinney's eyes. "Yeah. He was behind all of this. He wanted to kill the Moore girl. I don't even know why. But he blackmailed us into helping him. He thought the hostages were in the cabin, so he thought starting a fire would kill her and the kidnapper all at once."

Tinney—so awkward at faking innocence and victimhood—clearly saw the opportunity to get a lesser charge if he put all the blame on someone else. Especially a man who wasn't there to defend himself or tell another story.

"Where is he now?" Callum braced an arm on the roof and the other against the door as he ducked lower to see Franks past Tinney. The quiet guy looked at Tinney, but the bearded agent kept his attention on Callum.

"We didn't see him after he went to start the fire."

Had the Forster killer realized a gift had been handed to him? Someone he could kill off, dress with his own clothes, and leave behind to make everyone think he had died.

Callum thought back to the clothing on the body. The killer wouldn't have had much time to exchange clothes with the victim. Maybe he'd made a mistake.

Brown zippered down jacket, black jeans, black shoes.

Wait.

Callum thought hard, visualizing the moment when he'd scanned the victim to see if he matched the children's description of their kidnapper.

Callum hadn't gotten a close look at the shoes or paid much attention. But in his memory, they definitely had black, smooth, and thin soles. Like black dress shoes. Not the defined rubber grips of the kidnapper's hiking-boot footprints Phoenix had been tracking every day.

Callum dropped his gaze to Tinney's shoes.

Black dress shoes. Standard part of an FBI agent's uniform. Maybe Tinney and his pals had rushed so quickly to the rescue operation that they hadn't switched to more appropriate footwear.

"Was your partner wearing the same kind of shoes?"

"He wasn't my part—"

"Save it, Tinney." A spark of anger made Callum snap the words. This conman had already caused enough damage. Didn't need him wasting more precious time. "The shoes."

Tinney looked down at his footwear. "Yeah, I guess so."

*Dear God, help us.*

The Forster killer was alive.

Who would be his next victim?

# FORTY-FOUR

Callum's heart pounded in his ears as he ran to Phoenix's white van, which someone had parked while he had questioned Tinney.

The back doors were open.

He checked inside.

No one was there. The team members must have already gone to the visitor center.

He whirled around, almost crashing into a slim blonde.

"Callum?"

"Cora?"

They said each other's names at the same time, both blinking at the near collision.

"Are you all right?" Cora's forehead lined with concern.

His alarm must be showing. "I just realized something. I don't think the Forster killer died at the ranger station."

Her eyes widened. "You don't? But Phoenix said there was a body there."

"Tinney admits one of his partners in crime went to start the fire behind the cabin and never came back. And he was wearing shoes like those I saw on the man I had thought was the Forster killer."

Cora's eyebrows drew together as she pushed her hands into the pockets of her pale blue jacket. "But he was wearing the kidnapper's clothes. You're saying the kidnapper exchanged clothing with the FBI agent but in his haste, forgot to switch shoes?"

"Or chose not to. The agent's shoes weren't practical for hiking. Maybe the killer thought no one would notice his shoes since they'd be too busy trying to ID him. Looking at his bloodied face." Callum clenched his jaw. "A face the killer intentionally marred so much that no one could tell it was the agent we had already seen."

Callum shook his head. "That facial damage bothered me from the beginning. I should've gotten suspicious. Figured it out."

"But Phoenix was there with you, correct?" Puzzlement shaped Cora's delicate features.

"Yes. I shot him to keep him from shooting her. I thought." Had he even hit the guy? Probably not, given that the Forster killer must have already murdered him. And the Forster killer himself had apparently ducked in time to avoid Callum's shot.

"Phoenix was there." Cora looked at something beyond Callum's shoulder, but her gaze was distant as if she wasn't seeing anything. "Oh, my."

The concern in her voice made Callum's nerves stand on end. "Cora?"

"We all wondered why Phoenix sent the FBI agents on ahead." Her blue eyes met his gaze, worry filling her irises. "The crooked agents, as it turned out."

Realization rushed through Callum in a wave. "Oh, man. You don't think she planned that, do you? Sent them to become bait?"

"To let their evil play out against each other the way they chose, yes." Cora nodded as she pressed her lips together. "I've seen her use the evil instincts of such people against themselves before."

"And she knows the Forster killer so well, she would have

predicted what he'd do." Callum pushed back the hair that had fallen onto his forehead. "She knows he's still alive."

A smidgen of relief relaxed some of the rigidity in his muscles. Phoenix would already be prepared to catch the killer again. She didn't want him to hurt anyone else either, and she wanted him brought to justice. Of that, Callum was certain.

Maybe she was already out there somewhere, capturing him and bringing him in. "She must have a plan." He looked at Cora with renewed hope. "Maybe she's already caught him. Do you know where she is?"

"She called me on the satellite phone when we were hiking to meet our transportation. She asked where we were and told me to send the team members home as soon as we reached the base."

"How long ago was that?"

Cora lifted her hand and pressed the backlight button on her wristwatch. "Let's see. We stopped on the way to pick up the PK-9 van. I believe it was approximately four hours ago."

Longer than he would like. But Phoenix could handle herself. If she was after the Forster killer, even alone, she would come out on top. "So she didn't give any indication of where she was going or say anything about the Forster killer being alive?"

"No." Cora slipped her hands into her pockets again. "Though I wouldn't expect her to. She keeps a great deal of information to herself."

A half smile tugged at Callum's mouth. "Yes, she does."

Cora tilted her head, her expression turning peculiar as she watched him. "You appreciate her, don't you?"

The unexpected question robbed him of a quick answer as he blinked at her.

"I'm sorry." She smiled. "Forgive me for being so direct. But I noticed it earlier, as well, at the campsites. Until now, I haven't seen a man look at her the way you do or interact with her as you do."

Oh, boy. Had he been that transparent?

"You seem to…" Cora moistened her lips, "understand her, perhaps."

At least she hadn't asked if he liked Phoenix romantically. Though Cora could be dancing around that particular question out of tact.

"I don't know." He looked away, seeing Phoenix's face as she'd watched him lift the children into the rescue helicopter. And he had seen her watching. He'd wondered what she was thinking, what she was feeling since the Forster killer was dead. So he'd thought.

But all the time, she'd known the truth.

Callum sighed as he returned his focus to Cora. "She's the most complex person I've ever met. I doubt anyone understands her."

"Perhaps not." Cora studied his face as if trying to see beyond his surface to something beneath. "But I believe she needs someone who cares enough to try."

His insides twisted with the desire to do what Cora said, to get to know Phoenix enough to truly understand her. To get close enough that she would let him.

But she had disappeared.

"If only she hadn't vanished again." His tone held the defeat he hadn't meant to reveal.

"She respects you more than I've seen her respect any other man. You couldn't have earned that honor without having special gifts and insights. I would guess they are insights into Phoenix herself, and perhaps you share her powers of deduction. I can't imagine her showing you such respect for anything less."

Callum wasn't sure he could agree with that. Especially since he didn't even have enough insight to know what Cora had observed that had led her to conclude Phoenix respected him.

"Use those gifts to find her now." Cora's lips curved in a gentle smile. "I know she likely wants to bring in the kidnapper by herself, and usually, I don't interfere with her plans. They always turn out right. I wonder if in this case, though, she might not realize she needs your help. Not physically with the capture. But in other, more important ways."

Was Cora right? Callum's heart squeezed. He hoped so.

But Phoenix wouldn't want him to get in the way of her strategic plan to catch the killer. She was incredible beyond belief, realizing the FBI agents were crooked and there to kill Marnie, then using them like pawns in a chess game. Using even the Forster killer himself as another pawn, as she predicted he'd kill one of the agents so everyone would think he was dead, and he could get away undetected.

She would have predicted what he would do next.

So if Callum wanted to find her, he also needed to determine what the Forster killer would have done.

The killer's driving goal the whole time had to have been what it usually was—to kidnap his intended victim by destroying her sheltered family structure, then abuse and murder her. In such a way that he wouldn't get caught.

Then why kidnap a busload of children at a national park? The same question Callum hadn't been able to answer before loomed like an impassible wall, obstructing any conclusions about the Forster killer's actions.

What had changed between the Forster killer's last murder and the attack at Timber Park?

No one knew with certainty when the Forster killer's last crime was, since no one had been able to identify the perpetrator. But the FBI suspected he was responsible for the murder of the Teague family in Wisconsin three years ago. The daughter had been taken after the murderous home invasion and never found again.

Given that Phoenix was listed as a consultant on that case, Callum deduced she was the one who had identified the perpetrator as the Forster killer.

If that were true, the killer had performed his usual crime—an almost identical repeat of all those since his first attack of the Forsters.

And now, twenty-six years later, he made drastic changes.

In the month of November. Only nine days after the discovery of his first victim, Rose Forster.

Callum mentally shook the dust off the idea he'd had what felt like a lifetime ago—when the school bus kidnapping first took place, and the rescue operation began. Why had he discarded the theory that the discovery of Rose's body was relevant?

He searched his memory to recall his reasoning. He had speculated that finding her remains could have bothered the killer, given him a sense of incompletion that had drawn him to the Twin Cities area so he could replicate the original killing in the same location.

But Callum had dismissed the idea because geographical location hadn't seemed significant to the Forster killer before. And because something had happened just when Callum had thought of the possibility. Oh, yes—they'd found Hayden.

What if Rose's remains and the geography were significant, but not in the way Callum had thought?

"You remind me of her." Cora's voice startled him.

He'd nearly forgotten she was there. "Of..."

"Phoenix. You process and come to conclusions silently, as she does, and use words sparingly."

"Now that is the nicest compliment I've ever received."

Cora smiled, her eyes warming with too much perception.

But he didn't mind if she knew he admired Phoenix. Anyone who didn't admire, respect, and appreciate her was a fool.

The image of Phoenix after God had enabled Callum to rescue Dag appeared before the eyes of his memory. The way she'd looked at him differently then. How she had let him sit next to her on the bluff and tell her his testimony of coming to Christ and letting go of hate for his stepfather. How he'd ventured to explain what drove him in life.

*"What are you living for, Phoenix?"* The question Callum had dared to ask echoed in his mind.

And her quick response, full of the meaning born of trauma and pain, was still imbedded in his heart. *"Justice."*

"Oh, no." The deductions Cora had encouraged him to make finally emerged from the layered complexities of this case, of the Forster killer. And most of all, of Phoenix Gray.

Cora's eyes widened. "What?"

"I've made a mistake. I shouldn't have tried to figure out the killer. I should've tried to figure out Phoenix."

"You said no one understood her."

"I do." Shock ricocheted through him. "I understand her. I only hope it's not too late."

# FORTY-FIVE

The time had come. The moment Phoenix had planned for, dreamed of, longed for since she was fourteen years old. Since the day she'd stopped grieving and realized there was only one thing she could do for them, for herself, and for others. Only one thing that would change anything. Only one thing that would matter.

Justice.

All of her dogs were safe outside except for Azami, who was tucked away in her room, and Dagian.

Phoenix's faithful partner stood by her side, as always, as she paused in front of the closed steel door. Took in a breath. Let it out.

She would not rush. Twenty-six years of surviving, training, study, dedication, and planning had led to this moment.

She would savor every second. Set aside the future, where law enforcement would take issue with what she was about to do.

That didn't matter. All that mattered was Rose. Their dad and mom. The horrors they had suffered. Their lives, snuffed out.

And the many innocent girls since. Tortured and murdered.

The fire deep inside flamed hotter with every reminder of the reasons for this night. The reasons she must mete out justice to the fullest extent.

The blaze climbed higher in her body, reaching her throat as she punched in the passcode on the keypad, and the door slid open.

She marched through, Dag entering with her.

But her gaze went to the window in the wall. She walked to it, her pulse picking up speed with excitement.

She stopped and stared through the glass to the room on the other side.

The monster's cage.

He sat where she'd left him, on a chair in the middle of the more brightly lit room. Chains wrapped around his body, securing his arms and legs with unbreakable force.

She'd removed the jacket and sweater he had stolen from the FBI agent he'd killed. The white T-shirt that remained left little protection against the chains she had tightened to an exact pressure.

His shaved head, bare of the hat she had taken, started to list to one side. The effort to avoid leaving DNA by shaving his body hair wouldn't help him now. Nothing would.

He lifted his head.

Adrenaline rushed through her veins.

The sedative was wearing off exactly in the time frame she'd planned. Perfectly timed for her to watch him awaken.

He blinked drowsily as he rotated his head to see his surroundings.

The muscles of his shoulders flexed as he tried to move his arms.

His gaze snapped down to his lower body. He took in the heavy chains that kept him prisoner. His hands were secured behind the chairback, as well, tied with chains over handcuffs, while his ankles were bound, one to each chair leg. The chair itself was made of steel. No chance he could break any part of it to escape.

His gaze jerked to his right, then his left as he checked the room.

Small, rectangular. Concrete walls and floor. It was devoid of furnishings except for the chair and one long table against the wall to his right.

He swung his head to look forward. At the two-way glass that appeared as a mirror from his side.

His eyes were wide. Full of fear.

A smile curved her lips.

It was time.

She walked slowly to the door to the far left of the window, the only door that remained between her and the end of it all.

She pressed her whole hand against the print reader she had installed herself, only for that room. No one—even if Cora or Marion accidentally got lost in the house or someone managed to overcome her other security—no one but Phoenix would ever access that room.

The door slid open.

She stepped through with Dag. He had been with her for the last ten years of this mission. He deserved to be there for the end.

The door shut behind her, the click of locks signaling it had secured itself properly.

Those eyes, the eyes of her nightmares, locked on her.

But they weren't deadly now.

They weren't glistening with enjoyment—delight in her suffering. In Rose's suffering.

No relishing of his power.

Fear glittered in their depths. Only a hint. But that would grow.

She would see terror by the end.

"You." His voice was raw. Slightly raspy. The sedative and unconsciousness had likely dried his throat.

Let him feel the thirst. Only a small foreshadowing of the discomfort to come.

"You're Phoenix Gray."

She walked in front of him and turned to face the monster head-on.

Dag let out a growl, but she put her hand on his head. Her silent signal that she had the situation under control.

Only two feet between her and the monster, she stared hard at the creature she'd faced so many times in her nightmares.

As she'd expected, his features no longer made her squirm or want to flee. Now she saw the wrinkles that weren't there before, the gray stubble growing on his chin, the pockmarks, the increased fat in his cheeks.

A sickly pallor tinted his skin. He was weak, aging more rapidly than a man of forty-eight should. The evil of his ways was consuming him from the inside out, as it did with all such demented humans.

He strained against the chains, then winced. They were squeezing him, digging into his skin, especially painful where Dag's teeth had torn the monster's flesh.

Satisfaction slid through her. It was only the beginning.

"Where am I? Why am I tied up?" A tremor shook his voice.

Delightful. Her mouth tugged up at one corner. She hadn't realized how much she would enjoy this.

"You're not a cop." The skin bunched where eyebrows would be if he hadn't shaved them.

She didn't blink. But she let her pleasure show in the curve of her closed lips.

"You can't keep me here."

Was that the best he could do?

His confusion gave way to a glare. "You've seen what I can do to people. I'll do the same to you unless you let me go right now."

She stepped closer.

He flinched. An almost imperceptible movement.

But she saw it.

A thrill shot through her.

She closed the distance even more. Leaned forward, resting her hands on the arms of the chair on either side of his body.

She stared into his eyes, only inches away.

The fire within raged hotter than ever before, scorching her insides until she felt it sear her eyes as she looked into the heart of the monster.

The fear in his gaze increased. He looked away. The coward couldn't withstand even her scrutiny.

He tried to turn back to her, his focus aiming at her cap instead of her face. "If you have a family, I'll kill them all. But they'll suffer first." His lips moved, forming the threat.

She couldn't hear the words at first. Not past the roar of the fire blazing in her ears.

But she understood their meaning before they became sound, what seemed like minutes later. Her heart understood.

She pulled off her cap and tossed it to the floor a few feet away, then planted her hands on the armrests again to keep him trapped beneath her. "You killed my family." She delivered his guilty verdict in a low voice as hard as steel. "You killed me. Robin Forster."

Confusion and disbelief contorted his features. *"You're Robin?"*

She had removed the blue contacts. Her naturally brown eyes were visible, the same as they'd been when she was a child. When he'd filled them with horror and pain.

His turn now.

"I'm your worst nightmare." She watched him as she spoke the triumphant truth.

A flicker of fear sparked in his irises. He tried not to look away, the twist of his mouth showing he wanted to.

"I'm going to make you pay. For every pain you made Rose endure. For every fear you made her suffer. For every child after her to which you did the same." Phoenix's jaw clenched as she let her anger through, let it intensify her voice.

The fire devouring her soul overflowed, and she didn't try to hold it back. She let it show in her eyes, allowed the blood to rush to her face, allowed the fury to raise her voice with strength and wrath. "Then you will pay with your life. For Rose's life. For all your victims' lives."

And for Robin's. She didn't speak the last, private purpose. For justice to be complete, he had to pay for Robin, too—the young, innocent, happy girl she'd been until he'd destroyed her.

"I am an expert on people like you. Those who prey upon children." She straightened, switching to a calm, placid tone he would find as frightening as her wrath. She gestured with her hand toward the table by the wall. "I have collected the tools of your trade."

She stared at him a few, silent beats. "Now you will learn how they feel. You will learn what it is to be the victim of yourself."

His gaze flitted from the table and jumped to her face.

There. Terror.

It filled his widened eyes. As he looked at her.

She smiled.

# FORTY-SIX

"If I do this, I could lose my position at Phoenix K-9." Cora looked at Callum as they stood on the dark threshold of Phoenix Gray's house. "Far worse than that, I would destroy the trust she has in me. It would end our friendship."

Cold air whipped through the leafless trees and darted around the gloomy, two-story house made of stone blocks, chilling Callum like the dread that coursed through his bloodstream. "I know. I'm sorry to ask you to shut down her security. But it's like you said—she needs our help."

He could imagine the loud barks of the two dogs—a Great Pyrenees and a Doberman pincher Cora had introduced as Birger and Apollo—were a call for help. But more likely, the barking was intended to scare the visitors away.

Though the intimidation factor was undermined by the way fluffy Birger hopped and wagged his tail as he barked at them through the gate in a chain-link fence that jutted out from the side of the house, dividing the backyard from the front.

"It is odd she has the dogs confined to the back instead of patrolling all the property." Cora cast her gaze into the darkness of the land that was surrounded by a ten-foot chain-link fence with a front gate about an acre away.

"But are you one hundred percent positive she has him in there?" Cora moistened her lips. "And that she's going to... torture him?" Her tone tilted up with disbelief.

"Ninety-five percent. This is Phoenix." Callum lifted his shoulders. "But it all fits. She's been wearing that pendant, a Phaistos Disc replica, and fiddling with it whenever she sits or stands out in the open. As if she wanted it to be noticed. Had you ever seen it before the park kidnapping?"

Cora's eyebrows pinched together. "No. She never wears jewelry."

Exactly what Callum had thought. "It took me a while to remember, but I saw her wearing it at the press conference after she found Rose's body. The pendant must have been buried with her, and Phoenix removed it before she called in the FBI."

"But why?"

"Because she knew it was important to Rose's killer. Important enough that he buried it with her. It must have significance to him and the killings he's obsessed with doing. Digging up Rose and the Phaistos Disc would destroy his sense of completion in that first killing. Phoenix knows him better than anyone, and she would know that. She knew he would do anything to get the pendant back."

Phoenix had probably recognized the pendant from when she'd been kidnapped with Rose. The killer had likely worn it or carried it with him.

But Callum kept that information to himself. Cora might not know Phoenix was Robin Forster, and it wasn't his secret to share.

Cora's eyes widened. "Is that why he kidnapped an entire class of schoolchildren at Timber Park? To lure Phoenix there so he could steal the pendant?"

"I think so. It explains why he suddenly changed his MO after twenty-six years. He must have seen Phoenix at the press conference, wearing the pendant, and learned she headed an agency that did search and rescue."

"I wondered why she spoke at the press conference. She's never done that before."

More confirmation that Callum's theory was on the money. "It also explains why she was so certain he wouldn't take his target victim and leave the park. She knew he wouldn't leave without the pendant that she had the whole time."

Cora's lips pressed together. "But how do we know she found the killer at the park? She could have come straight home."

"The phone call."

"The phone call?"

"When you were on the way to meet the transport for Tinney. You said she asked where you and the team were. She knew the Forster killer's only option when she left in the rescue helicopter was to follow the rest of her team in the hope that would lead him to her."

"He wanted the Phaistos Disc that badly?"

"Apparently even more than his next chosen victim. Your information enabled Phoenix to know where he was and intercept him."

"And she must be here now." Cora glanced at the dogs, still barking from behind the fence. "She let the dogs outside. But I still can't believe she would do what you suspect. She wouldn't hurt someone out of revenge."

"She would for justice. Trust me. I know." Because the same desire drove Callum. It was the only way to set things right.

The thought made him pause before urging Cora to shut off the security. Maybe it wasn't so bad he'd had to take the time to explain the evidence to Cora.

The Forster killer deserved justice. He deserved to suffer for the cruelties and atrocities he'd inflicted on others. On the most innocent and vulnerable of humanity.

If Phoenix carried out the plan Callum suspected, this one serial killer would receive what he deserved. Justice would be done.

But God's Word was clear. He was supposed to take care of that. Humans were not.

"All right." Cora looked down at the smart tablet she held in her hands. "I'll turn off the passcode requirement for all doors throughout the house." She tapped the screen with her finger. "It's done."

Callum gripped the doorknob and turned.

It opened. No security alarms went off.

Callum kept the opening small as he stepped through, and Cora slipped in behind him, shutting the door.

The moment she did, a shiny, steel door appeared from seemingly nowhere and slid over the outer door, sealing it with a resounding bang.

Callum blinked. That was unexpected.

Cora had already turned away and started up the short, narrow passageway.

Callum hurried to catch up, reaching her at yet another door. It was heavy-duty steel but with a normal knob. Next to what appeared to be a fingerprint reader.

Not exactly a welcoming entryway into a home. But it was Phoenix's house.

Cora pressed a small red button at the bottom of the reader, and a quiet click sounded. She opened the door only partially and leaned her head through the opening. "Phoenix?"

Callum winced. Hadn't planned to announce their arrival.

She opened the door wider and stepped beyond it, giving Callum space to enter.

Sensing the weight of the door in his hand, he turned with it as he closed it, careful to prevent a free-swinging slam. Then he spun back around and scanned the shadowed interior.

Recessed lighting that must be set low on a dimmer switch highlighted a kitchen with an island. To his right, a space probably meant to be a living room held only one armchair, a rug, three dog beds, and a medium-sized dog crate.

No Phoenix anywhere in sight.

"Cora." Callum whispered as he followed her across the open space. "Probably best not to call out to her."

"Why?" Cora tossed the question over her shoulder, lowering her volume to just above a whisper. "Phoenix would never hurt me."

"I know." But she might hide the Forster killer. Hide that she had taken him.

"And she'll likely have seen us coming on her security cameras."

Good to know. Callum hadn't spotted cameras outside or inside the house. She must have them camouflaged or hidden from plain sight.

Cora led the way through one hallway, then another. And another.

The relatively short passageways turned corners several times, challenging Callum's attempt to create a blueprint in his mind.

As they made another turn, he spotted two doors, one to his left and another farther down the hallway on the right.

Cora walked past the first one without pausing.

"Shouldn't we check this?" He kept his voice quiet.

She stopped and looked back. "I don't think she'd keep him here. I was at her house once before, and the passageways continue, to a place where I saw things that didn't make sense to me then. But now, I think I might know what they were."

Callum nodded and followed Cora as they walked on into the labyrinth.

They turned another corner, passed through a hallway, and then turned into another.

Steel bars, like those in a prison, stood in their way.

"I wondered." Her quiet tone held a note of gravity he hadn't heard from her before. "Perhaps I should have known. Should have prevented this somehow."

Callum stood beside her at the bars.

She turned her gaze to him. "I saw the tracks in the floor and the pockets where these gates, these bars cross the hallway. I thought she had all of this for security. For protection." Moisture glistened in Cora's eyes. "But it's not to keep people out. It's to keep them in. It's a prison."

A chill shot down Callum's spine. And it was where Phoenix lived.

"We had better hurry." Cora pressed the *Enter* button on a keypad attached to the wall.

The barred gate trembled, metal clanging as it retracted into the recessed pocket.

Cora hurried through at a faster pace. "We passed several of these before reaching the guest room where she had me stay. I would guess she didn't have me stay where she planned to put him. It's probably somewhere beyond that room."

They trotted through the next two hallways, pausing only to open the barred gates.

"There." Cora stopped, and Callum braked beside her. "This is the room I stayed in."

"Okay. Then let's keep going. Maybe we're almost there." He kicked into a jog as he made the next turn into another hallway. Glanced at a door on the right.

No, double doors. Elevator doors. "She has an elevator?" He glanced at Cora.

She lifted her shoulders. Then pressed the button below the fingerprint reader.

The doors slid open.

They stepped inside, and Callum scanned for the buttons to choose floors.

Only two options. *1* and *B*. The elevator must not go up to the second floor. But *B* must stand for *Basement*.

What better place to keep a serial killer. Callum punched the button, and the doors closed.

He looked at Cora as the elevator started downward. "I'd better exit first. Just in case."

She nodded, her complexion paler than normal.

"Not because of Phoenix, but because he might be there."

Callum didn't want her to think he believed Phoenix would hurt her. He knew she wouldn't. He even trusted she wouldn't hurt him, though he was an intruder in her home.

"I know. We both care about her."

Callum opened his mouth to protest Cora's statement, but the way his heart squeezed at her words meant he would be a liar if he tried to deny that he cared. A great deal.

The doors slid open, and Cora stayed back as he pulled out his weapon, positioning himself off-center of the opening.

A concrete wall and floor greeted his gaze as he checked the angles, clearing only the few feet of lit hallway that he could see since it ran perpendicular to the elevator.

He swung out to the right, planting his feet and aiming.

Nothing but five feet of concrete floor and a blank wall in front of him.

He pivoted to face the other direction, Glock raised.

Empty hallway, stretching about three yards straight ahead to a closed door, lit with a few bulbs spaced evenly down the center of the gray ceiling.

He lifted his hand and signaled to Cora she could come out.

The elevator doors slid shut behind her as Callum lowered his weapon. "Looks like the right place."

"Yes." Her response came out as a whisper.

"It might be best for you to stay here. I don't know what I'll find in there. If he's there, it isn't safe."

"I must go." Cora turned her blue eyes on him. "If what you suspect is true, Phoenix may need us both." The worry in her gaze was undergirded by a resolve he knew not to argue with.

And she was probably right. She'd known Phoenix much longer. It was more likely Phoenix would listen to someone she knew and trusted. But as Nguyen had mentioned that first night, Cora was the only one from the Phoenix K-9 Agency who didn't wear a weapon. At least not a visible one.

"Okay. Stay behind me. And if he tries to attack, get yourself out as fast as you can."

She nodded.

Callum started up the hallway, his gaze on the closed door as he kept his Glock in a ready position.

No handle or knob on the steel door.

He stopped in front of it, and his gaze landed on the fingerprint reader secured to the wall. He pressed the red button below the scanner to bypass it.

The door slid open.

He shifted to the right, weapon lifted.

A dimly lit room of gray concrete, only a blank wall to the left and straight ahead.

He moved to the left of the doorway, scanning the right side of the room.

Or rather the front of the room, since a framed window—or maybe a mirror—took up three feet of the wall there, drawing the eye that direction.

The room was empty, so he gestured with a tilt of his head that Cora should follow him in.

He kept his gun raised as he spotted a door in the same wall, just beyond the window.

"Is this an interrogation observation room?" Cora's quiet question trailed him as he approached what must be a two-way mirror.

Phoenix.

His heart lurched at the sight of the woman he'd been longing to see more than he'd realized.

Her back was turned, but he would recognize that long, honey-blond braid anywhere. And she wore the same dark gray pants and black jacket she'd had on when he'd seen her last.

She seemed to be facing something away from the mirror. Or someone.

She turned to the left and walked away, allowing Callum to see what—

His breath choked.

A man sat in a metal chair, covered in chains that wrapped around him.

The Forster killer.

His shaved head matched the description his hostages had given. He wore a white T-shirt and black cotton pants that appeared too small for him. Likely stolen from the FBI agent he'd murdered.

The worry and sense of urgency that had driven Callum to invade Phoenix's home melted away as he stared at the murderer.

Phoenix had done it. She had caught perhaps the vilest, most perverted serial killer in existence that had evaded capture for twenty-six years.

She had apprehended the man who had destroyed her family and nearly destroyed her.

She was bringing him to justice. The man who hurt the innocent in the worst ways possible and enjoyed every minute of it.

He was finally getting what he deserved.

The frustration Callum had been carrying for years, the despair that had brought him to the brink of quitting his job, of giving up, seeped away as if Phoenix had pulled the plug on the drain of his pooled failures.

At last. One of the evildoers would receive the justice that was his due.

Phoenix came back into view, carrying something in her hand.

Was that—

Callum's gut seized, panic instinctively pulsing through him.

An electroshock device. The kind his stepfather had used on him. Over and over again.

Phoenix walked closer to her captive.

She was going to use it on him.

Horror rippled through Callum. He pressed close to the window, his gaze jumping from the device to her face.

Emotion showed in her eyes and in every feature. Even in the curl of her mouth as she spoke words he couldn't hear.

But it wasn't the compassion, kindness, or love he'd imagined seeing on her face one day. No, it was the same hatred and anger that had overtaken his stepfather—the cold, hard evil that had driven his cruelty.

"Dear Lord, no." Cora's frightened whisper was a weak echo of the dismay that pierced through Callum's ribs, stabbing his heart.

What had he done?

# FORTY-SEVEN

"Where's my Phaistos Disc?" The monster's anger warred with the fear in his eyes as Phoenix moved closer with the shock device.

She stopped a foot away and reached under the collar of her sweater to pull out the pendant that hung from the chain around her neck. "I've decided to keep it. To wear it for Rose and my parents. A reminder of how you suffered for what you did."

"You can't wear it." His mouth twisted in a sneer, but his voice trembled.

"Only those who look like her can wear it, you mean. Your mother."

"No! Sadie. Sadie was my best friend. Until her parents made her move away."

A childhood friend. The girl could have been three or seventeen. Didn't matter to Phoenix in the slightest. No childhood pain, even abuse of the worst kind, justified or excused the horrors he or any other criminal inflicted on the innocent.

People became what they chose to become. Or they chose to overcome.

Callum had overcome his terrible childhood abuse.

Phoenix had overcome her devastating trauma. She'd risen again. Rebuilt herself into something greater than before. Into a person who had the courage, intelligence, and ability to bring justice to the worst. Justice to this illusive, unremorseful monster.

"The disc is mine now. And so is your life." She switched off the safety on the stun gun, setting it to a voltage that would cause significant pain but not stop his heart. She couldn't have that.

He had much more suffering to undergo before the scales of justice even came close to being righted.

"Phoenix, don't." The male voice burst into the room.

She jerked toward the door.

Still closed. Dag had apparently moved away at some point to sit in front of it. He wasn't growling or warning her.

The reflective overlay of Phoenix's specialized two-way mirror setup began to pull away.

Someone had hit the switch on the observation side. The overlays Phoenix had made removable were simultaneously retracting in the captive's room and observation room, revealing clear glass beneath.

Cora and Callum stood by the window on the other side, watching her.

They'd seen.

They knew.

She immediately schooled her features as she rapidly deduced how they'd arrived there.

Cora must have overridden her own security system to access the house and the secured prison section. She didn't have a passcode, but she had no doubt built a backdoor into the metadata of the software in case of malfunction or emergency. Never thought Cora would use that against her.

Normally, Phoenix would have seen any such attempt to enter the premises by monitoring the cameras on her smartphone. But she hadn't brought it into the room for security reasons.

And then there was Callum. He'd become the liability Phoenix had suspected he would be from the very beginning.

He had apparently pieced everything together to determine she would be at her house with the Forster killer, where she would enact justice. He was indeed dangerously intelligent and intuitive.

She should have chased him off. Never allowed him to join her on the rescue operations. Never let him get so close. Never allowed him to see...her.

She drew in a slow breath through her nostrils.

No matter. He couldn't stop her. Couldn't give her an impossible choice of going through him to reach the monster.

The lock on the door to that room was not connected to Cora's security system. They couldn't get through the steel unless Phoenix let them in.

Nothing would stand in the way of her plan.

"Phoenix, please." Cora's sweet voice came through the intercom. "You aren't going to do this, are you?"

A pang shot behind Phoenix's ribs.

Cora shouldn't witness this. It would be too much for her. Too traumatizing.

Phoenix stepped in front of the window and faced the unwanted visitors, ready to send them away. But what she saw froze the words on her tongue.

Shock tinted Cora's big blue eyes as they flooded with shimmering tears. Horror crimped her eyebrows and mouth, her skin ghostly white.

But she wasn't looking at the monster. She was staring at Phoenix.

Unease and something Phoenix had never felt before curdled in her stomach. Her gaze darted to Callum as if seeking an escape.

He stared at her, too, his greenish brown eyes darkened with a mixture of disbelief, desperation, and...repulsion.

They both looked at her the way good people looked at killers and rapists.

The terrible feeling surged up from her stomach, painfully curling through her chest and hitting her throat.

She saw herself as they must. Standing there, ready to torture a human being. Ready to enjoy it.

Her horror turned in on herself, intensifying the awful feeling consuming her insides until the stun gun felt like it would singe her fingertips if she didn't drop it.

But something else kept her grip strong. Despite the feeling that must be regret or guilt—things she'd never experienced before.

The other emotion was stronger. One she knew from of old but had conquered. Until now.

Fear.

No disgust at her own behavior, what she was about to do or what she might become, could mitigate the threat of the inconceivable alternative if she stopped.

He would go on living.

There was no chance of the death penalty in Minnesota. Even if he went to prison, he would not begin to suffer to the degree he deserved. His suffering would be nothing compared to the children he had victimized. Not at all a just punishment for the slaughter of families and torture of children.

No. He must pay for what he had done.

Phoenix could not live with any other outcome. She turned toward him with the stun gun, her back to the window.

"Phoenix, this isn't right. Please, stop." Cora's voice, pleading and frightened, matched Rose's cry in Phoenix's memory.

*Please. Stop.*

She'd said that to him. The monster. And he hadn't stopped.

The devastating memory flared in Phoenix's mind, blocking out all else.

He'd shown no mercy to Rose.

Phoenix would do the same to him. For Rose. Even if it made Phoenix a monster, too.

He had to suffer as Rose had suffered.

If it made Phoenix into what he was, so be it. Justice must be done.

---

He could have prevented this. The repulsion Callum had instinctively felt at the sight of Phoenix, looking like his abusive stepfather, had transitioned into repulsion aimed inwardly. Where it was most deserved.

Phoenix walked away, going toward the table along the left wall without first using the shock device. Was she going to stop?

*Please, Father, make her stop. Don't let my own sin be the cause of her destruction.*

She spun away from the table and started toward the Forster killer again. A knife gleamed in her hand. Sadistic pleasure curled her lips.

"Phoenix!" The shock and trepidation in Cora's cry sounded like the voice of his heart.

Phoenix paused, slowly turned her head toward Cora.

*Father, what have I done?*

If Callum hadn't been so bent on justice, no matter the cost, he wouldn't have wanted to believe so badly that the dead man in the ranger station was the Forster killer. He wouldn't have so quickly dismissed the obvious anomalies of the bloodied face and the wrong shoes.

He would have connected the dots faster to discover Phoenix's plan, and he would have raced into Phoenix's house as fast as possible instead of taking time to explain his evidence to Cora.

He would have brought Nguyen and other FBI agents with him to take the hostage from Phoenix by force if necessary. Even to arrest Phoenix for kidnapping, assault, torture, and attempted murder if she committed those crimes.

But he didn't do any of those things he should have. Because part of him wanted this.

He wanted to see a bad guy, someone who'd done horrible things, get the justice he deserved—to suffer for what he'd done.

The desire for justice wasn't wrong. But what Phoenix was about to do—that was.

Callum was guilty of the same thing. He'd wanted to take vengeance himself. And because he hadn't wanted to stand in the way of that deserved vengeance, he had hesitated to stop what he knew was coming.

But his mistake had resulted in this—the imminent downfall of the woman he…loved. Yes, loved. There was no denying the strength of his feelings that had begun as compassion and empathy for the young girl he'd seen only in a photo.

She was no longer Robin Forster, the damaged young girl he wanted to save. She was Phoenix, the unbelievably heroic, intelligent, beautiful, and compassionate woman he had somehow come to love.

He didn't know how it had started with admiration and respect, then exploded in a love so strong it couldn't be stopped. But his actions, his desire to let her take vengeance and justice into her own hands the way he wanted to, could lead to the destruction of her life and her soul.

*Father, forgive me.*

"You don't have to do this." Cora's voice broke through Callum's anguish, though he had the impression she'd already been speaking before.

Phoenix stood closer to the window, looking at Cora. "I do. I will not let him go unpunished. Justice must be done."

"But this is revenge, Phoenix. Not justice."

She shook her head in denial, fury glinting in her eyes. "The monster getting what he deserves—that is justice."

"She's right."

Both women switched their attention to Callum.

"Revenge is like vengeance. God takes vengeance on evildoers. And He's always just."

Cora's eyebrows lifted. "I hadn't thought about it that way

before." She transferred her gaze to Phoenix. "But the difference is that God does the vengeance. Only He can mete it out justly. If we try to take vengeance on others, we'll be destroyed by it."

An ember of hope, like a flickering flame must appear to one lost in a pitch-black cave, flared in Callum's mind. Was Cora a Christian?

Phoenix stared at her through the glass. "Your God takes vengeance on evil people?"

"Yes." Cora nodded. "He promises in the Bible that He will. 'Vengeance is mine; I will repay.' He also said, 'Evil will slay the wicked; the foes of the righteous will be condemned.'"

The Scripture quotes sent another pang through Callum's raw conscience. God promised to repay evildoers, to enact perfect justice in His timing and His way.

When had Callum forgotten that? When had he stopped trusting in God, in His justice?

Callum knew the answer. When he'd learned he couldn't prevent the crimes he had tried to—when he couldn't protect children even from repeat offenders he had locked away—Callum had begun to blame himself and the broken system.

He'd started limiting God. He forgot that God controlled the system and overrode and ordained all human actions according to His will.

Callum had stopped believing, at the deepest level, that God made all the decisions about the crimes and evil He allowed and even who suffered.

And worst of all, Callum had stopped trusting that every one of those decisions were right and good. Even the people God allowed to be released from prison to commit crimes again were only freed for God's purpose and perfect plan.

What an arrogant fool Callum had become without realizing it. God didn't need Callum's help to bring about justice.

God's justice was enough and would be brought about in the end, with or without Callum's help.

Justice was guaranteed. And it didn't rely on Callum. It only relied on God.

Relief rolled through Callum, washing away the frustration and blame—the heavy burden he had been carrying. The consequences of trying to take on a responsibility that he wasn't meant to bear.

*Thank you, Lord.*

"I thought your God was a god of love." Phoenix's firm statement grabbed Callum's attention, recalling his attention to the violent rage in her eyes.

Dread cinched his ribcage.

No. Her fate was not his burden either.

God had a plan, and Callum would trust Him with Phoenix's present and future.

*Father, use me if you will. But either way, please save Phoenix.*

# FORTY-EIGHT

Cora held Phoenix's gaze with her soft, unwavering blue eyes. "God is love, justice, righteousness, and so much more. His characteristics never contradict one another. They are always in harmony. His love is shown in His justice and vice versa."

His love was shown in His justice? Phoenix had never heard the Christian God described in such a way.

People talked about Him being compassionate and loving. Her parents had often spoken of His love. The song Rose and Robin had learned at church was called, "Jesus Loves Me."

Christians also talked about God's forgiveness. Ad nauseum. As Callum had with his story of the concentration camp survivor, and his own tale of forgiving his abuser.

As if forgiveness were an adequate substitute for justice.

"Look at yourself, Phoenix." Callum's voice, ragged with emotion she would not identify, beckoned her to look at him.

But she did not. She stared at the knife in her hands. The instrument of torture she was going to use on the monster who deserved that and so much more.

"You haven't risen from the ashes of your past. You're buried in them. You're buried in death."

The words snuck through her defenses, hitting a raw nerve.

She jerked her gaze to his. "Then so be it. I'll die a thousand deaths to see this monster suffer what he deserves."

"Phoenix." Pain glistened in Callum's eyes. "Listen to what you're saying. You want to torture another human being. I saw the pleasure on your face. You're taking pleasure in his suffering. You enjoy it. That's the twisted thinking of the serial rapists and murderers we've both spent our lives pursuing. I can't watch you become one of them." His tone tightened, as if the thought caused him anguish.

Her ribs crushed inward. But she would not be swayed from her purpose. She would push him into a safer category, into being her adversary. He would end there, regardless, if he continued to oppose her. "Because you'll need to arrest me?"

His jaw clenched. The blow had hit its target. "By your own measure, you would deserve it. You would deserve punishment and suffering. Just like him." Callum looked beyond her shoulder. To the monster.

Anger fanned the fire within her. "You know what he's done."

"The *why* for what you're doing doesn't matter. He's intentionally hurt others and enjoyed their suffering. He's taken lives. Isn't that what you're about to do?"

Phoenix's heart thrashed against her ribcage with rising fury. "You said God takes vengeance."

"*He* does. Not us. We can't do it justly. We can't do it with pure motives. But God is perfect and good. Only He knows what punishment is just. Only He can mete it out without being tainted by evil in the process. Without perverting justice."

"Please listen to him, Phoenix." Cora placed her palm against the window as she pleaded. "You see what this is doing to you. We should never enjoy making others suffer or taking someone's life, no matter the reason."

Her mouth tightened at the corners. "I always wondered why you treated me with special kindness. When you asked me to research the killer's target victim, I finally realized. As a child, I would have been the type of victim he would have chosen. You're Robin Forster, aren't you?"

Phoenix stared at her. She'd known when she had described the monster's preferred target's traits that Cora would come to the conclusion she had. True to Cora's patient sensitivity to others, she hadn't blurted out the discovery or questioned Phoenix about it. But now, she would try to use it to dissuade Phoenix from what she had to do.

"I must remind you, in some way, of Rose. Your sweet sister." Cora's sad eyes searched Phoenix's face. "I don't want to ask you this, Phoenix, but I must. What would Rose think if she saw you now? If she knew what you're about to do?"

The question was exactly what Phoenix anticipated, but it still stung. Rose, like Cora, would be horrified to see Phoenix do violence to anyone, even someone as deserving as the monster. Even though he had hurt her.

"Rose needed protection." Protection Robin had been too young and untrained to provide. "You need protection. Whether or not you want to see it accomplished, you need others to keep you safe, whatever that takes. All the vulnerable will be preyed upon unless others have the courage to end the threats."

Which was why Phoenix would not let them distract her any longer. They were wasting precious time. Stalling as they waited for the FBI to arrive. Phoenix wouldn't be warned now when the agents easily invaded her house, thanks to Cora shutting down her security. She had kept Birger and Apollo confined to the back portion of her property for just such a contingency, ensuring no agents would harm them to gain entry.

But the FBI would be too late to thwart the justice she would give the monster.

She spun toward him, raising the knife. She would begin somewhere highly sensitive. Excruciating.

She stepped closer.

His nostrils flared in panic, reigniting the fire inside her.

Yes, this was right.

A rumble filled the room.

She jerked toward Dag.

But he wasn't at the door, warning her of an intruder. He stood at her elbow, lips curled above his teeth as he emitted another low growl. At her.

His bright blue eyes pierced her soul.

Her fingers trembled on the knife. She regripped the hilt before it fell.

Dag?

He was behaving as if he had perceived her intent and judged it evil.

He saw her as the villain. The monster.

Was he right?

The possibility nearly choked her.

"You need protection, too, Phoenix."

Shaken to her core, she flinched at Callum's voice. But she couldn't tear her gaze from Dag—her partner and friend. Couldn't look away from the stare that froze the fire inside her as if his eyes were shooting ice into her soul.

"You're vulnerable to yourself. Dag sees it. He wants to protect you as desperately as we do. And it's clear God is protecting you. Just like He sent you to protect Cora and others, He sent Dag for you. He sent us to be your protection in this moment."

Something shifted in Phoenix's mind, as if a door that had always been sealed cracked open. Could Callum be right?

She watched Dag.

His lips had lowered, but he still gave her the icy stare of warning that he leveled at criminals. The stare that said if she acted on her violent thoughts, he would intervene.

"You've done so much for me, Phoenix." Cora's soft tone, thickened with tears, reached for Phoenix's heart. "You've changed the lives of every woman at PK-9 for the better. You helped us all overcome our pasts. But do you see how your efforts wouldn't have been enough on their own? Every one of us needed God to do the work of saving us in the end. Of bringing us to Him so we could truly be healed."

Phoenix's gaze pulled to Cora.

Tears trekked down her cheeks as she watched Phoenix.

"You're amazing, Phoenix." Callum braced his hands on the sill of the window and leaned forward as if to stare into her more deeply. "You create elaborate plans and predict what people will do and say, all for one aim—to help others overcome their pasts and ensure justice is done. But where do you think that desire and your abilities came from? They were hardwired into you by God Himself. He is even better at planning and strategy than you are."

Callum straightened, gesturing at Cora and the observation room with a sweep of his hand. "Why do you think we're here, right now? Because He knows you need us, and we need you. He made our lives intersect at just the right time for both of us."

Phoenix's ears perked. *"We need you...for both of us."* Had she done something for Callum?

He held Phoenix with his intense gaze. "God is the One Who enabled Dag to find Rose at exactly the right moment. He's the One Who let the searchers recover all the kidnapped children so not one of them was lost. He had you train Marnie and then placed her with the other hostages so they would be saved."

Callum's hands lifted in front of him as passion infused his voice. "He kept you from finding this killer all the years you've tried. And He ordained the killer's attack now, orchestrating all the events to allow you to capture him and end up here. In the very place that God gave Cora access to well in advance so we could reach you just in time."

Callum stepped even closer to the glass. "He's the Creator of the universe, Phoenix. He can predict every human's behavior, not because He knows what they'll do, but because He controls everything. He ordains all that comes to pass. He can strategize and plan much better than even you because He controls the future."

Callum's lips formed a straight line, matching the gravity in his gaze. "He causes people to be reborn out of sin and darkness into light and eternal life. He can do that for you, Phoenix. He can give you the rebirth you've been trying to bring about yourself for twenty-six years. He can raise you up out of the ashes."

Phoenix couldn't look away from Callum. Her pulse pounded, echoing in her ears as if in an empty chamber. Her throat dried. Scratchy. Her breaths came shallow and short.

That door in her mind opened farther still. Facts she hadn't noticed before spilled out, falling rapidly into place as they interconnected to form a shape she never could have predicted. So many instances in her life, in the lives of others. Inexplicable events, impossible timing, synchronicity. The transformation of the PK-9 agents, well beyond what Phoenix could explain. The course of her own life. The frustrated attempts to catch the monster, even when she'd thought she had him.

And everything falling into place now. The evidence. Rose's remains. The pendant. His mass kidnapping in a national park. His fixation on Phoenix to retrieve his Phaistos Disc. All of those events led to his capture, at long last.

She'd thought that was her doing. Her powers of deduction and predicting human behavior. Her tracking skills and intelligence.

But her intelligence told her something different now. Something she'd never wanted to see.

She wasn't capable of orchestrating all that had unfolded. No human was.

It would require a Divine Being. An uncreated Being. Someone outside time. Someone in control of everything, down to the very fabric of the universe. Someone like the God her parents had taught her about as a child. The God they'd cried out to when the monster invaded their home.

Was that part of a master plan? A painful part she didn't want and didn't believe was necessary—but all the while, it could have been vital. For the protection of the vulnerable. For her family. For her.

Could she trust Him, just as she asked the PK-9 team and all those she helped to trust her? Even when they didn't understand what she was doing or that it would be all right in the end.

"Phoenix, put down the knife. Please." Callum's voice was so gentle, it brought a prick of tears to her eyes.

She blinked them away as her gaze lowered to the weapon still in her hand. The instrument of torture.

She angled toward the monster.

He stared at her, terror in his eyes.

It didn't fill her with satisfaction this time. It twisted her gut.

"'Vengeance is mine; I will repay.'" Callum seemed to read her thoughts, giving her the assurance she needed. "Cora is right. God promised He will punish all wrongs in the end. That He'll bring justice and vengeance to the killer you have in chains and every person who does evil."

*Every person.*

Dag still watched her warily, the trust that had always been in his gaze when he looked at her replaced by guardedness.

She only wanted justice. But Dag saw the darkness in her.

The knife hilt was cold and heavy in her hand.

*"The why for what you're doing doesn't matter."* Callum's statement from moments ago rang in her conscience. Exactly what she always said about killers and abusers. It didn't matter if they'd suffered abuse or trauma themselves. Nothing justified the crimes they committed against others.

Nothing, not even her quest for justice, excused her enjoyment of causing suffering, the torture she'd been about to visit upon the monster.

The truth doused the last embers of the fire of hatred within. "It's too late." The confession slipped from her lips as a near whisper that perhaps only God could hear.

She lifted her head to see Callum. "You said it. I deserve punishment and suffering. I've become sick and evil in my thinking. Like him. I wanted to torture him. I would have, if you hadn't come."

Callum nodded. Something shimmered in his eyes. Moisture? "I deserve that, too. I should be destined for judgment in hell for all the wrongs I've done. Jesus said if we only think badly about another person, we're subject to the fires of hell. But He forgave me for my sins. And He'll forgive you, too, if you repent and ask for forgiveness."

"No, that can't be." Phoenix slowly moved her head back and forth in denial. "Not if He is just, as you claim. By that argument, serial killers could be forgiven and let off without punishment."

"If He chooses to save them, yes."

"That isn't justice."

"It is when He does it, because Jesus Christ paid the price for the sins of His children." Callum glanced at Cora.

She nodded, silently encouraging him to continue.

He returned his focus to Phoenix. "You're right. Sin must be punished. If God pardoned someone for doing evil, and no one ever paid for that, He wouldn't be just. So He sent his Son, Jesus, to live a sinless life, something only the God-man could do, so that He had no sins of His own that needed to be paid for. Then He went to the cross where God poured out on Him all the just wrath that was meant for me." Callum placed a hand on his chest with the words. "And for Cora. For every one of His children, so that we could be forgiven *and* the debt be paid."

Urgency intensified the green in Callum's eyes as he held Phoenix's gaze. "Jesus paid it all, Phoenix. Justice has been done."

Her heart lurched into her throat. *"Justice has been done."* The most hopeful words she'd ever heard.

Something moist slid down her cheek. A tear?

Phoenix Gray did not weep.

But for justice, for evil being repaid. For that, she would spend her tears.

All the truths she had overlooked, perhaps intentionally hiding in the secret vault of her mind, interconnected and rose as one shape in her mind. The shape of a Being she didn't recognize.

But He was just, He was perfect. He was in control. He could raise her from the ashes.

*Yes. God, I want to shed these ashes.* The unspoken prayer flowed up from her soul, where the fiery embers had been snuffed out and only dark ashes remained. *I want to be justified. Make me right before You. Grant me Your forgiveness for the evil I've fostered and acted upon, that You have paid for in full.*

Even as her prayer finished in her mind, His response came swift and strong.

A current blazed through her, sparking every fiber of her being, electrifying and awakening the dead corners of her heart and mind.

Life. That was what it was.

And it refused to be contained.

Phoenix felt her lips curve before she meant to smile.

"Phoenix?" Cora's voice lifted with a blend of hope and worry.

But Callum grinned. The first broad, happy grin Phoenix had ever seen on his face. It sent a jolt to her swelling heart.

"You've been reborn." His gaze found hers and looked into her soul.

"I believe I have."

"Oh, Phoenix." Cora pressed her hands together in front of her face as more tears spilled from her eyes. "You don't know how long I've prayed for this moment."

"I do." Since the day Cora had come to work for Phoenix, she was sure. Cora's passion for sharing her faith had been obvious from the first and had not waned with the years.

Cora laughed, a beautiful sound that sent a burst of something Phoenix didn't recognize through her chest.

Was that joy? Phoenix would have to work on identifying the emotions that apparently belonged to the new life pulsating through her. But so far, she didn't mind the change.

A whine cut the feeling short.

She looked down at Dag.

Gone was the warning and threat against her evil intentions. His blue eyes looked up at her with trust, once again.

She crouched in front of him and stroked his head. "Well done, Dagian."

"I hate to break this up, but do you think you could let us in there?" Callum's question was filled with a note of humor. "And maybe we should give the prisoner to the authorities before we get in trouble."

Something moved up Phoenix's throat. Was that a laugh? It didn't make it to an actual sound, but the idea that something as happy as laughter might be accessible to her was a shock. Another change she would have to ponder and adapt to.

She went to the locked door and placed her palm on the interior reader.

The internal latch clicked as it released, and the steel door slid open. She pressed the button to hold it open and stepped through.

Callum met her first. His hands moved away from his sides as if he considered embracing her.

A bolt of heat shot through her torso. Did he want to?

But he shoved his hands into his pants pockets instead and smiled—the small, sweet smile she'd come to know and...

She left the thought unfinished as her pulse skipped in an odd pattern.

"I can't tell you how glad I am to see you." The meaning of his words was not lost on her. Nor was the depth of joy in his eyes. He meant the real her, the new her. The Phoenix who was no longer twisted and tormented inside like the serial killers they brought to justice.

Emotions thickened her throat. New emotions she couldn't identify. But there was one of old. The longing for connection. The connection she'd only felt with one person—Callum Ross.

"Phoenix." Cora rushed around Callum as if no longer able to contain her happiness. Her smile beamed just before it disappeared from sight as she wrapped her arms around Phoenix in a gentle embrace. She pulled back quickly. "Forgive me. I know you don't like hugs."

Phoenix looked on Cora, the woman so very like Rose in all the best ways. The woman with her own brand of strength and courage that Phoenix had always valued but now admired more than ever. Phoenix owed her a debt she could not repay. "Thank you."

Cora tilted her head. Then she nodded, her mouth forming a watery smile as more tears pooled in her eyes. "Thank *you*."

Phoenix owed Callum a similar debt, added to the debt for saving Dagian's life. If it hadn't been for him sharing the truth alongside Cora, for him deducing where Phoenix was and what she had planned—which she was sure had been Callum's doing—she would still be dead in the truest sense and destined for a tormented future she did not want to consider now.

She turned to tell him, but he was entering the prisoner's cell.

Phoenix let Callum take the lead in unlocking the chains, for which she provided the key.

The prisoner was smart enough to keep silent and cooperate while Callum removed the bindings. Callum switched the handcuffs to the front, likely because he saw the bite wounds on the prisoner's arm would not rub against his side that way.

Phoenix's heart pinched as she marveled at Callum's compassion. Even for a child-killer.

Perhaps she would get there someday. But for now, she was content to let Callum take hold of the killer and follow her out of the deep dungeons of her house, upstairs through the labyrinth of hallways and barred gates.

As they came to the door that led to her living space at the front of the house, an unexpected feeling of anticipation added more lightness to the life that still pulsed through her.

Perhaps she would leave this dark and cold part of her house, that part of her old self, behind forever.

The door opened.

She took in a deep breath and stepped through.
A snarl.
Phoenix somersaulted as a shot pierced the air.

# FORTY-NINE

Phoenix came out of the somersault, pain searing her arm.

A bullet had hit its target.

She stayed low and snatched the Glock from her waistband behind her back.

"Move, and the blonde dies." A black-haired, tall man aimed a Glock at Cora's head.

Special Agent Grant Brayson.

Of course. The killer of Marnie's mother. There to finish the job, which now included eliminating Phoenix. He apparently thought his men had told her his identity. Big mistake.

The corrupt agent gripped Cora's upper arm, standing to her right with a foot between them. Putting him close to Callum.

Callum had stepped out of the doorway and held the prisoner's arm. His gaze found Phoenix.

Their eyes locked. Understanding lit his.

The second he released his grip on the prisoner, Phoenix slowly stood.

Dag growled at Brayson.

"You and your dog stand down, Gray. Or your friend here gets it."

"You clearly didn't plan to find more than me here. You'll never make it out."

"Oh, I will. I'll eliminate you and then take care of that brat, once and for all. No one—"

Callum lunged at Brayson, hitting him low and hard.

A shot went off as they slammed to the ground.

The prisoner sprinted across Phoenix's view of the fight.

Callum could handle Brayson.

"Cora. Open the access gate to the front yard."

Pale and shaken, Cora still rallied as always and pulled her smart pad from her purse. Two seconds of tapping, then she looked up. "Done."

Phoenix and Dag followed the prisoner out the door at an easy walk.

Growls and barks curved her mouth into a smile.

She followed the sounds around the side of the house, going through the opened gate to where her K-9s must have cornered the prisoner.

Not only the dogs. The new feeling that must be joy welled up in her chest at the sight of the prisoner standing against the wall of her house, Birger and Apollo holding him there with barks, and the PK-9 team providing backup.

"Hey, Phoenix." Nevaeh greeted her with a grin. "We saw this guy and figured he hadn't been shown out properly yet."

"The cuffs were our first clue." Jazz laughed. "Glad you must've let the boys loose just before he tried to take off, or they would've missed all the fun."

Phoenix and Dag walked by the two women and stopped at the center of the half-circle the agents formed.

Sofia flashed one of her giant grins. "Told him he must be a real loser for Birger to actually pull the guardian routine. Takes a whole lot of evil intent to earn a Great Pyrs' wrath." She laughed, completely unaware she'd hit the mark of Phoenix's conscience.

But her evil intent had been paid for. Justice was done.

The reminder brought a smile to her lips once again.

"Phoenix?" Bristol leaned past Sofia to peer at her. "Are you okay?"

All of the agents' attention shifted to Phoenix. These amazing women who fiercely cared about each other and Phoenix, who had been given new life by the same God Who had now given that life to her.

"Yes. I believe I'm wonderful."

---

"Are you sure you're all right?"

Cora answered Callum's question with a nod, her complexion slowly recovering some pink color.

Callum aimed the Glock at the man who was apparently another crooked FBI agent looking for Marnie, given the threat he'd thrown at Phoenix. Callum had been able to disarm him quickly and had him on his knees to wait for backup.

Holding the guy's own weapon on him carried a certain sense of satisfaction, but Callum would give anything for zip ties or handcuffs right then. Because he wanted nothing more than to be with Phoenix.

To make sure she was all right. To revel in the miracle he could hardly believe. Not only had God prevented her from committing a horrible crime, but He'd brought Phoenix to Himself.

A thrill shot through Callum as he tried to grasp the reality he hadn't even dared to dream could be possible.

"It's incredible, isn't it?" Cora moved closer to Callum's elbow.

He glanced at her and caught the wonder in her eyes—the same wonder that was filling his heart to overflowing. He nodded. "Incredible." He stopped with that, afraid he might not be able to get anything else out past the gratitude and happiness that bunched in his throat.

"Zip ties, anyone?" The familiar offer from the female voice brought a smile to Callum's face.

He turned to see Sofia saunter into Phoenix's house with Raksa. This time, he wasn't surprised that the Phoenix K-9 Agency had shown up when needed. "Perfect timing, once again."

"Always." She held up a black zip tie and lifted her eyebrows.

"Please." Callum took one hand off the Glock to gesture toward the agent.

Sofia walked to him and pulled his arms, one at a time, behind his back to tie his wrists. "Who is this guy?"

"No idea. He wants to kill Phoenix and Marnie, I think."

Sofia rolled her eyes. "Join the club."

"I believe he's the FBI agent Phoenix was trying to find." Cora watched the kneeling man. "The one who murdered Marnie's mother. He must have hired Tinney and his comrades, as well."

"Nice guy. I'll take him out." Sofia winked at Cora. "And you can interpret that however you like."

Cora shook her head with a smile.

"Supposed to greet the FBI anyway." Sofia hauled the man to his feet.

"How's Phoenix?"

Sofia shot Callum a curious glance, then cast a mischievous, knowing look at Cora.

Heat crawled up the back of his neck. Though there shouldn't be anything innately romantic about the question, given the circumstances. "The gunshot wound."

"Gunshot wound?" Sofia's brow crunched into incredulity. "No way. Phoenix never gets injured." Her mouth shifted to one side. "Though she was acting a little weird."

Weird. And Sofia didn't know Phoenix had been shot? That meant she wasn't getting any medical attention.

"You believe Phoenix was shot?" Concern shaped Cora's tone.

"His bullet got her in the arm. Her sweater ripped." Callum started backing toward the door and looked at Sofia. "You've got this?"

"Sure." Confusion and a bit of suspicion, like one might have when watching a crazy person, still filled her eyes.

But Callum didn't want to stay another moment to explain his worry. "Where is she?"

"Around the south side of the house."

"Thanks." Callum dashed out the front door.

A man pulled up short in front of Callum as he darted to the side, narrowly avoiding a crash.

Kent. "Where's Cora?"

Callum thumbed over his shoulder. "In there." He took off again, his heart rate double-timing as he veered away from the FBI vehicles approaching the house, the rising sun backlighting them and bathing Phoenix's property in an orange glow.

Callum sprinted around the corner.

Nevaeh's curls and red jacket caught his eye. She stood next to Jazz, both of them watching something. Their dogs were beside them, staring in the same direction.

Shouldn't Nevaeh be treating Phoenix's wound?

He hurried through the open gate, his gaze swinging past Bristol and Toby to see what held their attention.

Phoenix.

Her long, blond braid dragged on the brown grass as she lay on the ground behind the Forster killer, Dag waiting a few feet away. Her arms wrapped around the prisoner. In a choke from the looks of it.

Callum's mouth twitched as his pulse slowed. He should have known a bullet wouldn't stop Phoenix Gray.

"Would you believe he tried to attack her?" Nevaeh shook her head and rolled her eyes. "With handcuffs on."

Callum walked closer to Phoenix, his heart driving his feet, apparently unable to wait any longer to be near her. "I thought you weren't going to kill him." The humor was probably irreverent and totally inappropriate given what she'd just gone through. But he didn't seem able to contain the mirth and joy bubbling in his chest.

She didn't look at Callum or show any surprise he was there.

"He went for the pendant. I suppose you're about to tell me the FBI frowns on chokeholds."

A full smile cracked his mouth. So Phoenix did do humor. Even a joke. "Here I thought Phoenix Gray was always right."

She pulled away, sliding out from under the man and getting to her feet as the prisoner stayed still. "Bristol."

The brunette headed for the unconscious prisoner, apparently assigned to deal with the serial killer.

Phoenix turned her gaze on Callum.

His heart stopped. Then jumpstarted with a horse kick that nearly knocked him over.

He couldn't move.

But she did, walking slowly toward him until only three feet separated them.

He stared into her beautiful eyes. Brown eyes. Robin's eyes.

Except they were so very different now. Where there had been a dark void—an utter destitution of emotion—a radical change had taken place.

Now the brown orbs radiated with a vibrant intensity, perception, and intelligence—all softened with a brightness, as if a great light were shining from inside her and casting out all the darkness of before. And so it was.

"Boss, were you shot?"

Phoenix slowly looked away, as if she didn't want to, as Nevaeh hustled to her with Alvarez, Jazz, and Flash trailing closely behind.

Nevaeh gently parted the sweater sleeve where it was torn and peered at the wound. She let out a whistle. "I'll be. Looks like a bullet grazed you." Her eyes widened as she looked up at Phoenix and then glanced at Jazz. "We all thought you were invincible."

Jazz nodded. "Indestructible."

"She pretty much is." The words came out before Callum considered saying them. Filled with too much admiration, apparently, given the secret smiles Nevaeh and Jazz exchanged.

But he didn't care. Because just then, Phoenix turned her attention on him, and he forgot everything else.

Until a throat cleared. "You know, this injury isn't too bad." Nevaeh's tone sounded completely inauthentic, but Callum couldn't look away from Phoenix. "I think we'll help Bristol with the prisoner, and I can patch it up later."

Phoenix turned her head, quickly scanning. She must have been satisfied everything was in order, because she brought her focus back to Callum.

His heart thudded against his ribs as the truth struck him. Life would never be dull with Phoenix Gray. And he wanted to be there for all of it. To earn her permission to be part of her life. Her future. Maybe, someday, to earn her love.

He knew he'd be waiting a long time for her to say anything, to give him an indication of where he stood. To tell him if there was any hope for his crazy dream.

So he wouldn't waste any time getting started. "It's going to take a while to finish everything here. Debriefs, wrap-up investigations, building the case for trial…"

He moistened his dry lips, staring into those gorgeous brown eyes. They held so much now. So many emotions and thoughts he wanted to explore for the rest of his days. If she'd let him. "I'm thinking I'll stick around for a while." A very long while, hopefully. He kept that thought to himself. For now.

"I'll bring Jewel here." Callum took a step closer to Phoenix, his heart urging him to close the gap between them completely. But that would be moving way too fast. Especially when he didn't even know how she felt about him.

"I'd be honored if…" He considered for one crazy, split second asking what his mind leaped to—for a future with her, for her love. But he held back the impulse just in time. "…If you'd allow me to introduce Jewel to you."

Phoenix watched him for a moment. A long, silent moment. Was she not going to answer him again?

Slowly, her mouth lifted at the corners, and her smile

dawned, one hundred times more radiant than the sunrise that bathed her in its light.

Then he knew. God had given him a new purpose he could never have imagined and hadn't known he needed—loving Phoenix.

And he knew, with a predictive certainty that could belong to Phoenix Gray herself, that someday, she would love him, too.

# EPILOGUE

*Six months later*

"Come on, Phoenix." Marnie marched across the grass that was sprinkled with the green beginnings of spring. "Mom says you should join the party."

The girl smiled up at Phoenix as she took her hand, a new gesture Phoenix had allowed since the kidnapping. Since the changes that had started in the dungeon of her house and continued in the deep recesses of her heart. The work of the Holy Spirit within, according to the Bible she'd been studying after Cora had given her a copy.

Among the changes He'd wrought was a willingness to show her love and affection for others, and to let them do the same in return. It was an ongoing struggle and effort for Phoenix to risk such vulnerability.

But it wasn't actually a risk now. Not with a sovereign God in charge Who controlled all things and had a perfect plan He was bringing to completion.

The reminder made Phoenix grip Marnie's hand in return as the girl tugged her toward the long table between two benches that Eli had built to hold his large family. With the PK-9 team and their families present, as well, the lawn chairs clustered in two circles would be needed to supplement when they all sat down to eat.

Dag followed alongside Phoenix, and Jewel, Callum's tall Great Dane, stayed within inches of him. For some reason, she'd bonded with Dag and Phoenix at their first meeting, despite Dag not being sure what to make of his new shadow. But he let her stay close without protest, perhaps a sign he would consider reciprocating the friendship someday.

As they reached the table and chairs on the east side of the Moores' home, Phoenix's gaze went of its own accord to the grill where Eli and Callum stood and talked. Eli's boisterous laugh carried easily on the cool breeze as he rotated the meats on the grill.

But it was Callum's quiet smile, and his glance in Phoenix's direction, that awakened the ache in her chest. The ache that only he seemed to stir, often with his mere presence recently. And with his absence, too.

The scents of hot dogs, brats, and hamburgers reached Phoenix's nostrils.

Then it was her dad who stood behind the grill, Mom making him laugh. Phoenix tickled Rose until she fell to the grass, giggling.

Hot moisture pricked Phoenix's eyes as the memory, so vivid one second, pulled away to reveal the present in the next. She blinked the tears back.

The memories still had value, she'd learned. As did the tears. So she let them come more often, allowing the memories and tears free passage to interrupt her days with feelings and parts of herself she'd forgotten. Parts that hadn't been destroyed but only hidden out of fear.

But the fear that justice wouldn't be done, that the staggering pain of loss could never be relieved—those fears no longer kept her from the memories. Because now she knew the glorious truth. Her mom, dad, and Rose weren't dead. They were alive. They'd simply gone ahead to the eternal home where she would join them someday.

"Phoenix, can I get you anything?" Marion smiled as she set plates on the white tablecloth with one hand while cradling baby Hannah against her shoulder.

"No."

"Want to come watch us play baseball with Uncle Branson and Uncle Mike? Aunt Sof is playing, too." Marnie squinted in the sunlight as she looked up at Phoenix. "She says we're going to show the boys how it's done."

Uncles and aunts already. Although that day was the first time Marion had met most of the PK-9 team and their spouses, she had already decided they could be family to her children. The woman's open, loving heart was astounding. At least Phoenix understood better how and why Marion could be so willing to love all people. It was God's love in her, overflowing to others.

Perhaps, someday, Phoenix would get closer to sharing His love so courageously.

"No, we'll wait here." Phoenix sat in a lawn chair near the table.

"Hey, Marnie!" Joe's shout and wave from the makeshift baseball diamond staved off any disappointment.

"Coming!" Marnie sprinted to join the other children, Sofia's daughter, Grace, the first to welcome her. Given the two girls' challenging backgrounds, it was no surprise they had connected immediately upon meeting.

Dag lay down beside Phoenix, and Jewel quickly dropped to the damp grass next to him, drawing a pointed look from Dag. But he didn't move away.

Phoenix seemed to have the stronger urge to stand up and leave. To go stand at the perimeter, watching for danger and observing the interactions of the women in her care from afar. But she'd been trying to change that, too. Trying to live in the truth that they were in God's care, as well. And His protection was more effective and foolproof than hers.

Barks drew her attention to Toby, Raksa, and Gaston as the off-duty K-9s jogged around the children with Marion's dogs, Lily and Hercules. Even Flash was comfortable enough to choose a rare separation from Jazz to play with the children. Like his human partner, Flash showed signs every day that he was learning to embrace his new PK-9 family.

Nevaeh's and Sofia's husbands shouted and waved as they tried to corral the children and assign positions.

Bristol laughed from the lawn chair where she sat next to her husband, Remington, watching the chaos in the yard as she held her baby daughter. "I don't know how you manage, Marion. I'm worried I'll mess up our first little one, and you make eight look so easy."

Marion smiled at Bristol. "How old is she?"

"Two months." Remington beamed like a proud father as he caressed his daughter's dark hair. He looked at his wife. "And I told you, we'll do just fine. Neither you or God are about to let me ruin our first child."

Bristol playfully slapped his arm, and he laughed.

Marion's smile widened at the couple. "If you both follow the Lord and teach your daughter to love Him, too, you're doing the best anyone can."

"Potato salad and cherry salad, coming through." Jazz's call carried past the screen door as her husband, Hawthorne, pushed it open, then held it for her, Nevaeh, and Cora, all three of them carrying bowls. Kent and Jana slipped through after Cora, both staying close to their favorite person, as usual.

"And cheese puffs for Nevaeh." Cora smiled at Nevaeh as she stepped around Jana and Cannenta to set the bowl on the table, squeezing it between the fruit bowl and platter of vegetables. "Is this where you want it, Marion?"

"Anywhere you can find room is perfect." Marion pushed aside a pitcher of milk to create space for the bowl Nevaeh held, then went around to the same side of the table as Cora. "Thank you for bringing food."

"This is an amazing feast, Marion, without our contributions." Cora straightened and smiled at their hostess. Odd to see them together, these women who had been the first people Phoenix had cared about—had come to love—after her family was gone. Keeping them apart, two protected worlds that never met, where one barely knew about the other, had been so much safer. But doing so had prevented this, the special moment Phoenix was watching unfold. The connection of two kindred souls. Two sisters in Christ, as Cora liked to say.

"You are so kind to open your home to all of us. Thank you." Cora smiled.

But Marion reached out and touched Cora's arm with her mouth drawn in a serious line. "No. Thank *you*." She cast her gaze to include Nevaeh, Jazz, Bristol…and Phoenix. "Thank you to all of you. I thank God for each of you every night and every morning." Her eyes shimmered, and her chin trembled. "And every time I look at Marnie."

Cora rubbed Marion's back with a comforting hand. "I think I can speak for all of us when I say it was truly our honor and privilege. And when I say it wasn't us—it was God. He chose us for the task."

Marion's gaze found Cora's, and she nodded. "Amen. You look so familiar, I feel like we've met before. Are you a follower of Jesus?"

"I am." Cora nodded. She glanced at Phoenix first, and then the others standing near. "We all are, praise the Lord. And I can tell you must be, too."

Marion nodded, a smile stretching her mouth as she wiped away an escaping tear. "Thanks to a lovely woman who visited the orphanage I lived in one Christmas when I was a little girl. She told me about Jesus and how God chooses to adopt His children. And she gave me a baby Jesus figurine I still have to this day."

Phoenix listened carefully to the story. Marion had never shared it with Phoenix before, likely because she hadn't wanted to know. But now, the account of another's journey to justification held a great fascination. There seemed to be no end to the ways God worked and brought His children to Himself.

"I didn't come to faith then..." Marion reached for the plastic cups clustered at the center of the table and began to set them by plates, one at a time.

Kent grabbed the remaining cups and took over the distribution with his usual expediency.

"Thank you." Marion cast him a smile, then brought her focus back to Cora. "I came to Christ years later as an adult, thanks to the seeds she planted and the memory of what she told me. I wish I could tell her the impact she had. But I know God will tell Mrs. Isaksson and reward her richly someday when she gets to heaven."

"Mrs. Isaksson?" Cora's surprised response came at the same time the name triggered realization in Phoenix's mind.

It couldn't be.

Cora cast a glance at Phoenix, then darted her gaze back to Marion. "Do you know if her first name was Elizabeth?"

Marion blinked. "I don't know. Why?"

"My mother was Elizabeth Isaksson, and she used to visit orphanages at Christmas time with other ladies from her church."

"Oh, my. Do you look like your mother?"

Cora nodded, her eyes widening, full of amazement.

"That's the reason I thought of telling the story. Because you remind me so much of her."

"That's incredible." Jazz looked at the women, then at Nevaeh, who also stared in disbelief.

The hairs on Phoenix's arms stood on end as Marion and Cora laughed and embraced around the baby on Marion's shoulder. Then they cried as Cora shared that her mother had passed away when Cora was young.

Until six months ago, Phoenix had no idea she was only a small part in the unfathomable plan of the Master Planner. Of the God Who worked all things for the good of those Who loved Him. A God Who knew all the connections, the causes and effects, the details and the broad strokes that were necessary for the plan of redemption and for moments like these that meant the world to the people living them.

God was truly wondrous and incomprehensible. Which gave Phoenix further confirmation that He was truly God. Big enough and mighty enough to control all that she couldn't and vastly more. To bring to justice those who did evil, and to pardon those He chose to justify.

"Brats and hot dogs are ready, hon!" Eli called to Marion with a wave as Callum headed their way, carrying a platter heaped with meat.

"Okay." She returned the wave.

Still always on alert with excellent situational awareness, Sofia started leading the children, dogs, and coaches toward the house.

"We'll have to call the baseball crew to—" Marion halted as she looked toward the yard. "Oh, Sofia's already bringing them in." Marion turned to Callum and pointed to the spot on the table she'd cleared. "If you could set it there, please, I'll cover it with this foil to keep everything warm."

Marnie and Grace ran ahead of the other children, Flash and Toby prancing alongside them, having the time of their lives.

"Can I have hot dogs?"

"Me, too, please." Grace's request came on the heels of Marnie's.

"It's 'may I,' and, yes, you both may." Marion held up a finger. "But only after you go inside and wash up. Marnie, I want you to show Grace where she can wash and then help all the little ones."

"Okay."

Pride swelled in Phoenix's chest at Marnie's uncomplaining response.

Becoming the protector and advisor for forty-seven kidnapped children had made the girl grow in maturity by leaps and bounds. But her smiles and laughter proved that the additional confidence, and the security provided by her parents' love, enabled her to enjoy her childhood more than ever.

"I told Eli an outdoor party wasn't the best idea in these muddy conditions. The snow only just melted two days ago." Marion shook her head as Marnie and Grace ushered the other children inside, all of them spattered with dirt.

"Hey, this is May in Minnesota." Eli grinned at his wife as he carried a platter of hamburgers to the table. "It's all the spring we're going to get. And we couldn't let this occasion go without a celebration."

All eyes went to Phoenix as a hush settled in the cool air. They all knew the truth now. Knew she was Robin Forster, the only survivor of the famous serial killer. And they knew she had nearly tortured him to death in an effort to see that justice was served.

The only measurable change after they knew was that they behaved with less caution and more happiness when they interacted with her. Though perhaps that was due, more than anything, to her becoming a Christian.

"Phoenix, do you want to make a toast before the kids come tearing out here?" Eli lifted a plastic cup of lemonade off the table.

A toast. She looked on the expectant faces as she stood and accepted the cup offered by Cora. They would expect a toast to celebrate the conviction of Jim Nullop.

The man who had murdered her family felt the wrath of the community and justice system when his highly publicized case was expedited, and he was sentenced to life in prison. Even with no possibility of parole or abbreviated sentence for any reason, and his location in a maximum-security prison, the punishment was not enough recompense for the crimes he had done to her family and all the others.

But whatever justice was lacking would be meted out through God's wrath. That assurance made all the difference, allowing Phoenix to experience a daily sense of peace she'd never known before.

And she could be patient for Marnie's attackers to be tried, praying that they would be brought to justice. It was incredible to know God's answer to that prayer was already *Yes*. Whether in the courts or at their final judgment before God, the two FBI agents Brayson and Tinney, as well as Franks, the FBI-impersonating sidekick who had survived, would receive justice.

But none of those outcomes, positive or lacking, seemed worthy of the gathering of these individuals—the gathering of this Christian community that God had wrought.

She lifted the cup. "To the God Who is sovereign over all things." The line from the hymn they often sang at Cora's church leaped to Phoenix's tongue. "And Who saved a wretch like me."

"Amen." Eli's response was echoed by the others in the group as they nodded, and Cora wiped a tear from her cheek.

"We're ready!" Marnie and Grace burst from the house and screeched to a halt by Eli as the other children tumbled out after them.

Eli laughed and rested his large hand on his daughter's head. "Okay. But we're going to pray first. Though Phoenix already did a pretty good job of that." He aimed a warm smile at Phoenix before switching his focus to Branson. "Care to lead us, Pastor Branson?"

Nevaeh's husband chuckled as he lowered his arm from his wife's waist and folded his large hands together. "I'm not officially a pastor yet, but I would be honored." Branson bowed his head, and Phoenix joined in the prayer filled with gratitude for the many blessings God had bestowed upon the people gathered there.

The moment Branson ended the prayer, chaos ensued as the children begged for their favorite foods while Marion herded them toward chairs to let their guests sit at the table and start eating first.

Phoenix used the commotion to disappear.

A honed instinct she had not abandoned entirely. And she wasn't sure she should. Although she had to admit to herself that disappearing now may not have been for legitimate security reasons.

She stopped at the edge of the woods on the Moores' property, hidden beneath the trees as she watched the joyful gathering by the house.

The impulse could have come because the ache had increased during the prayer. Or perhaps when she'd seen the laughing, happy couples and families. Or had it been before, when Callum had watched her during her toast?

She hadn't met his gaze. Her relationship with God was so new. She had never thought she'd needed Him. And now that she knew how much she needed God, she had to spend all her time with Him. He was all she needed. He was completing her. And He could satisfy the longing the ache stemmed from.

But she hadn't minded the way Callum had integrated into her life in the past six months. Within a week of Jim Nullop's arrest, Callum had moved into a Minneapolis apartment with Jewel. A day later, he'd asked Phoenix if she and Dag would meet him and Jewel at one of the city's parks to become acquainted.

Once the introduction to Jewel had been achieved, Callum had wasted no time in creating new excuses to come around. First, they needed to compare notes about Jim Nullop, and Callum wanted Phoenix to review his statement and trial preparations.

Then, Callum had dug persistently enough into Phoenix's normal activities that he'd learned of her work at the prison and in self-defense training for women and teen girls. Proclaiming, with a sincerity Phoenix couldn't deny, that he had always wanted to become involved in such efforts himself, he somehow convinced her to let him be the so-called bad guy for her female self-defense students to practice on.

He'd then suggested they start a self-defense class for girls and boys of younger, elementary ages. She hadn't been able to deny the idea was a good one, and Marnie joined them as a student instructor in their new co-ed self-defense program for kids.

Given that Callum also attended Cora's church where Phoenix went, she saw Callum at least three times a week if not more. Clearly by Callum's design.

He explained his schedule flexibility and availability to often take walks in the park with their dogs by reminding Phoenix he'd taken a leave of absence from the FBI. And he excused his frequent requests to join her for dinner at her home by saying he'd never tasted cooking as good as hers.

Those reasons could be true, but they both knew he wasn't inserting himself into her life out of boredom or hunger. His eyes, his attention, his respect, and even the space he was giving her without pressure or expectations said there was a much deeper reason for the closeness he pursued.

The ache deep inside Phoenix throbbed. God would fulfill that longing, wouldn't He? If He didn't, she would live with it as she always had. She didn't know how to do anything different.

"You're not leaving, are you?" The male voice—Callum's voice—jolted her heart.

She turned to see him walking toward her with Jewel through the trees, twenty feet away.

No one surprised her at that distance. Had part of her wanted him to follow?

She faced forward again, her attention returning to the activity by the Moores' house.

Jewel's paws padded along the ground as she jogged to reach Dag. And Callum's steps halted about a foot from Phoenix.

He turned in the same direction she faced and stood beside her. Silent.

Her pulse sounded in her ears, beating erratically. Something it had started to do when he came near.

"Where are you going, Phoenix?" He asked the question in the soft, thoughtful tone she'd come to recognize. He intended more than the surface meaning of the words.

Where was she going to go? What was she going to do?

The questions had been constantly on her mind for the past six months. She'd always had a plan, since the age of fourteen when justice had become her mission.

She was looking at the fruit of one of those plans now—the Phoenix K-9 Agency. She had always intended it would become more than an agency. That it would become a family for the remarkable women who had conquered and become strong together.

Now, as she watched the smiling, laughing women with their husbands and children, there was no doubt she had succeeded in building the PK-9 family.

No, God had. He had simply used her to accomplish His purpose when she had no idea He was behind it all, bringing her simpler version of a plan to completion in ways she'd never predicted.

They were a family that could stand on their own without her. She had already thought as much, given how well Sofia had stepped into the leadership role. But now, Phoenix was even more certain they no longer needed her because God had and would continue to support them better than she ever could.

She would leave them as planned, only returning when they needed her help.

But leave to do what?

She had intended to move on in search of her family's killer. But that lifelong purpose was finished. She hadn't given thought to what she would do after that if the day came. Perhaps because she'd known daylight would not dawn for her if she had descended into the darkness of her intentions for the serial killer.

But she hadn't. Thanks in no small part to the man who stood beside her, patiently waiting for her response. Waiting for her. Something he had been doing for six months.

She couldn't give him what he wanted. But she could give him what he deserved. What she owed him.

She took in a slow breath, then turned to him. "Thank you."

He faced her, his greenish brown eyes skimming over her features. "For what?"

"Saving Dagian."

Callum held her gaze, not speaking for several seconds as the green in his irises intensified. "You're welcome. But you should know that as much as I wanted to help him, I did it for you."

Phoenix hadn't known that then. But she had deduced as much when he'd talked her down from ruining her life and her soul. Since then, he'd demonstrated nearly every day that he cared about her. How much, she wasn't certain.

"I've been praying a lot, trying to find out what God wants me to do with my life next. And His answer keeps getting louder and clearer." Callum stepped an inch closer, narrowing the gap even more.

Phoenix's heart rate spiked in response. She didn't move away, though she never stood that close to anyone. With his tall height, she had to tilt her head up, and his angled down toward her. Somehow, the positioning didn't put her at a disadvantage with Callum. He would never look down on her psychologically or make her feel vulnerable in any way. She knew that.

"But I need your answer, too."

She couldn't look away from the intensity in his gaze and the other emotion she hadn't yet wanted to name.

"I was content in my life, with my singleness and job. Then God brought you into it. And you exposed a void I didn't know I had. A longing I didn't know I had." His mouth curved in that sweet, closed smile. "It's like God suddenly created a Phoenix-shaped hole in my heart. And only you can fill it."

His arms moved slightly away from his sides toward her. As if he wanted to take her hands or touch her arms.

Alarm snaked through her, tension pinching her muscles.

But he didn't touch her. His arms returned to his sides. "What I'm trying to say is that I love you, Phoenix. I've loved you for a long time now."

Heat surged through her, speeding her heart rate as she searched his gaze.

The love was there in his eyes. Strong, deep, powerful.

The emotion she'd been feeling for him increasingly in the past six months rose within her. But was it love?

She didn't know. She had never loved a man like he would want her to. And she was only beginning to learn how to express friendship love more openly.

The feelings she had for Callum—the ache and longing he awakened deep within—those were different. So very different.

But he had said the same thing. That God had given him a longing he'd never had before, so she could fill it.

The longing for connection and understanding wasn't new for Phoenix. It had been there since she was a teenager, when she'd realized she must ignore it, keep it buried forever because she had a different purpose.

But could God have a greater purpose in that desire? It would explain why the longing for deep human connection, the ache that throbbed most painfully when Callum was near, hadn't been alleviated by her new relationship with Christ.

And why Callum felt the same thing. Was he right, that God had destined them—designed them—for a life together?

Her pulse skittered. She didn't know how to do that. Didn't know if she could.

Callum still watched her. Waiting for her.

"I don't know how to be in a relationship. To live life with someone else."

A spark lit his eyes as if she'd said she loved him in return. His hands slowly went to her forearms, resting gently on the sleeves of her black PK-9 windbreaker.

The warmth from his touch permeated through the nylon and the cotton of her sleeves beneath. Then the almost electric sensation kept traveling, through her skin, her arms, seeping into her chest where it found her racing heart.

Callum's touch felt nothing like she'd expected. It was like nothing she'd ever experienced.

She didn't mind it a bit.

"You know what I think?" His smile broadened. "God has a

plan for us, and He's going to make it happen no matter what. I'm more than happy to wait for that."

There it was again. Another declaration of love, though not in the same words.

And he was right. God had a plan. Was His plan for both of them to be together? Could God change her enough for even that?

Her phone vibrated loudly in her pocket.

Callum's gaze held her.

Another vibration.

"You should take that." The brown in Callum's eyes grew darker, his smile vanishing as he glanced down toward her pocket.

She stepped back, angling slightly away from him as she pulled out her phone and checked the caller ID.

*Wendy Arndt.*

Phoenix tapped to answer. "Go."

"Phoenix, I'm so glad I caught you. This is Agent Arndt. We have a situation. A seven-year-old girl has been kidnapped in Wheaton, and we think she's been transported outside state lines to Ohio. Can you help us get her back?"

Phoenix's jaw firmed. "Send me all the details you have. I'm on my way." She pressed the button to end the call and slipped the phone into her pocket.

Righteous anger, as the Bible called it, flared in Phoenix, leaving no doubt as to what her life's mission still was.

She'd normally be stalking away with Dag already. But something held her back.

Someone.

She lifted her gaze to Callum.

"Kidnapping?"

She jerked a nod.

"Where do you want me, Phoenix?" The same question he'd asked her once before.

"Your call." Her heart thumped against her ribs as she waited for his answer.

His eyes found hers, plunged deep inside her, to the hidden parts no one else understood. He saw her.

That sweetest of smiles curved his closed lips. "I'm going with you."

Joy, that emotion she was learning to recognize, burst from her heart and flowed through every fiber of her being. Her mouth stretched in the unfamiliar feeling of a smile. "Keep up."

She spun away and started off, Dag instantly by her side.

Then Callum fell in step with Jewel at Phoenix's other side, throwing her a knowing grin.

The soaring sensation in her chest lifted to even higher altitudes, and she had to struggle to focus on what she would need to rescue the girl and apprehend the kidnapper as quickly as possible.

Until she remembered, within a few seconds, that she had an advantage now that was greater than the mind of Phoenix Gray.

She had Callum and God. With Callum's support and God's plan in place, her quest for justice and her mission to rescue the victims of evil would never fail.

At last, she was truly Phoenix—reborn from the ashes of death, justified, and destined to live forever.

Turn the Page for a Special Sneak Peek of
WINDY CITY WESTONS, BOOK 1

# WAYLAID

**PREORDER NOW**

# WAYLAID

## CHAPTER ONE

*Chicago. August 28. 9:26 p.m.*

A pop pierced the night.

A gunshot? Spring Weston's stomach clenched as she ducked lower over the handlebars of her bicycle and peddled hard. A shooting wouldn't be a surprise in that neighborhood, but she'd rather avoid a run-in with a stray bullet.

She glanced into the hazy darkness on either side of her as she kept her pace steady, light raindrops mixing with sweat on her face.

Nothing moved in the glow from streetlamps.

A white van waited next to some business with barred windows. The building's sign was a yellow blur as she whizzed by, maintaining her racing speed.

She tapped the backlight on the timer attached to the handlebars. Great pace. Faster than she should be at mile ten. Adrenaline and nerves must be driving her legs.

Drugs. Doping. On *her* team.

The anxiety wadding in her stomach threatened to choke her.

She puffed out a breath, willing her muscles to relax as she kept pedaling at the same clip.

She glided through a curve into the headwind. Rain pelted her face.

"*Doping? Are you kidding me?*" Cliff's denial echoed in her ears, louder than the wind that rushed past. "*I run a clean team. You know that.*"

"But I saw Megan...popping pills." Spring had watched her coach, desperately hoping he would offer some explanation she could believe.

"How do you know they were drugs? She takes supplements all the time."

"Megan told me what the pills were."

Cliff laughed. "She told you? That'd be pretty dumb if she was doping, wouldn't it?"

Spring frowned at his jovial grin. "Megan didn't think I'd care. She thought it was expected. She said—" Spring moistened her lips. "She said the whole team is doing it."

"Well, there you go."

Spring raised her eyebrows.

"Obviously, she was just joking. She knows you don't take drugs." Cliff's grin angled sideways. "You know what a kidder Megan is. You gotta learn to lighten up and not take things so seriously."

She stared at him. Why couldn't he be more convincing? Offer some explanation or at least a denial that he was involved?

He had stepped closer to her, his grin softening into a smile that seemed to hide something. "Come on, Spring. Don't you trust me more than that?"

She had trusted him. But she knew what she had seen Megan take, what Megan had said. It wasn't a joke. At least not to Spring.

She shifted her shoulders, trying to relax as she surged through the neighborhood she was moving too fast to see.

The rain weakened, but her tense thoughts pelted her from the inside.

If only it wasn't true. If only she hadn't met Megan for a training run and seen her take those pills.

Spring pressed her lips together, trapping her breath longer than she should. She had no hard evidence to prove doping on the team. Only what Megan had told her. Would anyone believe her if she reported it? She could hardly believe it herself.

But she couldn't knowingly compete on a team that was doping. Every win would mean nothing. And the scandal could come out once she made it to an elite team. Everyone would think she had doped, too.

*Lord, give me wisdom.* Calm slid through her chest with the prayer, soothing the tension and allowing her to breathe more evenly.

She would have to report what she knew. Whether or not anyone believed her wasn't her responsibility.

Relief flowed to her fingers with the confidence that she'd made the right decision.

Readjusting her position over the handlebars, she focused on pushing her pace back up. A praise song from church started to play in her head, lending a driving beat to her pedaling rhythm.

She sailed into the curve under the overpass, the road wet enough to make her slow just slightly.

She sped into the straightaway.

A rumble behind her.

*Ugh.* Traffic. Unusual for the area at that time of night.

She drifted closer to the curb to let the driver pass, not slowing her pace.

The rumble grew louder. Why wasn't the car passing?

She glanced back.

A white blur slammed into her bicycle. Catapulted her.

She flew, airborne.

Her breath caught as time stood still.

A concrete abutment waited for her.

She was going to die.

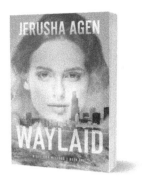

Someone wants to kill her. She wants the killer to finish the job.

Spring Weston will do anything to rise in the ranks of pro cycling and prove she isn't the one failure of the five Weston siblings. Anything except cheat. When she learns of doping on her cycling team, she's determined to uncover the truth. But she can't if she's dead.

Sergeant Torin Cotter may not be the hero the public thinks he is, but he recognizes fear when he sees it. When he takes over the investigation of the collision that landed Spring in the hospital, he's compelled to protect her from whatever danger she's in, even though he knows he might fail. Again.

Spring's faith in God isn't enough to help her face the living nightmare she awakened to after the accident. But neither she nor the handsome sergeant see the greater threat that's coming until it's too late.

If they're going to survive, Spring and Torin will not only have to confront their worst fears—they'll have to find a reason to live.

Shop *Waylaid*
at WaylaidBook.com

She never invites visitors. But visitors sometimes invite themselves.

When a winter storm brings more than snow, May Denver is forced to flee from her home and fight for her life. Can she trust an unwanted neighbor and risk her greatest fear in order to survive?

GRAB THIS ROMANTIC SUSPENSE STORY FOR FREE WHEN YOU SIGN UP FOR JERUSHA'S NEWSLETTER
www.FearWarriorSuspense.com